JINGLE BELL HEARTS

Jillian Hart

Copyright © 2014 by Jill Strickler
All rights reserved.
http://jillianhart.net

Cover Design by Kim Killion, Hot Damn Designs
http://hotdamndesigns.com

E-book Formatted by Jessica Lewis, Authors' Life Saver
http://authorslifesaver.com

This is a work of fiction. Names, characters, places, brands, media, and incidents are either the product of the author's imagination or are used fictitiously. The author acknowledges the trademarked status and trademark owners of various products referenced in this work of fiction, which have been used without permission. The publication/use of these trademarks is not authorized, associated with, or sponsored by the trademark owners.

ISBN: 1496184424
ISBN-13: 9781496184429

CHARACTERS IN THE MCPHEE CLAN

Adam	courting Annie
Alice	Penelope's mare
Annie	McPhee cousin
Aumaleigh	aunt to McPhee sisters
Bea	McPhee cousin
Beckett	engaged to Daisy
Burton	wrangler at the ranch
Buttons	Aumaleigh's mare
Cal	stable boy at the ranch
Carl	owns the feed store
Charlie	Seth's horse
Clarence	works for Seth
Clarice	friend to Bea
Daisy	2nd oldest McPhee sister
Dobsons	enemy bakery owners
Dottie	mercantile clerk
Elise	friend to McPhee sisters
Ernest	Verbena's former beau
Fanny	competing baker
Fred	post office guy
Gabriel	Aumaleigh's former love
Gemma	works at mercantile.
George	Ernest's buddy
Giddy	Junior's brother
Gil	works on ranch
Hartwell	town doc
Hailie	Beckett's daughter
Ian	Rich guy
Iris	oldest McPhee sister
Jane	horse
Josslyn	cook at the ranch
Junior	stranger new to town
Lawrence	a desperate bachelor
Leigh	Gabriel's daughter
Liam	Gabriel's son
Liz	Seth's former love

Louisa	ranch's kitchen maid
Lucile	customer, Clarice's ma
Maebry	wife to Gil
Magnolia	2nd youngest McPhee sister
Marlowe	horse
Marvin	horse
Maureen	deceased grandmother
Milo	sheriff
Miss Ginger	ranch horse
Mr. Michaels	lumberyard owner
Nathanial	town lawyer
Nora	Tyler's mother
Odie	ranch horse
Orla	maid at the ranch
Oscar	homeless guy
Penelope	new schoolteacher
Poppy	horse
Rose	middle McPhee sister
Sadie	Milo's oldest daughter
Samuel	Sarah's husband
Sarah	former schoolteacher
Seth	Josslyn's son, owns livery
Travis	brother to Tyler
Tyler	engaged to Magnolia
Verbena	youngest McPhee Sister
Victoria	Gabriel's wife
Vivian	Gemma's grandmother
Wade	deputy
Wally	one of Seth's horses
Wilhelmina	Hailie's elderly nanny
William	Wally's brother
Wilson	deceased grandfather
Zane	married to Verbena

CHAPTER ONE

December, 1876, Bluebell, Montana Territory

"You've gotten a late start today." Gemma looked up, smiling in greeting from behind the mercantile's front counter. "It's understandable, considering."

"It was a wild weekend, what with Verbena's wedding and all." Rose McPhee stumbled through the doorway loaded down with her basket full of bread. The fresh doughy scent of the loaves wafted into the air every time she breathed. Too bad her stomach growled in response because lunch was a long time away. Ruefully, she elbowed the door closed behind her, making the bell overhead jangle in protest. "A wild weekend, but a wonderful wedding."

"It was so romantic." Gemma sighed wistfully, As if it were her dream to have a dashing man fall madly and devotedly in love with her, too. "Such a whirlwind match. The way Zane fell for her so fast, how he proposed, and then he couldn't wait to marry her. I'll never forget the look on his face when she walked down the aisle. You could just see his deep commitment to her. It renewed my faith in love."

"Oh, I've always believed in that kind of devotion. It would be impossible not to, actually." Rose ignored the hitch in her chest, where her feelings were at war, and slipped the basket of wrapped bread onto the counter. "I grew up with four sisters who are nothing but romantics, even Daisy who says she's too practical for that, but I know the truth about her. She's a secret romantic, too."

"And she has a wedding coming up, as well." Gemma gave another sigh as she scooted the basket closer to her for a better look. "She found a good one, that's for sure. Beckett is one of the best men I know. She's a lucky lady."

"She really is." Rose stepped back from the counter, dusting a little bit of flour off her hands from the basket. There went her chest again, twisting tight, as if it were too full of too many conflicting things. She felt great, great happiness for her sisters—Verbena, newly married, Daisy about to be and Magnolia engaged. But on the other hand, there was the loss. Verbena had already moved into her own home with Zane, of course. Daisy would be going next.

Change was good, she reminded herself. Verbena's life was going to be fantastic. But that didn't stop her from missing her sister. The morning had felt empty without her. It was like a piece was missing.

"Beckett is so good to Daisy," Rose continued with a smile. "After what we've all been through with Ernest, we value good men quite highly."

"No kidding." Gemma tossed a sympathetic look Rose's way before plucking a loaf from the basket. "Hmm. These smell wonderful. My stomach is growling, and it's a long time until lunch."

"I know! That's my exact problem, too." Rose laughed. With the sunshine tumbling into the store through the big front windows, slanting with gentle mid-morning light, she felt sunny again, the ache of missing her sister vanishing. "I couldn't help noticing you did quite a few turns around the dance floor at the reception with two handsome bachelors."

"Mercy dances." Gemma rolled her eyes in good humor, as if being over thirty and a spinster didn't bother her at all. "At my age, folks feel sorry for me and offer to dance with me so I'm not standing on the sidelines alone. That's why Nathaniel asked me. He isn't interested in me."

"Well, you are pretty and kind and fun," Rose pointed out. "Why shouldn't our local attorney be interested in you? He's single. He needs a wife."

"Please. Don't even try to read anything into this." Gemma shook her head, eyes sparkling with mirth. "I've lived in this town for over ten years. Nathaniel moved here not long after. If he was interested, he would have come courting long before this, not hold me as far away from him as his arms would allow during that dance."

"Oh. Well, that doesn't mean I won't stop being hopeful for you." Rose felt for Gemma. She knew exactly what it was like to be considered only a little pretty, because she had so many gorgeous sisters. Men tended to look past a regular girl. The male gender was easily dazzled by beauty. Sometimes it felt lonely to be overlooked like that. She shrugged. "Burton danced with you, too."

"Burton? Right." Gemma looked ready to break into hysterics as she piled the bread onto the counter. "He's fifteen years older than me. Plus he's notorious for his dim thoughts on marriage."

"True, but sometimes opinions change." Rose rescued the empty basket from the counter. She felt sad for Gemma. Gemma had become a friend, and Rose knew her well enough to guess there was a lot of sadness hidden down deep inside. She wished she could do something to help with that.

"Oh, that's easy for you to say," Gemma gently teased as she fussed with the loaves, getting them just right in the display. "You have that handsome deputy beauing you."

"Wade?" Rose's chest tightened up again like a belt was cinching tighter around her ribs. She liked Wade. He was a good beau to have. Determined to be content with that, she gave a little sigh. "He's nice, that's true. And, hey, you never know what's up ahead. Maybe the perfect man for you will come walking through that door this very minute."

"You wouldn't say that if you were standing where you could see who's just driven up." Gemma grabbed another armload of bread from the counter. She gestured toward the front windows with her chin. "Don't even try to tease me about Lawrence."

"Oh, no. I wouldn't. I like you way too much for that." Rose glanced over her shoulder and spotted the local bachelor climbing down from his wooden cart. His donkey stood placidly in front of the hitching post, the animal's big ears perked up with curiosity. "Well, I hate to do this to you, Gemma, but I'm going to get out while the getting is good. I do *not* want to be stuck here talking to that man."

"I wish I could go with you," Gemma laughed mischievously, settling the loaves into a big basket next to the counter. "That man is the bane of my existence."

"Too bad you can't go hide in the back of the store." Rose quickened her step, trying to judge how fast she had to move to escape before Lawrence was done tying up his donkey. "I'll see you tomorrow."

"Wait! Before you go." Gemma gathered up the rest of the loaves, tucking them neatly in the crook of her slender arm. "A friend of mine works at a mercantile over in Deer Springs and her father, who runs the store, is looking for a new baker. I put in a good word for you and your sisters."

"That's wonderful. Thanks, Gemma. We're hoping to expand." She sailed out the door, wishing she could stay and talk more, but, honestly, Lawrence was giving the knotted reins a test tug to make sure they would hold. She was out of time—he'd be heading this way any minute. "See you tomorrow! Good luck."

"Thanks, I'm going to need it." Gemma rolled her eyes.

Heart pounding, Rose didn't hesitate or pause or even glance over her shoulder at him. It was the best strategy for coping with poor Lawrence. On a mission of escape now, she looked neither right nor left but focused on the boards at her feet as she rushed along.. Too bad she'd parked her horse so far away from the front door.

"Miss Rose, is that you?" Lawrence called, his puffed-up sounding tenor booming rather irritatingly.

"Good morning, Mr. Latimer." She avoided the steps, which would have brought her closer to him, and leaped off the boardwalk into the knee-deep bank of snow. Icy cold closed in on her feet and soaked her shoes, but so what? As important as shoes were, getting away from Lawrence Latimer was top priority.

"And good morning to you, my fair lady!" Lawrence swept off his bowler hat and made a sweeping bow, fit for a duke greeting the Queen of England.

Afraid he was about to launch into forty minutes of non-stop talking, she yanked at the mare's reins tied around the hitching post. Drat. That only knotted them more. Just her luck. Desperate, she frantically worked at the tangle as boots *scrunched* in the snow behind her.

"Seems as if you have a bit of a problem, my dear." His shadow falling on the glittering snow beside her came closer. First his bowl-shaped hat, then his stooped, narrow shoulders. "Maybe I can help."

Okay, she was starting to imagine what would happen if she let overeager Lawrence "help" her. She'd never be able to get rid of him, that's what. Would he start following her around town like a puppy, the way he did with Verbena? Oh, probably. Rose blindly gave a frenzied yank on the leather straps—which came loose! Yay.

Victorious, she gave a little hop of joy and, hauling the reins with her as she swirled to avoid the still-approaching Lawrence, leaped into the little sleigh. Ooh, she'd escaped in just the nick of time.

"Looks like you've forgotten something, beautiful lady." Lawrence swept the empty basket from the snow bank where she'd dropped it (she'd been in too much of a panic to have remembered doing it). His handlebar mustache twitched as he stalked closer, strutting along as if he was the tallest man on earth even though he was rather short. He managed a debonair pose (or what he probably thought counted as one) as he handed over the basket. "Here you are. I see you're all by your lonesome this morning. One of your sisters usually comes along with you on your morning deliveries, if I'm not mistaken."

Rose bit her lip, refrained from commenting on the fact that he seemed to be spying on her family, took the basket and managed what she hoped was a cordial half-smile. "Thank you, Mr. Latimer. Yes, I'm alone this morning. All my sisters are busy."

"It's a busy time for your family, what with Verbena newly married and Daisy about to be. Then there will be Magnolia's wedding to come. So many of your sisters have found their match." His brown eyes sparkled hopefully. "Does it make you start wishing for a husband of your own?"

Not in a thousand years, Lawrence. Rose dropped the basket on the floor at her feet, biting her lip again to keep her thoughts unsaid. Look at the man, such a little guy, thin and forlorn in his secondhand clothes, hopeful he might catch himself a bride, even me, Rose thought. He really must be lonely.

See, the thing about Lawrence was that he was an annoyance, but he was also a sad man. You had to feel sorry for him, even if you wanted to run in the other direction.

"Well, I would like a husband one day," she said benignly, gathering the reins, one in each hand. "But Wade and I have only been courting a few months. I don't think we're ready to tie the knot just yet, but it's kind of you to ask. Have a good day, Mr. Latimer."

"But I—" He began, puffing up his skinny chest and looking like a man about to start a long discourse, but Rose wisely sent the mare bolting away. The mare gave a huff as if she'd had enough of poor Lawrence, too.

"I don't think his prospects of getting married are very good," she confided. "What do you think, Jane?"

Jane gave a horsy snort, as if to say *fat chance of that.*

"I totally agree." Rose glanced over her shoulder now that she was out of the danger zone. She was much too far away for Lawrence to shout out to her, for instance. There he was, narrow shoulders slumped with a bit of defeat. She felt sorry for him, she couldn't help it.

"Poor Gemma," she sympathized. "It's not like she can escape him. He's a customer."

Jane's rhythmic *clip-clop* on the hard-packed snow gave a jarring note. Something metallic went clunk and the old mare skidded to a halt, one foot cocked. A steely horseshoe sat all by its lonesome on the side of the town street, glinting in the morning sun.

"This is a problem." Rose draped the reins across the sleigh's wooden dash, debating. "Can I drive you if you're missing that shoe? Or would it be super bad and lame you or something?"

If Jane knew the answer, she couldn't communicate it. The small brown mare stretched her neck to look down the street behind her at her lost shoe. Was that worry in her brown eyes? Or simply surprise? Rose had no clue.

"Something tells me I'd better err on the side of caution." She climbed out of the sleigh, her shoes sliding slightly on the icy street. Town was quiet this morning. No one else was on the street. The handful of stores nearby looked open, with lamplight golden in their windows. Probably poking her head into one of the shops sounded like the best plan. Surely she could ask one of the shopkeepers if it would be okay to continue on to her sister's house or if her morning travel plans were thwarted.

"Stay here, Jane." She gentled her voice, hoping she sounded reassuring. "It will be fine. I'll just go fetch—"

That's when she spotted him. Lawrence Latimer had hesitated just outside the mercantile's front door. His hand was even on the doorknob, but did he turn it? No. Instead he was gazing down the street at her, alert, as if he sensed an opportunity. She watched in horror as

Lawrence drew himself up to his full (albeit short) height, squared his (thin, slightly rounded) shoulders and strutted in her direction like a knight on a rescue mission.

Zounds! If she let him help her, then she'd never get rid of him. Not ever. Panicked, she bent and snatched the horseshoe off the snow, gave a fast turn intending to get off the street and into the safety of one of the nearby stores before Lawrence could arrive, but her shoes had another idea. They hit a patch of especially slick ice and her feet swooped out from under her. Suddenly she was going down, her skirts puffing up with a gust of wind as she smacked against the ground, lying dazed, flat on her back.

The force sent shockwaves of pain through her whole body. Air shot out of her lungs and stayed that way, leaving her gasping like a beached salmon, and all she could do was stare at her red wool long johns, the only thing hiding her bare legs from view. Worse, her skirt was up to her thighs, showing off her knees and part of her petticoats. *In full view of half the town.*

Embarrassment charged through her like adrenaline, *rat-tat-tatting* in her blood. She tried to push herself up but her lungs were bursting, gasping for oxygen and not getting any. So she stayed collapsed on the chilly snow, seeing nothing but doom. Think of the gossip. *Remember the day that McPhee girl flashed her undies to the entire street?*

And worse, Rose thought ruefully, she would never be rid of Lawrence then.

Footsteps clomped behind her—heavy, like a man's. Coming quick, no doubt Lawrence on his way to her rescue. She mentally groaned (since she still wasn't breathing it was the only kind she could manage) and rolled her eyes to the merry blue skies staring down at her. Why, she thought. Why me?

"You went down hard." A friendly baritone rumbled from behind her as those boot-steps came to a stop—not Lawrence's breathy tenor at all, but a familiar voice. Seth Daniels. "Are you all right?"

"I am now." Her seizing lungs relaxed, and relief surged through her in one warm rush. She blinked, staring up at the tall, strapping man, brawny of chest and shoulder, with his black, slightly curly hair and handsome, sculpted face. He tipped his hat to her cordially, always the gentleman even, apparently, when her long johns were showing. She started blushing. "I can't believe I did that. I'm usually not that clumsy.

How many people saw?"

"Hardly anyone," Seth said in his easy going way, a hint of a smile curving the corners of his chiseled mouth. He knelt down beside her and offered her his gloved hand. "Let's get you standing up and your skirt going the right way. Does that sound like a plan?"

"In other words, everyone saw, didn't they?" She slipped her gloved fingers against his offered palm, and her heart skipped when his bigger, stronger fingers closed over her own. She felt the power of his muscles rippling as he tugged her gently into a sitting position, and before she knew it, she was on her feet, her skirts swishing into place around her ankles. "Everyone saw my knees."

"Well, the long johns disguised them somewhat." Seth looked her over as if checking for any sign of damage—blood or broken bones, maybe. "But you do have nice knees."

"Shocking that you should say that," she teased him, feeling a little breathy and dizzy. Likely from standing up too quickly. "I thought you were a gentleman, Seth."

"I do my best, but I have lapses," he confessed with a good-natured wink. When he smiled, little attractive crinkles dug into the corners of his black eyes.

Strange, that she would notice them right now, when she was still breathy and lightheaded. She must have hit the ground harder than she'd thought. Seth was—well, *Seth*. They'd known each other eons ago when they were both babies and then toddlers, playing together on her grandmother's ranch where she'd lived and his parents had worked. Her family had left Ohio not long after that, and she hadn't seen him since, not until she and her sisters had arrived last summer. He owned the local livery.

"Uh oh. Looks like I got here just in time." Seth jutted his chin in the direction of the street behind her, where Lawrence stood, looking indecisive. His handlebar mustache drooped as he took in the sight of Rose with her hand still tucked in Seth's much larger one.

With a shrug of his narrow shoulders, Lawrence's chin lowered, he turned around and retraced his steps back to the mercantile, his feet dragging with disappointment. He really was a sad figure, Rose thought, her sympathies tugging. But honestly, she was really, really glad he hadn't been the one to reach her side first.

"I owe you, Seth." She gave him her best smile. "In fact, I don't think I can ever repay you for this act of kindness."

"Saving you from Lawrence?" He arched one dark brow, and the lean lines of his face, the slash of cheekbones, the straight nose, the dimple carved chin would make any girl swoon.

Good thing her head had stopped spinning, or she might have started to think it was spinning because of him.

"Believe me." She brushed snow off her coat. "Lawrence caught me at Verbena and Zane's reception and talked my ear off for forty-two minutes—I know, I had a perfect view of the mantel clock—before Magnolia spotted my plight and dragged me away. Literally."

"I did notice all that time you spent with him." Seth took the horseshoe Rose was still holding in one hand and studied it, leading the way back to the sleigh and the waiting horse. He eyed her jokingly. "Here I thought you were two-timing Wade."

"Yeah, right. That's a terrible joke and you know it." She stared up at the sky helplessly. "You have the worst sense of humor of anyone I've ever met."

"Fine, okay, I'm sorry. I know you aren't interested in Lawrence." He resisted the urge to reach out and brush tiny bits of ice from the soft blond curls tumbling down to frame her face. Her blue hat was askew, though, so he told himself it was the gentlemanly thing to straighten it for her, so she wouldn't drive around town with it off kilter.

He reached with his free hand, leaning in close enough to smell the lilac scent of her hair, her warmth and her sweetness. His chest cinched tight uncontrollably. He did his best not to let his feelings show as he caught hold and gave her hat a light tug. "I would have come and rescued you at the party, but Doc Hartwell was telling me about his son who'd just finished up his medical training, and I couldn't get away."

"Sure, likely story." She swept alongside him, light as a breeze, as sweet as a snowflake. "I guess the thought of helping counts for something."

"I should hope so." He tucked the horseshoe into his coat pocket, trying to force his gaze to the mare standing patiently in the road, her right rear hoof cocked, not bearing weight. "Hmm, you seem to be in need of a blacksmith."

"True. Gee, I wonder where I can find a good one?"

"You're in luck. You happen to be looking at the best in town."

"You're the only blacksmith in town."

"True."

"And I did say I wanted a good one, but beggars can't be choosers." Rose leaned back against the side of the little wooden sleigh, polished to a gleam in the sunlight. Mischief danced in her blue-green eyes. "But I suppose, since this is an emergency, you'll have to do."

"I'll try not to disappoint." He knelt down to take Jane's rear hoof in his hands, leaning in to get a look. "Are you out doing deliveries?"

"Just finished the last one for the morning." She swiped an errant curl out of her face—her beautiful, high-cheekboned, oval face. No one in the county was as striking. "I don't like that frown on your face. Is something wrong with Jane's foot?"

That crinkle of concern was adorable. He tried not to notice. She was off limits, and that was just as well. He carefully lowered Jane's hoof to the ground. "I want to clean this up and take a good look. It won't take long if you want to spend some time shopping. I can bring her back to you when I'm done."

"Oh, I'm not stepping foot inside the mercantile, not now." She shook her head prettily, scattering those gossamer, golden wisps. "I was on my way to Verbena's."

"Sure." That's when he spotted the baskets sitting on the seat. Zane and Verbena's wedding had been quite a big event. Most of the town had attended, pouring into the enormous McPhee Manor, the stateliest house he'd ever seen. It was the McPhee sisters' inheritance and somehow they had made the monstrous structure into a home, full of warmth and coziness. Of course, she was going to visit her sister this morning.

"Then I'll lend you a horse, and we can trade back when it's easy for you," he offered, doing his best to sound casual as he stood up and ran a hand along the mare's flank to reassure her. "It would be no problem."

"Oh, I don't mind walking." Rose breezily snatched one of two wicker baskets from the seat. "It's a beautiful morning and honestly, I don't want you to go out of your way. Just fix poor Jane's foot for me."

It was a hoof, but he didn't tell her that. No, his chest twisted up with all kinds of sweet feelings for her—for how cute Rose was and how nice.

"Thanks, Seth. You really are a lifesaver." She smiled up at him, all golden curls and sweetness.

"Nah, I'm just doing my job. Blacksmithing is more heroic than you might think," he joked.

"Sure, I knew that all along. Forget the Canadian Mounties or the Texas Rangers. They probably dream of being blacksmiths."

"You know it," he called out, watching her spin away from him and walk down the side of the street. "Be careful. You don't want to slip and fall and give the folks in this town another show."

"Thanks for that helpful advice," she teased back, calling over her slender shoulder before trudging through the snow and up onto the covered boardwalk. Her shoes tapped a merry melody as she hurried away out of his sight.

His chest gave a little wince. He had a sweet spot for Rose. He couldn't help it. But that was all it could ever be.

"C'mon, Jane." He grabbed the horse by the bridle. "Let's get you fixed up."

Jane seemed agreeable, so he led her across the street to his livery.

CHAPTER TWO

Verbena's house towered ahead of her as Rose tapped up the shoveled walkway, the basket hanging from the crook of her arm. It was a pleasant two-story home, mantled in white and tucked beneath two giant cedars. Lamplight shone in the big front window, giving the rented house a cozy look. Rose knocked the snow off her boots before trodding up the porch steps. So romantic how Zane had rented the nicest house in town for his new bride. They planned to build on land he'd purchased come spring.

"Rose!" Verbena threw open the door, looking radiant in a lavender calico dress. Her dark hair was down, tumbling around her shoulders and her sapphire blue eyes twinkled with happiness. "I saw you walking up. Where's your horse and sleigh? What about the deliveries? Where's Magnolia? Isn't she supposed to be with you?"

"Magnolia and I split up the delivery route today because there's just so many of them. She's on her way to Deer Springs delivering two cakes. I took care of the ones here in town but, Jane threw a shoe."

"Oh no. Poor Jane." Verbena swung the door shut against the icy air and accepted the basket Rose thrust at her. "Hmm. Blueberry muffins. You are spoiling me."

"Really, it's Zane we want to spoil," she teased sweetly, removing her hat. "We're so grateful to him for taking you off our hands. Here we feared that we were going to be stuck putting up with you forever."

"I know! That had to be terrifying for you to worry about, but it's over now. I'm happily married." Verbena peeked beneath the basket's lid and inhaled deeply. "I have some fresh coffee to serve with these. Come on into the parlor. We'll have Zane go fetch Jane for you and take care of that shoe. He's really handy, you know."

"Oh, he doesn't need to bother. Seth is seeing to it." Just saying his name brought it all back—the strength of his grip, the size of his much larger hand engulfing her own, the way he'd towered over her, blocking the sky, larger than life.

She rolled her eyes. There she went feeling breathy again. Likely from that brisk walk from Main Street. She shucked off her coat and hung it on the nearby coat tree. "How is married life treating you? From the looks of it, pretty badly."

"Yes, it's been awful." Verbena beamed, whisking the basket with her as she led the way into the cheerful parlor. "Somehow I will manage to endure it. Ooh, you look half frozen. Come warm up by the fire. I'll fetch the coffee."

"Thanks. I really am in need of a thaw." Rose arrowed straight for the fireplace where flames cracked and popped, radiating wonderful, welcome heat. "I'm going to have to thaw out before I can feel how cold I really am."

"That can't be good." Verbena plopped the basket in the middle of the polished coffee table. "When we all dreamed up the idea of starting a baking business, it was summer. Those morning deliveries were warm and sunny."

"Yes. I didn't think far enough ahead to make Iris do the deliveries instead," Rose teased lightly, turning around so the heat could warm her back first—and hopefully it would warm away some of the ache from the fall too. She was really starting to feel it. "I wonder if it's too late to switch with her?"

"Funny." Verbena swiveled her gaze to the ceiling. "You can't fool me. You wouldn't do that to our beloved Iris. If she even suggested it, you'd refuse to let her out in the cold."

"Too true." Rose thought of their oldest sister at home, probably working on the next batch of deliveries for the afternoon. They only had one order, but that wouldn't stop Iris from throwing herself whole-heartedly into it. Sadness crept into Rose's chest, thinking of Iris's past tragedy, the one that had changed her forever. Verbena had come close to a similar tragedy, but the sheriff and the men in town had intervened just in time. And when Zane had came to hunt down Verbena's former suitor, Ernest, he'd put a stop to the danger and had captured Verbena's heart.

But it was too late for Iris, Rose feared. And she wasn't alone with that. She sighed. "I worry about letting Iris drive by herself. She might feel scared."

"I know." Verbena stared down at her shoes, sad too. "That's why I'm so glad she has the bakery business. It's not like she'll be getting married."

"No." Rose blew out a breath, staring at the big area carpet at her feet. Iris's tragedy would keep her from marrying for many reasons— one being her ability to trust a man. "That's why I'm determined to do all I can to make our bakery a raving success."

"Even though I'm married, I can still help out," Verbena offered over her shoulder, weaving her way through the room. "I've been doing a lot of thinking—oh, Zane." She skidded to a stop, her lavender skirts swishing around her elegant frame. Her dark hair bounced, cascading over her shoulder and down her back. "Look at you. You brought us coffee."

"Least I could do," Zane Reed said in his deep baritone. He stalked into sight, a big bear of a man, muscular and rough and intimidating— unless you knew him. Then you thought, what a great guy. He was handsome with a thick mane of dark hair falling past his collar and a rugged, chiseled face that would make any woman stop in her tracks for a second look. He carried a small tray with the coffeepot, two steaming cups, sugar and creamer. He'd added plates for the muffins.

Rose filled with adoration for this man who treated her sister so well. She watched as he stopped to brush a light kiss on Verbena's cheek.

"That's so thoughtful of you." Verbena gently pressed the palm of her hand to her husband's whiskered jaw.

Zane gazed down at his wife with such tender love, it brought tears to Rose's eyes. Now *that* was fairy-tale love, the real thing. Something out of a dream.

"I'll just set this down right here," Zane said, his voice gruff, thick with emotion. He gave Rose a friendly smile. "You two ladies can visit. But forgive me for stealing one of those muffins. They smell good.

Thanks for bringing them, Rose."

"You can thank Iris. She made them." Rose cleared her throat, still touched by the love she'd witnessed. It was a rare thing, she knew, not your average everyday kind of love, and it was encouraging to see. True love did happen, and it made the world a better place.

"Well, then, thanks to Iris." Zane gave a gentle smile as he opened the basket's lid. "You brought two whole dozen. Maybe I'd better take two."

"Yes, we wouldn't want you to starve." Rose bit her lip to keep from laughing. Iris really did make excellent muffins. She scooped up both cups of coffee and handed one to Verbena.

"Thanks." Verbena took the cup. Her heart-shaped face blushed with delight. "Tell me all about what's new with you. Did Wade come to take you on a Sunday drive yesterday?"

"He couldn't. He was busy helping his brothers. He's been busy a lot lately." Rose stirred two sugar cubes into her coffee, trying to pretend it hadn't bothered her. "Then again, he came to the wedding and reception on Saturday, so he had less free time for the weekend."

"I see. I saw you two together at the reception," Verbena said sweetly. "He had you in his strong arms for more than a few dances."

"True, I can't deny it." Rose's face heated. She took a sip of her coffee, uncomfortable confessing her feelings. She liked Wade. Waltzing with him, being that close to him, gave her a comfortable feeling. But was it love? She was pretty sure it wasn't. "It was nice."

"Nice?" Verbena waggled her brows, sitting back on the sofa, cradling the cup in both slender hands. She looked elegant sitting there in her pretty dress with her rich brown hair shot with red highlights tumbling over her slim shoulders. Her beauty stopped men in the street, and the man who'd married her loved her so deeply, he was prepared to die for her. But not every girl could warrant that kind of affection in a man. And honestly, that was the last thing Rose expected. Mutual love, genuine caring. That was realistic. It was what life was about for the rest of us.

Verbena took a sip of coffee, blue eyes full of mischief. "It ought to be a good deal more than nice. I know you have feelings for Wade."

"I absolutely do." That much was true. She liked him. She couldn't deny that. Her stomach growled, reminding her that she'd worked up an appetite on the walk here. She deserved a muffin, too. She leaned forward to grab one from the basket. "He makes me feel very nice things."

"There's that word again. *Nice.*" Verbena shook her head disapprovingly like a wise old schoolmarm. "I'm not believing a word of it. My guess is that you'll be engaged soon. Christmas is coming up, and you know it's the traditional time when a courting man gives his beloved a ring."

"The thought hadn't crossed my mind," Rose confessed, nibbling on the edge of the muffin. (So good with the sweet, plump blueberries breaking apart in her mouth, combined with the light cake surrounding it). Unable to resist, she took another bite.

"What do you mean? It's crossed mine." Verbena took a dainty bite of her muffin, careful not to drop any crumbs. "I've already planned it all out in my mind. Next is Daisy's wedding. Magnolia's will be in the early spring. So that means a May wedding would be perfect for you. What do you say?"

"I say, let's not rush things." She didn't know why her ribs constricted and she couldn't get any air—just like when she'd been flat on her back on the street with her skirt up around her thighs and the wind knocked out of her. Which was an odd way to feel because Wade was a nice guy. He was a dependable sort who worked hard and seemed kind. So, there wasn't a great love between them, like Verbena and Zane shared, but that didn't matter. She didn't want a fairy-tale. She wanted something real.

Except lately it had begun to feel hollow. She didn't know why.

A knock rapped on the front door. Verbena crinkled her forehead. "Hmm, I wonder who that could be? I see a man's shadow falling across the porch."

"A man's shadow?" An instinctive kick of alarm rocked through her. Rose set down her cup before she spilled it. She turned toward the large front window, full of dread and fearing the worst. The image of Lawrence rushing down Main Street to rescue her flashed into her brain. Maybe he'd come to offer her a ride home in his donkey cart. It would be just the kind of thing he'd do, and he'd talk both of her ears off on the way. "Can you tell who it is?"

"Not without peeking out the window." Verbena set down her coffee and muffin on the table and stood, her skirts rustling. "What's with you? You have sweat beading on your upper lip."

"It's just panic." Rose waved away Verbena's concern with a weak hand. "If you can't see who's out there, can you at least see what kind of hat the shadow is wearing?"

"Now you're being ridiculous. It's probably someone for Zane." Verbena gave a light laugh, crossing the room.

"I had an encounter with Lawrence this morning," Rose confessed. "What if he followed me here?"

"He *is* persistent," Verbena agreed, perhaps remembering all the times Lawrence had attempted to beau her over the past few months. There were far too many times to count. "From what I can tell, the shadow is wearing a Stetson, not a bowler hat. You're safe."

"Good, because I didn't want to hide in the kitchen with Zane." Rose blew out a sigh of relief. "Not that I don't like Zane, but I don't want to feel cowardly. And I can't take being trapped with Lawrence for the rest of the morning."

"I've been there, and I don't blame you. He's like a poor, lost little skunk you feel sorry for but you don't want to get too close to." Verbena nodded with deep understanding before she opened the door. "Hello, Seth. Always good to see you."

Seth. Rose's knees went weak. Good thing she was sitting, or she'd be on the floor. Just knowing he was out there made her feel slightly dazed, as if the aftereffects of falling on the icy snow had returned—which was totally puzzling. It was as if she could feel his solid, dependable presence, although she couldn't see him. The moment he crossed the threshold, her heart leaped, pumping fast and skipping a few beats. This wasn't normally how she felt around men—even Seth. What was going on?

I know! Rose thought, buoyed by the realization. *Perhaps it's because I'm worried about Jane.*

"That's what a man like me likes, a warm welcome. I don't get it often." With a good-natured wink and a grin, Seth strode into the parlor, shucking off his coat. His black gaze shone with a warm shimmer. "I'm just lucky the lovely ladies in this town don't see me coming and run the other way. Or pretend not to be home and don't answer the door."

"It was tempting," Verbena teased. "But then I remembered you have our horse."

"Yes, you do." Rose sat up straighter in her chair. From this vantage,

Seth loomed so tall and large in the room, he seemed enormous, with thick ridges of muscle bunching beneath his blue flannel shirt as he folded his coat over one arm. He was a likable guy, which was probably why she smiled at him. "If you didn't bring Jane over, then there has to be a problem."

"Yep. A big one. Sorry to be the bearer of bad news." He closed the distance between them in three long-legged, powerful strides. His nearness was like the fire radiating scorching heat. She gasped as he knelt down beside her, looking her in the eyes. Sympathy shone there. Seth was a guy with a good heart. "Your mare—"

"Technically, it's the ranch's mare but Aumaleigh lets us use her when we don't have enough of our own horses," Rose found herself saying, leaning a little closer to Seth. She just felt at ease with him. Comfortable. Like she could just relax and be herself, which was totally nice. "But I'm completely responsible for her and her bill. She was in my care when this happened."

"Unfortunately, she has a severe crack in her hoof. It was probably there for a while, but sometimes those suckers can hide on you, even when you're taking good care of a horse's hooves." Seth raked a hand through his thick black hair, tousling it, making it curl a little more. "She's going to need rest. I don't recommend her pulling your sleigh back home."

"Of course not, poor thing." Rose's heart twisted. "Jane didn't seem to be in any pain when I was driving her, or I would have stopped."

"Don't worry. I'll get her fixed up, but she needs to keep off that hoof until some of that swelling goes down." Kind. That was Seth. Confident in a humble way. There was just something likable about a big strong but gentle man. "Jane will get the royal treatment at my barn, just like always."

"Why am I not surprised?" Rose asked. Warm fuzzies filled her up. "Thanks for taking such good care of her."

"No problem. But unfortunately you are horseless for your journey home."

"And our sleigh is stranded," she agreed, rolling her eyes ceiling ward to try to think of a quick solution. "Well, Verbena is here. Zane is here. He has a couple of horses. He could run me home. After all, as my new brother-in-law, isn't that his duty?"

"I heard that." Zane's voice, thundering from the kitchen, echoing with a note of amusement. His heavy boot-steps knelled closer. "Nobody told me about any duties. Now that I know, I'm rethinking this marriage."

"Sure you are." Verbena's trill of laughter rang with joy, beaming, simply beaming. Their gazes locked. "Too late for you, buddy. I have you for life."

"Darn. I didn't know about the lifelong rule either," Zane quipped, striding into the room, seeming to dominate it. He held an empty cup, which he set down on the tray next to the steaming coffee pot. "Pull up a chair, Seth, and stay awhile."

"Thanks, Zane. But I've got to get going. I have some horses to shoe at the Landry's ranch." Seth stood, pulling himself up to his full height, giving powerfully built Zane a run for his money. Both big men seemed to shrink the room, making it feel tiny.

"But I will run Rose home," Zane assured her, glancing her way. His dark eyes glinted with kindness, which was a remarkable thing in a man who had the reputation as one of the toughest bounty hunters in four territories (as rumor had it and Rose didn't doubt it a bit).

"No need." Seth shook out his coat and hauled it on. "I've got one of my horses tied at the street and blanketed, ready for Rose when she's done here. But Rose, you'll have to swing by the livery and pick me up. I'll drop you off at home. Does that sound like a plan?"

"Absolutely. I really appreciate it, Seth." She hopped to her feet, leaving the basket. "I wasn't going to stay long anyway."

"Wait, does this mean you're leaving now?" Distressed, Verbena's forehead crinkled up. "But we didn't get much talking in."

"We can always talk later." Rose wrapped her arms around her sister, her baby sister, and gave her a squeeze. "But you've been married, what, two days? I think you need to spend time with your new husband. Am I right?"

Verbena blushed. "Well, we are treasuring our time together. It's awfully nice being married."

"I can see that." Rose let go, snaring her coat from the coat tree. All those loving looks, the happiness sparkling in Verbena's eyes, the feeling of home already in this beautiful house. It was everything she'd ever wanted for Verbena, and everything she'd feared Verbena would never find. Thank goodness Ernest was dead, his body sent back to Chicago to his family, and the trauma and fear he'd caused everyone was gone. With any luck, it would never come their way again.

She stuck her arms into her coat sleeves. "You and Zane have a wonderful day. I'll swing by tomorrow with some more baked goods. You know Iris. If she loves you, she bakes for you."

"Tell her I love her and her baked goods. I'll take more muffins any time." Verbena lit up with bliss when Zane came up behind her and wrapped his arms around her, holding her close as Seth opened the front door.

"I will." Rose took one long look. This was what happiness looked like. Contagious, it filled her right up. She was more grateful to Zane than she knew how to say. She buttoned her coat, stepping out the door. "See you tomorrow!"

"Stay longer next time," Verbena called out before Seth pulled the door shut.

"It's nice to see a happy couple," Seth commented, keeping pace beside her as they tapped down the steps. "Makes you think not all marriages are a bad decision."

"Oh, are you one of those anti-marriage men?" She crooked a playful brow. "Afraid of commitment? Too tough to be vulnerable?"

"What? It's not obvious?"

"Well, it's not written on your forehead or anything." She pulled her gloves from her coat pockets, working them onto her small, feminine hands. "Although that would be really convenient for us girls. All it would take is one look at a guy, read his forehead and we could say, *nope, reject that one.*"

"I could fix that. All I'd need is a chisel and a mirror. I have one at the livery. We could swing by and get it."

"Tempting." She stopped beside the sleigh, tilting her head to gaze up at him. Her sunny, gold curls danced in the gentle winter wind. Graced by sunlight, she'd never looked more beautiful. Like a sweet, sugarplum fairy, full of Christmas surprises. "Come to think of it, yes. Let's get that chisel. Maybe we can start a new trend."

"Something tells me it might not catch on." He offered his hand, palm up, to help her into the sleigh. Her fingertips grazed his, light and feather-soft even through her gloves, and the impact rocked him to the core. Sweetness filled him up as he helped her onto the seat. Boy, she was nice. His feelings strengthened, beyond his will and out of his control.

When he'd first spotted her again after a lifetime of being apart, he'd liked the look of her. Then he'd been drawn in by her gentle, winsome smile and her quiet beauty. When he gazed at her, he felt less lonely. Unaware of his feelings, she scooted onto the seat and took her fingers from his palm.

"That's a man for you," she said cheerily. Her sea colored eyes, a swirl of blue and green, mesmerized him, and just drew him in. "Never wanting to sacrifice. What's a little pain after all?"

"Yes, it would only be a little pain to carve words into my forehead," he agreed, rolling his eyes, laughing as he circled around the back of the sleigh. Wade was a lucky man to have claimed her heart. No doubt about that. He hopped onto the seat beside her and reached for the reins. "I only meant it's nice to see two people happy. Verbena and Zane seem made for each other."

"Yes, they do." Rose gave a sigh, turning toward the house for one last look. Surely she saw as he did, the newly married couple through the window, alone in their parlor, talking to one another. The big ex-bounty hunter reached out to pull his pretty wife into his arms, bringing her in for a passionate kiss.

Seth blushed, looking away and slapped the reins. It would be nice to be in Zane's shoes, a happily married man, fortunate enough to have a kind wife to love and take care of. Life for many bachelors was a lonely place in this neck of the woods, for this remote part of Montana Territory didn't have a whole lot of single, marriageable women. So when the McPhee sisters had rolled into town, it was like hope rising in the east with the sun for a lot of men—and he wanted to be one of those men. But he knew how important it was to choose a woman wisely. Funny how three of the sisters hadn't lasted long as single ladies either.

Nor would Rose. That was a simple, plain fact. Seth snapped the reins again and picked up his pace, zipping along the icy street. She was already spoken for.

CHAPTER THREE

"Although, teasing aside," Rose said, turning toward Seth on the seat, above the cheery ring of the sleigh bells. "I understand what you mean about seeing a happy marriage. I've witnessed too many of the other kind too."

"Then you know where I'm coming from." Seth leaned back on the reins, slowing his big tan-colored mammoth of a horse at the intersection. There was nothing coming, everything was silent and still along the tree-lined lane. Cozy houses lined up neatly in a row, mantled with snow. Nice. He loved winter. He gave the reins a little shake and his gelding picked up speed, black mane rippling. Seth gave a broad-shouldered shrug. "I watched my ma struggle through a lot of unhappiness. But, honestly, what have you seen? Listening to my mother tell it, your parents were made for each other."

"At one time they were," Rose confessed, leaning back against the cushioned seat, wincing at the knot of old pain tangled up deep inside. Her parents were gone now, but she loved them dearly. Theirs had been a tragic story. "I don't remember them happy, but everyone assures me they were truly in love. All I remember is the bitter, wounded silence in the house whenever they were in it together or the disappointment in their words to one another."

"That's a shame." Seth's voice dipped sympathetically. When he cut his gaze sideways to meet hers, understanding and sadness shadowed his dark irises. "My pa and ma started out happy too, from what I hear, but all I ever saw was the struggle."

"Yes, that's what I remember of mine, too." Rose sighed, the images from that time rising up unbidden and unwanted. Of Ma standing at the stove boiling chicken bones to get every bit of nutrition she could for their watery soup. The handed-down dress Ma patched one more time, the tip of her sewing needle darting in and out of the faded yellow calico. Pa sitting up late at night in the dark of their shanty, his head bowed, his face buried in his hands, shadowed by hopelessness. "Their love was broken by the world. Life was just too harsh."

"Sometimes it is. I'm sorry for them." Seth cleared his throat, sounding genuine. "I'm sorry for you, too. That had to be a hard way to grow up."

"Pa had a long string of bad luck in Chicago." She agreed. That couldn't be denied. And it had looked as if she and her sisters had inherited the propensity for bad luck until they'd received a letter from Grandmother Maureen's attorney telling them of their inheritance. It had changed their lives, but that didn't mean she would forget her past or the lessons of it.

She had a lot on her mind and questions to ask, but a cute yellow cottage was coming up on the left. It was plain but still charming and no longer looked lonely with the dark-windows-and-abandoned-look that empty houses had. No, golden light shone in the large front window, casting a glow out onto the small porch and snowy yard below.

"It looks like Adam got the house." She leaned forward, full of happy hope. "It's wonderful he's moving here so he can court Annie."

Annie, their cousin, was endearing and with her sad history, she truly deserved a shining knight like Adam. Because wasn't that what a shining knight was—a truly good man? How fortunate Annie was to have found such a devoted and kind beau. Anyone could tell simply from looking that a proposal would be coming soon. That meant there would be another wedding in the McPhee Clan. Happiness and true love was breaking the old family pattern of unhappiness and lost love. It gave a girl hope.

Maybe she could find that kind of happiness. The real and true kind, and it would last.

"Hey, there!" A deep baritone called, ringing in the still, bright day. Adam, burly, dark-haired and self-controlled stepped through the open door and onto the porch. His Stetson shaded his eyes, but he was smiling. "I'm trying to keep this a surprise."

"Oh, and you think I can't keep a secret?" Rose answered merrily as Seth drew the horse and sleigh to a stop. Think how delighted Annie would be. The thought made her smile so wide her face ached. "Not a worry with me, but you never know about Seth."

"Me?" Seth argued good-naturedly, giving a head shake. Dark locks shifted around his face, some caught by the wind and rippled against his wide shoulder. "Give me some credit. I'm an excellent secret keeper."

"Glad to hear it." Adam buttoned his big wool coat, pounding down the stairs, his gait easy, his smile tentative but friendly. He was a quiet, almost shy man, which was pretty endearing in Rose's opinion. Adam's humbleness was deeply likable. "I've just signed the papers. This is the house she was dreaming on one day. I thought I'd make that day sooner rather than later."

"I like it." Rose nodded with approval, hoping he could feel the appreciation bright in her heart. "I approve of how you're treating my cousin."

"Well, it's easy to be good to her. She's pretty great." Adam blushed, a little bashful of his strong feelings, which was endearing too.

"You've moved to town, which means you're starting up your teaming business here." Seth looked interested as he knuckled back his hat, revealing his fine, handsome features. "And now that you've bought this house, you have to know what we're all expecting."

"I imagine Annie is expecting it too." Adam shrugged, as if they wouldn't be waiting long for some more really excellent news. Someone in the house called Adam's name (it sounded like the middle Montgomery son, who handled most of the family's real estate business) and Adam sighed. "Got to go. Have a nice day."

"You too," Seth found himself answering, tipping his hat before reining Wally down the street. He shook his head, wondering how any man in his right mind could take on the prospect of marriage as if it were no big deal. Personally, Seth was more cautious about that. He liked to think things through carefully, consider ever angle first.

"I know something not one of my sisters knows." Happy, Rose relaxed back against the seat. "It's a rare event. My sisters are really nosy."

"I don't have that problem. My brothers are all back in Ohio." Seth couldn't say why his gaze kept cutting sideways to look at her. Maybe because she was so pretty. You just had to look. "When Ma's second husband died and she went back to working for Maureen, my brothers were settled down in jobs and marriages. So I agreed to move out here with her. It was a dangerous journey back then. We went by wagon driving cattle. Maureen and Wilson's men came along, too. That meant a lot of gunpowder so chances were she'd be safe. But this was my ma. I wanted to make sure."

"That had to be an amazing and hard trip." Rose's soft alto dipped down with concern. "It was tough enough going by stagecoach, the way we did. And even we were robbed, frightened by the possibility of Indian raids and outlaw attacks. I can't imagine what it had to be like for you."

"We had the cattle, so we weren't moving fast." Seth leaned back, reining Wally left onto Main. The sleigh whizzed along, the runners almost soundless on the hard-packed snow and ice. His chest felt tight, remembering leaving everything he knew behind and heading for the unknown. "We had enough guns and men, armed and ready day and night, so we were safe, but it didn't feel safe. We only had one shoot out with a tribe. I took an arrow to the arm. Nothing bad, but it left a scar."

"How awful. I'm glad you were all right." Rose had a mesmerizing, compassionate smile. Not because it was the brilliant, look-at-me kind, but more like it was subtle, gentle in the way the first beam of sunlight comes to a summer dawn. Quiet, but when you notice it, you've never seen anything more beautiful. Unaware of her rare beauty, she brushed a lock of golden hair out of her face with her knit glove. "Aumaleigh and your mother have never talked about their journey here to Montana."

"It wasn't a happy time." He gritted his teeth, sending Wally into a faster walk. "My stepfather was gone, Mom was not the same after that marriage. Not for a long time after, anyway. Maureen's illness was worsening, so Aumaleigh's burden had increased greatly. She didn't want to leave their home in Ohio."

"I didn't know that." Rose bit her bottom lip, surprised and curious. "Aumaleigh seems happy here and so settled. She likes Montana."

"I'm sure she does. Time has passed and she's made this place her home. Her friends are here and her family." Seth scrunched his mouth up, like a man debating the merits of revealing a long held piece of secret information. "But according to my ma, Aumaleigh fought leaving for years. As the family's finances dwindled, they discussed leaving their ranch to start over with homesteaded land in the West, but Aumaleigh resisted."

"Did your mother say why?" Okay, call her curious but she had to know. Although down deep, she had a clue. Because honestly, how many hours had she and her sisters spent wondering or discussing their aunt's mysterious and long-ago love affair that they knew almost nothing about? "Did it have to do with her Gabriel?"

"That's what I've heard." Seth nodded once, definite, sadness and empathy softening the shadowed depths of his dark, obsidian eyes. "Although my uncle Gabriel had moved on—"

"He was your *uncle?*" Rose's jaw dropped. Shock raced through her like a punch, nearly knocking her off the seat. "Did I know that? No, I don't think I did. How could we not know? Because Aumaleigh hasn't told us much of anything, that's why. I can't imagine how hard it must have been for her. She's so close to your mother."

"And she was way back in the day too." Seth's tone softened, as if respectful of the past and of Aumaleigh's broken heart. "What I know, I know secondhand or from overhearing my mother speak of it. My uncle Gabriel moved to town because work was scarce and my ma knew one of the local ranchers was hiring. He met Aumaleigh and started courting her. Word is that he loved her very much. With every piece of his heart."

"Well, how could he not? Aumaleigh is adorable." Rose's chest felt tight and scratchy, hurting for her aunt because she knew how it ended. In utter heartbreak. "What was he like?"

"A good man." Seth's answer came quick and sure—there was no doubt. "I can't count all the times he helped out Ma. He loaned me part of the start-up costs for my livery and refused to accept a penny of interest when I paid him back. I sent it anyway."

"That doesn't surprise me." Some of the shock was wearing off and Rose turned to the man beside her—big, strong-strapping. Dark-haired, dark-eyed, iron jaw. He was Gabriel's nephew. She wondered if he looked anything like his uncle. If so, then no wonder Aumaleigh had fallen for him. She squinted at Seth, trying to see him through unbiased eyes—through a single woman's eyes.

Totally stunning and manly. That sculpted profile, those steely good-looks, that kind, likable charm. No wonder Aumaleigh fell hard.

Any girl would.

"I don't know you very well, Seth," Rose admitted. "But you come across as an honest, good guy."

"You've got me all wrong. You gotta be careful," he quipped, blushing a little at the attention. Perhaps he was the humble sort, too. "Looks can be deceiving."

"I'll remember that." She laughed lightly, and suddenly it felt as if she were with an old friend. It was a comfortable, totally at ease feeling with someone she truly trusted. "Now, back to your uncle and my aunt. Do you know what happened? Why they didn't wind up married and happy?"

"No idea." Seth shook his head, scattering his black hair. His mouth turned down in a sad frown. "All I know is that it broke Gabriel's heart beyond repair. Aumaleigh's too. I think Maureen had something to do with it."

"Considering what I've heard of her, that sounds exactly right." Sad, too, Rose thought, her chest hitching hard. Aumaleigh must have really loved Gabriel. She'd spent her life alone. She'd never loved again. She'd never married. Perhaps no other man could compare.

"My uncle was terribly sad for a long time. He moved away from that Ohio town," Seth confessed. "He couldn't stay in the same place as Aumaleigh, bumping into her now and then. He said it was too painful. So he settled down in a different part of the state and eventually started courting Victoria and married her. She was very nice, and we loved her so much for making him happy again."

"Victoria." Rose repeated the name, instinctively not wanting to like the woman who had taken Aumaleigh's place, but truly, that wasn't the woman's fault. It was a tragic tale. "Were they happy?"

"Yes. Very." Seth fell silent as the town rolled away and the snowy countryside rose up to meet them. Sun glittered on miles of snow and kissed the nearby mountain tops with such blinding brightness it felt as if there could never be any sadness anywhere.

But the sorrow in Rose's heart took over. Poor Aumaleigh.

"They had three children, my cousins." When Seth finally spoke, his baritone was thick and scratchy. As if he felt that old pain too, as if he were touched by the sad tale. "Gabriel's story is a happy one, in the end. But my mother says he was never the same, not after Aumaleigh broke his heart."

"I suspect she was never the same either," Rose said quietly, hanging her head, sad in a way she'd never been before. The image of Verbena and Zane together through the window, caught in a private, cozy and loving moment, flashed into her mind, reminding her of what her aunt had lost. Love was hard, she thought, just like life. Some things just weren't fair. Deeper sympathy for her aunt carved its way into her heart.

"So, after my uncle and watching both of my mother's marriages fall apart, I'm glad I'm a bachelor." Seth winked, as if trying to lighten the moment. "No surprise there, huh?"

"No kidding." She gave a weak smile, because the sorrow lodged in her heart was stubborn. "It makes me glad I'm not going after the fairy-tale kind of love."

"What does that mean? Isn't all love a fairy-tale?" Seth's forehead scrunched up, his eyebrows drawing into a puzzled but curious arch. His black eyes twinkled inquisitively. He was teasing her.

"I'm after something more practical," she confessed, as her driveway came into sight and Wally turned onto it, prancing proudly, mane and tail flying. "Something that's less earth-shattering but nice all the same."

"You play it safe. Smart. I like that." When Seth smiled at her, his entire face lit up.

Something funny happened inside her chest—a combination of her heart skipping a beat and tumbling downward, out of place. Odd, very odd. Maybe it was hunger? It was almost lunchtime and she'd been tormented both by the delicious scents of the baked bread she'd delivered and the muffins. Not fair at all. She pressed a hand to her stomach, but it wasn't gurgling or growling.

McPhee Manor came into sight. The sun winked over the top of the grand, two-story house, glinting on big bay windows, highlighting turrets and gracing gingerbread trim. The porch gave the house a smiling look.

Home, Rose thought, still a little awed that such a glorious house was really hers. A year ago, they'd been struggling to pay for the extra coal to heat their one rented room in a Chicago boardinghouse. Now they could afford to heat an eighteen room estate. Amazing. It was incredible what one year and a good turn in one's luck could do. She really was incredibly grateful.

"The renovation looks great. Better than new." Seth drew Wally to a halt at the edge of the shoveled walkway. "Tyler's men must almost be done with their remodeling work."

"Oh, they finished up just in time for Verbena's wedding supper." Which had been held at the Manor, of course, stuffed full of most of the people from town. It had been a fun time, full of laughter, frivolity and delicious food (Aumaleigh's kitchen staff had done the cooking. Yum). "I think Tyler's men have moved on to work on Beckett's cottage. They're adding a few rooms. Oh, look. Here comes my nosy sisters."

"They didn't waste any time getting out here, did they?" Seth gave a light, soft bark of laughter. The sound seemed to skittle through her all the way to her toes and made them tingle. He held out a hand to help her out of the sleigh.

What a gentleman. A warm feeling settled dead center in her chest as she took his offered hand and hopped off the seat. When she looked up, the front door was wide open and two of her sisters had crowded onto the porch, likely full of questions. Everyone was eager to hear how Verbena was doing as a happy newlywed, no doubt.

"My sisters are a formidable force," she told Seth. "And did I mention meddlesome?"

"Makes me glad I don't have any sisters." He winked in his amiable way, and his smile brought out two deep dimples in his lean cheeks. Striking. Really striking. It really was too bad some woman hadn't snatched him up.

"Thanks, Seth. I owe you," she called over her shoulder, heading down the walkway.

"Yes, you will owe me, and don't think I'll forget," he called above the *chink-chink* of Wally's steeled shoes on the snow. "You owe me big time."

"I always pay my debts," Rose answered easily, hardly noticing the ice under her shoes or the wintry breeze knifing through her coat or the fact that her backside felt achy from her fall in town. Seth, too far away to answer, held up one gloved hand in both an acknowledgement and a goodbye wave. She didn't know why she turned to watch him go, disappearing down the tree-lined lane, jingle bells ringing. Maybe because she couldn't help wondering about him, this man she'd known as a small child. Maybe there was a friendship bond there still, after all this time.

"Rose!" Magnolia shouted from the porch. She'd wrapped her arms around herself, because the wool shawl she'd tossed on wasn't warm enough for the chilly December day. She stomped her feet, presumably to stay warm but more than likely from impatience. "Stop staring into space and get in here. We have questions."

"Big questions," Daisy called out. Her engagement ring sparkled on her left hand as she held open the door. Her molasses-dark hair was tied up in a relaxed knot on her head, and soft tendrils had fallen down to frame her heart-shaped face. She radiated with the contented bliss of a bride-to-be. "Aren't you freezing?"

"Uh, yes." Rose answered, realizing she was. She ripped her gaze from the shadowed lane, now that Seth was gone, and hurried toward the front porch. "I'm really freezing, by the way. We spotted snow clouds in the northwest. I think we're in for more snow."

"She's trying to change the subject," Magnolia realized, spinning on her heel with a swirl of her sapphire-blue wool dress and led the way into the house. "She probably thinks we aren't going to ask why a man other than her beau drove her home."

"And where's Jane?" Daisy asked, blue eyes snapping with nosiness. "Magnolia got back from her deliveries nearly an hour ago."

"Jane had some trouble, but Seth is taking care of it." Rose swooped in, unbuttoning her coat. "But we won't be able to drive her for a while. Something's wrong with her hoof."

"So, we're down one horse?" Daisy frowned, her forehead furrowing with thought as she closed the door and shrugged off her coat. "That's not convenient. Well, we'll just have to juggle the horses a bit more."

"Which is really too bad," Magnolia commented, waggling her brows, always quick to humor. She hung up her shawl on the coat tree. "Horses are so heavy to juggle. My arms get tired really fast."

"Funny." Rose laughed. She adored her little sister's humor. But then again, it didn't take much to amuse her. She hung up her coat. "My arms get tired, too. Maybe we should let Daisy juggle the horses."

"Punny." Daisy rolled her eyes, heading down the hall. "Well, today won't be much of a problem. We only have one delivery for the afternoon. One of you can drive, but we need one of you here. We have a lot of baking to do for tomorrow."

"I'll go," Rose said, because she had an ulterior motive. "I don't mind going back out in the cold."

"Only because you love to drive," Magnolia commented, tapping down the hallway behind her. "Which I completely get, because I do too. I love our horses."

"No kidding." Rose sighed. She really did love horses.

"Now I'm worried about Jane." Daisy led the way into the large, beautiful kitchen. Red-oak cabinets lined the walls and towered over gleaming counters. In the far nook, a round table and five chairs basked in the waning sunlight of a big bay window view overlooking the orchard and breath-taking mountains.

"What's wrong with Jane?" Oldest sister Iris asked from the stove, wooden spoon in hand. Slender and tall, she was delicately beautiful with strawberry blond hair and periwinkle blue eyes. Her lovely features crinkled with concern. "Did something happen to her?"

"Seth is taking care of her," Rose said confidently. "She'll be all right. She has to rest her hoof is all."

"Oh, the poor dear." Iris, tender-hearted, set down her spoon. "Is there something we can do?"

"I'll ask Seth," Daisy offered. "I hate to think of her in any pain."

"She's in capable hands," Rose assured them, her toes tingling again. Probably due to chilblains. Her feet were beginning to thaw in the warm house, which proved exactly how cold it was out there. "Verbena is happy. Isn't that what you were all wanting to know?"

"We *know* she's happy," Magnolia said, stealing a cooling cookie from a wire rack on the counter. "She's with Zane. How could she not be happy?"

"Did she and Zane like the muffins?" Iris asked, lifting the small pan of melted butter from the stove. "We're sending supper for them too, Rose you'll take it on your delivery run. I don't want her to have to do a lot of cooking. She should be spending time with her husband."

"They looked as happy as two lovebirds in a tree, all lovey dovey." Rose pulled out a chair and plopped onto the cushion, remembering. It sure had looked wonderful, just the two of them so happy together. Her heart yearned for that kind of bliss—although that was a yearning she kept secret. No one needed to know.

Not every wish a woman had could come true. She'd learned the truth about wishes. So few of them actually were fulfilled. In all of her life, Rose could only think of a handful that had—and those she'd reserved for when it mattered most. For instance, she'd wished for Iris, who'd been near to dying, to survive her serious bout with scarlet fever. She'd wished for enough income to meet their basic living needs.

And for happiness for her sisters when they'd moved here to Montana Territory.

Yes, a wish coming true was a rare thing. But when she looked around her, so many of them lately had come true. Verbena was married. Daisy about to be. Magnolia engaged. A lump caught in Rose's throat—gratitude, yes, but something more. Everything was changing. Verbena was no longer with them. Next it would be Daisy. Soon it would only be Iris and her rattling around in this enormous house. And one day, if her feeling for Wade turned into something much larger, then it would be only Iris.

Sadness wedged into her chest, tight between her ribs. Yes, that was life, always changing. So she took a long moment, just watching her sisters—Iris, face blushed from working over the hot stove; Daisy giving instructions as she whipped up a bowl of vanilla icing; Magnolia sneaking a clean spoon into the bowl to taste-test.

These were the loves of her life, Rose thought, her heart full. Her sisters and this time with them was precious. She savored the moment, remembering the small things—the feel of contentment in the room, the ring of laughter—and imprinting it deep in her memory and onto her heart.

"What are you doing just lazing around?" Magnolia demanded with mischief in her blue eyes. "Get over here, Rose. There's work to do."

"You know me," she said, pushing out of the chair and landing on her feet. "I'm the frosting queen."

"Queen? I don't think so," Magnolia argued playfully, taking the icing bowl from Daisy. "I don't see your tiara."

"I left it upstairs," she quipped, joining in on the laughter and the fun as she washed up at the sink.

CHAPTER FOUR

By mid-afternoon, snow was falling steadily across the Bluebell valley. Rose squinted out the parlor window at the pummeling white stuff. Gorgeous, sure, but it looked mighty cold out there.

"Better wrap up the cakes really well," she called loud enough to be heard in the kitchen. Iris didn't answer, so she spun around, wool skirt and petticoats twirling and sidestepped to avoid tripping over Magnolia, who was hunkered down on the floor in front of the fireplace absorbing all the heat. Rose crooked an eyebrow. "What are you doing?"

"I'm organizing the list for the Christmas gifts we are making and giving." Magnolia shoved a lock of blond hair out of her troubled eyes and stared down at the paper she was scribbling on. "With all the sewing and knitting we've been doing on them, it's been hard to keep track of what we've got and what we still need to do so I'm making a list."

"A long list by the looks of it." Rose peered over her sister's shoulder at the impressive tally. "That's a lot of gifts—or is that the list of gifts we have yet to make?"

"Yep. We've gotten a little behind, but no worries. We can do this." Magnolia blew out a breath and the lock of hair she'd just tucked behind her ear fell across her face once again. She shoved it back. "If I get this organized, then the gift making will go faster. That's my theory, anyway."

"That's a good theory. I'm just surprised you came up with it." Rose couldn't help joking.

"Sometimes I even surprise myself." Magnolia grinned, tossing down the list. She was a doll—quirky and flawed, but then who wasn't? "Aren't you supposed to be spearheading this? It was your idea after all."

"I know, I'm full of brilliant ideas," Rose teased merrily, although her inspiration for how to best celebrate their first Christmas as non-poor-people really was one of her very best ideas ever. "Maybe I should do more of this—thinking up ideas and letting you do all the work to implement them."

"You'd better make Iris do all the work." Full of mischief, Magnolia rolled her eyes. "You know I'm lazy."

"That'll be the day." Rose twirled into the hallway, snatching her coat from the tree, careful of the bulging pockets. "Are you coming on the delivery with me?"

"No. Tyler is coming by after work. He's joining us for supper." Magnolia lit up, beaming with precious happiness.

Now that was how Rose wanted her sister to look—brimming with joy and desperately blissful. She could kick Mrs. Montgomery in the shin (okay, not very hard, but hard enough for her to notice) for not being grateful her son had found Magnolia. No other woman could love Tyler more. Not one.

"Did you hear me?" she asked Iris the second she popped into the kitchen.

"Not only did I hear you, but I'm one step ahead of you." Sweet Iris worked busily at the counter, where she'd lined up a row of small bakery boxes in perfect order. "I grabbed two crates from the attic. We'll fill the crates and cover them with a tarp to keep everything snow free."

"Excellent." Leave it to Iris. She was full of ingenuity. Which was why their bakery business was flourishing—and a good thing too. Rose slipped into her coat and started buttoning up. "It's a long ride and we don't want anything to be snow-soggy. These are new customers. Think of the impression that would make."

"We're getting a lot of new customers lately." Iris plunked the last, small individual Christmas-tree shaped cake into the small box and secured the lid. "Before we know it, this will be a full-time thing."

"A real business," Rose agreed, working on the last coat buttons before pulling out her hat and gloves from the stuffed-full pockets. "Isn't that what we've been working for?"

"I just never thought it would happen so fast. It's like a little dream." Iris smiled. She looked a little brighter, stood a little taller. These days she was more like the older sister Rose used to know—before the tragedy that had changed her, that had ruined her life.

Sympathy mixed with love as she buttoned her coat. "It's proof dreams do come true. But keep in mind that if we get any more business, when we lose Daisy to marriage, we're going to have to think about hiring help."

"It's exciting to think about *when* we can afford it." Iris beamed, giving the box she'd just closed a loving pat. "I'll get these crated up."

"Be careful of my frosting job." Rose couldn't help being overprotective. She'd spent hours frosting those little cakes green and decorating them carefully. The Deer Springs lady's book club would be delighted—so delighted they would never want to order another baked good from anyone else. She marched over to help set the small boxes into the bottom of one of the crates, keeping a careful eye on Iris the whole time (even though she knew Iris was the careful sort). She couldn't help it. When she did a job, she did it right, all the way, one hundred percent. Customer satisfaction guaranteed.

"Cal's here with the sleigh!" Magnolia's voice rang through the house, although she sounded distracted. Probably still troubled by her Christmas-gift-organization mission.

Maybe I'll lend a hand after I get back, Rose thought. She set the last cake in her crate, gently nudging other boxes aside so it would fit in. It was so thrilling to think about Christmas this year. Yes, this year they were going to do it right. Big time. They were going to celebrate as if there had never been a Christmas before. They could afford it, thanks to their enormous inheritance.

"I'll help you to the door." Iris scooped up one of the crates. "Are you sure you can do this alone? I'd go with you, but I have more baking to do for tomorrow's orders."

"I'll be fine, and I'll be back in time to start frosting." Rose hefted up her crate, leading the way down the hallway through the house.

"And, before you ask, yes, I know the way. I got clear directions when I took the order last week. No worries."

"You know that won't stop me." Iris's sweet smile lit up her heart-shaped face. "I'm not sure I like you driving alone all that way."

"I'll be perfectly fine, don't worry." Rose paused in front of the archway into the parlor, winking at Magnolia who was still sprawled out on the floor. "I transferred the snake stick from the buggy to the sleigh when it got snowy, so I'm well-armed."

"The snake stick." Magnolia sighed fondly. "It is a great stick. I miss whacking things with it."

"Snakes, you mean." Rose shivered. Ew. "I'd rather not have to whack anything with it. I take comfort in the fact that there are no snakes out and about to scare me and the horse. It's one of the best things about snowstorms."

"I'm with you on that," Magnolia agreed, turning her attention back to her list, her forehead furrowed in concentration.

"Be careful of strangers," Iris advised, balancing the crate on one hip as she freed a scarf from the coat tree. She looped it around Rose's neck. "Just because Ernest is gone doesn't mean you should throw caution to the wind."

"Iris, Ernest is *gone.*" Rose freed two fingers from the crate to wrestle open the door.

"And George is in jail—" Iris shuddered in memory of the ordeal Ernest, Verbena's former ex-beau had put them through. Not to mention his accomplice, George Klemp. "We're rid of them, but you just never know about men. I mean it, Rose."

"You worry too much," Rose said gently, because Iris wasn't wrong. There were bad men in this world, men who found pleasure in harming innocent women. But this wasn't Chicago, and she did have the snake stick, after all. She wasn't afraid to use it. Besides, she wasn't going to live in fear, the way they'd been forced to do when Ernest had been stalking Verbena.

"I'll be fine." She managed to pull open the door without dropping the crate. "Keep baking. Oh, and what are we having for supper? Something good?"

"I was going to make chicken and dumplings." Iris gave a start when a male shadow emerged from the thickly falling snow, crossing the yard (Cal, their aunt's stable boy). She recovered and politely handed her crate to Cal, staying in the doorway where it was warmer. "Rose, why don't you stop by and invite Wade to supper? We're already having Tyler over. We'd like to get to know Wade better, since he's courting you."

"Beauing me," Rose corrected, her face heating even in the bitterly cold wind. She tromped down the snowy steps and down the walk to where the silhouette of a horse and sleigh stood waiting for her. "Marvin, is that you?"

Marvin, the gentle old gelding, turned toward her, ears up and gave a friendly horsy nicker. His rich brown coat and black mane and tail were dappled with white, poor thing, but his brown eyes shone, eager, as if happy to be the one to help her with the deliveries. He really was such a good horse. She stopped to give his cheek a kiss on her way to the sleigh.

"It's starting to feel like Christmas," she told Marvin merrily, wedging the crate into the foot space on the passenger side. "All that's missing are jingle bells and a Christmas tree."

"I'd be happy to cut you down a tree. You just say the word." Young Cal tromped through the snow, handily setting the other crate onto the driver's side floor. "Is it okay if I stow this here? Otherwise, it'll just slide off the seat."

"Yes, I'll make do." She settled onto the seat with her feet off to one side. Not exactly comfortable, but the safety of the baked goods were the priority here. She waited while Cal spread out the tarp Iris had also given him. "Thanks. We'll get back to you about the tree. We'll definitely take you up on the offer."

"Have a good drive, Rose." Cal tipped his hat ever so politely.

All it took was a shake of the reins and a few steps from Marvin and the stable boy was nothing but a shadow in the downfall...and then he was nothing at all as the gelding took off down the lane. Soon, even the cozy glow of the lamp-lit windows disappeared, and there was just her and Marvin alone in the storm, traveling the snowy roads together.

An adventure. Just what she loved. Rose shook snow off the buffalo robe folded up on the seat beside her and huddled beneath it. Snow flew into her eyes as she reined Marvin around the corner and onto the county road. She kept the reins in her left hand so she could check her pockets with her right hand—yep, the things she'd snuck in after lunch were still here. She felt encouraged, on a mission now, as the snow began blowing hard, almost straight-line.

"You know where I'm coming from, don't you, Marvin?" she told him. The gelding pricked his ears, swiveling them back to catch her every word. "You had it rough before you came here, being a rental horse, doing without a lot of comforts and even enough food by the looks of you. But you're safe and warm and well fed now, aren't you, boy?"

Marvin nickered again. If he didn't understand her words, then he definitely grasped her sentiment. He held his head high, his neck proudly arched and his step quickened as a fork in the road came into sight.

Instead of turning him left, which she should have done, she detoured toward town on her secret mission. Swiping snow out of her eyes with her gloved hand, she pulled Marvin into a slow walk before the first official block of town and turned him onto a forgotten lane cutting through a grove of trees.

"Oscar!" She drew Marvin to a stop in a desolate clearing, surrounded by more trees. Overhead their limbs writhed and danced in the hard wind, rustling and whooshing. She couldn't see anyone so she dropped the reins to cup her hands to her mouth. "Oscar. Are you here?"

No answer. The wind howled, the trees thrashed, the snow hailed down like white fluffy bullets. A sinking feeling settled in her stomach as she looked around, squinting through the snow. Maybe he'd moved on. Maybe his pride kept him from accepting her help.

Poor Oscar. She'd met him awhile ago, but she hadn't told anyone about him. Not even her sisters. Ignoring the pelting snow, she hopped out from beneath the buffalo robe, shivering as the wind punched her, plowing through the snow to the little shelter built beneath one of the trees. The dwelling was nothing but cut boughs tied together to make a hut. No smoke rose from the makeshift steel pipe poking up through the thatched-bough roof, so she pulled the cloth-wrapped bundles from her pockets, set them against the door.

Perhaps he would be back to find them before a stray or wild animal did. At least she hoped so, remembering how it felt to go hungry. That deep, dark gnawing, endless and strident, would never leave her, not completely. She would always remember that week as a child when her pa had fallen ill and there'd been no paycheck and they'd squeezed by on one slice of bread each—just one meal a day.

"Oscar!" She hesitated by the sleigh, cupped her hands to her mouth and called one last time.

Still no answer.

Concerned for him, she climbed back beneath the buffalo robes.

"Rose?" A man's familiar voice broke out of the storm, deep with surprise. Wade Wetherby, the most handsome deputy in town, emerged from the white fall—first a shadow, then a silhouette, then full flesh-and-blood man. Snowflakes clung to his collar-length blond hair and crowned his dark Stetson. His navy jacket and tin lawman's badge emphasized the fine cut of his shoulders and chest. He frowned, puzzled. "What are you doing out here?"

"Well—" She hesitated, remembering her pledge to Oscar. A promise was a promise and she couldn't break it. "I'm on a cake delivery."

"And you've gotten lost." Wade jumped to conclusions, reining his fine red roan gelding to a stop by her sleigh. He towered above her, handsome in the right light. His hazel eyes crinkled in the corners pleasantly. "Come this way. Follow me. I'll get you headed in the right direction."

"Thanks, Wade." She sighed inwardly. At least she wouldn't have to explain. Let him think that, as a woman, she was hopeless when it came to directions. "How is your afternoon going?"

"Pretty quiet. Most troublemakers are staying in because of the storm, so it's not all bad." He flashed her a boyish smile. With his angular face and chiseled chin, he did have a certain charm. "I'm surprised you didn't wait until better weather to make your delivery. It's only a cake. This here is a pretty serious storm."

"Oh, I couldn't do that to Iris." She turned Marvin around, getting him going back down the lane while Wade kept his gelding at her side, pacing them. "She is counting on this business succeeding. She hasn't said it in so many words, of course, but I know the truth. She's relying on me. Besides, Marvin isn't afraid of a little snow. Are you, Marvin?"

The gelding arched his neck even more, all fortitude, plunging through the deepening accumulation. Truly a horse a girl could depend on. Hard not to love him for that.

"Then maybe I should accompany you, if it isn't far." Wade tipped his hat, knocking snow off its brim. Kindness softened his hazel eyes.

"I'm on duty, but the sheriff won't mind. Milo is awfully fond of your cakes."

"It's good to have the law on my side." Rose pulled Marvin to a stop, since they'd reached the end of the overgrown lane, where the outskirts of town stretched out around them in a white, storm-covered haze. "But I'm on my way to Deer Springs."

"I'm afraid that's out of my jurisdiction." Wade's voice dipped gently.

He was a good man and Rose hoped he was the right man for her—but she didn't know. She didn't feel tingly and shivery, the way Magnolia always said she felt whenever she was with her Tyler. Nor did she feel a deep connection to the man, a powerful bond, which Daisy had with her Beckett. Verbena always felt captivated by her Zane, held by the heart and soul. Rose experienced none of that.

She didn't expect to. But the pleasant comfort that came from the sight of his smile, of the strong look of him sitting protectively on his horse, a man of the law and so dependable seeming—well, that was rather nice. Not earth-shaking. Not soul-binding.

But nice.

"That's okay." She swiped snowflakes from her eyelashes. "I know the way. Besides, you know me. I love zipping around in this little sleigh. And Marvin looks up for an adventure. Right, Marvin?"

Marvin gave an amiable nod, always ready to be of service.

Wade gave a low, rumbling chuckle. A really nice sound. The kind a girl could get used to.

"But I *can* escort you as far as the town limits." Wade reined his big roan down the street. "I'd go farther, but I promised Milo I'd keep an eye on things here in town. We've got a few vagabonds slinking around, looking for opportunities to steal. Got to keep our stores and citizens safe."

"Right." Rose swallowed hard, worrying about Oscar. Judging by the way Wade set his shoulders a little straighter and drew up taller in his saddle, this was an assignment he took seriously. She liked that about Wade, that he was a hard worker and did a good job for the town, but she feared he wouldn't have compassion for Oscar if he knew about him.

Good thing he hadn't noticed the tree-bough shelter built into that cedar. She bit her lip, hoping Oscar would be all right.

"Oh, I almost forgot." She slackened Marvin's reins, allowing him to set the pace, to keep up with the deputy's horse. "You're invited to supper tonight. Iris is making chicken and dumplings."

"That sounds awful tasty." Wade gave a nod of approval, but only a small nod. His gaze drifted off down the hazy road, as if staring at the mountains, invisible today, shrouded by clouds and snowfall. He seemed to hesitate.

Hoping to entice him further, she hurriedly added. "You won't be the only guy there. Tyler will be there too."

"Tyler, huh?" Wade gave a bigger nod at that, his lean face furrowing with thought. "I'd like to, but I already have something going on. I promised my sister. I'm not sure at this late notice if I can get out of it. Although I sure would like to."

"Oh, all right." A little disappointing, but she knew that Wade had family obligations, always helping out with his brother and widowed sister. She liked that about him. "Maybe another time?"

"Absolutely. I'll look forward to it." He drew his gelding to a halt in the middle of the road. Snow dappled him, clinging to his shoulders and hat, catching on his thighs and knees. "You drive safe now. Marvin, don't you go too fast for the lady, you hear?"

Marvin swiveled his ears at the friendly words and gave a little nicker, as if he already had it covered. With a light touch of the reins, the big horse took off at a good pace, trotting through the snow like a warrior on the march.

Rose glanced over her shoulder, lifting a hand in a farewell wave. It had to be a positive sign that Wade still sat in his saddle, watching over her as she drove away. He lifted his gloved hand in return, growing fainter as the storm closed around him, stealing him from her sight.

She wished her heart gave a little sigh, but it did not. Maybe in time, she thought, settling back against the seat as the frosting-white countryside sped by. This was no fairy-tale love. The regular kind—the one for average girls like her—progressed differently. She would just have to be patient. It would happen in time.

* * *

Seth gave the knotted rein a tug, standing in the lee of the covered boardwalk. At the hitching post, he'd had a good view of Wade and of Rose, talking together before she'd driven off in her sleigh.

"What does she see in him?" Nathaniel Denby asked from the boardwalk above. The town's attorney gave his spectacles a shove up his nose. "I had first shot at them, you know. When the McPhee sisters came to town, they stepped foot in my office first. Not one of them seemed interested in me. But why Wade?"

"Don't know." Seth shrugged, giving Wally and his brother William a pat on their noses before climbing up the slick steps. "Maybe it's the badge?"

"A badge does not a man make." Nathaniel shook his head. He was a good guy, the kind who always did the right thing. Honest. Dependable. "Guess we're both out of luck. Again."

"Hey, I'm not looking." Seth held up both hands, an innocent gesture as his boots struck a rhythm across the boardwalk. Well, he wasn't *seriously* looking, anyway. It was more like window shopping. He looked, but he wasn't prepared to buy. He was far too cautious for that. Not to mention he'd tried love once.

Disaster.

"I'm looking." Nathaniel gave a heavy sigh. It wasn't easy being a bachelor in this town where eligible single ladies were few and far between. "What do you think she sees in a man like Wade?"

"Probably whatever he wants her to." Seth grabbed the brass knob, hauling open the heavy wood and glass door. "But I don't think she'll end up with him."

"Why do you say that?" Nathaniel seemed curious. Not because he was probably interested in Rose, so much as wondering why he was still a bachelor when he didn't want to be.

"It comes down to money." Seth shrugged. "Wade might have had a real chance back when Rose was just Rose. Now she's an heiress. Wealthy in her own right. Maybe she hasn't quite realized that, but when it sinks in, that'll change. When she gets used to being rich and starts seeing herself that way, she'll want someone equal to her. Someone who can fit the bill."

"Guess that leaves me out entirely." Nathaniel gave a good-natured shoulder shrug. "I'm just a regular working guy."

"A working guy with an office," Seth corrected, stepping across the threshold and into the post office. "That's a step up from a regular guy like me."

"I'm not too sure about that." Nathaniel shook his head. "Have a good one, Seth."

"You too." Seth grinned, pushing all thoughts of Rose and Wade out of his head. He wasn't quite successful.

"Afternoon, Seth." A boisterous voice boomed through the tiny storefront. "I saw you had your hands full earlier with one of them McPhee sisters."

"Rose, you mean?" He huffed out a breath. So much for trying to get her out of his thoughts. He ambled over to the front counter, where the postmaster, wearing a white shirt, black trousers and a green cap, looked eager for the latest gossip. Who knew what version of the tale was already circulating through town? Seth might as well set the record straight. "Rose slipped. I helped her up. That was the end of it."

"Not from what I hear." Fred, eager-eyed and grinning wide, absently wandered over to the mailboxes mounted on the wall behind him. "I saw the whole thing. How you rushed over to help, beating out that poor Latimer fella. He's never gonna find him a wife at the rate he's goin'. He'll talk any available woman to death and after that, even if she was interested, she'd change her mind. Anyway, the way I see it, there's got to be only one reason why you'd hurry over to beat him out with Rose."

"Yes, you're exactly right." Seth splayed his hands against the countertop. "I wanted to spare poor Miss McPhee from being talked to death by Lawrence. It was an act of gallantry, nothing more."

"I know what I saw." Fred grabbed a few envelopes and moseyed back to the counter. "You, taking her by the hand. You, trying not to look at her underthings. It was very gallant. Too gallant, if you ask me. You're sweet on her."

"She's a sweetheart. Who wouldn't like her?" It was best just to be honest, Seth decided, to tell the truth. "She's a likable girl. Her aunt and my mom are friends. Rose and I are friendly. But as for anything romantic, count me out. I'm more of a lone wolf."

"Why, that's just too darn bad." Instead of handing over the letters, Fred kept them, studying the return addresses. "And here I was rooting for you, Seth. You deserve a good woman."

"I'd rather have a poke in the eye," he quipped.

Fred gave a friendly scowl, shaking his head. "You young people. You don't know what life's about. Marriage is wonderful. Of course, I gotta say that. If word got back to my wife I said anything different, I'd be in big trouble. Hey, it looks like you got a bill from the steel supply over in Bear Hollow. And here's something for your ma. Want me to keep it for her? It looks real important, though. It's from Ohio."

"Ohio?" That got his attention. Seth thought of his uncle, remembering his conversation with Rose. "I'd better take it. It's probably from Ma's brother."

"That it is." Fred handed over the mail, looking as if he was mulling over that piece of news, like he wanted more information. "She and that brother of hers write each other a few times a year. It's nice when families stay in touch."

"Thanks, Fred." Seth glanced at his mail—yep, a bill and a letter from Gabriel. He pocketed both. "You have a good afternoon now."

"You too, Seth." Fred looked disappointed he hadn't gotten more of a scoop, but it wasn't his business.

No way, no how, Seth thought, letting the door shut behind him. He paused on the boardwalk, breathing in the crisp, clean scent of snow. The arctic air burned his lungs, and he felt alive and invigorated. He stared down at his uncle's envelope. Gabriel's story had been a sad one, too, before he'd married Victoria. Love was a hazard, no doubt about that. He tromped down the steps, chest tight, and a shadow walking along the street through the snowfall caught his eye.

He'd seen the man before. Down on his luck, limping along with his head down, shivering in his layered clothes. Back in September, Seth had looked the other way when he'd gone to open up his livery stable to catch sight of this same man skedaddle out the back door—he hadn't wanted to involve the law. No harm was done, the barn was exactly as Seth had left it. But that was back in September. He hadn't seen him since.

"How's it going?" Seth called out, concerned. Bad luck came around to everyone.

The man, looking a little surprised, shrugged and gave a small uncertain smile. "Okay, I guess. How's it with you?"

"It could be less stormy." He wondered about the man. Had he found work? Food? Shelter? Seth reached into his pocket and offered a coin or two, but the man was gone, lost in the snow. Well, maybe next time, he'd be faster with those kinds of questions and the coins. Troubled, Seth turned his attention to freeing Wally and William from the hitching post.

"Guess a trip out to visit Ma is in order," he told his team. "We've got a letter to deliver."

But the wind gusted, with a haunting, angry note that warned of worsening conditions. He thought about Rose out there on the road, worrying about her when he had no right to. She wasn't his to worry over, but that didn't stop him. Not one bit.

CHAPTER FIVE

"These cakes are *darling.*" Mrs. Caster, the leader of the book club, praised as she peered into one of the dozen boxes. "They are absolutely perfect and they smell *divine.*"

"I'm so pleased you're happy." Rose set the last bakery box on the lady's kitchen counter, thrilled at a job well done. "I couldn't resist adding a few extra touches."

"Yes, I see. The frosting ornaments are delightful." Mrs. Caster grabbed her reticule and loosened its strings. "The ladies are going to enjoy these so much. Thank you to you and your sisters for making our little pre-Christmas party so special."

"It's been our pleasure." Rose stacked the crates, setting them by the kitchen door.

"Here's what I owe you and a little something more." The buxom, genteel lady handed over a generous fold of greenbacks. Not a little tip, but a really awesome one. "You'll definitely be hearing from me again. You have yourself a Merry Christmas now."

"You too, Mrs. Caster. Thanks so much!" Beaming, she hauled her crates outside and pulled the door closed behind her. The payment felt delicious in her hand. She stuffed it carefully into her coat pocket before traipsing down the steps to where Marvin waited faithfully in the snow. It was coming down so hard, he was nothing but white.

"You poor baby." She tossed the crates onto the sleigh's floor and hurried over to him. "You're not a snowman, but a snow horse."

Marvin nickered low in his throat, as if he appreciated her sense of humor. Yes, she thought, swiping snow off his lashes and brushing it off his dear gray muzzle, he was easy to love.

"I'm going to leave your blanket on because it's gotten horribly cold out here," she told him, giving him a kiss on the nose. "If you don't mind, I have an errand to run, since we're in Deer Springs anyway. I won't be long, I promise. I'll hurry as fast as I can. I have fabric and yarn to buy to make Christmas gifts."

Marvin didn't seem to object, the gentleman that he was, so she climbed beneath the robe, picked up the reins and directed him through town to the store she had in mind. After tying Marvin up on the sheltered side of the street, she dashed into the lovely store, quickly chose a dozen skeins of lofty wool yarn and yards upon yards of wool fabric in different colors. It was already late by the time she untied Marvin and hurried him out of town. Knowing twilight would soon be falling, he set a quick pace on the road home.

It was dusky, with the last strains of gray daylight left, when she spotted him. A solitary figure limping along the road, leaning on a crooked branch he was using as a makeshift crutch. The stranger, upon hearing the horse's gait, moved over to the snow-drifted shoulder, dragging his right foot, keeping his head down. Limping along with heart-breaking slowness.

It was Oscar all over again. Sympathy welled up. This wasn't Chicago—this was small town Montana Territory, where neighbors helped neighbors.

"Are you all right?" she called out, tugged Marvin to a stop in the middle of the road.

"Just fine, Miss. Don't trouble yourself over me." The man had pleasant lines crinkling into the corners of his big blue eyes when he gave a small smile. "Walking is good for the constitution."

"True." She wiped snow out of her eyes. "But have you noticed the terrible storm? It's nearly a white-out."

"Is it snowing? I hadn't noticed." Light, as if he was the kind of man not about to let hardship or a threatening blizzard get him down. He stumbled, his wounded leg giving out on him in the uneven drifts. Down he went like a boulder—thud, face down, right in the middle of the icy snow. He hit hard. His stick flew onto the road and landed with a *crack*. Marvin startled. Air whooshed out of the man in a painful sounding groan.

Concerned, Rose watched, hurting for him, as he lay too stunned or too pained to move. She remembered back to the days in Chicago when they'd been desperately poor, struggling to pay off their parents' medical and funeral debts, and how Iris had been too sick and then too weak to work for a long time. Others had judged her harshly. Rose was not about to make that mistake.

Fearlessly, she launched out of the sleigh, sinking into the fresh snow. Winds pummeled her, wrapping her skirts tightly around her ankles as she fought her way to the fallen crutch. She snatched it up, fighting the winds to get to the man's side.

"Are you all right?" She had to shout to be heard above the wailing wind. "You hit pretty hard. I know just how that feels. I did the exact same thing just this morning."

"I'm fine, Miss." The man was about her age, she decided, although it was hard to tell because he was so snowy. He had sad eyes.

That got her every time. Empathy rushed up and she knelt to grab his elbow. "Can I help you up?"

"Thanks, Miss, but I can manage." He had a deep, strong voice as if he were a man of inner strength. He pushed his way to his knees and took his crutch from her. "It was kind of you to fetch this for me. Although it was a little foolhardy to stop and help a stranger like this. I could be dangerous."

"You didn't look dangerous." She hovered nearby, clasping and unclasping her hands, wishing to help but not wanting to injure his pride as he struggled onto his feet. She shrugged. "Besides, there's not a lot of crime around here. Especially not anymore."

She thought of Ernest, dead now, and of George Klemp, who'd confessed to his crimes in exchange for a lighter sentence. Both men had caused a lot of harm to her family, but that was an isolated incident. She thought of all the men in this county who'd joined the posse that night not too long ago when Verbena and Magnolia were kidnapped. Gratitude was too small of a word to describe what she felt toward those brave men who'd helped them. Now it was her turn to help others.

"It seems like fine country here." The stranger straightened his knit cap and leaned heavily on his crutch. He had a direct look, not shifty at all. "I've come to start fresh in a new place. After the accident."

He gestured toward his lame foot.

The poor fellow. She winced, biting her lip to keep from asking what had happened. Maybe it would be painful for him to have to relive the accident. And while she accused her sisters of being nosy, she had a confession to make. She was nosy, too.

"This is a wonderful place to start over," she assured him. "My sisters and I did the same thing."

"Did you now?" His smile was sad too, just like his eyes. He had a lost dog look about him. "I've sort of inherited a house and some property not far from here. I'm told it isn't much, but as I'm down on my luck, I'm awful grateful for it. Hopeful, too."

"That's exactly what happened with me and my sisters." Oh, this was a sign if ever there was one, Rose thought, gesturing toward her sleigh. "Why don't you let me drive you? It's likely the storm will get nothing but worse and it's a good ten more miles to the next town. I'm only going as far as that, but driving you is the least I can do."

"Why, I'd be awful obliged, Miss." The stranger dipped his chin in a humble sort of thanks. He retrieved a small, snow-covered rucksack from the side of the road and slung the strap over one shoulder. "Bluebell just happens to be my destination."

"What a coincidence." See, now this was more than a coincidence, she thought as she hurried to move her packages off the seat to make room for the stranger. It was fate. She was meant to help him. "I'm Rose McPhee. It's so nice to meet you, Mr.—?"

"Most folks just call me Junior." He held out his hand to help her into the sleigh.

Her heart warmed. For a long time, when things were at their worst back in Chicago, she'd forgotten there was good in people. Life had simply been that bleak. But lately, the goodness in humanity was everywhere she looked. She accepted his help, noticing he had several holes in his fraying gloves. She'd once had gloves like that too.

"Things will get better for you, you'll see." She slipped across the seat to take up the reins. "It happened for us, and it will happen for you."

"That's encouraging, Miss Rose." He shrugged in a modest, ordinary way, settling onto the seat beside her. His mouth tilted upward in the attempt at a smile. "I appreciate it very much."

"Good times always come around again, of that I'm absolutely sure. You just have to hold on until they get here." She tightened her grip on the leather straps as Marvin took off down the road, eager to get home. Not that she could blame him.

Boy, was it coming down! The falling flakes felt like ice bullets diving into her face a dozen at a time—needling her eyes, her cheeks, her nose, her mouth and making it impossible to speak. Junior seemed to be having the same problem, for he fell silent too, huddling on the edge of the cushioned seat, as if determined to keep a respectful distance, like a good gentleman ought to do.

It was a good thing she'd given him a ride, she reflected later as she pulled Marvin to a stop in town. The white-out had worsened. You couldn't see a single glow from any of the lamp-lit windows along the street. She could hardly make out Marvin's tail, much less the road in front of them.

"Thank you kindly again." Junior gripped the side of the sleigh, struggling to his feet. He leaned on his crutch as he hiked his rucksack onto his back. "Good fortune to you, Miss Rose, for helping me. Just you be careful driving home in this storm."

"I will." She waved goodbye to the town's newest resident, hoping he got settled in to his new house all right. Marvin seemed terribly impatient to get home. The poor dear must be half frozen. She would ask Cal to spoil him with some warmed oats.

"I've been keeping an eye out for you." A man astride a big buckskin draft horse broke out of the haze of thick snowfall and into sight. His Stetson sat at a confident angle, his invincible shoulders unbowed by the beat of the storm. Seth tipped his hat to her with one gloved hand. "Now I get to head home."

"You've been waiting out here all this time?" she asked, disbelieving. "No, that can't be true. You'd be an icicle by now."

"I was watching from the new building Tyler's company just finished." He sidled Wally close, coming into full focus. Light from the post office window faintly lit him. His friendly eyes just drew her in, warming her up from the inside out like the pleasant heat from a crackling hearth. "I had a few errands I was running while keeping an eye out. My mother would have killed me if I hadn't made sure you made it back. The roads are bad."

"And getting worse," she agreed. "But we're almost home. And since it's nearly suppertime, I'd better hurry."

"You had someone with you in the sleigh." He didn't move away, just kept his horse even with her as she drove along. "Who was it? Anyone I know?"

"Someone new to town, that's all. I'm sure you'll meet him soon enough." The road curved, taking her out of town and down the road toward home. "Have a good night, Seth, and don't you dare think you'll see me home. I can get there perfectly fine."

"What if it's the gentlemanly thing to do?" He arched a questioning brow.

"Too bad there's not a gentleman around," she teased him.

"I could take offense to that." He crooked up a smile, one that revealed perfect round dimples in his lean cheeks. "Okay, so I'm not really a gentleman. I have gentlemanly qualities."

"That's debatable."

"Ouch." His hand was on his chest, over his heart, feigning injury. "You wound me."

"You'll recover," she shouted, not sure if he heard her as the wind kicked up a notch, stirring the snow so hard, she lost sight of him. She twisted around in her seat, searching the shadows for him, but there was only a quick glimpse—the angle of his hat, the straight, strong line of his body—invincible. Something sighed deep inside her—probably because Seth Daniels was the kind of friend a girl could always count on, and that was a nice thing to have.

The storm and darkness closed in around her, making her feel alone, as if it was just her and Marvin together in the snow-driven world. She settled down with a sigh, aware of the warmth and light from her unexpected encounter with Seth fading away. She didn't know why she felt a little hollow as she snuggled more deeply into the buffalo robes. Maybe it was because she knew she wouldn't be seeing Wade tonight.

This was the third time he'd excused himself from a supper invitation with her sisters. Sure, he was busy, she knew that, and devoted to his family, but still. She sighed, a little wistful, turning her thoughts to the evening to come. A tasty supper, lively conversation and laughter, and then putting on the final touches for their dresses for Daisy's wedding. Fun times ahead. She should be concentrating on that and glad that her beau was the kind of man who put so much effort into helping his family. Family was important to him, just as it was to her. But she couldn't help feeling like something was wrong. She didn't know why.

* * *

The morning stayed silent and still, frozen under the blanket of a heavy snow. Seth shivered as he upended the wheelbarrow and forked out the last batch of soiled bedding into the stack behind the livery. His breath rose up in great foggy clouds as he tossed the pitchfork into the bucket of the wheelbarrow, gripped the worn wooden handles and heaved it into motion.

Schoolchildren paraded down the street on their way to school, their high-pitched voices, talk and laughter crisp and clear in the icy air. Easy to remember those days when he was a schoolboy, of lunch pails and spelling tests. He didn't miss it much. He took a moment to watch the kids march by, trying to ignore that part of him down deep inside that wouldn't mind being a father.

Sure, it was a strange longing for an affirmed bachelor, but somewhere out there, there had to be the right woman for him. He'd been so sure with Liz, courting her with blind devotion, not even considering she might not be as committed as he was. So staying a bachelor and not letting his heart fall until he was sure—now that was a real wise plan.

"Hey, Jane." He stowed the wheelbarrow, noticing the doleful mare watching him. She looked confused, as if she didn't know why she was here and not home in her stall at the Rocking M. He ambled over to her stall and rubbed her silky nose. "How's the foot feeling today? Better?"

She eyed him warily instead of answering him, and he remembered the man who used to be in charge of horse care at Aumaleigh's ranch. George Klemp. While Klemp had been fired a good while back, he'd taken out his anger and his sloppiness on the horses. Jane was a helpless victim of that lack of good care, and Seth was determined to make sure she would recover fully. She deserved that much.

"I'll whip up another poultice in a bit," he told her. "Then you'll be feeling even better."

Big brown eyes studied him. It must be hard to be a horse, completely dependent on how others treated you. He rubbed her cheek and then up over her ears, loving her up. He figured she was used to a lot of attention, since she was often the horse the McPhee sisters borrowed from the ranch when they needed an extra one. It was pretty clear how those women treated their animals—they spoiled them rotten, which was a good thing in his view.

"Howdy there, Seth." Deputy Wade Wetherby ambled into sight, framed by the half-open barn door. The tall, lanky man looked a bit green around the gills this morning and pale, with dark-circles under his eyes. Slumping and rubbing his head like a man who'd had way too much to drink last night, he blinked against the light. "Got my horse ready?"

"He's saddled and good to go." Like always. Seth gave Jane a final pat and headed over, walking considerably faster than the beleaguered deputy. "Got him cross tied in the aisle, but judging by those bloodshot eyes, you aren't feeling your best this morning."

"Right, I see him now." Wade looked like his head was about to explode as he changed directions, heading over to his horse. The gelding didn't seem surprised by Wade's condition. It wasn't the first time.

"Had a rough night again, huh?" Seth asked. Most folks didn't know about Wade's hung-over mornings or his fondness for cards. He doubted Rose did either.

"A rough night?" Wade gave a moan, grimacing as if his head had begun splitting in two. "It was worse than that. I lost most of my last paycheck and what I didn't lose, I drank in whiskey. It was brutal, but it was worth it. Had a rip-roaring time."

"I see that." Seth untied Wade's gelding to save the man the trouble. It didn't look as if the deputy would be able to manage untangling a simple knot. "You need coffee, man. I could pour you a cup. I've got some in my office."

"Nah. I'll just get some over at the feed store. Carl owes me." Wade swept off his hat, raked his fingers through his blond hair to comb it. He could almost pass for respectable once he'd made it into his saddle. "I stopped that break-in last week. Someone was going through the window into his store when I spotted him. If only I hadn't been two blocks away, I could have caught him."

"We've had a lot of problems lately." Seth frowned, shaking his head. As a business owner, he wasn't happy with the spike in petty robberies, but he knew the sheriff was on top of it. "I thought once Ernest was caught and George was put away, it would stop. They seemed to be the cause of a lot of problems around here."

"There are a lot of bad men in this world." Wade tipped his hat, struggling to look like a respectable lawman. "It's my job to apprehend them. I'll get whoever this troublemaker is. Probably some vagabond. Don't you worry, I'll catch that varmint."

"I'm not worried at all." Okay, that was a little sarcastic, but Seth couldn't help it. He didn't mind Wade, but he didn't like that he was beauing Rose—and Rose had no idea who the man really was. Not that many folks did. Wade was good at presenting the face he wanted the whole town to see. Not that he was a bad sort, just a man with a little weakness.

Wally gave a snort once Wade had ridden out the door. The gentle gelding arched a horsy brow as if to say, *do you believe that guy?*

"Tell me about it." Seth rolled his eyes. He started to turn around and head deeper into the barn to get back to work, but something stopped him. The back of his neck prickled strangely—not in foreboding or like a chill snaking beneath his collar. More like a tingle, an awareness.

Huh. He went with his gut feeling, stepped out the door and spotted Rose McPhee zipping down the street in his direction, tucked in the horse-drawn sleigh, holding a bakery box on her lap as her sister Magnolia drove one of their old bay geldings.

"Hey, Seth!" Magnolia called out as they approached. "How's it going?"

"No complaints. How about you?" He addressed both of them, but his gaze latched onto Rose. She looked lovely this morning, sweet as could be, pink-cheeked from the cold, her head crowned by a light blue knit cap, bundled up beneath a warm buffalo robe. Her blue-green eyes lit up with friendliness when she saw him.

"I've got lots of complaints," Magnolia answered cheerily. "You know, I thought we got a lot of snow in Chicago, but this is ridiculous. I want to have a word or two with the person in charge of the weather here."

"Good luck with that," he called out, feeling that tingle at the back of his neck calm. Everything within him went calm as Magnolia drew the horse to a stop and Rose smiled at him, amused at her sister.

Out of the corner of his eye, he caught sight of Wade crossing the street, two streets down, keeping his focus on Rose as if making sure she didn't see him in a hung-over state. The snake.

"How are you feeling after yesterday, Rose?" Seth found himself asking, managing to sound almost normal despite his gritted teeth and rising anger. He flicked his attention across the street, but Wade was gone, taking the back way to the feed store so he'd keep out of Rose's sight.

"Not as sore as I thought I'd be. That snow is harder than it looks." Her gaze sparkled merrily, as if a fall and a little pain didn't trouble her at all. "But that was yesterday. Today you are just the man I want to see."

"I get that a lot." He tossed her a smile, unable to resist a little fun. "I'm in demand with women. I don't know what it is about me. It's just charisma, I guess."

"It's not charisma," Rose assured him. "You have Jane."

"I'm crushed." He chuckled, liking it when her soft laughter seemed to meld with his, like music, two notes ringing in harmony.

"Why would you be sore?"" Magnolia turned in the seat to ask her sister. "What happened? Is something wrong?"

"Oh, I slipped on the snow and fell down." Rose blushed furiously, turning strawberry red. He knew she was remembering her skirt flying up, exposing her long johns to the entire street. "It was nothing serious. Just surprised me more than anything."

"And I'm just learning about this now?" Magnolia shook her head, scattering blond locks over her shoulders. "Seth knows it, but not me. Your own sister. I'm disappointed in you, Rose."

"I'm not." Rose's soft mouth twitched in the corners. Trouble danced in her eyes. "If Seth hadn't said anything, maybe I could have kept it to myself. I don't want any fussing."

"I totally get that." Magnolia nodded, rolling her eyes skyward in thought. "Our sisters can be like a flock of chickens descending on you. They go overboard with the fussing thing—peck, peck, peck. But are you sure you're all right? Now *I'm* worried."

"You're fussing, Magnolia." Rose's smile grew, upturning in the corners, showing all of her sweetness. "Why don't we keep this incident as our little secret? Just the three of us? It'll be fun."

"I can try," Magnolia said. "But I'm making no promises."

"It's a start." Rose shook her head as if to say, *sisters*. "So, Seth, how's Jane?"

"Better. You can see her if you want. She's going to be just fine."

JINGLE BELL HEARTS

"Thanks to you." Rose beamed at him. "We've got a cake to deliver, but can I stop by on my way back? I've got something else to ask you."

"Sure thing." He wasn't about to deny Rose anything. She was a sweetheart. You couldn't help liking her. As the sisters whizzed away in their fast little sleigh, he couldn't take his eyes off her, even when all he could see was the blue of her cap in the distance. He didn't know what it was about her that drew him, but it did. It didn't let go.

CHAPTER SIX

"That's three more successful deliveries today." Magnolia looked ready to float with happiness as she reined Marvin down the residential street. "It's really awesome that Mrs. Dunbar was so happy with the cake that she placed a huge Christmas order, isn't it?"

"Yes, it's awesome. That's what we work so hard for, to have happy customers." Rose shivered, drawing the buffalo robe more tightly around her. While the skies were a crisp, clear blue and the sun shone merrily, it was still well below freezing. As in single digits. "But Christmas is going to be pretty busy as it is. I told her we would manage such a large order, I mean, we're a new business, we can't turn down orders, but with the wedding and everything–"

"Oh, it'll be fine." Magnolia didn't seem troubled by it. "You and Iris are both whizzes in the kitchen. Plus, you've got me and Daisy to boss around."

"You know I like to boss," Rose teased.

"And I'm sure we can get Verbena to help out in a pinch." Magnolia slowed dear Marvin as they passed by the schoolhouse. You never knew when a kid would come bopping out onto the street chasing a ball or on a toboggan. "Look, there's Bea. Hi Bea!" She leaned over Rose to shout out.

The schoolyard was busy with snow activities. Darling little girls made snow angels. Little boys were building snowmen. Bigger boys were throwing snowballs and chasing each other all over the place. But on the schoolhouse steps sat two girls all by themselves. One of them was Bea, their fourteen-year-old cousin.

"Hi Magnolia! Hi Rose!" Bea waved, dear with her blond braids and wide blue eyes. When she smiled, she could be a cherub (with clothes, of course), angelically cute.

What a gift it was that Bea and Annie, her older sister, had moved to town. Rose already loved her dear cousins. She waved back, twisting around to keep Bea in sight just a few moments longer as their sleigh picked up speed.

"And Annie can help too if we need it," Magnolia added, reins held lightly in both hands. "She could use the extra money, I'm guessing. It won't be long until Adam proposes."

"True," Rose agreed, warm joy filling her up, chasing away the cold. Another happy couple, she thought, because although Adam had only begun to court Annie, anyone with eyes to see could tell what was to come. That man was over the moon for Annie. A proposal would come; it was only a matter of time. Especially since he bought that house she was dreaming of.

Traffic in town had picked up. Now that the storm was over, shoppers were everywhere, bustling down boardwalks and maneuvering down the streets. Christmas was coming up fast, and there was a sense of urgency in the air, not to mention a few jingle bells. Some of the passing sleighs had bells on them. Rose smiled, loving the merry sound as Magnolia headed toward Seth's livery.

"Hey, Rose!" Elderly Vivian Gunderson called out from the boardwalk, leaning on her cane, as they passed by. "How are you feeling this morning after that fall?"

Great. Rose's shoulders slumped. So yesterday's embarrassing incident wasn't forgotten after all. "I'm fine, Mrs. Gunderson."

"Young girls these days. Far too brazen." Although her tone was scolding, the elder woman's eyes glittered with amusement. "Back in my day, if a lady showed her underthings to the whole street, she'd be too ashamed to show her face the next day."

"Sorry, Mrs. Gunderson." Rose called out over her shoulder.

"What's this about your underthings?" Magnolia's slender eyebrows had arched up so far they were hidden behind her bangs. "You showed them off to the street?"

"When I fell down, my skirts didn't come with me." Mortified, Rose covered her face with her gloved hands. Did she have to relive it all over again? As if the embarrassment of being so klutzy wasn't enough? "It was only my flannel petticoats and wool long johns."

"Still, I'm not sure I should be seen with you." Magnolia teased, drawing Marvin to a halt. "Think of my reputation. It suffers enough as it is. But to be seen with such a brazen woman showing her undies—"

"Red undies," a deep voice answered. Seth stepped out from the shadowed barn doorway, looking amused.

Oh, he was having fun at her expense, was he? Rose arched a brow at him. She wasn't about to forget this slight. Didn't friends stick together?

"Although it was nothing scandalous," Seth conceded. "Embarrassing, but not scandalous."

"Talking about my undergarments. This is totally inappropriate. Honestly." Rose rolled her eyes. Okay, it was funny….or it would be if it wasn't her underthings. "Is this a good time for you, Seth?"

"For you, anytime is good." He circled around the sleigh, his shadow falling across her as he stopped at her side. "Are you both coming in?"

"No." Magnolia quickly shook her head. "I'm going to peek in on my fiancé. Rose, when you're done, come find me at Tyler's office, and I'll give you a ride home."

"No need." Seth spoke up, his hand engulfing Rose's as she climbed out of the sleigh. "I've got business at the ranch. I can drop her off on the way there."

"Excellent. More time with Tyler." Magnolia waggled her brows as if a kiss or two might be involved and gently slapped the reins. Marvin obediently lunged forward, taking her away.

"Come see Jane." Seth still had hold of her hand, his grip firm, unrelenting.

Wow, he was strong. Rose hadn't really given it much thought before. He was brawny and big, sure, it was obvious. All you had to do was look at him. But to *feel* his strength, that was something entirely different. He towered over her, powerful and commanding. Lucky was the lady who one day would win his reluctant heart.

"You can see she's getting my best care." Once inside the barn where it was no longer icy and she could fall, he released Rose's hand, staying beside her as he gestured toward the stall midway down the aisle. "She's been an excellent patient."

"Not surprising, as she is an excellent horse." Rose reached out to stroke the mare's velvety muzzle. Jane lapped at her sleeve cuff affectionately with her whiskery lips. "We've been short-handed without her. Today we were lucky because the deliveries were pretty close to one another, so Magnolia and I could double up, but that's not going to work tomorrow."

"Let me guess. You need to rent a horse?" Seth's brow furrowed in surprise. "But your aunt has a ranch full of horses. Why not borrow one of those? It would be more economical."

"She offered us use of her dear Buttons." Rose thought of her aunt, so eager to help, as always. "It's generous, but it's her mare. Then she offered us any of the ranch horses, but it doesn't feel right. Because what we need is another horse of our own."

"Oh, I get it. You want me to help find a horse for you and your sisters?" He nodded in approval, his mouth tucking up in the corners as if he was already giving it serious thought—and liked the challenge.

"Not exactly," she told him. "Just for me. I want my own horse. Not that my sisters wouldn't be able to borrow him or her, but I've always wanted a horse of my very own since I was small. Of course, we were so poor, we didn't have horses at all. But, as you know, we're not poor anymore."

"That's the truth." Seth smiled at her in understanding. "Well, trust me. I can find the right horse."

"I knew I could count on you." Relief swept through her, thinking of how much easier it would make things for her sisters—okay, and a big thrill for herself because she was getting a horse! "We haven't needed this until now, but the bakery business is growing. We have more business than we know what to do with."

"I'm glad for you." Seth gave Jane a pat on the neck. "If things keep on like this, you ladies will have to hire help, especially with Daisy getting married."

"I know. Changes are coming, and they are going to be excellent." What a good feeling, being able to look at her future and knowing it would be bright. There would be so many happy times, times of hope. "Do you have a horse here that would fit the bill? Can I look around?"

"I'd be happy to show you what I have, but I don't have much of a demand for a lady's driving horse. Mostly, I keep draft horses for ranch or hauling jobs. Let's start with the gentlest one of the lot." Seth gestured across the aisle, where a black and white pinto watched her from beneath spiky lashes. "This is Patches."

"Patches. Really? For a pinto?" Rose gestured toward the patchy black and white coat. "It's not too imaginative."

"I name a lot of horses," he explained with a smirk. "Sometimes I run out of brilliance and come up with a few dull ones."

"Brilliance?" Rose arched a brow, fighting a grin. "That's debatable."

"You won't be the first one to think so. Patches is a good guy, but he's not much of a snuggler. He's more reserved. Likes to keep his emotional distance." Seth held out a hand, palm up, and the gelding didn't move closer. He just gave a sniff and a look that meant, *that's close enough, buddy.*

"I see what you mean." Rose scrunched up her nose, debating. He was a gorgeous horse, so stunning with his black and white coat. "But for my first very own horse, I want a snuggler."

"See, I knew that about you." Seth shot her a dashing grin. Really dashing. Like wow. Unaware of his own stunningness, Seth moved on down the aisle, past a few boarders to the next candidate. "This is Patrice."

"Patrice?" Rose sidled up beside him, considering the mare who had her bottom facing them (she was busy looking over her stall gate to the paddock outside). "Isn't that a little formal for a horse name?"

"It suits her. She's very particular." Seth sighed, watching the mare expectantly. "I'm hoping she turns around. That means she likes you."

"Hmm. Her tail is facing us. Maybe it's you she doesn't like."

"Well, that too." Seth shrugged good-naturedly. "You can't win everyone's affections. Let's see who else we have. How about Dudley?"

"I hope Dudley isn't a dud?" She considered the mud-colored horse in the neighboring stall. He swished his tail, studying her with uninterested eyes. The gelding looked as if he might be thinking about coming up to her for a nose pet, but then shook his head, as if it was too much effort.

"He's a little sloth-like," Seth confessed. "You probably want a horse who can go faster than a slow walk."

"You have some real winners here, Seth." Rose reached out, her hand landing briefly on his forearm. It was a natural thing, something between friends, to let him know that while she was teasing him, she saw the truth about him too. "Where did you get all these winners?"

"I frequent a lot of horse sales," he confessed, dipping his chin. There was something both manly and vulnerable in the gesture, like a guy doing his best not to show the soft side of his heart. "I like to pick up deals. It's smart business. Buy low, sell high."

"Right." Knowing Seth, he bought up the ones no one wanted, so they wouldn't be sold for slaughter. She considered the next horse over, swayback and rather homely, the poor thing. He charged the gate, eager for affection, bouncing up and down like a dog, hard enough to shake the building. "Let me guess. This one isn't broken."

"Not even a little bit, but he is affectionate." Seth reached out, his powerful hands gentle as he cupped the horse's muzzle. "He's not ready to pull a lady's sleigh. He's not ready to pull anyone's sleigh. I think if he ever got going, he'd be at the Canadian border before anyone could stop him."

"No kidding." Rose leaned in to stroke the soft nose. "One day he is going to be a sweetie."

"But we need one for you right now." Seth turned away, mouth puckered up in one corner, considering the rest of her choices. "It's too bad. I just sold the perfect horse last week to the Montgomerys."

"I'm a week too late for the perfect horse?" She glanced around, considering. Most of the animals were boarders, the rest big draft horses built for work, horses he rented out or sold when the need arose.

"It'll take me a bit, but I'll find it." Seth's promise boomed low like winter thunder, uncompromising. "I have a few leads I can follow and there's always the auction in Deer Springs on Friday. If you can wait that long, I might find something good there."

"Thanks, Seth. I appreciate it." It was time to go, she had things to do, but her feet felt stuck to the ground. Strange how she couldn't seem to move away from him. "If things keep going the way they are, we might need two horses."

"I'll keep that in mind." What sounded like mischief layered his voice as he hauled open one of the stalls. Wally ambled into the aisle, heading straight for Rose. His big brown eyes flickered with fondness as he lapped her across the face with his rough, horsy tongue.

"I think he likes you." Seth's wry words were the understatement of the century. "C'mon, you big lug. Get over here so I can hitch you up."

At the thought of having to go, Wally gave a sorrowful sigh. He nibbled on Rose's bangs with what could only be equine adoration before complying, clomping down the aisle at Seth's command.

Her heart gave a little tug. For the horse, she thought quickly. Not for the guy. Although Seth *was* a sight, all strong and well-built man, muscles rippling under his gray flannel shirt as he backed Wally into the traces of his sleigh. Elation filled her, slipping into her blood like fine wine.

She was getting her own horse! It was official. She felt like hopping with excitement. So many wonderful things were yet to come, and this was only the beginning. She could just feel it.

* * *

Seth closed the front barn door up good and tight and flipped the sign over to *closed*. Folks around here knew if they needed something, he'd be back. Rose waited for him, all bundled up in his sled, looking pretty as the day with the blue knit hat she wore, emphasizing the blue shades in her ocean-colored eyes. In the full kiss of the sun, her blond hair sparkled like rare gold, her complexion light and flawless.

"Oh, I'm going to need a sleigh too," she told him, as if it had just occurred to her. "Something cute and really fast. I want to be able to beat Magnolia in a race. You know, if we ever have one."

"Got it." He'd already thought of that, but he only hiked up one shoulder in response, tipping his hat against the slanting sun as he paced over to the sleigh. Once he was beneath the furs beside her, he took up the reins.

Funny thing, how he always felt self-conscious around ladies. It had even been that way when it came to Liz. But with Rose, he felt completely at ease. As if they'd been lifelong friends. Maybe he could chalk it up to being buddies when they were toddlers—like something about her was familiar after all this time. He shrugged, not able to come up with another explanation. He reined Wally down the town street, navigating around the back of Carl's slow-moving delivery sled filled with hay.

"Howdy to you, Seth," Carl called out from the driver's seat, his salt and pepper hair tidy beneath his black wide-brimmed hat. He was a kind man, sturdy but strong, fit from years of lifting one hundred and fifty pound bags of feed in his store. "How are things with you?"

"Good." Seth drew back on the reins, slowing Wally down enough to keep up a conversation. "That's a big delivery there."

"Yep. A small fire in the Hutchinson's barn, no terrible damage, but the smoke and water ruined some of the feed they have. I'm comin' to the rescue." His gaze slipped over to Rose and then back again. "This is twice I've seen you two together in two days. How are you doing, Rose? After that spill you took, I'm surprised you're up and around."

"Did everybody see that?" Rose shook her head, looking more amused than embarrassed. "Maybe you could just erase that from your memory? You know, like chalk on a board. It never happened."

"I'll be happy to." Carl gave a good-humored wink. "But I'm not so sure about others in this town. Seth, you say hello to your lovely mother for me, will ya?"

"Sure." Seth chirruped to Wally, who immediately obliged by pulling them around and away from the friendly feed store owner. His sleigh bells gave a merry jingle. "Is it me, or does Carl seem interested in my mother?"

"I was thinking the same exact thing." Rose lit up, glancing over her shoulder. "Ooh, this could be exciting. Carl seems like such a good man. He makes a nice living. Everyone thinks well of him. Do you think he has a chance with your ma?"

"A chance?" Seth arched an eyebrow. He didn't even have to think about it. "Nope. Not even a ghost of a one. My ma has sworn off marriage. It's why she works long hours on the ranch and has for more years than I can count. When it comes to marriage, she says never again. She means it."

"Hmm, that's too bad." Rose settled back onto the seat, snuggling beneath the warm furs. A little dimple dug into her cheek while she thought. She really was adorable. "What if Carl is her true love, her one perfect match? She'll let him get away."

"I don't think that's how Ma sees it." Seth tried to sound amused, but what Ma had gone through was no laughing matter. *Even good men made poor choices*, she'd told him once. *They let down their wives and families, and then it becomes a habit they can't break. Don't ever treat your wife that way*, she'd said with sorrow in her eyes, knowing the emotional pain of what happened when a man's weakness defined his character and a marriage. Sad, he cleared his throat, trying to rid himself of the impact from the memory. "She said if another man ever tried to come calling, she would chase him off with a broom and aim to hit and hit hard."

"Wow, she has a bad attitude toward dating." Rose's mouth crinkled playfully. "Do you think we can change it?"

"We? Oh, no." He gave a soft laugh, amused at the idea. "There's no chance of that either. Ma won't change her mind. Trust me."

"Sorry, I can't. I'm going to need a reason why." She focused her blue-green eyes on him, full of mischief and caring for his mother.

Hard not to like Rose more for that. The steel walls around his heart creaked open just a smidge. "If I tell you about my ma, you are going to know some things about me I've never told anyone."

"I can keep a secret." Gentle, no longer playful, her smile fading as she gazed up at him. "Or I could tell you one of my secrets and we'd be even. We'd be secret keepers together."

"Tempting." A man could fall forever into those soulful eyes, swirled with green and blue, colors of the ocean, he thought, or of earth and sky. That crack in his heart opened a little wider.

All around them the magnificent landscape sped by—white rolling fields sparkled in the sun. Snow-shrouded trees lined the road, still and proud. Breathless, rugged mountains glinted pure white at the horizon, their peaks so near and so stunning, they dominated a slice of the sky. Seth bit his bottom lip, breathing deep, feeling the memories stirring beneath the surface, memories he'd worked long and hard to keep buried.

"Ma's second husband treated her like a servant." That was the nicest way he could think of to say it. His chest ached, that old bitter anger rising up, knotting his stomach. "She married him because she had sons to raise and no way to support us. What she made working in the ranch's kitchen wasn't enough. She did it to do right by us."

"Oh, Seth. You feel guilty." Rose's voice gentled with understanding. Her gloved hand landed on his arm, and the comfort from her touch rushed through him like pure sweetness. He'd never felt anything like it. She shook her head, adamant. "It wasn't your fault. You can't hold yourself responsible. You were young."

"Our stepfather didn't treat us any better. I was the oldest, so I did my best to figure out what would set off his temper so he could never find fault with us." Seth's baritone cracked once, a single show of his true feelings, but that was all. His jaw tightened, he set his chin and he went on with his tale. "We were early with our chores, doing them right so he would find no complaint. We helped Ma with the housework, so the house would always be spotless the way he wanted it. We had to grow up early, taking care of our ma so Arnold couldn't find a fault, not a single one, or he'd lose his temper."

"You protected everyone." Rose saw that easily. "He was violent. He hurt her, and he hurt you and your brothers."

"Mostly me. I'm the oldest, I made sure I took the worst of it." He gave a casual shoulder-shrug, as if it was no big deal. Anyone would do the same.

But she wasn't fooled. Not at all. What he'd done for his mother and his brothers had cost him. And he'd never complained. He'd simply done everything he could to better his loved one's lives as much as he could.

Okay, I really like this guy, Rose thought, so glad they were friends. So glad she'd gotten this chance to know him better.

"But as hard as we tried," Seth continued, "we couldn't protect Ma from a lot of things. Arnold treated her like dirt. The things he called her, the way he spoke to her. She didn't deserve that."

"No, she absolutely did not." Rose thought of Seth's mother, Josslyn, who worked in the ranch's kitchen. Josslyn had been a life-long friend to Aumaleigh and a loyal employee at the ranch. Rose thought of the spunky, fun and kind older lady with her red hair and warm brown eyes. Affection filled her. She had no idea Josslyn had been through so much. "I'm sorry. It had to be especially hard on her, after losing your father."

"As Ma said, she lost Pa long before he passed away," Seth answered. "That was the true tragedy. Watching their love die. Watching him turn self-destructive and change into a different man. I was old enough to remember when his inner demons won."

"That is really tragic." She had watched her beloved father fail in life, fail himself and lose the man he used to be—so she knew. Her heart broke for Seth, for what he'd been through and what he'd lost. Sympathetic tears filled her eyes—both for him and for her pa. It still hurt to remember the father she'd lost. Likely it always would. "I can't imagine how hard this has all been on your mother. And on you."

"I'm tough, don't worry about me." He tugged on the right rein, instructing Wally off the road and onto a tree-covered lane. "But Ma has had some difficult times. I can't blame her for not wanting to give marriage a third try."

"No, I suppose not." Rose glanced over her shoulder wistfully, as if Carl Thomas and his load of hay were still in sight. "That's too bad. But what if the third time is the charm? What if she could find real and lasting happiness?"

"I would like that for her," he said honestly. "But the choice is hers."

"In other words, you don't want me trying to set up your mother with Carl." Rose squinted as if she was trying to see through him, deep into the place where he held his secrets.

"Exactly. Don't set her up. Maybe someone else, but not Ma." He didn't know why he was laughing. "And not me. I don't know why, but I suspect I was the first one who popped into your mind."

"I wish I could deny it. You're a good man and not bad looking."

"Oh, not bad looking? I'm flattered."

"You should be." Mischief flashed in her eyes. "I've seen some really ugly men in my time, and you're not one of them. Close, but you could attract a desperate woman or a really ugly one."

"I feel so much better now." Laughter rolled up, and it felt good. Very good. "Most women are too contrary to trust. They change on you, they make you love them and then they break your heart."

"Ah! Now we're getting to the truth about you. Finally." Rose turned toward him, so full of caring, he'd never seen anyone more beautiful.

The sun sifted through the trees arching overhead, tossing dappled light across her, dazzling her with its golden goodness. His heart lifted, open now, and began to feel. Caring rolled through him as she leaned in, so close it was as if they were completely alone, the only two people in the entire world—just her and just him, two kindred hearts.

"What made you want to fall in love with her, the one who broke your heart?" Rose asked, luring him closer with her compassion and sincerity. He was helpless, he had no choice. His heart, so open, ached with sweetness for her.

"I believed it was worth a try," he confessed, his voice raw and gruff, laid bare with honesty. It would be easier to pretend he was too tough and macho to have let himself be that vulnerable. It would have been less embarrassing to leave his foolishness buried, but he wanted to tell Rose. "Liz seemed so sweet. I'm a sucker for that. She had such a good heart, or so it seemed, which made her the prettiest girl to me."

"Why, you're a romantic, Seth Daniels." Rose gazed up at him, and in those blue-green depths he could see her truly, so tender and kind. It drew him in, drew him closer. She smiled at him. "Down deep beneath all that rugged manliness, you are a snuggly bear."

"Not true. I deny it absolutely." His entire world stilled as he leaned in a smidgeon more. When he breathed, he breathed her in—scents of lilacs and the warm silk of her hair.

A stray golden lock fell forward onto her soft cheek and without thought, as naturally as if he'd been made to do it, he brushed that silken strand off her satin skin, so warm and incredibly soft, and tucked it behind her ear. Unable to breathe, unable to think, one desire rose up as pure and bright as the sun—the unquenchable, sweet need to kiss her on that cheek.

I care about her, he realized. Really and truly. His heart rolled over, too full of longing to beat.

But the feeling was not mutual. Rose looked past him, and only then did he realize Wally had drawn them out of the cover of the arching tree branches to a stop at the edge of the front lawn. Worse, they weren't alone. A man dismounted from a red roan gelding, his tin badge catching the light.

"Wade!" Rose smiled his name with such cheer, it was like a wound piercing through Seth's chest wall.

He sank back against the seat, a little dazed and embarrassed, glad beyond measure that he hadn't acted on that insane impulse to kiss her cheek. Talk about luck. Now he was horrified at himself, wanting another man's girl. What was wrong with him? He clamped his molars together hard, gripping the reins as Wade crossed over to Rose's side, helping her from the sleigh.

"Howdy, Seth." Wade nodded at him with gratitude, completely unsuspecting the truth. "Thanks for seeing her home. You're a good friend."

"That's me," he said, his voice scratchy sounding, the words rising up in his throat like a knife, cutting deep. "A good friend."

"Thanks for the ride." Rose smiled, skirts swishing as she took her place at Wade's side.

That same compassionate look in her eyes is what had cracked his defenses wide open in the first place. Such an innocent thing, and yet it had changed everything.

"Any time," Seth told her casually, carelessly, as if he were still that good old friend. "See you later."

"Sure. Looking forward to it." She tossed him a smile, the friendship she had for him remained etched onto her face. So lovely, so amazing.

His chest inexplicably ached too much to try to say anything more, so he slapped the reins, letting Wally take him away. A quick getaway seemed like the best course. What he felt for Rose was wrong. As strong as it was, it had come as pure surprise. He was going to make sure he never felt that way again.

CHAPTER SEVEN

Junior shouldered open the door of the rundown cabin, his stolen groceries in hand. The place wasn't much—just one room with the kitchen on one side, the living area and hearth on the other. Two bunks were stacked against the dark back wall. That was it, but the roof was tight and the walls solid. That was what mattered.

Weary from the walk, he leaned his crutch against the wall by the door and set their food down on the rickety table. It felt good not to be leaning on that infernal crutch all the time. He stretched out his back before unwrapping the fresh bread he'd taken along with beans and coffee at the town mercantile. He broke off a hunk of the loaf and stuffed it into his mouth. Chewing, he moseyed over to the whiskey bottle he'd stashed on the pantry shelf.

"Junior, is that you?" A sleepy voice drawled lazily from the bottom bunk.

"Yep, Giddy. A bear could have walked in here for all you know." He scowled, annoyed by his younger brother who seemed to do everything better—he'd always been faster, smarter and their parent's favorite, even if he was more than a little lazy. "You sleep like the dead. It's the middle of the day."

"Well, I was tired." Giddy yawned loudly, stretching like a dog on a hot summer afternoon before drawing himself up to his lanky height. Yawning again, he ran a hand through his shaggy brown hair. "Did you bump into the sisters when you were in town?"

"Not a one of them." Junior scowled, clenching his teeth. He was frustrated. "They're always driving around delivering their baked stuff. Maybe I'll see one of 'em tomorrow. Maybe even that blond who gave me a ride. She's a bleeding heart and easy on the eyes."

"It was genius having you walking along that road, I knew she'd pick you up. Glad I thought of it." Giddy moseyed over, arms up in another stretch as he yawned away. "I say, know your enemy. It's the best way to bring 'em down."

"You shoulda seen that sleigh she was driving." Resentment built like a fire beneath Junior's sternum as he twisted the bottle's cap. The strong, reassuring scent of whiskey wafted up, stinging his nostrils as he poured a healthy dollop into one coffee mug, then the other. "That vehicle was top of the line. Brand new. Expensive, let me tell you. Burns me up she can afford something like that and all we've got is one swayback horse and a third-hand saddle."

"Me, too. I snuck around and got a good look at that mansion they're living in." Giddy snatched up his cup, sloshing whiskey over the rim. "It ain't right. We're here in this rundown shack and they got every convenience. It just riles me up."

"Good." Junior didn't always like his brother, but they were together in this. United in their hate of the wealthy McPhees who had done their family wrong. It wasn't fair, and that's why he and Giddy were here. To right old wrongs. To find justice and even things out—at any cost.

* * *

In the warmth of the foyer, Rose shrugged off her wool coat. McPhee Manor was alive with voices rising and falling in conversation. One peek into the parlor told her why. Aumaleigh had come to visit, and she wasn't alone. She'd brought their cousin Annie.

"There she is! Rose!" Aumaleigh brightened, turning toward the foyer instantly. She was a lovely woman in her fifties who wore it well. Her sleek molasses-dark hair was pulled back in a soft bun, leaving gossamer tendrils to fall down, framing her heart-shaped face with delicate curls. She raised her slender arms, rushing forward, the skirts of her tasteful butter-yellow dress rustling with her quick gait. Before

JINGLE BELL HEARTS

Rose could hang up her coat, Aumaleigh had wrapped her in a brief, warm hug. "We were just talking about you."

"Me?" Rose kissed her aunt on the cheek. "What did I do?"

"Word travels fast in this town." Aumaleigh stepped back, fussing in a motherly way, taking Rose's coat from her to hang it up. "Excuse me, Wade. Here, let me hang up your coat too."

"Thank you, ma'am," Wade answered politely, but Rose couldn't seem to pay him any mind because something in the parlor drew her attention.

"You finished the dress!" she exclaimed, soaking in the beauty of the gown Daisy was holding up. The soft red chiffon shimmered with a silken luster. Rose gasped, rushing forward, forgetting everything but the gown and the soft ruffle neckline and graceful drape of the narrow skirt that belled out elegantly, the touches of matching lace.

"It's breathtaking." She swept it from her sister's arms, holding it up in front of her, imagining wearing it to the wedding. "It's the most beautiful thing I've ever owned."

"And it will look incredible on you." Daisy reached out to brush a strand of hair out of Rose's eyes. Oh, she looked joyous. "Annie and I sewed all morning on it, so fast I think our fingers were nothing but blurs. My shoulder is aching, and I poked myself more than a few times with the needle, but it was worth it."

"Thank you." Rose clutched the garment, turning toward their cousin to include her in the thanks.

"It was my pleasure," Annie said in her darling way. She was such a lovely girl with her sunny blond curling hair, light blue eyes and heart-shaped face. She had come to town wearing nothing but patched, secondhand clothes, but they had fixed that problem, Rose remembered with satisfaction. She and her sisters had pilfered their closets to contribute their best garments to Annie.

The lake-blue dress she wore complimented her complexion perfectly and emphasized her petite, slender form. It was heartening to see her beaming with happiness, too. Rose thought of the cottage Adam was buying as a surprise and shivered with anticipation. Think of how much happier Annie's life was about to get. Rose loved nothing more than a happy ending.

"We heard about the town incident." Iris tapped into the parlor carrying a small silver tray. Steam curled above the china cups, spiraling into the air. "Why didn't you tell us?"

"Oh, that I fell down?" Rose waved one hand as if to dismiss the whole thing. "It was nothing. I fell. I got back up. End of story."

"You *fell?*" Iris startled, nearly dropping the tray. "When did this happen?"

"And are you okay?" Daisy snatched the dress away, looking just as surprised.

"Oops. I guess there was more than one incident in town." Rose took one of the tea cups from Iris's tray. "What one are you talking about?"

"There's more than one?" Daisy rolled her eyes. "That's it. There's no more driving alone. You and Magnolia go back to pairing up. Both of you attract more trouble than a magnet does nails."

"I need a hint here." Rose took a sip of tea. The blistering liquid scalded her tongue. Hot, hot, hot. She immediately set the cup on an end table and plopped into a wing-backed chair. "What did I do?"

"You were seen in the company of a man," Aumaleigh informed her, not looking troubled at all, unlike the rest of the room's occupants. Aumaleigh took a tea cup from the tray and settled down on the sofa next to Annie. "A man who was not your beau."

"Which is why I brought it to their attention." Wade lumbered across the room to warm himself at the hearth, his long-legged steps purposeful, his boots pounding against the floor as if to accentuate the gravity of the situation.

"Hmm." Rose considered the man she was dating. Tall, handsome and decent. Just the kind of man she'd always hoped for. And yet, he wasn't perfect. No one was. Perhaps he didn't mean to be so, well, underhanded.

"Wade," she said gently, because she knew he didn't have a lot of experience with girlfriends. Ma always said a man needed training up. "It would have been better to have talked to me first."

"Oh." He looked puzzled at that, his forehead furrowing, his mouth tucking downward as he considered her statement. He turned his back to the fire, listening to it pop and crackle before he nodded. "I guess I can see that. I'm sorry, Rose. I got so concerned is all."

"It was just Seth." What was there to be concerned about? She shrugged, stymied by the unease in the room.

Iris had set the tray on the coffee table and settled into a chair in the corner, her arms wrapped around her middle, deep lines of distress carved into her face. Annie had gone pale, her forehead rutted with furrows, her mouth one tight, worried crease. Daisy's joy had faded. She'd slipped onto the edge of a couch cushion, looking ready to take charge and right all wrongs.

"What's the problem?" Rose asked everyone. "Seth's a friend. I've known him since we were born. Okay, not every year since, but we were little together. He just offered me a ride home so Magnolia could spend more time with Tyler."

"It's not Seth," Aumaleigh said quietly, glancing around the room at all the worried faces.

Okay, now she was really puzzled. "Then what's the problem? I haven't been riding around with any other man—wait." The memory popped into her head of the brutal snow and the stormy ride back from Deer Springs. "Are you talking about the lame guy?"

"What lame guy?" Daisy wanted to know.

"He was lame, leaning on a crutch and walking along the road. In a snowstorm," she added, a touch defensively because she wasn't getting a single look of compassion from her overprotective sisters, or, it seemed, from her beau. "What was I going to do? Just keep on going after he slipped and fell?"

"Yes," Wade bit out. "Rose, you can't go around picking up strange men."

"He was limping along," she pointed out. "He was suffering, struggling through the snow. He looked poorer than we were back in Chicago, remember that? His coat was ancient and patched, so thin it couldn't have been any better in that cold than a shirt. And you should have seen his boots. Sewn and patched and even then the leather was coming apart."

"He could have been dangerous," Iris uttered, looking ashen. The stricken shadows in her blue eyes said more than any words could. Something terrible had happened to Iris back in Chicago, years ago now, and it had ruined her life. It had changed who she was.

"He wasn't dangerous, Iris. I promise you that." Although she spoke to Iris gently, she shot to her feet, feeling agitated, hating that she'd brought such unhappiness to everyone. And during this wonderful season, too, she thought, when they were working on Christmas plans, sewing tons of Christmas surprises, not to mention the imminent wedding. That wasn't all right, not at all. She fisted her hands, marching over to Wade at the fireplace.

"Poor Junior was lame and exhausted and polite. I thought about it before I offered him a ride." She stared Wade straight in the eyes. "If I thought he was anything less than a harmless man, I would have kept on going. And yes, there are men in this world who either like to hurt women or think it is their right. After what we've been through with Ernest, how could I not know that?"

"You're too kind, Rose." Wade's jaw muscles bunched, his gaze hardening as he turned defensive. "You don't understand what you did."

"I do. I saw a man down on his luck. One who meant me no harm. I've been down on my luck, so I know how it feels." She caught sight of Daisy's shoulders slumping, of Annie staring down at her hands, blinking hard, of Iris finally nodding with understanding. "I gave him a ride. It cost me nothing. No harm came from it. I used my judgment. If you don't trust my judgment, Wade, then you and I have a big problem."

"I see." Cords stood out in his neck as he tore his gaze from hers, staring out the window. Anger seeped from him, but not a harsh anger or one that was out of control. He'd only been concerned for her, acting in the way he'd thought best.

He really did need training up, she thought, biting her bottom lip. Men were not perfect. She remembered her ma's words on more than one occasion. Maybe Wade needed a break too. She wouldn't hold his temporary anger against him.

"I know you want me to be safe," she said, firmly but gently too. Because it was nice to have a man who cared so much about her. He wanted to protect her and take care of her. He just needed a little fine-tuning is all. "I promise I won't pick up any strangers who could be dangerous. You have my word of honor."

"All right." He shrugged, looking like a man who'd lost a battle and didn't like it. "Guess I ought to be getting back to work. See you ladies later."

He gave a chin jut of farewell before crossing the room. He must have still been a bit angry, because he didn't look back, didn't acknowledge Rose on his way out of the room or out of the house. She couldn't help feeling a little miserable, watching him stride down the walkway and out of sight. She leaned one shoulder against the wall, wondering if she could have handled that better. Men seemed to be a lot of work—and one big puzzle. Not to mention a little controlling. She'd have to work on that.

"I want to know more about you and Seth." Aumaleigh rose from the couch, waltzing closer. Her bluebonnet blue eyes brightened with caring. It was easy to see she'd understood about the Junior incident. "You and he seemed pretty cozy driving up."

"Because we were on the seat together, huddled beneath the furs." Rose shrugged, grateful to her aunt for changing the subject. "And don't tell me you know all about the falling incident."

"I did hear a rumor," Aumaleigh confessed, leaning close. "But I decided to keep it to myself. Look at all this fuss over helping a disabled man. Imagine what would happen if they knew about your exposed underwear."

"It was only my long johns, which are basically like pants," she argued, resisting the urge to laugh. Tiny lights danced in Aumaleigh's eyes, as if she were trying not to laugh, too. "It's not funny. Jane was hurt."

"Which explains why you were with Seth. How is she doing?"

"Better. He's taking good care of her. She should be home in a few weeks." Now it was her turn to feel bad. "I should have taken more care with your horse."

"Nonsense. Sometimes these things happen. Come to find out that when George was second-in-command at the ranch, he took a few shortcuts on the horse's care." Aumaleigh looked down, saddened by that. "I've asked Seth to check every horse we have, just in case another animal's problems are overlooked or too subtle for the men to notice. So, no worries. Are you home to stay for a bit, or will you be running back out on deliveries? After lunch, Annie and I are coming back to help with cleaning. We have another wedding reception to throw in this house."

"Cleaning. Yay." Rose's mouth twisted in a wry smile. "It's my favorite."

"I know it is." Aumaleigh patted the girl's rosy cheek, deeply fond of her. She had such a tender heart. "With all of us here, we will make short work of it. Maybe I can talk Josslyn into helping out."

"Now I feel really guilty," Rose confessed. "I have a cake to frost and two deliveries. Isn't that right, Iris?"

"Oh, I'm thinking you should stay here and clean, and I'll do the deliveries," Iris teased, taking a sip of her tea. "What do you think?"

"Oh, I couldn't take the privilege of scrubbing floors away from you," Rose teased in return. "I know how you especially love that."

"It is one of life's great pleasures," Iris quipped sweetly. "Aumaleigh, do you really have to go? You and Annie can stay and eat with us."

"And leave my poor kitchen workers alone with the horde of cowboys?" Aumaleigh shook her head, stepping into the foyer to rescue her coat from its hook. "No one deserves that kind of treatment. It would be cruel and unusual punishment."

"Yes, the cowboys are a wild bunch," Annie agreed, joining in as she pushed off the couch. "And it's bean and bacon soup day. You should see them lap up that soup. They're like wild dogs, all tongues and teeth."

"Surely not my cowboy," Daisy joked as she rose to her feet. Love warmed her words. "My Beckett has better table manners than that."

"Beckett is perfect," Aumaleigh assured her dear niece. She imagined their wedding day, Daisy and Beckett, hand-in-hand standing before the town's minister. Hope welled up, filling her until she could burst. She wanted Daisy's life to be so, so good. She wanted Daisy to have everything—everything Aumaleigh had never had. True love and family and children to delight in. A real happily-ever-after. "We'll be back, girls. Annie, be sure and button up all the way. It's a short ride but a cold one."

"I've just got a few more buttons," Annie replied, bowing her head to deal with them.

Oh, how she loved her nieces. After a few hugs and goodbyes, Aumaleigh led the way down the walk and untied Button's reins from the small hitching post. Then, snuggled with Annie beneath the warm flannel robes, she steered her mare down the lane and onto the country road in search of the next driveway, which would bring her back to the ranch.

"It's really something to see Daisy so happy." Annie broke the silence, her words muffled by the scarf wrapped halfway up her face due to the cold. "She's going to make a glorious bride."

"That she is. No argument there. She's going to be beautiful. Now that we've got all the wedding sewing done for the girls, it's time to think about what you and Bea are going to wear to the wedding."

"Oh, this dress is fine enough for me," Annie said, referring to the handed down, but unbeknownst to Annie nearly new dress that Iris insisted she have. "But Bea does need something. I was hoping to buy some fabric from the store in town and sew it up. After payday, that is. I think I have just enough time to get it done if I sew every evening."

"Oh, I don't think your free time should be full of work too." Aumaleigh reined Buttons up to the kitchen house's back door. "Why don't I check with Cal and see if he can drive you and Bea to Deer Springs after school. You can find something for both of you from my favorite dress shop."

"Oh, no. I couldn't." Annie blushed, aghast at such an expensive offer, no doubt. "That's way too much, much more than we need."

"Consider it an early Christmas present." There, Aumaleigh thought, that ought to halt any argument. She set the reins on the sleigh's polished dashboard. "It's a practical gift too. We are going to have more than one wedding in this family, and you'll need something to wear for each one."

"Magnolia's isn't until spring," Annie argued as she slid out from beneath the robes. "A sensible wool dress for Bea would be best. She could wear it to church, too."

Aumaleigh bit her lip, because she had a few Christmas secrets. Several wool dresses, very pretty ones, were part of that secret. "I'm your employer, Annie. You'll do as I say if you want to keep your job."

"I'm not fooled by you." Annie shoved a curling lock of blond hair out of her eyes. Gratitude shone there, warm in her words, tender on her face. "You won't fire me. You're just trying to get me to accept a far too generous offer."

"It's for Bea." Aumaleigh slid across the seat, planting her feet, so thankful for this chance at love in her life. Romantic love had passed her by, in fact, she had a part to play in the blame for that. And with that lost chance at love, she'd lost the hope for children of her own. But her nieces, now they were her second chance. "You and I want the same thing, Annie. Happiness for Bea."

"I can't argue there." Annie blinked hard, looking away, taking a moment to accept the offer which might be hard on both her conscience and her pride.

"We're all family," Aumaleigh told her, waving to Cal who'd poked his head out of the barn door, noticing Buttons standing in the cold.

He nodded, promising to rush right over and fetch the mare. She also spotted a familiar sled and horse parked near the barn. Pleased, Aumaleigh took Annie by the elbow, making sure she didn't slip on the slick snow. "We help one another. That's the way it is around here. It's a rule."

"Then I have to say yes, if it's a rule." Annie gave a weak laugh, one of resignation and a little bit of discomfort. She'd been on her own a long time and wasn't used to accepting help. "Do you think Rose and Wade will be next to get married?"

"I think it's a possibility," Aumaleigh hedged, not quite certain herself. She would like to see Wade be more enamored with Rose, mesmerized and captivated by her. A woman deserved to be loved like that, cherished by the man she married. "They have only just begun to date, but I am confident, there will be more weddings ahead. We have Iris and we have you."

"Oh, yes. Me." Annie blushed, bowing her head as she tromped up the icy steps onto the porch. "Adam does seem serious. I know he wants to marry me."

"I know it too. Everyone does. One look is all it takes to see that man is devoted to you, heart and soul." Just the way it should be, Aumaleigh thought, glad for Annie but worried for Rose. It seemed to her something was missing in that relationship. Perhaps Wade and Rose would find it along the way?

She opened the door for Annie, letting her into the house first.

"I didn't used to believe in happily-ever-afters," Annie confessed from the shadowed foyer, as she unwrapped her scarf. "But I do now. They can even happen for girls like me."

"Especially for girls like you." What a sweetheart. Aumaleigh patted Annie's cheek in reassurance, full of love and hope. "You deserve Adam, Annie. You deserve the best. Now, hurry and go warm up by the stove. Your skin is like ice."

With a brilliant smile, sweet Annie hurried away, petticoats rustling. Voices rose from the kitchen as Josslyn and Louisa greeted her.

If only the afternoon wasn't so busy, Aumaleigh thought as she unwound her scarf. Then she could go to the dress shop with Annie and Bea. But helping get the mansion ready for Daisy's wedding party was important. It was a promise she aimed to keep.

"There you are." Josslyn barreled around the corner with a wooden soup spoon in hand. "I was starting to wonder if you were going to show up at all. You know it's bean and bacon soup day."

"How could I forget?" Aumaleigh hung up her coat. "You were afraid I'd seek refuge if I could from the wild dog cowboys, right?"

"It crossed my mind. Anywhere is safer than here." Josslyn's warm eyes twinkled. "The bread just came out of the oven. It's almost cool enough to slice and serve, which means it's almost time to ring the bell. You don't want to be standing there for much longer, because the cowboys will be descending. You'll be trampled."

"That would be bad for me." Aumaleigh pulled off her hat and her mittens. "I spotted Seth's horse and sleigh at the barn. He should stay for lunch."

"I already asked him." Josslyn waved her spoon in the air, for emphasis. "Now, there's something else, but I don't know if I ought to tell you."

"That doesn't sound good." Concerned, Aumaleigh studied her friend and employee. She'd worked side by side with Josslyn for too many years to count. Time had taken its toll on both of them—gray was trying to slip into Josslyn's red hair and wrinkles had worked their way into her face, but time could not change one thing. She was still the good, amazing friend she'd always been, and she looked troubled. "What's wrong, Joss? I can see something is."

"My stomach has been in a knot ever since Seth gave it to me." Josslyn glanced over her shoulder, into the kitchen as if to check on everyone's whereabouts before leaning in, lowering her voice. Her words were laden with sorrow. "The letter. It was from Gabriel."

At his name, Aumaleigh's chest wall clenched tight, wrenching her lungs so hard she couldn't breathe. Her heart couldn't beat. She clutched the wall for support, her head reeling. Gabriel? Pain arrowed through her, from heart to soul. Why was Josslyn talking about him after respectfully staying silent for so many years?

"I don't know how else to say this." Josslyn took hold of Aumaleigh's arm, helping to support her, an apology written on her face. "It won't do any good to keep this from you, because that would be worse in the end. He's coming. Gabriel is coming to visit me and Seth for Christmas."

Aumaleigh opened her mouth, searching for something to say, but nothing came. Her brain spun, unable to engage. There was nothing but shock and silence spreading through her skull. She wasn't prepared for this. Not at all. Finally, she managed to draw in the tiniest of breaths.

"I know it's a shock," Josslyn apologized. "It is for me, too."

Somehow, she had to get her breath. She had to stop standing here, slouched against the wall, like she'd suffered a mortal wound. Look at Josslyn, worried and dismayed when this was good news for her. Her brother was coming to see her after decades of being apart.

"You will have to take time off over Christmas, no argument," she managed to croak out. There was no way to hide the pain stark in her voice, resonating in her words. All she could do was to go on. "You need time to spend with your brother. What a nice thing for you and Seth."

"This is killing you, isn't it?" Josslyn bit her lower lip.

"I'm fine. I will be fine. What I felt for him was a long time ago." She raised her chin, a determined and stubborn woman when she put her mind to something and right now, she was going to be glad for Josslyn. That was what mattered here. "You must be very excited to see him. Come, let's get the food on the table because the cowboys are bound to be starving."

Josslyn didn't look fooled. Tears stood in her eyes, but Aumaleigh didn't want to talk anymore about it. She took off, marching deep into the kitchen, determined to carry on as if she wasn't falling apart. Some loves, when lost, you could never recover from.

Gabriel had been that love for her.

CHAPTER EIGHT

The May breeze whispered through the wild grasses, caressing the wildflowers—the fragrant rambling roses, the friendly yellow-centered daisies, the bright orange butterfly weeds, the stunning black-eyed Susan's. It was like a painting, Aumaleigh thought, freshly done and ready to be framed. With the meadow stretching toward a green tree line, and the small lake glittering as blue and flawless as the sky above.

She stopped walking, still and silent, trying to memorize the details, just drink them in, so she could remember this day forever. Her first date with Gabriel. One day in the far future, she hoped they would be sitting on a front porch together, old and gray, and speaking of this moment, when she knew he was the man she wanted to spend her life with.

"It's quite a sight, isn't it?" Gabriel's baritone rumbled deep and intimate, already her most favorite sound in the world. Her heart responded as he towered at her side, strong and powerful, his wide shoulders braced and the wind ruffling his collar-length dark hair. "It's got to be one of the prettiest places in this side of the county, and it's mine."

"Yours? You mean, you own it?" She hadn't expected that. She gazed around the property with a new appreciation—the lush meadows perfect for grazing livestock, the pleasant copses of trees to shade a house and yard one day. "I didn't know you were a property owner. Then why are you working on someone else's ranch?"

"To earn money. Building your own place doesn't come cheap. I worked in the West as a cattle hand, driving animals to market to save up enough for my own land. But the animals, the buildings, the start-up costs, that's another thing."

"So you're a man with great plans." As if he wasn't already perfect enough, he had the strength to work for his dreams. Her estimation of him rose, it just took flight. As if it wasn't already high enough.

"I don't know about great plans. I just want a place of my own, to raise some cattle and horses, and have a wife and family one day." His tone dipped low, ringing clear with the quiet, unspoken hopes of a man smitten.

She blushed, staring down at the toes of her shoes, black against the green grass. A buttercup danced nearby, brushing the hem of her dress. Gabriel knelt to pick it, handing it over in a sweet gesture. His smile, slanted up in the corners and bordered by deep dimples, seemed to say more. That when he looked at her, he saw his future, too.

Her heart simply came alive. The world brightened—the sun blinded, making her eyes sting. The rustle of the wind through the grasses and the melodic songs of larks and sparrows felt like the most beautiful serenade as Gabriel took her by the hand, his much bigger one enveloping hers, making her feel safe and protected, making this feel so right.

They chose a spot near the lake's shores to open the small wicker picnic basket he carried. Inside, he took out a blanket and spread it over the clean grasses, offering his hand to help her onto it. Thoughtful, the way he took care of her, pouring her a cup of lemonade, waiting for her to take the first sip and then the first taste of the cookies he'd picked up at the bakery.

As sweet as the treats were, nothing could compare to his company. Being with him was like being fully alive for the first time. It was like being with your other half. She'd never felt more at ease or more comfortable with anyone. He was the missing piece of her heart, found after all this time. They talked of little things—the places he'd lived and worked, childhood stories, funny tales from her parent's ranch. She hardly noticed the sun slipping toward the western horizon until the shadows had lengthened, falling over her as she sat on the blanket, her lemonade cup drained of every drop.

"The time has flown," she confessed, hauling herself to her feet. She fought down the wild distress that gripped her every time she feared her parent's—especially her mother's—wrath. "I need to get back."

"Sorry, I should have been keeping an eye on my watch." Calm but concerned, he handily tossed everything back in the basket, working fast but relaxed. His gray gaze studied her with what had to be sympathy. "I know your mother runs a tight ship. My sister has mentioned it often."

"My mother is uncompromising." It was the most positive but accurate word she could use to describe Maureen McPhee, who wanted everything her way without exception. "I really do need to get back. I'm expected to be helping in the kitchen about now."

"You didn't tell her about me?" He closed the lid, grabbed the basket's handle in one capable hand. His words weren't accusing. No, they held a hint of pity.

That got to her. It made her feel ashamed. Heat scorched her face as she retreated back through the wildflower speckled grasses. She could see the tip of her nose turning strawberry red. Here, she'd been so enamored with him, her lonely and needy heart so quickly filling up with love for him. What if he'd asked her out because he felt sorry for her? And here she'd thought he'd been sweet on her too, that he was hoping for a future with her. Mortified, her chest knotted up. She tromped through the grass, walking fast, blinking hard so her eyes wouldn't fill.

"It's okay if you want to keep me a secret. I can't blame you there." He lumbered behind her, his voice resonating with a brand of kindness she was not used to. It was steady and gentle.

Nothing could be more alluring to her. She hesitated, touched by it, needing that kindness the way a drowning person needed air or a starving person food.

He strode up to her on long, denim-encased legs. A green muslin shirt covered his muscled arms and torso. His black hat framed his face—the straight blade of his nose, sculpted mouth and iron-hewn jaw were sheer perfection. But what was even more striking was the tenderness shining in his gray eyes.

"I know I'm not the kind of suitor your folks would want for you." He reached for her hand, slowly taking it in his, his touch certain and comforting and thrilling all at once. "But I promise you, one day I will be. I'll work hard and do what it takes to be good enough for a fine lady like you."

"I'm not so fine." Her voice broke, all raw feeling. She couldn't hide her emotions from him, but it was time he knew the truth about her. Because if this courtship went any farther between them, she would lose her heart entirely, forever and for good. It was self-preservation that made her utter the cold hard truth. "I am no fine lady. I am a kitchen worker, just like your sister. In fact, she is my supervisor."

"I know." He leaned in, the calloused tips of his fingers grating roughly along her cheek, and yet softly too, as he leaned in, cupping the side of her face. What she saw exposed in his unguarded eyes weakened her knees and stopped her heart.

"But you are such a fine lady, the most beautiful and most sweet I have ever seen." He fastened his gaze on hers, gazing to the depths of her soul. "Don't break my heart, please. Will you let me come calling again?"

His words moved her, chest wrenching with physical pain. To have a good and handsome man see her in such a way, and to feel for her so much, it was a dream *come true. A dream she never wanted to end.* She nodded because she did not trust her voice and he moved in, leaning so close her skin tingled and she could feel his body's heat. His lips brushed her cheek in a respectful kiss, making her feel so cherished, so loved.

"Come on," he said, tugging her toward the horses. "Let's get you home. Should I drop you off at the fence where I found you?"

"Yes." Gabriel Daniels was going to be her little secret. Mother must never know. Mother would hate him, Mother would chase him away faster than all the others. As they hurried along, she tightened her fingers around his, holding on, never wanting to let go.

"Aumaleigh?" a voice intruded into her thoughts.

Pulled out of the memory, Aumaleigh blinked. The vivid day vanished, the memory of Gabriel's voice and presence faded, and the past was gone. She stood in the present, in the shadowed kitchen, staring vacantly into space. She shook her head, realizing that Louisa looked a little worried as she straightened her ruffled apron.

"Are you all right?" she asked, pushing a strand of light brown hair out of her face.

"Yes. I'm perfectly fine." It was all behind her, in the past, where it needed to stay. Where she needed to put it to rest and leave it be. The only problem was what to do when Gabriel visited? That was a solution that would take time to find. Aumaleigh shrugged. "I was just lost in thought. Is it time to ring in the cowboys?"

"Yes." Louisa's worried look didn't relent as she marched past Aumaleigh and yanked open the front door. "I can hold off ringing the dinner bell, if you need time."

"No, best not keep the hungry horde waiting," Aumaleigh quipped, forcing her sadness away and pasting what she hoped passed for a smile on her lips. "I'd better go lend a hand. Oh, looks like they are coming anyway."

"That's what we get for running a few minutes late," Louisa despaired, sighing at the look of three dozen cowboys stalking across the yard with fierce expressions and purposeful gaits. They had been working hard in the bitter cold all morning, and they meant business. Louisa shrugged and scurried back into the kitchen. "They're coming! I'll get the bread!"

Aumaleigh laughed to herself because the cowboys amused her. She hurried to lend a hand, grabbing an extra ladle to help Josslyn fill the bowls.

* * *

A knock rapped on the manor's front door, echoing down the hallway. Rose looked up from the cookies she was icing, spatula in hand. She glanced over her shoulder—no sign of Iris. Where had her sister gone?

"Hey," she called out. "Iris. Magnolia. Someone answer the door. I'm sticky."

Her words resonated in the high-ceilinged room, but were not acknowledged. Looked like her sisters had abandoned her. Good, because honestly she got very little alone time and bad, because sisters were useful for opening doors. Rose set down her spatula, stepped away from the counter and wiped the icing from her hands onto her apron.

The knocker knocked again, so she sprinted down the long hallway, past the library and sunroom and into the spacious, light-filled foyer. She yanked open the door, surprised to see a perfectly strange woman—well, a stranger, there was nothing particularly strange about her—standing on the doorstep.

"Oh!" the pleasantly plump lady said in surprise. She had a button face and a warm smile. She tugged her scarf a little higher around her neck. "Hello. I'm Lucile Breckenridge, and I was hoping to speak with one of the McPhee sisters. I'd like to place an order, please."

"Sure. Come on in." She held the door open wider, shivering in the chilly wind. "Did you want to order a cake, or cupcakes or cookies?"

"My thought was to get a cake." Lucile tentatively stepped across the threshold and into the foyer, wide-eyed, looking around with interest at the ornate wainscoting and soft, floral wallpaper and soaring ceiling. The woman seemed uncomfortable, staring down at her modest coat and well-worn shoes. "I'm really not sure. My daughter has had the specialty cakes at a friend's party and wants one with our Christmas dinner. To make it special."

"I see. I'm Rose." She gave the door a push closed, recognizing how Mrs. Breckenridge must be feeling. Maybe overwhelmed by the grandeur of the house—it was quite grand—like stepping into something in a book. She gestured for the lady to follow her. "Come with me. I was just about to box up a few orders and get them delivered. You might as well take a peek and see what you think."

"That's very kind of you." Lucile tapped down the hallway, a few paces behind Rose. "You're one of the sisters. I should have realized that right away. My daughter Clarice is friends with your little cousin Bea."

"Oh, Bea says such nice things about Clarice." Rose led the way to the far counter, where several cakes and a batch of cupcakes were finished and ready to go. "She sounds like a lovely girl."

"Thank you, I think so too, but then I'm biased." Lucile bit her bottom lip, debating, carefully keeping her hands firmly planted in her coat pockets as she leaned over the counter, assessing the baked goods. "These are just exquisite. I didn't know a person could do this with just frosting."

"I worked in a bakery for many years," Rose admitted, already plotting how best to make little Clarice happy. "These cakes are for a large group of people. The cake with the frosting Christmas trees and holly garlands is for a wedding. The other two cakes are for a company party here in town. The lumber mill."

"That's where my husband works." Lucile lit up. "It's a big to-do. The owner is very generous to his workers. He's bringing in a cook from Deer Springs to fix us all a fancy meal. Now I can't wait. I'll get to have a slice of your cake."

"Excellent. Hmm, I'm getting another idea." She was full of them today. Rose smacked her lips together, thinking harder. Yes, she could see it now. Little boxes of baked samples, all tied up with a cheerful red ribbon. Inspired, she rushed to the lower set of cabinets to dig through their supply of bakery boxes and chose the smallest one. "Why don't I send a few cookies home with you? We have extras. We always bake extra just in case something happens, like I drop one or something, besides the fact that we like to snack on them."

"That's very generous, but I can't afford—" Lucile fell silent and chewed on her bottom lip, blushing. She was of modest means. Her coat and the dress ruffle showing beneath were in good repair and fairly new, but nothing high class. Hers was an average family.

"Think of the cookies as an early Christmas gift." Rose selected some of the gingerbread men she'd been working on, carefully laying them in the bottom of the box. "How many children do you have?"

"Four. But, that's more than enough. We can share. I—" Lucile truly seemed distressed. Perhaps because she hadn't asked the question that really troubled her.

"We have affordable prices," Rose went on to explain, adding a layer of paper before selecting two more cookies, for a total of six. "An elaborate cake with so many layers and design can be quite pricy, but for a family of six, we can do just one layer, a simple pan cake to keep it affordable. We can cut it in half and add filling, and it will be every bit as delicious as our bigger cakes. I'll do a little extra decorating to fancy it up. I don't have a cost for that, but I could work something up, if you're interested."

"Oh, I am." Lucile lit up with relief and happiness. "Clarice has her heart set on this. She's such a good girl. I don't want to let her down."

"Neither do I." As Rose closed the lid tight, she thought of the girl who'd been sitting with dear Bea on the schoolhouse steps. "Let's see if we can't figure something out to make this special for your daughter."

Thank you." Lucile meant it, eyes bright with gratitude. She accepted the bakery box, hands trembling. "You have a good day now, Miss Rose."

"Just Rose." She shrugged, liking this lady very much. Anyone could see how hard she worked to make her family happy. Rose gestured toward the hallway, intent on seeing their newest customer to the door. "Why haven't I met you before? I didn't see you at my sister's wedding, although everyone was invited."

"It seemed mighty fine," Lucile said with a blush as she worked her neck scarf into place. "Although I was curious. I heard it was a simple wedding, but terribly romantic with the way the groom acted with his bride, so in love with her. And the dinner party was held here, in this house." She glanced around, hesitating in the hallway to peer into the parlor. "It's like a castle in here."

"I know, I can't get used to it." Rose laughed, opening the door. "We all shared a single room in a boardinghouse before we came here. It's been quite a change. Lucile, Daisy's wedding is coming up. I hope you and your family can make it. You would be welcome, and it's not fancy. We're just a regular family and we want to celebrate our Daisy's marriage. Please join us."

"Why, I just might talk to my husband and see." Lucile nodded once, as if she were truly considering it, as she stepped onto the porch. "It really was nice meeting you, Rose."

"You, too. I'm so glad you stopped by." It was true, and it was a perk of this job—getting to know people. There were so many good folks in this world. "I'll be sure and drop by with an estimate."

After a few more pleasantries, Lucile made her way across the yard and climbed into a horse-drawn, homemade wooden sled. Smiling to herself, Rose shut the door.

"Who was that?" Iris peeked over the rail of the grand, curving staircase that rose up to the second floor. She had a kerchief tied over her strawberry blond hair and a streak of dust on one cheek.

"Sure, now you show up," Rose teased. It was, after all, a sister's duty. "Funny how you were nowhere in sight when there was work to do."

"Was that a customer?" Iris clutched the polished wooden banister with excitement. "And I missed it?"

"Which was really too bad, because I came up with another brilliant idea." Rose leaned back against the door, mind spinning, excited by the prospect. "Remember that dream you and I used to have when we worked at the bakery in Chicago?"

"The one where we had our own storefront?" Iris went dreamy, her gaze drifting ceiling ward and she gave a little sigh. "It was a sweet dream. Totally out of reach, completely impossible. I can still see the front window display we planned. The green striped awning over the boardwalk. The little tables along the window for customers to sit and relax."

"Have you considered that maybe it's not so impossible after all?" Rose pushed off from the door, seeing that dream, too. The happy customers nibbling on cookies and sipping tea or coffee and hot chocolate. The scent of sugar and chocolate and cinnamon rising up from behind the display case full of delicious things she'd decorated. The contentment of working alongside her sisters in their own business. "There's that new building just off of Main. It's still vacant. Not to mention there's a few empty storefronts in town. We could check them out, figure out which one would be best for our purposes."

"We're not spending money on a losing proposition." The dreaminess faded from Iris's gaze, and her wistful smile twisted down into a terse, no-nonsense frown. "Because we inherited that money doesn't mean we should spend it willy-nilly. A penny saved is a penny earned, and I won't have us losing our financial stability over a business. Not when we have a perfectly wonderful kitchen right here to bake in.

What we're doing right now is financially responsible."

"Okay, that's sound thinking, I can't argue with it." Rose pounded up the stairs. "But Lucile Breckenridge just stopped by."

"Do we know her?" Iris's nose scrunched up as she thought about it. "I don't think we do."

"We do now. She's a wife and mother, and her husband works at the lumberyard." Rose swept to a stop in front of her sister, wishing Iris would catch some of her excitement. "We've been targeting the fancier side of Bluebell."

"They are the ones who can afford to pay for specialty cakes." Iris arched a brow warily, not one to be taken in by exciting new ideas. "That's the way it was in the Chicago bakery, too."

"I know, but Lucile's daughter wants a special cake for Christmas. She wants one of our cakes, and she needs an estimate." Rose sidled up to Iris on the step below and leaned on the rail. "This is for a nice little girl."

"You know I have a soft spot when it comes to children." Iris, the former schoolteacher, sighed. "I'll do it after supper and see if I can make the numbers work. You are thinking about expanding, aren't you?"

"I have some plans." Rose smiled, keeping them inside like a wonderful secret. "Think of all the people we can make happy with our baking."

"I would be happy if we operate at a profit," Iris answered ruefully. "But it's a nice dream. I've been so content here in this wonderful house, watching my sisters fall in love and planning weddings, and baking my cakes I guess I've forgotten to dream."

"You deserve dreams too," Rose told her gently, her throat tightening up into one big sore ache. What happened to Iris all those long years ago had devastated her. But she was finally coming back into her own, being the always-smiling, sunny Iris they used to know. "It just so happens we share this dream, and I'm going to make it happen. Profitably."

"We'll see." Iris sounded pessimistic, but the spark of hope lighting her periwinkle blue eyes said something more.

This can work, Rose thought, pushing away from the rail. This could make her sister happy. Wouldn't that be worth the effort? "I'm going to go finish the cookies. Does Cal know to bring Marlowe around for me?"

"Daisy has Marlowe," Iris said, padding up the stairs lightly, full of grace. Her blue wool dress shivered around her, rustling softly, emphasizing her petite, slender frame. "And Magnolia has Marvin. They're out on another delivery, you know."

"Then I'll borrow Phil." Phil was the ranch's errand horse.

"That's a problem." Aumaleigh waltzed into sight, a mop in hand. "Annie and Bea took Phil to Deer Springs. I can run down and have Cal hitch up one of the other ranch horses for you."

"No, I can do it. You stay in here where it's warm." Rose jumped over a few steps, landing in the foyer and took off for the kitchen. Honestly, she really did need her own horse. Here's hoping Seth would find the right one on Friday, because she couldn't afford to wait much longer. She had things to do, a business to run and plans to make. Yes, she had lots and lots of plans.

CHAPTER NINE

The ranch's horse, a big gray gelding by the name of Odie, pricked his eyes and shook his head disapprovingly at the eerie, lonely feeling of the little clearing near town.

"Don't worry," Rose told him, carefully grabbing the cloth-wrapped bundle of sandwiches off the seat beside her. She'd made good use of having the kitchen all to herself and even added one of the gingerbread men as a treat.

Oscar was nowhere in sight as she approached his makeshift home, but there were fresh tracks. She recognized his thread worn boots and his uneven gait imprinted in the snow and felt a whoosh of relief. At least he was okay. She worried about him in this weather.

She set the cloth-wrapped bundle in front of his door, spotting a folded pile of white napkins, ones she'd left him from before. They were carefully washed, spot free and precisely folded. That was Oscar. She grabbed them up, intending to return them before her sisters noticed they were short on napkins.

"Rose, is that you?" A voice broke the stillness, and several branches rustled. Oscar, wearing several thick layers of worn and handed-down coats over his clothes to keep warm, limped out of the undergrowth. He was coming from the direction of town. His square face, splotched red from being out so long in the cold, broke into a troubled frown. His gaze shot to the doorway. "You didn't have to do that. You do too much for me."

"It's just a sandwich." She gave Odie a reassuring pat, for the horse was not at all sure about the ragged looking man. "When you're back on your feet, you'll do something helpful for someone who needs it, and I'll consider this paid."

"You know I will do it." Oscar took a moment, standing still, swallowing hard to marshal his emotions. He was maybe in his early thirties, but hardship and homelessness made him look ancient. "It helps to think of better days to come."

"They'll get here, I know they will." Rose climbed back into the sleigh and tugged the robes over her, feeling guilty because she had so much. "Is there anything else I can get you? Anything you need?"

"No, Miss. I was just out gathering firewood when I heard your horse." Oscar glanced over his shoulder, squinting down the lane. "I was afraid it was the sheriff. There's a law against squatting. You know this isn't my land."

"I know. Your secret is safe with me." She reached for the reins, wrapping her fingers around the thick leather straps, turning Odie in a circle so he was headed toward town. "I'll see you tomorrow."

"You're my lifesaver, Rose. I won't forget this." Sincerity rang in his pleasant tenor as he lifted one gloved hand. Sadness shrouded him, this man down on his luck.

Since she didn't know how to tell him there had been a few times in her life when she'd feared winding up homeless—after her parents died, for one, and another time when she and Iris had been laid off from the bakery due to hard times for the owners and they couldn't pay for their rented room. She'd been lucky—she had her sisters. They'd pulled together and figured out a way. They'd helped one another. But who did Oscar have? He had no family. He had no one.

It must be hard to be so terribly alone, she thought as Odie emerged onto the main road. She reined him to their next stop—Mr. Michael's lumberyard. She'd never been alone. She'd always had her sisters, and now she had Wade. She wanted to like him so much. She smiled at the thought of the reliable deputy as Odie pranced along. Maybe one day soon, love for the deputy would touch her heart, and her life would never be the same.

Town was busy, full of folks who'd traveled in from the countryside on this sunny day to do their Christmas shopping. She waved at people she knew—Elise Hutchinson coming out of the mercantile with her mother, and a few shops down, Penelope Shalvis, the schoolteacher, ready to cross the street in front of the feed store.

"Penelope!" Rose pulled Odie over, straining across the boxed cakes set carefully on the floor to talk to her friend without shouting. "Just the person I wanted to see. Will you be coming over this evening?"

"Wild horses couldn't keep me away." Penelope peered out from beneath her woolen hood, which framed her nearly round face. A few stray strands of brown hair tumbled down her forehead. "I love our sewing get-togethers, and it's such a pleasant way to spend time."

"Especially now when there's so much to do," Rose agreed. Their sewing parties were total fun. "Christmas is coming so fast. We have to get it all done."

"It will be, don't worry." Penelope smiled in her teacher-ly way, so gentle it was impossible not to adore her. "Will Verbena be there too, or will newly wedded bliss keep her away?"

"Rumor has it that she's coming." Rose didn't add exactly how great that newly-wedded bliss looked. "Did you see the house Zane rented for them?"

"I did. I drove past it once when I got lost and went down the wrong street," Penelope confessed cheerily. "It's gorgeous and exactly what Verbena deserves. I'm so happy for her. Everybody should find true love. It makes the world right, you know?"

"I do."

"How about you and Wade?" Penelope waggled her brows. "Things must be getting serious with you two. Doesn't he take you driving every Sunday after church? Is it getting serious?"

"I'm content to take my time. I just want to enjoy being courted." Rose noticed Odie was looking bored, like he had better things to do than stand around so a couple of women could talk. That's what you get for driving a horse used to being around cowboys. "I have am impatient horse, so I'd better get going."

"Good idea. He's looking ready to revolt and take off on his own." Penelope's hazel eyes twinkled. "Then your handsome deputy beau would have to come rescue you."

"He is rather handsome," Rose agreed, tightening her grip on the reins. She was still a little unhappy with him, though. She ignored the sinking feeling in her stomach, hoping everything would work out.

"You're lucky," Penelope told her with a wistful look.

"Who, me? Have a good rest of your day!" The instant she gave the command, Odie launched into action, storming down the street as if he had better things to do than this and couldn't wait to get back to the ranch to do them. It was impossible to get a good look to see which storefronts were vacant as he dashed by, his neck arched and his feet flying. It was all she could do to yank him to a stop in the residential street behind Michaels Lumberyard. He didn't look impressed with his surroundings as he waited at the hitching post for her to get out of the sleigh.

"You don't seem to be enjoying yourself," she told him, plunging toward him through the drifted snow to tie him up.

Odie didn't answer her. He stared at her with one disapproving eye. Probably the cowboys didn't talk much to their horses. Odie didn't look as if he approved of unnecessary conversation. Not the talkative type.

"Okay, I won't torture you with more chitchat." She tethered him up good, double checking the knot before circling back to the sleigh. "Just stay right there."

He didn't look thrilled, but he waited obligingly as she swept one of the cakes off the floorboards.

"Miss McPhee!" Mr. Michaels, a strapping lumberjack sort of man, bounded through the front door of the two-story house, storming down the walk toward her. His thinning black hair flew up, caught in the breeze, before he pulled on his hat. "So glad to see you. We've been thinking of nothing else since lunch. Can't wait to dig into your cake. Here, let me take that for you."

"Fine, then I'll go get the other." She whirled around, loving her job. Really loving it. "This is a nice thing you're doing for your employees."

"We've had a banner year." Mr. Michaels called out over his shoulder, stomping up the walk. "Christmas bonuses are nice and they'll be plenty large this year, but I wanted to do something personal, treat them like family. Let my workers know how much I appreciate 'em. Your cakes will help make it a special night."

"I hope so." Rose bent to lift the bakery box from the sleigh floor, careful to keep it level. All the time she'd put in helping Iris bake it and in getting the frosting just right was worth it. She followed Mr. Michaels into his house, made sure he and his wife were happy with the finished product (they were beyond the moon) and after pocketing her payment, she returned to the sleigh.

To find it missing.

The tracks in the snow told the story. The indentation of the leather rein hitting the snow beneath the hitching post and of it dragging along as Odie's big hooves marched down the street, retracing the route they'd taken. The problem was that she had one more delivery to make. Panic popped through her. She needed help and she needed it fast.

Seth. The image of his ready, dimpled smile and his amused, dark eyes popped into her brain. She rushed down the side street, along the lumberyard's tall wooden fence, around to Main. Seth's livery stood directly across the way. He would help her. The panic pouring through her veins began to fade as she charged across the street.

"Rose!" A man's voice called—not Seth's. "Are you looking for this?"

Wade, astride his red roan, looked wonderful— strong and official and handsome. One gloved hand was wrapped around a leather rein, holding Odie firmly in place. "When I saw him heading down the street on his own, I raced to the rescue."

"You are a lifesaver." Relief swelled through her, especially when she saw the big, tall bakery box still tucked safely on the floor. It hadn't moved an inch. She tilted her head to gaze up at Wade, so tall and imposing astride his horse, and she felt grateful. Why didn't she feel more for him? How did you make your heart love someone? She had no idea. None at all.

"Thank you so much." She took the rein, holding onto it firmly. Wade grinned down at her, easy-going with a touch of pride and a hint of charm. There was like in his eyes, a certain amount of fondness. Was he struggling, too? She lifted her chin, trying to push down the disappointment overtaking her. "You saved the cake, Wade. I owe you big time for that."

"You could bake me something, you know, after your Christmas baking rush is over." He winked at her and knuckled back his hat. His blond hair ruffled in the breeze, giving him a slightly untamed look. Definitely handsome.

Shouldn't her heart be fluttering? she asked herself. Shouldn't the sight of his smile make her weak in the knees? She really wished it did. She climbed onto the seat, taking up both reins firmly. "I'll put it on my to-do list after Christmas. I'll do my very best baking for you."

"I'm counting on it." Wade tipped his hat. He was a good man—easy to please, relaxed and amiable, easy to get along with. He should be easy to love. Why was her heart having such a hard time of it?

Confused and let down, feeling like she was failing, Rose yanked the robes over her, watching as her beau rode off down the street, his back straight and shoulders braced.

"What were you thinking, Odie?" she asked the gelding in a scolding voice. "I was counting on you, and you let me down. How did you manage to untie yourself?"

If a horse could look guilty and indignant all at the same time, that was Odie. His ears sank back against his head even as he lifted his nose, clearly proud of himself, clearly intending to do it again. Perhaps he thought being driven by a woman to deliver cakes was damaging to his rugged ranch horse reputation.

"Are you all right, Rose?" A voice called above the *clink, clink* of horses going by on the street and a nearby conversation of two ranchers meeting up in front of the hardware store. She knew that voice, knew it so well that she turned toward it without thought, anticipating the sight of him standing in the barn doorway, his dark hat shading his face, his boots braced, looking long, tall and dashing in denims and a wool shirt.

"Seth." She was surprised by the way her heart leaped when she saw him. Perhaps it was that way with old friends, there was an amazingly strong bond that nothing could compare to. "Yes, I'm fine now that I have Odie back. Can horses untie themselves from a hitching post?"

"Depends on the horse. I've seen it done before." Seth ambled closer, stopping at the edge of the street. He didn't come any closer. "Before you ask, yes, I'm working on a horse for you. I've been putting out feelers, just in case I don't find anything at the auction."

"I appreciate that more than you know. I may have to bake you cookies, too." She didn't know why she said that, why the words came so easily with Seth. Talking to him felt as natural as breathing. Why couldn't it be that natural with Wade?

"I never turn down cookies." Seth's smile looked strained, not quite reaching his dark eyes, usually so expressive, but today they were like black glass, giving nothing away. "Well, I'll let you get on with your delivery. I see you're busy. Talk to you soon."

"Right." She intended to thank him for being so conscientious about finding her a horse, but he'd already turned away, striding through the open, shadowed barn door. Walking fast, as if eager to get back to work.

Hmm. Maybe he was really busy. Her chest grew tight and uneasy, like something was wrong. She hated the thought of him having a hard day. Seth was really a nice man.

"Okay, Odie," she told the horse, lightly slapping the reins. "Do you think you can survive one more delivery?"

The horse gave a beleaguered sigh, as if the indignity was too much to bear. But he obediently trotted down the main street, his ears pinned angrily against his head.

Rose settled in, relaxing against the seat, keeping a tight grip on the reins just in case the gelding decided he wanted to misbehave again. They had a long way to go, for the customer was far out of town. The cold wind blew over her, making her feel lonelier than ever as she zipped along, on the country road now. Yes, realizing what she didn't feel for Wade made her feel more alone than ever.

* * *

Seth kept his back turned, even when he was safely in the barn. Even when he knew Rose had driven off with Odie, hurrying on to her next delivery. His chest ached with knotted-up emotions he couldn't name. It wasn't as if he wanted to feel this way.

He *wasn't* going to feel this way, he told himself firmly, pacing down the main aisle, doing his best to purge his emotions, just erase that caring for her right out of him. He wasn't going to go sweet for a woman that wasn't rightly his—and it wasn't as if he wanted any romantic entanglements anyway, especially with a woman as wealthy as Rose. It was just his stupid heart, feeling what it wanted to feel.

"Forget her," Seth muttered to himself, fisting his hands. "Just do it. She's not for you."

That seemed to do the trick. The ache began to ease. If a man wasn't in charge of his heart, then what was he in charge of?

"Wally." Seth arched an eyebrow at the big gelding. His sparkly brown eyes were focused on the road, all his attention zeroed in on the outside world. Seth glanced over his shoulder, studying the view through the open barn door. "I don't see anything, you nut. What is wrong with you?"

Wally didn't bother to answer. He was too busy straining eagerly against his stall gate, like he was desperate to get out. Crazy horse. Seth shook his head.

"Can you believe him?" he asked the horse in the neighboring stall. "Talk some sense into him."

Inga blew out a horsy raspberry, giving her clear and undiluted opinion of Wally. It didn't look as if she approved of the gelding's embarrassing show of emotions.

"I'm with you," Seth told her wryly, on his way to the door. "Keep feelings controlled. That's the best way to go."

That's the way it had to be. Seth strong-armed the heavy door partway closed. With his view of the road cut off, Wally settled down and harmony filled the barn, but Seth had other things on his mind. He propped one shoulder against the door, staring out at the street where Rose had been.

When he'd talked to her, he'd tried pulling back on the friendship, tried keeping things distant but amicable. He didn't like being abrupt and cool with her and she'd looked confused. Troubled, he scanned the street, letting the chilly wind blow across his face, trying to settle his feelings. He'd be smart to stay uninvolved and unemotional, not to mention hunt down that horse for her.

He'd follow all of his leads tomorrow. The sooner he found Rose a new horse, the faster this would all be over, and he could go back to his life, back to the days when he rarely talked to her at all.

* * *

Her mood had put a damper on the afternoon. By the time she'd delivered the cake (the customer was delighted), the sun was hanging low above the horizon, giving one last glimpse of the world before surrendering to the inevitable. Rose pulled Odie over in front of the post office, her last stop before heading for home. The gelding gave a horsy snort and stomped one foot. He didn't look happy.

"I'll just be a minute," she told him, hopping from the sleigh and keeping a tight hold on him. "You can be a gentleman and wait for me that long, right?"

He arched a horsy brow as if to say, *lady, I'm no gentleman.*

"Don't think I'm going to be fooled again." She didn't double-tie the knot. She triple-tied it. "I can keep an eye on you from the post office window, so don't even think about getting loose. Got that, Mister?"

Odie lifted his chin defiantly.

Maybe she'd ask Cal for a different horse next time, Rose thought as she gave Odie a pat on the nose (it seemed to annoy him rather than make him fonder of her) and dashed up the steps. She didn't have much time before Odie worked his way through those knots. Oh, she wasn't fooled by him. Once a male showed you his true nature, you had to believe him.

"Miss Rose!" Fred called out gregariously from behind the counter. "Glad you stopped by. I've got mail for you and your sisters. How have you been?"

"Busy." She glanced over her shoulder, thankful to have a perfect view of Odie through the glass. The horse was smart enough to watch her—perhaps waiting until her attention was directed elsewhere. Good luck with that! She ambled up to the counter. "How about you?"

"Oh, no complaints." Fred whipped a handful of envelopes out of a cubbyhole on the back wall, his eyes warm with amusement. "Of course, today's been on the boring side. Nothing much out of the ordinary goin' on out on the street. No one showin' off their petticoats, for instance."

"You saw that, too?" Rose's eyebrows shot upward as she shook her head. Why wasn't she surprised? "You see everything, Fred."

"Not everything. I heard about it though." Fred set the batch of letters on the counter.

"I'm trying not to think about it. It's less embarrassing that way." She took them, wisely glancing out the window. Odie had a hold of his rein with his big horsy teeth and was yanking on the knot. "I'm waiting for something else to happen in town, some really great gossip so then everyone can forget my long johns. Maybe Daisy's wedding?"

"That's gonna be a big to-do." Fred leaned on the counter, his shirt sleeves rolled up, looking like he wanted something gossip-worthy. "You didn't have a lot of time with Verbena's wedding, but this one you gals have been planning for a long spell. I'm expectin' a doozey."

"We've got a week of baking planned," Rose confessed. "And cooking. You should tell folks we really mean it when we're inviting the whole town. There are so many people we haven't gotten to know yet. No gifts required, just come celebrate with us."

"I'll pass that along, sure. Me and the wife are already planning to come." Fred nodded, looking pleased. "Uh, looks to me like your horse is tryin' to get away."

"He's only got through one knot." Rose gathered up the letters. "But he is fast, so I'd better go. It's a long walk home if he gets away from me."

"You have that fine deputy to help you out. Bet he'd offer you a ride, right?" Fred called out, fishing for information. The gossip.

Rose laughed, amused. She really did like Fred.

"I'm not sure I want to rely on a man that much," she teased, sailing through the door. "Maybe I'll stay a spinster forever."

Fred scowled, as if he knew exactly what she was doing. Not giving him a single bit of information to pass on to folks. Served him right. She waltzed across the boardwalk, letters in hand, already looking ahead to the evening. A pleasant supper with her sisters, dishes to be done and put away and then sewing together by the fire (with Penelope, of course). Oh, it would be such a pleasant time. She couldn't wait. Not to mention the excitement of stitching up gifts for Christmas. They had so much to do this year.

"—yep, I'll be there." Wade's low, mellow voice rumbled down the boardwalk, cutting into her thoughts, carried by the wind. He stood at the end of the boardwalk, leaning against a post, his back to her. "Today, I'm feelin' lucky."

"Fine with me," a man answered, someone she didn't know. He wore a cowboy hat, a tailored coat, wool trousers and an expensive pair of riding boots. "I don't mind. Playing poker with you is like taking candy from a baby."

"Only on a bad night," Wade chuckled in that good-natured way of his that she liked so much. "My luck was off last time. I was on a losing streak. I lost my shirt. But tonight will be different. Are you cookin' supper again for all of us? If so, I'm bringing a sandwich or something."

Last night? Rose froze, too shocked to move. Her jaw dropped, her heart stalled, and she listened to his words rolling around and around in her head. *My luck was off last time. Are you cookin' supper again?* She blinked, gave her head a shake, wondering what had happened to his widowed sister that he had to help all evening? *He'd been playing poker with his friends instead?*

Shock turned to ice in her veins. She shivered, colder than she'd ever been. Had he lied to her? Or was there a good explanation? Maybe his sister had cancelled at the last moment, she rationalized, watching

Wade hike off the end of the boardwalk, into the cross street, heading away from her. He and his friend were talking like old buddies, not bothering to look behind them. Which was a good thing. She felt foolish. Tricked. And desperate not to feel those things.

Even as the rational part of her brain kept trying to find a reasonable excuse that would paint him in a good light, she turned around and skedaddled down the steps. She caught hold of Odie's rein just as he loosened the last knot with his teeth. Her eyes stung. She blinked, staring hard at the snow at her shoes.

Clearly, he really had lied to her. He hadn't wanted to spend time with her and lied about what he was really doing that night. What he would rather do. Hurt gathered behind her sternum, making it hard to breathe.

Someone called out a hello from the street as they drove by. She raised her hand with the letters in them, not even seeing who it was. Her pulse rushed through her head, thudding hard. She popped onto the seat, hardly noticing what was around her or that the sleigh was even moving. As twilight fell, Odie took them home at a fast and determined trot. Wade was not the man she thought him to be—the man she wanted him to be. Whatever hopes she'd once had for happiness with Wade disappeared like smoke on a moonless night.

CHAPTER TEN

"You forgot these in the sleigh the other day." Cal, the ranch's stable boy stood at the door, envelopes in hand. Behind him on the far side of the covered porch, delicate flakes of snow wafted down like the lilting notes of a waltz. Farther out, on the other side of the white lawn stood three horses and three sleighs. Marvin, Marlowe and another ranch horse Rose didn't recognize.

"Thanks, Cal." Rose took the envelopes, frowning at herself. She didn't even remember leaving them behind. That went to show how upset she'd been that evening when she'd arrived home.

That hadn't changed. An entire day had passed, spent baking with her sisters, frantically trying to get both their orders and their wedding treats done. She was still upset. With a heavy heart, she cast her gaze on the third horse—the unknown. "Is this one easier to handle than Odie? I'm not very experienced as a driver."

"I know, Rose." Cal gave a sympathetic shrug. "If the cutting horses won't do, we don't have a lot of other choices. Most horses we have are young, the ones we breed here on the ranch, and they have a lot of spirit or aren't broke yet. The older ones have been put out to pasture for a long time, mostly brood mares and they haven't been harnessed in a long time. Aumaleigh wanted me to be sure and ask again if you wouldn't want to use Buttons. I'd be happy to ride back and hitch her up."

"No, that's more work for you." Rose went up on tiptoe, squinting to get a better look at the horse. "Tell me about this one."

"Her name is Miss Ginger." Cal tipped his hat, backing away. "She hasn't been driven in years, but when I took her on a test drive, she seemed to do okay, so she should be good for you. I put the whip in the socket just in case."

"In case of what?" She had to ask. After Odie, she wasn't going to assume all would go well. "What aren't you telling me, Cal?"

"Look, she's the best we had for a fairly new driver." Cal hopped down the steps, lean and lanky, little more than a kid. He held out his hands helplessly. "I did the best I could. She should do what you tell her. If not, bring her back and we'll try something else."

"That's encouraging." She wasn't sure if she meant that sarcastically or not. "Thanks."

"No problem." Cal clomped down the walk, moving fast, looking eager to get back to the barn and away from the questionable mare.

Hmm. Rose turned her attention to Miss Ginger. The little red mare looked docile. The gray around her muzzle was a promising sign. Maybe, as an old lady horse, she wouldn't be so prone to antics. It was entirely possible she might be settled and obedient, just like Marvin and Marlowe were. At least, that's what she told herself as she eyed the whip. The whip really didn't bode well.

"What's the hold up?" Magnolia wanted to know as she bustled down the hallway. "And what do you have there, our mail?"

"I forgot it in the sleigh the other day." Rose blinked, realizing she was indeed holding onto several envelopes. She glanced at them. A bill from the dress shop in Deer Springs. A bill from the hat maker's shop in Deer Springs. A letter from Sarah Combs, the former town schoolteacher. It was postmarked from Oregon. "Hey, news from Sarah."

"I wonder if she got the Christmas box we sent her." Magnolia stopped, bakery box balanced in both hands, to glance over Rose's shoulder. "Well, open the letter. What are you waiting for?"

Before Rose could respond, a voice called out from deeper in the house. "You're letting in all the cold air. Close the door!"

Daisy. Rose rolled her eyes, elbowed the door shut and tossed the bills on the ornate entry table. She tore open Sarah's envelope eagerly, needing a little good news. Magnolia sidled closer, leaning to read over Rose's shoulder as she unfolded the letter inside.

Dear Daisy, Magnolia, Verbena, Rose and Iris,
I hope this finds you well. Thanks for the Christmas box you sent. It's tucked under the Christmas tree that Samuel cut down for me. This is our first Christmas as man and wife, and it's been such a memorable season, not to mention fun trying to hide each other's secrets. I hid his gifts in the last place he would look (behind the dirty laundry bin in the lean-to). I catch him now and then trying to search our little house, trying to figure out where his gifts are. Ha! Not a chance. I'm determined to stay three steps ahead of him.
Marriage has been wonderful, of course it helps when you marry a good and kind man. I'm excited to hear all about how your wedding plans are going, Daisy, and congratulations on your engagement, Magnolia. Verbena, I hope Ernest is caught by now—

"We'll have to write her about our latest news," Magnolia said, leaning back in to read.

—and, Rose, that Wade is getting ready to pop the question. You know Christmas is a popular time for beaus to propose.

Rose sighed. She was going to have to figure out what to do about Wade. Her chest constricted painfully, as if her ribs had clamped up and had no intention of letting go. She glanced down to finish reading the letter.

My Christmas box should be arriving with this letter, but if not (and since you never know about the post office) be sure and keep an eye out for it. It's a mystery what those postal people do with packages sometimes. Have the merriest of Christmases, my friends, and know that I am sending love and good wishes your way.
Lots of hugs,
Sarah

"Sarah sounds so happy." Magnolia gave a happy head bob, her blond hair bouncing along with her as she swirled away and opened the door. "I'm so glad. I love a happy ending."

"Me, too." Rose grabbed the edge of the door, holding it for Magnolia as her sister hurried past. Dubious, she cast a glance at Miss Ginger standing blanketed in the snow. The mare's eyes had drifted closed and her head had bobbed down. It looked like she was sleeping.

Well, that had to be a good thing. Like maybe she wasn't a horse prone to running away with her fairly inexperienced driver. That hope sustained her as she set the letter on the foyer table. They'd had an unbelievable busy day yesterday, baking from dawn until almost bedtime, which meant there would be a day full of deliveries today. She'd best get cracking. Plus, maybe all that driving alone today through the countryside would give her the thinking time she needed to decide what to do about Wade.

"This is for you." Daisy tapped down the hallway from the kitchen, bundled up in her winter gear, cradling a big, oblong crate in both arms. It was carefully stacked with bakery boxes. Several small sample boxes (her latest idea) were on the top. Daisy frowned. "Are you sure you don't want to take Marvin? I don't mind driving the other horse."

"No, I'm good with Miss Ginger. You and Marvin are buds." Rose fastened the last few buttons of her coat and reached for her scarf, excitement trilled through her like little fizzy bubbles in her bloodstream. Pretty soon she was going to have a horse of her own! She had complete confidence in Seth finding her the exact right horse—her perfect match. That happiness outshone all the other things troubling her as she relieved Daisy of the heavy crate.

"Drive safe." Daisy held the door for her. "I'm worried about you out there with a horse we don't know. Although she does look better behaved than Odie. The stories you told when you came home that night. I shudder every time I think about what might have happened to that wedding cake."

"You and me both, sister." Rose turned sideways to get the crate through the door and bounded across the porch. "This one is still asleep, so maybe she has a lower energy level."

"It looks promising," Daisy called out before closing the door.

Rose took one last look at her sister—the bride to be—and how radiant she looked, as if joy was just shining out of her. And for good reason. Daisy was marrying the finest cowboy in the county. Beckett was not only kind and strong and manly, but he ran the ranch for

Aumaleigh with care and dedication. Yes, Daisy was going to be happy as his wife and as a ma to his daughter, Hailie. Rose couldn't wait for Daisy to start her new life as Mrs. Beckett Kincaid.

Marvin and Marlowe nickered gentlemanly greetings as Rose tapped down the walkway. Miss Ginger was still fast asleep. Magnolia climbed into her sleigh, all ready to go and gathered up Marlowe's reins.

"I might be back a little later than expected," Magnolia called out as her little sleigh whizzed by. "Deer Springs is my last delivery, and I have some Christmas presents to pick up. I won't be too long though. So if I'm late, tell Daisy not to worry. She always does."

"I'll let her know." Rose thought of her gifts for her sisters, hidden in her room. Glad she'd shopped early, she gave Magnolia a chin jut of goodbye before lumbering over to the sleigh (borrowed from the ranch too) and carefully wedged her crate onto the floorboards. The sweet fragrance of chocolate frosting and vanilla cake wafted up, teasing her nose.

Once she had the crate in place, she ambled up to the sleeping mare. How did you wake a horse? Rose didn't know if there was an official and accepted way to do it, so she cleared her throat and gave it her best shot.

"Uh, Miss Ginger?" She waited, but the horse didn't respond. She kept snoring softly in and out, eyelids shut, velvety nostrils widening ever so slightly with each breath. Well, best to try again. This time she touched the mare's shoulder. "Miss Ginger?"

The horse startled. One eyelid shot up and a brown eye stared at her in surprise and then in annoyance.

"Sorry to wake you, but we have a job to do." Rose couldn't help patting that soft, soft nose. There was something amazing about horses. She loved everything about them. They were wonder and beauty and majesty, and there was nothing sweeter than horsy kisses. Although Miss Ginger didn't look like she was interested in giving any kisses. She seemed to endure the petting with a slightly miffed look. She opened her other eye to glare more strongly at Rose.

Hmm. It didn't seem she was the friendly type. Rose shrugged, turning on her heals. Well, that didn't matter, they didn't have to be friends to get the deliveries done. But it did make her look forward to the horse she would have one day very soon. Hadn't Seth hoped by the end of the week? She gave a little shiver at the idea as she settled on the seat and hauled the flannel robes over her (they were folded up neatly on the seat. Thank you, Cal). She grabbed the reins, her mind drifting, and gave them a hearty snap.

What would her future horse be like? Would it be a sweet old gentle gelding, like Marvin? Or maybe a dear little mare, like Aumaleigh's Buttons? Would her horse be a deep rich brown with a black mane and tail, which was so stunning, or a brilliant sorrel, whose red coat would gleam in the sun?

"Uh, Rose." Daisy's voice cut into her thoughts. "Why are you just sitting here?"

Rose startled, glancing around. She was still in the driveway. Motionless. It looked like Miss Ginger had gone back to sleep.

This wasn't good. Not by a long shot.

"I told her to go." Rose blew out a frustrated breath. Honestly. She was going to have to really pay attention to this mare. She gave the reins a harder slap, so that they lightly contacted the horse's rump. "Let's go, Miss Ginger."

"Giddy up." Daisy lent a helping hand and gently slapped the mare's flank.

The mare's eyes popped open and she lowered her head, plodding slowly down the lane.

"Keep a tight rein," Daisy called out supportively, looking lovely with the wind scattering her molasses-dark tendrils. Slim and feminine, unable to hide her happiness, she cupped her hands to her mouth to add another helpful hint. "Stay right on her. Don't let your mind wander."

"That's near to impossible," Rose quipped over her shoulder, although she feared her sister was right. Miss Ginger had been out to pasture for a long time. Perhaps she just needed to be reminded how nice it was to be out on the road, enjoying the scenery with a person who cared. Perhaps a conversation was in order. You know, to build friendship.

"Town is to the left," she told Miss Ginger as the tree-lined lane was coming to an end and the county road approaching. "I bet it's been a long time since you've been to Bluebell."

Miss Ginger huffed out a sigh. Perhaps she wasn't in the mood to respond. The mare did seem to hesitate when Rose tugged on the left rein.

Very troubling. Rose tugged harder, and then harder still as the horse slowed down, perhaps intending to stop or fall asleep again. Afraid she was being too rough, Rose tugged hard enough to turn the mare's head. Thankfully Miss Ginger turned, dragging her feet (or would it be hooves?) in the snow as she angled onto the main road toward town.

Whew. Rose let out a pent-up breath. Her palms had gone damp, sticking to the insides of her gloves. Boy, this was a lot more stressful than she'd imagined. She was almost missing Odie.

"Our first stop is to drop off Lucile Breckenridge's sample." Rose resumed her conversation, determined to win Miss Ginger over. By the end of the day, maybe they'd be fast friends. "Iris worked up a price that I think will be doable for Lucile and her budget. Iris isn't sure we should bake at such a small profit margin, but she'll come around. When you've been poor and struggling for so long, sometimes you can't trust that the future won't be that way. Even if you have a whopping big savings account."

Miss Ginger gave a bothered sigh, swiveling her ears forward, as if not interested at all. Her hooves dragged as she slogged along—Rose figured if she got out and walked it might be faster. But at least the horse was moving forward. That was a positive, right?

"I have plans." She rubbed a couple snowflakes off her eyelashes. "I can see it now. Orders coming in, customers at the door, a few hired girls to help us in the kitchen. Delivery drivers taking off with the day's deliveries."

It became a picture in her mind—the fair and upbeat work environment (a change from back in the days when she held a job. Her boss was most difficult). Beautiful baked goods lining the counter, waiting to be boxed. A sense of fulfillment from work well done. A sign swinging above the door, *Welcome to the McPhee Sister's Bakery*—no, she thought, tilting her head in concentration. With everyone getting married, they would have different last names.

Maybe this would be better—*Welcome to the Bluebell Bakery*. Yes, that was much better, Rose thought, nodding with satisfaction. It was a fine image, this dream of hers. One she could feel coming true.

"And most important of all, I see Iris baking away, humming to herself the way she does when she's truly happy. We don't hear that anymore, but that's going to change. Mark my words." Rose blinked, realizing she'd let her mind drift and the mare was standing still in the middle of the road, eyes closed.

Sleeping?

Oh! Rose tamped down the rising anger at herself. How could she be so forgetful? She should have been paying attention. She knew better, but her daydreams had gotten the best of her. "Woo-hoo, Miss Ginger?"

The horse gave a small snore.

"Hey, wake up!" Frustrated, Rose shook the reins hard, waving them up and down, hoping it would be enough to wake the mare from her slumber.

Nothing. Not even a snort.

Now what did she do? Rose slumped back against the seat, at a loss. Her gaze slid to the long, sleek whip standing in its socket.

No! She bit down hard on her lip. No way. She couldn't hit an innocent animal. Miss Ginger was probably just really tired. She was old. Maybe she hadn't slept well last night...at least, that was a better explanation than the others that came to mind.

Well, she thought, casting her gaze over the top of Miss Ginger's head to the road. Town wasn't far. She could see the post office from here. But she could also see something else—a team of big buckskin draft horses pulling a sleek wooden sled. She recognized those horses—one of whom was Wally—and a smile broke out on her face.

Seth!

"Looks like you've got a problem." He pulled his team to a stop alongside her with a final chime of the jingle bells on the harness. Tiny flakes of snow danced in the air between them. "I know this horse. It's one of the brood mares from the ranch."

"Yes. Miss Ginger is a tad sleepy this morning." Rose ignored the rush of warmth in her heart when she smiled at Seth. It was such a relief to see him. He would know just what to do. He'd help her out because that's what friends did. It was a cozy feeling.

Wally, not to be ignored, gave a whinny of greeting and curved his neck around, brown eyes pleading and so sweet Rose couldn't resist. She stretched out as far as she could reach to give his big velvety nose a stroke.

"Is there some kind of horsy coffee? I don't know how to get her moving." She arched her eyebrows at Seth. Maybe there was a secret to dealing with a horse like Miss Ginger."

"No, sorry." He gave a soft chuckle, a pleasant sound, looking rugged this morning in his leather duster and black Stetson, his softly curling black hair tousled by the light wind. He hadn't shaved either, and dark whiskers layered his strong, square jaw. "You have to be firm with her."

"I *am* being firm with her." Her chin went up.

"Not firm enough." He gestured to the mare who slit open one eye as if to check and see if her ruse was still working. "You're too tenderhearted, Rose."

"Me? I've slapped her with the reins. Hard."

"Yeah, right." That made him laugh. Admiring, tender feelings rose up for this gentle lady. "Maybe your idea of slapping her hard and my idea of slapping her hard are too different things. Not that I—"

"I refuse to be cruel to her." Rose puffed up with indignation. "I can't believe you said such a thing, Seth Daniels. I thought you were a good man, not a man who endorses animal abuse."

"No, I just meant—" Actually, he didn't know what he meant, because his brain stopped working. His gray matter just skidded to a halt and refused to budge...just like a stubborn horse. He was left gaping, wordless and awkward as Rose went on.

"And it's not only you. It's Cal too." Ire swept across her face, turning her nose and cheeks red. "He expected me to use that whip. A *whip*. No way. I'm not touching that thing. You know good and well both Marvin and Marlowe have horrible scars on their backs from whips. I—"

"Whoa there, slow down." Maybe his brain was starting to work again, but it was hard to tell because his heart had taken the reins, letting him soak in the sight of adorable little Rose with her blond curls tumbling down from her knit hat and all full of righteous indignation. He'd never seen anything more dear. "I only meant you need to show her who's boss, not hurt her."

"But—" Rose's indignation ran out of steam as she thought over his words. "Well, I still won't hurt her."

"You don't have to." He climbed out of the sled, wondering what was up with Wally who gazed at Rose with bright shining eyes, as if he liked her even more for her stance on animal treatment. Seth slapped the mare on the flank, lightly. "Miss Ginger. You aren't fooling me. Open those eyes."

The mare gave a huff, very much like a sigh of resignation. But not willing to entirely lose the battle, she opened her eyes blinking, as if she'd just been woken up from a long winter's nap. Her gaze was entirely innocent as she looked around, as if startled she'd "fallen asleep," too.

"She's just trying to trick you to get her own way." He strode back to the sled, feeling awkward and maybe even a little embarrassed about his fondness for her. He couldn't seem to stop those feelings. "Shorten the reins. That'll keep her neck arched and her nose down. It'll be harder for her to pretend to sleep that way."

"She's pretending?" Rose's forehead furrowed up.

"Yes, and if you had let me finish, you would know what to do now." He tossed her a crooked grin. "Guess that's just too bad."

"Fine, I over-reacted." Rose rolled her eyes, so pretty in her blue hat and matching scarf, bundled up in her wool coat. "What do I do? I can't sit here waiting for her to stop pretending to sleep."

"Use the whip—" He held up one hand to stop her from protesting. "Don't hit her with it, snap the air beside her to startle her. That should do the trick."

Or, that was his hope.

Rose didn't look any more convinced of that than he was, so he grabbed the whip from the socket and held it out to her. Her small hands wrapped around the base. He hardened his chest to keep from feeling anything as he leaned in, still holding the whip.

"You give it a little flick, like this." He jerked the handle, aiming it a good foot from the horse's shoulder. Miss Ginger gave a startled neigh and took off at a fast clip—he let go of the whip just in time. Rose looked startled as the sleigh carried her away, and she wrestled the whip back into the socket and grabbed the reins off the dash. She twisted around in her seat. "Thanks, Seth!"

"Any time." He watched her go, seeing nothing of her but the blue pom-pom on the top of her hat over the back of the seat. He had to struggle to keep his heart like stone. Unfeeling. "I hope to have a horse for you by tonight."

"I sure hope so!" Rose called out, the wind carrying her words back to him as Miss Ginger pulled them down Main and he lost sight of them in the early morning traffic.

He stood there, a man alone in the road, covered with snow and shivering in the icy wind, his heart not stone at all.

He did okay as long as he wasn't near her. When he was busy going about his daily life, he could forget about this growing fondness he had for Rose McPhee.

But not when he was near to her.

Just get her the horse, he told himself, sure that would solve his problem.

"I guess I'm not the only one missing her," he commented dryly. "Wally, do you like Rose?"

The big, strong gelding gave a low, embarrassed nicker deep in his throat. As if it pained him to acknowledge it.

"Yeah, me too, buddy," he said, getting back in his sled. "Me, too."

CHAPTER ELEVEN

Only one more errand left for the day, Rose thought with relief as she climbed back into her sleigh in front of Bluebell's post office. Snow had been falling all day in light, sugary swirls and she brushed off the accumulation from the robes before drawing them over her, snuggling beneath their flannel-lined warmth.

She'd been going all day, returning home only to load up on more deliveries while she packed a big lunch (most of which she'd left at Oscar's front door). After driving far and wide, including six stops in Deer Springs, she was tired, hungry and yearning for the warmth of home. Too bad she'd saved the toughest stop for last.

"Okay, Miss Ginger, time to pretend to wake up." Rose stowed the handful of letters into the empty delivery crate at her feet (it looked like seven more orders had come in the mail). "Come on now. Open those eyes. Time to get moving."

The mare gave a perfectly timed snore.

It was actually pretty funny if you thought about it, but it had been a loooong day. A loooong day of trying to coerce Miss Ginger to move. Rose held back an aggravated sigh and reached for the whip. She didn't like to use the thing, (her worst fear was that she might accidentally hit the horse with it), but it had to be done. Miss G was not "waking up." Clenching her teeth, Rose lifted the whip from its socket and gave it a little flick. The long, frightening tail made a terrible snapping sound.

Smack! Miss Ginger's eyes flicked open and she gave a long-suffering huff before stepping forward a few feet.

Whew, Rose thought, replacing the whip and relaxing back into the seat. It was nerve-racking to use the thing, but it was effective. Now she could get on with tracking down Wade and having a very difficult discussion.

"Hi Rose!" Penelope called out, going the other way down Main Street. She looked cozy tucked into her little cutter, much lighter than a sleigh. "I'm heading to your house. You're going in the opposite direction. Your work day isn't done yet?"

"Technically yes, but I have to talk to Wade." That thought was depressing. It felt like Wally, in all his enormous glory, was sitting right on her chest, proof of how much she was dreading this upcoming discussion. "I'll be home soon, if Miss Ginger cooperates. She didn't respond to the whip when I used it the time before last—" Rose bit her lip, because it had finally dawned on her. Miss G had come to a full and complete stop in the road. Again. She'd squeezed her eyelids shut and gave a convincing snore.

"Is she *asleep?*" Penelope drew her darling little spotted mare to a stop, concern wreathing her lovely oval face. Snow dappled her fashionable gray hat and brown curls. "Well, I thought she was asleep, but she opened one eye just a bit to check on me."

"She's seeing if you believe her or if she—" Rose paused while the horse gave an even louder this time rumbling snore. "She's convincing, isn't she?"

"I'll say. She's behaving very terribly," Penelope said in her gentle, amused way. "If she were one of my students, I would make her write lines on the blackboard and sit in the corner through the day's recesses. But I don't know what you do for a misbehaving horse."

"Your mare is such a good girl. Where did you get her?" Rose remembered Seth's promise that he had leads to follow. Why couldn't he get her a darling little mare like Penelope's? She smiled at the thought, so ready for a horse that meekly did what she was told. In exchange, Rose would love and spoil her terribly.

"Seth found her for me. The Hutchinsons had a few for sale," Penelope volunteered. "Maybe they have another one. My Alice is so well-behaved. It might be a nice relief for you to have a horse like that."

"Oh, so you heard about Odie, did you?"

"Are you kidding? The whole town was talking about it, and you know my kids repeat everything, so I get to hear all kinds of interesting things." Penelope gave a soft, fond smile. Anyone could see she adored teaching. Joy glowed from her whenever she mentioned her students. "And I can always round out my information gathering with a visit to Gemma. She saw Odie running down the street without a driver. At least now the town has something new to talk about. Maybe they'll forget how you flashed your underwear to the whole street."

"It was only my long johns and petticoats. They successfully hid my drawers and bare legs." Rose still blushed, although now she could laugh. It really was funny.

"Hey!" a man called out from a wagon box mounted on runners. His four big horses went around Penelope, and as he drove by, he tossed them a disgruntled look of disapproval. "You're blocking the road. Women drivers."

"Oops, better go." Penelope gave a sheepish shrug. "I'll see you at your house soon. Have a nice talk with Wade."

The weight on Rose's ribs seemed to double. She opened her mouth to try to explain that it wasn't that kind of a chat, but nothing came. She could only nod as her friend sped away, drawn by her perfect little horse.

"Let's try this again, Miss Ginger." Rose reached for the whip, very aware that she was blocking one side of the street. Other horses and sleds were winding around her.

"Need help, Miss Rose?" Carl Thomas, the feed store owner, asked cheerfully from his seat as he passed by, a kindly older gentleman ready to assist a young lady in distress.

Not that she wanted to admit she was in distress.

"No thanks, Mr. Thomas." She tossed the sweet older man a smile. "I've got this."

"Okay. You have a nice evening now." He tipped his hat to her, driving off down the street.

A few shoppers on the boardwalk had gathered, huddling together to perhaps discuss her plight. A horse stuck in the road was big news in such a sleepy town.

Well, not for much longer. Rose used the whip. *Crack!* It made an angry sound, but Miss Ginger didn't startle. She didn't leap forward. She didn't even open one eye.

Grrrrr. Rose tried it again. *Crack!* Nothing. Miss G didn't flinch, but she did start snoring louder.

"Ooh, I can't believe this." Rose poked the whip back into its socket, shoved off the robes and landed on the snow. The road was icy from all those sled and sleigh runners rushing over it, but at least she remembered that this time and successfully slipped and slid her way to the mare's halter. The back of her neck burned, with the focus of all the eyes watching her. Were even more people stopping to watch? She was mortified. Didn't folks have anything better to do?

Then she spotted Lawrence Latimer coming out of the feed store, and panic charged through her like a speeding train. *Oh, no, not Lawrence.* She groaned, grabbed Miss Ginger by the bit and gave a mighty tug. "Come on."

With a snort of indignation, the mare opened her eyes. But instead of resignation, another emotion shone in those dark brown depths. Defiance.

Uh oh. Rose bit her bottom lip, stymied. What on earth did she do now? The animal outweighed her by hundreds and hundreds of pounds. It wasn't as if she could drag Miss G or plant both hands on her rump and push her down the road. Worse than that, Lawrence was getting closer. He was lumbering down the boardwalk with his bowler hat and narrow shoulders and eyes full of puppy dog hope.

She was afraid if she let Lawrence help her, she might never get rid of him. He was so lonely and desperate and such a talker. She tugged frantically on the mare's halter. *"Come on."*

"She musta figured out you weren't really gonna hit her with that whip, huh?" a familiar male voice called out. Junior! He limped toward her, crossing the street, leaning on his homemade crutch. He looked better today—his clothes were cleaner, his blond hair neatly combed under his worn, wide-brimmed hat. "How many horses do you have?"

"Oh, this one is a loaner," she explained, beaming a welcoming smile his way. "It's good to see you again. How are things in your new home? Are you getting settled?"

"Trying to. I'm almost there." He gave a mild shrug, one corner of his mouth tugging upward quizzically as he gestured toward Miss Ginger. "You've gone and let that horse think she can trick you, and that makes her the boss."

"I've heard this assessment before." Rose glanced over her shoulder, still a little worried, but Lawrence had been derailed by another woman he'd come across on the boardwalk (thank goodness! But too bad for her). Elise Hutchinson, with her sleek brown hair and impeccable manners, did her best not to look pained as Lawrence launched into a long-winded dialogue. Poor Elise.

"You've got to get back control," Junior advised, limping across the icy road and coming to a stop beside her. "If you want to get in, I'll get her started for you."

"Thanks, I'd be much obliged." Rose couldn't help feeling sorry for Junior. Look at him, doing his best to improve his life. His clothes, ironed, his jaw freshly shaven, and his mildly homely face scrubbed clean. She hoped he would find as much happiness here in Bluebell as she and her sisters had. "I'll just walk her from here. It might be easier."

"All right. You just take her by the bit ring like this." Junior grasped the bridle bits and pulled, hard enough to drag Miss Ginger's mouth forward, followed by her entire head. She dug in, her hooves planted in the snow, but he limped backwards down the road, hauling her by the bit—by the mouth.

Rose's stomach squelched, fearing he was hurting the mare, but the animal didn't complain or cry out. "Please be gentle with her, Junior."

"See, that's where you've gone wrong." He gave her a kind nod of respect. "You're awful nice, but remember, a horse ain't like us. Her mouth is made for this. Now, giddy up, horse. Stop your nonsense."

His stern, firm tone helped. Miss G grudgingly lifted her hooves, moving forward as slowly as possible. Her brown eyes beamed resentment.

Poor Miss Ginger. Rose took over, grasping the metal ring where the bit met the leather hardness and kept walking. No way was she stopping or she'd never get the mare started again. "Thanks for coming to the rescue, Junior."

"My pleasure, Miss Rose. It's the least I can do to repay your kindness the other day." He tipped his hat, leaning heavily on his crutch as he limped away, favoring his left foot. He made such a striking image, struggling on the ice and keeping his shoulders set, his spine straight, anyway. Full of dignity.

What was his story? she wondered, but that answer was for another time. She lifted her chin, trying to find the strength she needed for the task ahead. She had Wade to deal with, and her stomach went sickly feeling at the thought of it. This was not going to be easy. While she hoped there was a logical explanation, she suspected she wouldn't have a beau when this was done.

* * *

Just do it, Rose. Her hand trembled as she stood on the doorstep of Wade's shanty. Tucked back from the street, one block down from Seth's livery, the shanty was in good repair and well-built. She'd never been here before, but Wade had described his home to her on their numerous buggy and sleigh rides over the last few months.

Maybe this won't be so bad, she reasoned as she rapped her knuckles against the smoothly painted door. Inside the shanty, boot steps pounded closer. The hinges whispered open and there he was, without his hat and his badge and with a coffee cup in hand.

"Rose." Startled, he slammed the cup down on a small plank table behind him, sloshing the liquid inside.

It wasn't coffee, she thought with a sniff. Whiskey. That had been Pa's drink of choice when he was feeling down. It surprised her that Wade would be drinking alone like this. Was it a regular occurrence?

"What are you doing here?" He ran his fingers through his hair, trying to spruce himself up a bit. "I mean, it's a pleasure and all. Just a surprise. Come in. Will you, uh, be staying long?"

He cast a glance at his mantel clock, as if the time were a pressing concern. Since there was no fire in the hearth (the coals had been raked over) he must be planning on going out.

A sinking feeling dug into the pit of her stomach and stayed there.

"No," she told him, meeting his gaze directly. "This won't take long at all. I overheard you talking to someone the other day. You said you turned down dinner with me and my family to play cards and drink with your friends. Is it true?"

"Uh—" Wade stammered. "You sure don't beat around the bush, do you? When you say it like that, you make me look bad."

"I'm just repeating the facts as I know them." She couldn't help feeling sorry for Wade standing there, looking mighty uncomfortable as he scratched his head and rubbed the back of his neck. "If this is true, then you are the one who made you look bad."

"I just didn't know how to tell you is all." Wade straightened up to his full six foot height, giving her that vulnerable smile she liked, the one that made him look like a good guy—exactly what she'd been looking for. "I already had plans, and I didn't want you to think I was ducking out on supper with your family."

"It's interesting to me that I've invited you three times to have supper with us, and each time you had plans." Rose planted her feet and folded her arms over her chest. "It's starting to be a pattern, Wade. It's one thing if you are truly busy, but you are making excuses, aren't you?"

"See, you're thinking bad of me, and that's not fair. It's the man's job to do the inviting." A streak of anger layered his voice. His jaw snapped tight, his lips slightly curling as if he was fighting showing his true feelings, as if she'd hit a nerve. "That's the way courtship works. You can't go holding it against me if I play cards now and then."

"But didn't you tell me you were helping your widowed sister?" Rose was proud of herself. She'd almost said those words without a crack of emotion, without betraying how hurt she felt. "I trusted you, and you deceived me."

"Why, that's awful harsh." Wade's chin jutted up mulishly, but pain shone in his eyes. He sputtered, caught up in his emotions. "What about you? You're running to all four corners of this county, and I can't tell you the times I've heard about you in a sleigh with a different man. How's that for deceit?"

"Wade, I haven't deceived you." Disappointment curled through her, almost as heavy as the pain weighing on her heart. That's what the guilty did, they often accused you of their wrongdoings. "I haven't lied to you, but it's clear we can't trust each other. Without trust, what do we have?"

Wade opened his mouth, trying to think up a way to argue, but she didn't give him that chance.

"We have nothing, that's what." She said the words as kindly as possible. "I think we should end this. I don't want you to be my beau anymore."

Those words hurt, and she hated saying them. Rose squeezed her eyes shut, because she'd grown fond of Wade. She'd found so much to like about him—his humor, his gallantry, the fact that he was kind to her. He'd made her feel pretty, which for the plainest girl with four beautiful sisters, was a big deal. But that wasn't enough.

"Oh." Wade rocked back on his heels as if she'd struck him and hung his head. He stared hard at the floor, his jaw working, letting the silence thicken. Pain stood in that silence. This hurt him too. "I was going to propose to you on Christmas."

"I'd hoped that you would." Tears burned in her eyes, and she blinked hard and fast to keep them from falling. Part of her yearned for that dream of being married to Wade—he made her feel cozy and pretty and safe. She could have pictured it—him ambling through the door at the end of the day with all kinds of funny stories about what had happened at work, sharing supper and conversation over a table by a crackling fire, the kind courtesy he showed her, the thought of knowing she could always count on him.

But that was the good side of Wade. He'd taken care to show her the best side. This other side she was seeing—well, she didn't know that part of Wade at all. In truth, she didn't want to. And that plea in his eyes wasn't making this easy—he'd been her first beau—but she squared her shoulders and took a step back. "I'm sorry, but I'm not changing my mind. I can't date you anymore."

"I see." He blew out a sigh, heavy with pain. "I could stop spending so much time with the boys. Would that make a difference?"

"No." She said the word gently, her sadness sounding raw and strangled in her voice. "Goodbye, Wade."

He turned his back to her, perhaps wrestling with his emotions too. She quietly stepped outside and closed the door. The snow struck her cheeks like tears. Her heart cracked a little, but the saddest part of all was that it didn't hurt to walk away as much as she thought it should. Defeated, she eased down the snowy steps and across the yard to where Miss Ginger was waiting for her alongside the road.

"Let's go home, Miss G." That could not happen fast enough. All Rose wanted was the warmth and comfort of her house, of the soothing presence of her sisters, but when she reached to untie the mare from the tree branch she'd used as a hitching post, Miss G bared her big yellow horsy teeth threateningly.

The warning was clear. *Stay away from me.*

"Well, this is the last straw." Defeated, Rose leaned against the side of the sleigh and heaved out a long, frustrated sigh. Exhaustion weighed on her, she was beyond frustrated with the horse and on top of that her heart was sad. Not broken, but sad.

"We can't stay here all night," she told the horse. "If I untie you, you won't bite me, right?"

Miss Ginger eyed her furiously, as if she wasn't about to make any such promises. She gave an angry nicker, almost a growl, as if to make it clear being hauled by the bit down the road had been the last straw, and it was going to be no more Miss Nice Horse. Miss G lifted her top lip higher, as if to emphasize her point. *Come closer and I'll bite you. Hard.*

Great. What did you do with a horse that refused to move and might cause personal harm? Completely out of her depth, Rose buried her face in her hands.

"Rose? Is that you?" a male voice called out through the snowfall, so familiar and welcome he chased all the unhappy feelings away. A dark silhouette emerged from the shadow of nightfall. Seth. He strode closer holding something in one hand. It was reins, she realized, as a second shadow emerged into view behind him. A horse.

"Good, you're still here." He sounded relieved and upbeat as he marched across the road. "I saw you pull in when I was out in the back of my livery. I have a surprise for you."

"A horse!" She stared in disbelief as the little spotted mare ambled to a stop beside Seth, incredibly pretty with her sculpted head and full forelock and big brown eyes. Elation filled her. "You found me a horse."

"I'm not sure she's snuggly enough, but she's friendly and well-behaved and old enough to be mellow and easy to handle." Seth tipped snow off his hat brim, his smile was, well, only a little distant. All business, he turned to face the horse and laid a hand on her dainty nose. "The Hutchinsons are willing to sell her and I talked them into giving you a trial run. Since you know Elise, they agreed. The mare's yours to try out for a few days so you can see if she's a good match."

"Oh, she's lovely." The weight of the day slid off her shoulders, and the thrill of having her very own horse outweighed the sadness in her heart. Leave it to Seth to make things better. "What's her name?"

"Poppy." He gave the mare's nose a final pat. "I thought her name was a good sign."

"Poppy and Rose." Happiness hitched in her chest, and she felt the back of her neck prickle. When she turned around, she caught sight of the curtain in Wade's front window falling back into place. He'd been watching her, maybe hurting too. Boy, romance was sure painful, even when it was regular and ordinary instead of the fairy-tale kind. She forced herself to step forward and hold out her hand to Poppy. "It's nice to meet you, pretty girl. I hope we can be friends."

The mare gave a soft, tentative snort, as if she were considering it.

"Thank you for this, Seth." Rose's vision blurred with pesky, happy tears. "You have no idea how much I needed this right now. My own horse!"

"Hey, are you all right?" Seth's baritone dropped low, resonating with concern. "Are you crying?"

"With relief at getting a new horse," she confessed, because it was partly true. "I'm afraid Miss Ginger and I have gone as far as we can go together. She wants to bite me."

"That's an impediment in any relationship," he quipped, feeling more than a little uncomfortable, frustrated at how hard it was to hold his feelings still. "Go on, get in your sleigh and bundle up. It's cold out here. I'll get Poppy hitched up and tie Miss Ginger to the back and when you pull in at the ranch, Cal can deal with those big teeth."

"Speaking of teeth." Rose swiped her eye with the back of her glove and gave another try at a smile. "Looks like she's threatening to bite you too."

"No worries, I know how to handle a cantankerous female." Seth waggled his brows, friendly but firm. He left Poppy standing on the side of the street (she stood obediently, lifting her head to watch his every move). It wasn't easy, but he kept Rose out of his thoughts as he strode over to Miss Ginger, placing a firm hand on the near rein and drawing it down to keep her from using her teeth on him.

"Now you and me, we need to come to an understanding," he told Miss Ginger. "You don't bite me, and I don't bite you. That's fair, right?"

Miss Ginger curled her lip in answer. So, she didn't like a comedian. Some horses had no sense of humor.

"Then I guess we'll do this the hard way." He'd hoped for the mare's cooperation, but he could see she was in a mood. So he unbuckled her first, keeping a tight, short rein on her, drawing her nose down to the ground, keeping it there, while he worked.

"What do you think, Miss Ginger?" he asked softly as the last buckle fell free. "Are you done with the biting?"

The mare sighed an answer. He could feel the fight go out of her as the tension in her body relaxed. He eased up on the reins, stroking her shoulder soothingly and led her out of the rigging. "You're just tired. Everyone gets a little cranky when they've had a long day. Come with me, girl, that's it."

He loved horses. You always knew where you stood with them. As he led Miss Ginger around the sleigh, he caught sight of Rose. She'd settled onto the seat and bundled up beneath the robes. He could read the exhaustion on her face, and there was sadness there too. Was something else going on? He glanced at Wade's dark house and wondered some more—not that it was his business. And, fine, maybe he was a little jealous of Wade. Wade didn't know the jewel he had in Rose.

There he went again, feeling for Rose when his heart was supposed to be stone. Seth scowled himself, bending down to triple knot the reins on the tie bar at the tail-end of the sleigh. Miss Ginger seemed relieved, as if she understood the job she hadn't wanted in the first place was over. Poor old gal. He patted her neck in sympathy.

"I know the truth about you, Seth Daniels." Rose broke the silence, twisting around on the seat to keep him in sight as he snagged Poppy's reins.

"What truth is that?" he joked, because joking was easier. You could joke with anybody. Joking kept things light and fun and on the surface. Joking kept things well away from your heart. "That I'm an excellent horseman? That I know how to deal with ladies and their big teeth?"

"Miss Ginger's teeth really are big," Rose agreed. "But no, that's not what I meant."

"These are secrets I tell no one," he went on, backing Poppy into place between the rigging. "They're so secret I'm surprised you figured them out."

"Oh, I'm observant," Rose teased back. "Nothing gets past me."

"I'm worried now." He knelt down, buckling the harnessing, his fingers working light and fast, so used to the work that he could do it blindfolded. "What terrible truth have you discovered about me? Is it that I paid off the mortgage on my house? Or that I own my business debt free?"

"Much more shocking." She tipped her head to one side, letting the soft curls around her face brush against her cheek. Nothing and no one could be more beautiful. "You are a gentle guy."

"Me? I'm tough. Mean. There's not a gentle bone in my body." He had to deny it. He had to sidestep her well-meaning and heartfelt compliment, because otherwise it would get to him. It would make him care for her even more. He was already in too far. He drew the reins together, straightening them over the dash. "I have a secret past as a terrible outlaw."

She took the reins, gazing up at him, her Cupid's bow mouth crinkling up into a wry little grin. "What is it about men? You fib. Wade fibs. Is it so hard to tell the truth?"

Oh, so that's what was going on, Seth thought, taking a step back. His chest twisted up at the sadness in Rose's eyes—just a flash, but that flash was enough to get his protective instincts rearing up. Not to mention his tender feelings too.

"Relationships are rough." It was the simple truth. One he'd learned the hard way. "But you know I was only kidding, right? It was a joke. I would never fib to you, Rose. I'm not that kind of man."

"I know, and you're right. Relationships are hard." She let out a shaky breath, betraying how much she was hurting. That got to him, how much she'd tried to hide it. "I saw another side of Wade and I didn't like it very much."

"I've been there in a relationship. That same thing happened to me." He opened up when he should be keeping his heart safe and his feelings tightly reined. "I thought Liz was one thing, but she turned out to be another. I think sometimes people try hard to be what they want to be, but they just aren't ready, for whatever reason. They can't do it. They fail, and the hard part is that they end up failing you, too."

"Exactly." Tears shone in her eyes again, but she batted her curled lashes, fighting them down. "He was my only beau. What if he was my only chance at getting married?"

"You'll find someone, I promise you that." Seth reached out and brushed snowflakes out of her hair. They shone in the dark like rare diamonds, tiara-like, precious.

Tender, tender feelings came to life in his chest, taking over against his will and overpowering him with a mightiness he'd never felt before—might never feel again. He didn't even try to stop it.

"The right man will come along and all of this will be forgotten. He'll make everything right. You deserve that, Rose." He leaned in, more real and honest than he'd ever been with anyone. She deserved to know the truth. "You are beautiful and kind and so tender hearted, some man will be lucky beyond belief to have you as his wife. Don't you forget that."

"You are an amazing friend." Rose's hand landed on his, her touch as warm as her heart. "Thank you, Seth. I can't tell you what that means to me."

"My pleasure. Now you'd better head home. It's getting late and your sisters are likely to start worrying." He cleared his throat, steeling his spine and pretending his knees weren't weak. "Go on. If you decide to keep Poppy, just let the Hutchinsons know. I've worked out a good price for you, and they'll honor it."

"What about your fee?" She gathered up the reins in her delicate hands, nothing but shadow and sweetness in the deepening darkness.

"You drop me off a box full of cookies and we'll be square." No way was he taking her money, but he didn't know how to tell her that. He hadn't helped her for money or because it was his job. Not at all. "I have a sweet tooth."

"Ah, another secret revealed." Rose sent Poppy stepping forward obediently, drawing the sleigh away. "I'll know every one of them before I'm done, Seth Daniels. Beware."

"That *was* the last secret. I swear!" he called out, watching her go.

Okay, so that was another fib, but he couldn't help it. He had only one more secret, and it was buried deep in his heart, not for her to see.

As her sleigh and Miss Ginger disappeared in the shadows and snow, he let out a breath, relaxing, letting his guards back down. Those tender, tender feelings in his chest gained strength, pressing on the inside of his ribs. At a loss, he turned and crossed the street, heading back to the livery.

CHAPTER TWELVE

"**Y**ou went and did *what?*" Iris's eyebrow shot up so far in her forehead they disappeared behind her bangs. "But we already have horses."

"Not enough horses," Rose explained as she plopped into her chair at the dining room table. "Jane's injured, and some days we have too many deliveries for just two drivers. Like today."

"Then we borrow a horse from the ranch." Iris, who was excellent with money, poured herself a cup of tea and shot her best schoolmarm glare across the table. "It's economical and we're grateful to you, Aumaleigh."

"Why, I'm delighted to help." Aumaleigh looked amused from her guest spot at the head of the table. "I'm not sure I want to get in the middle of this. Rose, if you want a horse of your own, you have your pick from any of the horses we raise on the ranch. There are some very fine ones."

"Thank you, but there's a big problem there." Rose really didn't see what all the fuss was about. "You won't want to charge me, Auntie dear, and so it's better that I went to Seth. It's more fair. Besides, there's every hope that Poppy will be the horse I've always wanted. She's gorgeous."

"Very gorgeous," Penelope added supportively, taking a sip of tea.

"But she costs money," Iris argued, setting down the teapot with a *clink*. "Just because we have big savings accounts now doesn't mean we should be spending recklessly. That's not wise."

"Help me," Rose begged her other sisters, sitting around the table. "I've hardly spent a dime of my money at all, so it's not like I'm being reckless. And it's a lot of money, so I'm not likely to run through it because of one mare. Tell her, Magnolia."

"We *do* have a lot of money," Magnolia agreed, digging into her baked potato with gusto. "Frankly, I don't see what all the fuss is about, Iris. We have so much in the bank, we could spend it like crazy and I don't know if we could possibly spend it all."

"Don't talk like that. You're giving me heart palpitations!" Iris, whose money sense was the reason they'd always been able to make do, stretching their last few pennies and nickels until payday. When there were high medical bills and funeral debts, she'd been the one to figure out a way through it. Iris was a miracle at managing money. "You save money, you don't spend it extravagantly. Can you return the mare?"

"I haven't paid for her yet." Rose cast a glance at Daisy, who was looking like she wished she thought of buying her own horse before this, and Magnolia, who had a look like maybe she wanted to dig into her savings and spend some of it too. Well, at least she had sisterly support. "But it doesn't matter what you say, Iris. I'm buying a horse. It's my money. I notice you aren't out driving difficult horses. Do any of you know what I went through today?"

"Oh, I heard tales," Aumaleigh interrupted, laughter creasing her heart-shaped face, making her even more beautiful. She took a sip of milk and studied Rose over the rim of the glass. "I stopped by the mercantile to pick up a few things, what with the wedding coming up fast, and Gemma told the funniest story. About you dragging a horse by the bits down the street, walking her where you wanted to go."

"Most people just sit in the sleigh," Magnolia teased.

"Yes, definitely try that next time," Daisy joined in, laughing merrily. "That's what the reins are for, so you don't have to walk the horse where you want her to go."

"Rose, is that true?" Iris looked startled. "That can't be safe, being out on the road like that. Did you have to do this often? What if some unsavory fellow came along and you couldn't dash away in the sleigh?"

"It was a mite frustrating." Rose grabbed her knife and fork and dug into the fragrant slice of roast beef on her plate. "But the worst part was when she tried to bite me. So even if we're extra busy because it's Christmastime and we won't always need a third horse, I'm buying one. I want my very own Marvin or Marlowe to snuggle and love and adore."

Iris glared, not liking the sound of this reckless spending at all, and opened her mouth to say so.

"Speaking of Christmas," Aumaleigh smoothly changed the subject (was she a fantastic aunt or what?). "We haven't discussed how we are going to celebrate. Especially with both Verbena and Daisy married by then, we have to take into consideration how they want to spend the holiday with their new husbands and families."

"Yes, I'll want some time with Beckett and our little Hailie." Daisy's tone deepened with love as she said her husband-to-be's name and then her soon-to-be daughter's. "It will be our first Christmas together. I haven't talked to Beckett about it, but I was hoping the three of us could do Christmas Eve and Christmas morning together as a family at our house, and that would leave Christmas dinner for the extended family to get together."

"We could have it here," Iris offered, liking the idea. Her oval face blushed pink with excitement. Iris loved to plan. "We certainly have the room. We still need to get our Christmas decorations up—"

"Which we'll do anyway starting tomorrow," Daisy cut in. "For my wedding."

"I love the idea of Christmas trees for your wedding decoration," Magnolia commented gaily.

"We can do turkey, but we're doing turkey for Daisy's wedding supper—" Iris paused to consider other options, her slender eyebrows frowning together with the effort.

"And cranberries and potato casserole and buttermilk biscuits," Magnolia chimed in with a sigh. "It all sounds delicious."

"We need a Christmas cake, don't forget," Rose added, getting all tingly at the excitement to come. "I have some fantastic decorating ideas."

"We should have ham for Christmas," Iris decided. "I'll use Ma's recipe, and to think we can afford brown sugar and molasses and bacon to top it."

"I'll bring a pot of baked beans," Aumaleigh offered as she cut a dainty bite of roast beef from her plate. "It's your mother's recipe, too. I've used it cooking for the cowboys all these years."

"And we'll have Annie and Bea over, of course, with Adam," Daisy said with a nod, as if that was already a given. "So with me, Beckett and Hailie, then our cousins and Verbena and Zane, we'll have quite a houseful."

"It'll be the merriest Christmas ever." Rose stabbed her fork into her pile of mashed potatoes, feeling as light as air. The point of Christmas was not the number of gifts or the lack of them, it was the giving. It was family. In that respect, the McPhees had always had a meaningful Christmas. But this year—she thought of the fabric she'd bought, sitting in the parlor—this year was going to be spectacular.

"Knock, knock!" Verbena's sweet voice rang out over the whisper of the front door swinging open. A cool breeze blew through the house momentarily until the door closed again. "Are you slowpokes still at the table? It's long past suppertime."

"Blame Rose," Magnolia piped up, jabbing her fork in the air for emphasis. "She was late. We had to hold supper nearly forty minutes for her."

"She made the roast dry out," Iris teased, her periwinkle gaze gleaming mischievously. "It wasn't any fault with my cooking. Honest."

"Maybe it was a little," Daisy teased right back, and everyone laughed.

Footsteps tapped, coming closer and Verbena sailed into sight through the doorway. She swept closer, luminous in a new Christmas-red wool dress, which hugged her lean, willowy figure perfectly. With her brown-red hair, stunning beauty and the glittering diamond ring on her left hand, she was a fashion plate. She could have been a real-life princess walking into their dining room.

"It's good to see you, dear girl." Aumaleigh stood to wrap Verbena in a welcoming hug. "Married life suits you. Look at you. You're glowing."

"I am rather happy." Verbena squeezed their aunt right back and bopped over to her plate at the table and pulled out her chair. She plopped into it, reaching for the teapot which Iris had put in the middle of the table. "I highly recommend marriage. Then again, maybe it's Zane that has made it so wonderful."

"I suspect that's true," Rose agreed, filling with contentment at seeing her little sister looking so relaxed and peaceful. Verbena had found her fairy-tale, and she was right in the middle of her happy ending. What could be better than that? It was everything Rose had ever wanted for Verbena. Everything.

"Where's Zane?" Daisy asked, giving the honey jar a little shove so Verbena could reach it.

"He took the horses down to the barn." Verbena gave a little sigh, as if her mind had temporarily drifted. Likely to thoughts of her new husband. "He didn't want them standing in this cold for very long, but I really think he wanted to catch up with some of the men at the bunkhouse. He's been cooped up with me for days."

"A real hardship," Magnolia teased.

"Poor Zane." Rose tilted her head sympathetically, biting the inside of her bottom lip to keep from laughing. "We know what he's going through, having to put up with you."

"Yes, and we can't believe our luck," Iris added playfully. "We're finally rid of you."

"And I'm next," Daisy chimed in. "It's days away. Come Sunday I'll be Mrs. Daisy Kincaid."

"Poor Beckett," Verbena joked. "He doesn't know what he's in for. I feel for him."

"Me, too," Aumaleigh winked playfully, love shining in her eyes. "That poor man has no idea the gift he is getting with you for his wife, Daisy."

"Ah, Aumaleigh," Magnolia scolded, frowning comically. "You weren't supposed to go and say that. You were supposed to tease her. Now I feel like I have to say something nice, too."

"Don't change your ways now, Magnolia," Rose teased. "We've already got extra coal for your Christmas stocking. We don't want to have to change that."

"That's right." Iris took a sip of tea. "It's coal for you and nothing else."

"Again? But I tried to be real good this year." Magnolia wrinkled her nose, not worried at all. "So, what's for dessert?"

"Cupcakes. I'll get em!" Rose took a final bite of mashed potatoes before pushing out of her chair, but as her mind was going a million miles a minute, she was distracted and caught her toe on the rug. Christmas was in her thoughts, along with the wedding, and everything they still had to do. A thought formed and popped to full life right inside her head.

"Iris, my dear." She stopped in her tracks and gave her oldest sister her best, most charming smile. "Can you stretch the wedding budget a little more? I have an idea."

* * *

"Rose. You're early today." Oscar blushed, looking embarrassed as he pushed open the door of his hut. He looked half frozen, poor man, with white frosty patches on his coat and gloves. Frost even clung to his days old whiskers. It had to be extremely chilly living in a house made out of tree branches this time of year, even if he did keep a small fire going. How did he not get frostbite?

She was kind of curious, especially about how he managed a fire in such a flammable home, but she had other things on her mind to talk to him about. She reined Poppy to a stop. The obedient little mare halted precisely, her head up and pretty little ears pricked. When Oscar approached, Poppy arched a brow suspiciously.

"I need to talk with you, Oscar." Rose lifted the tarp covering the delivery crates on the floor beside her and rummaged around, beneath the bread loaves, searching by feel and found the sandwich she'd hidden there. "I notice that you're favoring your foot much less lately. That must mean its healing."

"That's what I think, too." Oscar shoved a lock of light brown hair out of his eyes. His chiseled face had gone beat red with embarrassment as he took the food. "Thank you, Rose. You don't have to do this. I caught some trout in the river. I'm getting by okay."

But not good enough, she didn't add, studying the man. Before he'd had a log crush his foot and lower leg in a logging accident, he must have been a handsome and well-built fellow. But homelessness and hard times had taken their toll, drawing deep, worry lines into his forehead, around his eyes and bracketing the corners of his mouth. He'd grown lean over the past few months that she'd known him, so much that his clothes hung on him.

There wasn't much a lame man could do to earn a living in this part of the country. Sympathy burned behind her eyes and she blinked it away. She had only a temporary solution (she wished it was more), but even a small solution could go very far when you were struggling.

"My sisters and I need some help in the next few days moving furniture and setting up tables and chairs at our house," Rose explained. "It's for my sister's wedding. It would only be a few days of work, but we will pay the going wage. Would you be interested? I think it's a job you could do even with your injury."

"You mean, you're offering me w-work?" Oscar's jaw dropped. He nearly dropped his lunch too. He caught it just in time, the precious bundle that it was. Disbelief darkened his blue eyes. "You mean, for real wages? Wait. No, I don't think I could accept money from you. I'd be happy to do it just to do it. For all the kindness you've shown me."

"Sorry, that's not how it works," she told him firmly, because she wasn't at all surprised by his answer. She expected this from goodhearted Oscar, but she intended to help him whether he liked it or not. "We're hiring someone, and you are my first choice. Someone we can trust to have full access to our home. If you won't take the job and the terms that come with it, I'll have to ask someone else. Maybe a stranger who wouldn't be as trustworthy."

"When you say it like that, you know I can't say no." Oscar's jaw clamped shut, and he looked troubled, staring off into the trees. It was hard on his pride, but he nodded. "Fine. I'll do it. You know I'll work as hard as I can for you, but I'm just not sure how much furniture I can move with this bum foot."

"We'll cross that bridge when we get there." Rose relaxed into the cushioned seat, relieved her idea was working. "I've got deliveries in Deer Springs to do this morning, but I'll pick you up on my way back, sometime after noon? I'll drive you out and introduce you to Iris and Daisy. They're the ones overseeing the big to-do list."

"Sounds good. I'm mighty grateful, Rose." Oscar's blue eyes turned bright, shining with gratitude and perhaps a hint of tears.

This meant the world to him, she could see that, and so she stared at Poppy and the road ahead as she lifted the reins, to give him privacy to compose himself.

"I'll see you in a few hours," she called out as her new little trial mare pulled her away.

"What do you think, Poppy?" She reined the horse onto the main road, heading down Main.

Poppy didn't comment. She picked up her pretty feet and clip-clopped along. The post office wasn't open yet, but the postmaster, Fred, was sweeping off the front steps. He lifted a hand in greeting as they zipped by.

"We need to stop at the mercantile, Poppy," she explained, turning her attention to the fresh baked bread loaves at her feet. The doughy, yeasty scent was intoxicating. "Our first delivery of the day. How are you liking things so far, girl?"

Poppy swiveled one ear in Rose's direction, as if deigning to listen in for a moment but offered nothing to say. The mare pulled across the street at the lightest touch of the rein and stopped dutifully in front of the hitching post.

"What a nice change of pace," she told Poppy as she heaved off the multiple robes and bounded out into the shocking cold wind. It cut like a knife through her many layers straight to her bones. Brrr. Teeth chattering, she gathered up the handles of the basket meant for Gemma, hauled it out of the crate and stopped to tie up Poppy.

"What a good girl you've been so far this morning," Rose praised, hoping that would do the trick and make Poppy warm up to her, but no. The mare eyed her curiously, as if she'd never seen anything as odd as a human being wanting to talk to a horse.

"Fine, be that way," Rose told her cheerily. "But you don't know me yet. When you do, we're going to be great friends."

Poppy arched an eyebrow, as if doubtful.

That was a little disappointing. Rose patted the mare's nose (who stood still and seemed to tolerate it), before traipsing up the icy steps and into the warm mercantile.

"You're early." Gemma looked up from her bookwork, her dark hair neatly pulled back into a tight, no-nonsense bun. "You must have another big delivery day ahead."

"With Christmas coming up fast, there are a lot of parties and festivities. We've been swamped." Rose heaved the basket onto the scarred wooden counter. "Iris, Magnolia and Daisy have stolen Annie from Aumaleigh's kitchen to help this morning. It's too much work for us."

"Things will likely calm down after Christmas." Gemma moved one loaf after the other from the basket, inhaling the good bread smell. "It's the same here, too. Harried customers, frantic work days, rushing to get everything done and stocked and sold and wrapped, and then January will be so slow I'll fall asleep sitting here waiting for a single customer to walk through that door."

"Ooh, getting paid to nap. I like it." Rose stared at the ceiling, trying to picture Iris's reaction if she happened to find Rose asleep at the kitchen counter. "No, I don't think Iris will put up with it. She'd prod me with a wooden spoon. Maybe even beat me."

"Yeah, right." Gemma laughed, lifting the last loaf from the basket. "I can't picture gentle Iris hitting anyone."

"I'm trying to get sympathy here." Laughing too, Rose scooped the basket off the counter and headed toward the door. "Oh! I've been meaning to thank you for the referral. The friend of yours in Deer Springs contacted us, and I'm delivering my first batch of bread to her family's store this morning."

"Excellent! So glad I could help." Gemma lit up. "Guess I'll see you at the wedding. Is Wade going to be your date?"

"Oh, Wade." She skidded to a stop at the door, one hand on the knob, her heart forgetting to beat. She hung her head, trying to ignore the renewed hurt in her chest, like a wound broken open again. She took a steadying breath. "Wade and I are done. I broke up with him. But I'm keeping that a secret until after the wedding."

"Okay, but I'm sorry to hear that. He's a nice man." Gemma leaned on the counter, looking stunned. "Here I was hoping you two would be the next couple getting married."

"I don't think Wade is ready for marriage yet," she said honestly. He wasn't ready to settle down, even if he wanted to be. "I'll be dateless for the wedding, but that's even better because I'll have lots of time to spend with my friends. You and I will have to sneak into the kitchen. I intend to stash the best cookies there."

"Excellent. You know I have a weakness for cookies."

"Me, too!" Rose sailed out the door, swinging the empty basket by the handle. Snow drifted down lazily from a white-gray sky, dappling Poppy where she stood in front of the hitching post.

What a good girl she was. She wasn't trying to untie herself and she wasn't feigning sleep, hoping to get out of work. So far, so good. She untied the mare, tossed the empty basket on the seat and before she could hop in and speed away, someone called out her name.

"Rose McPhee! Is that you?" Elderly Vivian Gunderson tapped down the boardwalk bundled up in a thick layer of winter wraps, her cane beating a merry rhythm. "Imagine the luck. I was going to talk with you girls at the wedding, but then I didn't know if that would give you enough time."

"Enough time for what, Mrs. Gunderson?" Rose couldn't help liking the older lady (Gemma's grandmother). Everything about her was lovable from her diminutive size to her gray curls and her no-nonsense attitude.

"To order a Christmas cake, that's what." Vivian came to a stop and peered over the boardwalk railing down at Rose, her eyes narrowing. "Word is all over town about that cake you made for the lumberyard's Christmas party. It was a sure-fire hit. Not to mention I heard you're doing a family size one for Lucile. For quite an affordable price, I hear. I want one of them cakes too."

"Excellent." Rose fished a small pink carton from one of the crates. "Here's a sample box of all the different cakes we make. There's an order form inside. Write up what you want and bring it to the wedding party. You and I can talk there."

"My, you girls sure have this all figured out." Vivian banged her cane against the boardwalk approvingly. "You're a real professional. Next thing you know you'll have a fancy shop over in Deer Springs."

"I don't know about that." Rose handed the sample box over the rail to Vivian. "But you never know what might happen next."

"And this smells delicious. Hmmm." Vivian took a deep whiff from the little pink box. "Oh, this will save me a lot of work. At my age, that's worth the cost. You have a nice day, young lady."

"You too, Mrs. Gunderson." Rose hopped onto her seat and took off, and her spirits were flying right along with the sleigh. The cake sample box idea was working absolutely perfectly. And as for Vivian's suggestion about a shop, it wasn't the first time she'd considered such a move. As Poppy hauled her down Main, past the feed store, Rose studied the empty storefront next to the hardware store. Plans started to brew.

A horse's friendly nicker broke through her musings. She blinked, looked around and spotted a very big, very gorgeous buckskin gelding waving his head up and down trying to get her attention.

"Hi, Wally," she called out, but it was the man in the sled behind him that seemed to make the day brighter, as if the sun had somehow burned through the clouds, chased away the snow and lit up the world. That's what happened when you unexpectedly came across a good friend.

Seth lifted a gloved hand in greeting. "How's the mare working out?"

"She's almost perfect." Rose tried to focus on the positive. "She does exactly what I tell her. It's a refreshing change."

"Excellent." He drew his team to a stop, looking dapper this morning with a black knit hat, black wool coat and a blue scarf that brought out the midnight blue flecks in his black eyes. "Will you be keeping her?"

"I still haven't decided," she admitted, which was ridiculous because Poppy was really the exact right horse—except for one thing.

"Has she warmed up to you yet?" Seth asked, as if he could read her mind.

"Not yet, but I hope that will change this morning," Rose answered, feeling optimistic and, well, shivery. Likely it was from all the excitement. Good things were coming, she could just feel it. It was what her heart needed. "We have a bunch of deliveries this morning, so Poppy and I will be getting to know each other. Maybe she'll even let me hug her."

"Where are you headed off to?" Seth asked as snow sifted over him, catching on his hat, in his hair, on the impressive span of his shoulders.

"Deer Springs." She turned Poppy around in the street, bringing her alongside Seth once again. "Where are you going?"

"Deer Springs." His smile widened, so familiar and comfortable and dazzling. "Want to drive along together?"

Like she was going to say no to that. Rose nodded, giving Poppy's reins a slap. "Let's go."

CHAPTER THIRTEEN

I can do this, Seth thought, watching the snow-driven landscape sweep by. All he had to do was to keep his guard up, his heart frozen as the world around him and he'd be just fine. That she'd broken up with Wade didn't matter. She may be a free and single woman, but it made no difference. Not to him.

Determined, he shifted in his seat, driving on the left side of the road so she could keep her horse and sleigh on the right. There was no oncoming traffic, since most folks weren't keen on running errands on a chilly morning like this. And as he tugged his hat more tightly over his ears, he didn't blame them a bit.

"You seem quiet this morning." He heard the low rumble of caring in his voice and winced. That caring was supposed to stay buried and secret. He cleared his throat. "How are you doing after your break-up?"

"Better than I expected." Her words came as light and sweet as the snowflakes falling. "It's nice that you're concerned about me."

"It's what friends do." It was just the truth.

She seemed to think so too because she grinned, her smile as lovely as a Christmas angel at the top of a tree. "I like that—that we're friends. I haven't told my sisters about Wade yet."

"Why not?"

"I don't want to detract from Daisy's wedding." Her eyes filled with love for her sisters. "They'll all be disappointed, I know they will. That's not what I want. And besides, I feel kind of embarrassed."

"You have no reason to," he told her firmly. "You didn't do anything wrong."

"You know when you told me about your Liz, that sometimes people try to be what they aren't?" Rose's eyes filled with sadness. "That even when they try hard, they fail and fail you, too?"

"I remember." His throat tightened, aching for her. He knew exactly what that was like. "With Liz, I waited too long to see it. By the time I'd accepted it, my heart was fully committed. And completely broken."

"I tried to be smart about it." Rose gave a self-conscious shrug, as if trying to hide her sadness. "It wasn't as if I was in love with him yet, but I could have been. And that's what hurts."

"It hurts to lose that possible future." He knew what that was like, too.

He looked away, gazing down the long stretch of country road, surrounded by rolling fields on either side. The snowfall veiled everything, hazing out the mountains and any sign of homes and barns along the way. It felt as if they were alone, just the two of them, so talking about secrets came easier. His ribs felt pressed, ready to shatter as he let those hard memories surface.

"Elizabeth, well, Liz, moved here with her family about five years ago." It still hurt to remember. "A pretty young lady, new to town, I was smitten. I rushed right in and asked her to go on a buggy ride with me before any of the other bachelors in town could do it."

"Don't tell me you were once like Lawrence, a desperate single man?" She arched a brow at him, lightening the mood. The glitter of understanding in her blue-green eyes touched him, burrowing right through his defenses and straight to his heart.

She was trying to make it easier for him to talk about this wound to his heart. He bowed his head, grateful for that.

"Yes," he joked. It felt good to laugh. "I confess. There was a day long ago when I spotted a single woman, regardless of her age, and talked her ear off for hours, whether she was interested or not."

"Poor Lawrence." Rose bit the inside of her cheek, trying not to laugh. "He used to be such an annoyance, but now he's sort of a tragic figure. He's never going to find a wife and he has no idea why."

"Uh oh, I see that look in your eye." Dimples bracketed Seth's manly smile as he shook his head, scattering snow off his Stetson brim.

"You feel sorry for him. You aren't going to let him beau you, are you?"

"Lawrence is not my type." Rose sighed, realizing she hadn't been paying much attention to driving. It looked like Poppy didn't need a lot of direction, she knew to follow the road and was matching Seth's horses' pace perfectly. Chalk it up to another plus in the "keep Poppy" column. "I've always wanted to find someone reliable, that I can depend on."

"That covers a lot of ground. As far as I can tell, Lawrence fits the bill so far."

"He does." Rose met Seth's gaze directly. She could tease, too. In fact, she'd spent a lifetime bantering back and forth with her sisters, so she was totally accomplished at it. "Maybe I should say yes next time he asks."

"So you like men with bowlers?"

"Absolutely. They are less manly than Stetsons, but it looks like a big upside-down bowl. Entirely attractive."

"Then maybe I should get one." Seth slung an arm over the back of his seat, turning toward her. The wind caught the ends of his dark hair, tousling it, giving him a rakish, pirate sort of look. "What do you think? Would it look good on me?"

"Unquestionably. You would be the talk of the town. You could start a new trend."

"I've always wanted to. Think of it. The cowboys and ranchers in town might follow suit. Bowlers have a few plusses aside from being stylish. With a narrow brim, a hat like that wouldn't catch snow the way my Stetson always does."

"Plus you could always use it for a bowl if you get short on clean dishes."

"Or a big cup. It would hold a lot of coffee. If you don't have a bucket, you can just turn your hat over and use it to carry water or bail out a boat."

"Now I know what to get you for Christmas." Rose threatened mischievously.

"I thought I was getting coal, as usual."

"Hey, even though we're doing Christmas up right this year, Magnolia's getting coal too. I'm not surprised because, like her, you deserve it."

"True," he agreed with an easy grin. He had such a handsome grin, but it was comfortable at the same time. Dazzling and cozy. (Strange how she kept noticing). He shrugged. "But maybe Ma will spring for a real present this year. With my uncle coming, she might want to hide the fact that she has a black sheep for a son."

"It must be a burden for her. A great embarrassment."

"I feel for her," Seth joked. "I'm still a carefree bachelor, the only son she has who hasn't settled down. She worries she hasn't raised me right. What's my uncle to think?"

"The worst, I'm sure," Rose said dryly. Then it hit her like a rock to the head. "Your uncle is coming *here*? To Bluebell? For Christmas?"

"That's what his letter said to Ma." Seth turned his attention to the road. There was a faint shadow up ahead. Someone was coming their way. "There isn't a hotel in town, so I'm giving up my house for them to use. I'll be sleeping on my ma's couch."

"Them?" Rose asked over her shoulder, because Seth was slowing his horses to fall back and move into the lane behind her. "Oh, you mean your uncle and his family."

"Yes." Seth said it quietly, because he had to know what that meant. He had to be thinking the same thing she was.

Aumaleigh. How would she feel about seeing her long lost fiancé with his family? Rose blinked hard, feeling her eyes sting at the thought. Aumaleigh had loved her Gabriel truly. There was no doubt about that. It was going to hurt terribly. Just terribly.

I'll have to tell my sisters, she thought as the oncoming horses trotted by, pulling a big wagon. A teamster's wagon. That's when she recognized the horses (Adam's horses) and the man on the seat, white with snow.

"Hi, Adam!" she called out, pushing aside her sadness for Aumaleigh. "Have you already found some customers in town?"

"Yep. I'm hauling in product for the feed store," he answered as he sped by. "Good seeing you, Rose."

And then he was gone, lost in the curtain of snow, another good, strong and wonderful man. Annie was so lucky. Rose sighed happily. There was going to be another wedding in the family soon. No doubt about it. Annie would be a lovely bride as she made her way down the aisle (likely borrowing Aumaleigh's wedding dress). She, Adam and Bea would make a darling family, living in that charming cottage (which was still yet to be a surprise for Annie).

Happy-endings were all around her. Rose settled back against the seat, encouraged and hopeful. Maybe she would have one of her own one day when she was ready to look again. Not with Wade, that was for certain, but with someone. Someone kind and strong and good. Maybe someone who made her laugh.

"You didn't finish telling me about Liz," Rose reminded Seth when he'd pulled alongside her again. "How long did you court her?"

"For nearly two years. I proposed at Christmas." He pretended like it didn't hurt him to talk about her, it was simply water under the bridge.

She wasn't fooled. "She didn't say yes?"

"Not quite." A muscle jumped tight along his jaw as he stared straight ahead. "She laughed at me, thought it was a big joke that I'd asked her to marry me."

"She *laughed* at you?" Rose couldn't imagine. "How could something like that be a joke? Especially after you'd been courting her for so long?"

"I was serious about her," he explained succinctly, without emotion, like his heart wasn't involved at all. "She wasn't serious about me."

"Oh." Rose stared down at the buffalo robes, watching snowflakes land. She felt sucker punched, hurting for him. "How could she not be serious about you? You're a good guy, Seth."

"She explained that she was just having fun." Another muscle bunched along his jawline. "I wasn't the kind of man she would ever settle for. I was a blacksmith, I owned a livery. It wasn't like I came from money the way her family did. I felt like a fool."

"She didn't just break your heart, she shattered it." That was easy to see. "Then she humiliated you. You didn't deserve that, Seth. You deserve someone who will love you for who you are. Not someone who doesn't see you as good enough."

"I think she used dating me to get back at her father," he added, his broad shoulders tight, his back rigidly straight. "Come to find out later, she'd been spending some time dating another man in Deer Springs the last three months or so we were together. A rich guy, so I'm told. As it turned out, I'm lucky she turned me down."

"But she made you feel foolish while doing it." Rose's throat felt tight, her chest achy. Her fingers yearned to reach across the small distance between them and brush away those deep, frown creases around his mouth. If only she could make it right for him, find a way to smooth away the pain from his heart. "That was cruel. I'm so sorry you were hurt like that."

"I've recovered." He tossed her a wry little grin, his mouth hooking up in the corners. "I'm just leery of romance. You can't always tell if the person you care about can be trusted with your heart. And even then, there are circumstances which might not make them the right person for you."

"Tell me about it." She rolled her eyes. Sure, she was still smarting over her disappointment in love, but it was nothing like what Seth had gone through. "No wonder you're an affirmed bachelor."

"Glad you get that. It means a lot. You're a good friend, Rose." His grin chased away all the sad emotion from his lean face. "We're here."

"Already?" She blinked, glancing around, recognizing the little farm, the last stretch of land before the outskirts of Deer Springs. "Time flies fast when you're with a good friend."

"That it does," he agreed warmly, and it felt incredibly cozy, so comfortable and effortless she wondered why romantic relationships had to be so rough. Friendship was much better with this natural ease and uncomplicated accord between them.

She liked that. A friend like Seth was exactly what she needed. She watched him slow his team, falling behind her again as another oncoming vehicle slid into sight, drawn by a pair of oxen. The steers looked like they meant business, hauling a big load of hay, so there was no more talking until they had passed, and then there was another horse and sled approaching, so Seth stayed in the lane behind her.

She pulled into a sweeping curve of a drive, pulling Poppy to a stop. Wally and William's hooves stilled on the road behind her.

"Guess this is where we part ways." Seth's warm voice held a note of regret.

She regretted it too. "Yes, I have a sample box to drop off here. You have fun at the horse auction."

"You remembered." He brightened, and it was as if the sun had come out, warming the arctic air and chasing away the snow. It felt as if it were spring. "I keep my promises. I'm on the lookout for a backup horse for you in case Poppy doesn't work out."

"She's doing...all right. She's a good horse." Rose wanted to be optimistic. Poppy was such a well-behaved mare. Look at how politely she waited in the middle of the lane with her cute head up and dainty ears forward, ready for her next command. She was perfect in nearly every way. "I don't want you to go to a lot of expense on my account."

"Don't worry. My stock is low." He tipped his hat in farewell as he reined his team on. "I always try to keep lots of different horses on hand. I need a lady's driving horse anyway to restock my barn."

"Yes, you definitely do." She couldn't help teasing him, realizing she was leaning over the back of the seat waving goodbye to him, watching him go. As Wally gave a parting whinny, Seth flashed an amused smile her way before turning his attention to his driving. It was curious how the shroud of snowfall and the curve of the road stole him from her sight, but the spring-like warmth inside her remained—even as the wind blew cold.

* * *

"I'm sorry to tell you this, Rose." The mercantile owner's daughter (Gemma's friend) rubbed her hands together, her round face twisting up with pure apology. "We have to cancel our standing order."

"Why?" Rose lifted the empty basket from the front counter, keeping her voice low because there were so many customers nearby. (It was a madhouse with Christmas shoppers). "Aren't you happy with the bread?"

"Oh, yes. I love it." Dottie's big brown eyes widened truthfully, but then her face crumpled up again, full of distress. "But my father says no, even if it is really good bread."

"Then why don't you want to order from us?" Rose asked. Talk about disappointed. And here she'd been all excited about getting this account.

"You see, the other bakery, the one that used to sell bread to us?" Dottie pushed a lock of straight, slightly scraggly brown hair out of her face. "They got angry you replaced them and came to Father with a lower price. So he took it. This is the last delivery he'll pay for."

"Oh." A little stymied, Rose didn't know what else to say. They'd given the Deer Springs Mercantile an amazingly good price. She doubted they could afford to go any lower.

"I feel bad, really, really terrible." Dottie swept out from behind the counter. She was a nice girl, probably Verbena's age, in her very early twenties. Dottie was rail thin and slightly awkward, but somehow terribly endearing. "It was nice to get to know you. Here's your payment, exactly what we agreed on. Father wanted to short you, but

I wouldn't hear of it. If anyone asks, please say that he did or I'll be in big trouble."

"That's really kind of you, Dottie." Rose took the fold of greenbacks and slipped them into her coat pocket. "I'll miss dropping by to talk to you. Hey, you wouldn't want to come to my sister's wedding, would you? Gemma will be there, and I'd make sure you weren't alone. It'll be a lot of fun and I guarantee the desserts will be tasty."

"That sounds like a lot of fun." Dottie hedged, glancing sideways at her stern-looking, narrow-faced mother behind the counter, ringing up numerous purchases for a customer. "I'll ask and see if I can borrow the family horse. It'll be up to Ma, but she might let me go. I mean, a wedding is always good luck and there are lots of single men at them. My mother is pretty eager to marry me off."

"Then I'll introduce you around," Rose promised. "I know a lot of single bachelors. Some are very nice."

"Really?" Dottie blushed, staring at the toes of her shoes peeking out from beneath her plain brown wool skirt. "I'm awful shy, though. It's hard for me to talk to men. My tongue gets all twisted up, and I look and sound like an idiot."

"I know. I've done that before too." Rose couldn't help liking this lonely-seeming girl. Business aside, she was starting to have another idea. "I'll help you out. Don't worry about it. I'm guessing Gemma wouldn't mind helping you out, too. So you'd have two friends looking out for you if you came."

"It would be fun to get away from the store." Dottie gave a single, definite nod. "Okay, I'll ask. Thanks for stopping by, Rose, and I'm really sorry about going with the other bakery."

"That's okay, you have a good day." Rose rushed off, weaving her way around customers and displays to the front door. The bell chimed overhead as she stumbled out onto the boardwalk. A little disappointed they'd lost an account, she tossed the basket into one of the empty crates on the floor.

"Well, Poppy. I guess that's business." She bounded up to the hitching post, but the little mare didn't seem too interested in hearing about the trials of growing a bakery. "I suppose you don't want another nose pat?"

Poppy sighed, lifting her head higher to make it harder for Rose to reach her nose.

It felt a little lonely being rejected like that. With a sigh, she untied the knot, hauling the rein with her. She settled into the seat and steered Poppy toward home. With all her deliveries done, she negotiated the busy street and her mind drifted to Seth. That spring-like warmth remained, like sunshine washing over her, remembering how they'd laughed together.

Her bruised heart felt better for it, and she smiled, reining Poppy right at an intersection and speeding through the town limits. It also felt lonesome to be leaving without him. How did the horse auction go? Was he busy finding just the right horses he was looking for? Or (as she suspected) was he feeling sorry for the horses no one seemed to want and had saved them from the slaughterhouse? See, that was just another reason why she liked Seth so much. He was kind to animals.

Poppy trotted through the gently falling snow, her head up and her ears pricked, the perfect horse. Seth stayed in the back of Rose's thoughts all through the long drive, even when she was pondering their loss of business to Dottie's father or how to win Iris over to the idea of a storefront.

By the time she pulled down the forgotten little lane that led to Oscar's tree hut, her brain was exhausted from thinking it all over. And she still had the wedding and Christmas and all kinds of Christmas surprises left to think on. Good thing she had an afternoon of work ahead, so her mind could ponder those things too.

"Oscar!" She hardly recognized the man. She blinked, did a double take and squinted at the tall, wide-shouldered man in an old leather duster. A worn Stetson, brim fading, shaded his newly shaven face. "You're ready for work, I see."

"Yes. I got gussied up some. These are some clothes I had back when I was working. I haven't needed them much until now." He was all uncertainty, blue eyes and stoic integrity as he climbed into the seat next to her. "I really appreciate this opportunity."

"And I appreciate the help." Satisfaction glowed inside her as she turned Poppy around and retraced their tracks. He wasn't dressed for the cold weather, not in that duster, so she made sure he covered up with the robes. "Don't worry about a thing. My sisters are going to like you."

"What if they ask about where I live?" A hint of shame sounded in his voice even as he lifted his chin a notch. "I won't be dishonest, but if they knew the truth, they might be afraid of me. Lots of ladies in town act like I'm a criminal or something."

"Just say you live near town. That's the truth." Rose gave a shrug. "It's as simple as that."

"Okay." Oscar seemed relieved.

As she steered Poppy toward home, Rose thought of all the good in her life—the fine and luxurious home, her enormous savings account and so many pretty dresses and comfortable things. She knew that as nice as they were, they were only possessions. What really mattered in life could not be measured in dollars and cents.

"Besides," she told Oscar with great certainly. "All anyone is going to be thinking about is the wedding. The wedding! I can't wait."

CHAPTER FOURTEEN

All the planning came down to this, all the sewing and fussing and worrying. The wedding day. Daisy sat in the back seat of Aumaleigh's two-seater sleigh, feeling storybook beautiful. She'd never felt like this before.

"Are you nervous?" Rose asked turning around in the front seat to rest her chin on the top of the seat cushion.

"No, I'm not nervous." Daisy waved her hand as if that was hardly her concern. "Terrified might be a better word. I keep wondering what can go wrong. What if I trip on my dress and fall down in the middle of the aisle in front of the entire church?"

"Well, it could be worse," Magnolia answered cheerily. "You'll be indoors, which means that if you land flat on your back there won't be a wind to blow up your skirt like with our poor Rose. Less embarrassing."

"Thanks, I feel better," Daisy teased.

Rose rolled her eyes and sank back against her seat. "The problem with sisters is that they have long memories. They forget nothing."

"That's right," Magnolia answered. "And don't you forget it."

The wind was bitter, although the sun shining made it a glorious afternoon. The snowy world spread around them like perfection, pure white and dazzling in every direction. A few winter birds had come out to chirp their delight as Aumaleigh's dear Buttons drew them toward town.

"Stop imagining disaster," their aunt advised sweetly, holding the reins in both gloved hands. She was a vision too—stately and elegant in her dove gray winter coat and matching hood, trimmed with soft white fur. "Everything is going to go just fine. You have us to see to that. Daisy, just concentrate on one thing and one thing only. Your handsome Beckett is waiting for you at the altar right this minute. Today your life starts anew. That's all that matters."

"It is." Daisy slipped forward on the seat, she loved their aunt so much. "And thank you for letting me wear your wedding dress. It means more than you know."

"For me, too," Aumaleigh admitted, keeping her eyes on the road ahead. No one would guess at the pain she hid. She'd made that dress for a wedding that had never happened. "It does my heart good knowing my dress will see you down the aisle to your own happily-ever-after."

"As if you could stop me from wearing it," Daisy teased, but she meant every word. In all the shops they'd visited in Deer Springs looking at wedding gowns, nothing had seemed quite right. She'd even thought of sewing her own, but when she'd first set eyes on Aumaleigh's dress, so delicate and lovely, she'd known why nothing else would suit.

It felt like destiny, this dress so lovingly made, sewn with endless love and a thousand wishes. What could be better? Daisy laid her hand on her chest, where under the wool of her coat the gossamer softness of the dress was a reassurance. She could feel Aumaleigh's love in every stitch.

"You're just lucky Verbena relinquished it." Magnolia fidgeted on the seat, sandwiched between Daisy and Iris. "I wasn't sure she would. She wanted to hold onto it forever, I think, and who could blame her. You know, I just can't get used to her not being here. It feels like something is missing. It's terrible."

"I know what you mean," Iris agreed, tightening the ties on her hood. "I can't get used to it either. And now Daisy is going to leave us too."

"Thank goodness." Daisy couldn't help rolling her eyes, feigning relief. "I've waited a long time to get away from you all. I cannot believe it's finally happening."

"Yeah, right." Rose wasn't fooled, nor was Aumaleigh who dabbed daintily at her eyes with the back of her knit gloves. "It's going to feel strange with just the three of us in the house. I miss you already,

Daisy."

"Me, too," Iris agreed with a sniffle. "I've changed my mind. We're not letting Beckett have you. You can't get married now."

"Okay, then, let's turn around." Although she was teasing, she teared up because marrying Beckett was the only thing she wanted. The only thing she was absolutely sure of beyond all doubt. Loving him was like a new sun shining when there had only been darkness before. But it was fun to joke. "Wait, don't turn around after all, Aumaleigh. There's no sense to it. There's the church."

"Too bad," Aumaleigh quipped as she drew her mare to a stop. "I guess you might as well get married, since we're here."

"Right. I'd hate to waste the wedding dress, since I went to the trouble of putting it on." Daisy drew in a steadying breath, studying the little white church, its steeple spearing up toward the blue, blue sky. There wasn't a cloud to mar that vast blue. The doors were open, as the last stragglers hurried up the steps and inside the vestibule.

"I've never seen so many horses and vehicles here," Aumaleigh declared as she slipped from the seat, smoothing her skirt as she stood up, always so fashionably put together. Her molasses-dark hair peeked out from beneath her hood, and her heart-shaped face was pink from the kiss of the cold wind. Her true blue eyes shone with joy. "So many people have come to see you married, Daisy. The church must be packed full."

"Now I'm nervous." She scooted off the seat, not sure her knees would hold her upright as she stood. The gorgeous dress swished around her as she took a step toward the church—a step toward Beckett. Aumaleigh was right. He was waiting for her inside, waiting to become her husband, her beloved. "Maybe nervous isn't the right word. I'm overwhelmed. Dreamlike. It doesn't feel real."

"That's exactly how it was for me." A voice carried toward them on the wind—Verbena, hurrying with her arm hooked around Zane's. What a couple they made with his handsome, raw masculinity and her stunning sweetness.

"It was like walking into a dream. It still is." Verbena gazed up at her husband as if he were her center, the reason for her life, her everything. "Daisy, this is the kind of happiness I want for you."

"I think I'm about to get it." Daisy whispered the words because they felt reverent, they felt true. "This is it. Hailie is waiting for me at the door."

The little girl with her brown braids, round face and midnight blue eyes could not be more charming in the princess-style purple dress she'd chosen. Daisy melted, full of motherly love for the child—for her child. As soon as the ceremony was over, Hailie would be her daughter to treasure and adore. There could be nothing sweeter than that.

"Hurry!" Hailie shouted, bouncing up and down in place. "I don't wanna wait anymore. I've got my princess shoes on."

"Which will be perfect for walking me down the aisle." Daisy led the way up the shoveled walkway, surrounded by her sisters and aunt. Aumaleigh was talking with Iris, Rose and Verbena and Magnolia were laughing away. Daisy squinted through the sun streaks arrowing down through the trees as she climbed the steps. Somehow her heart didn't seem to be beating, everything within her stilled as Hailie reached out and took her hand.

"This is the best day," Hailie beamed up at her, wide-eyed and serious. "I'm getting you for my ma."

"And I'm getting a princess for a daughter." Daisy knelt down, unaware of her hood and scarf disappearing, unaware of someone tugging off her coat. All she saw was the vulnerability and the hope in the child's eyes—so blue and dark, just like Beckett's. Love just kept strengthening inside her as she rose and took Hailie's hand. "Let's go get married."

There was music. She was vaguely aware of the packed church or what happened to her sisters and aunt as Hailie gripped her by the hand. They walked down the aisle together to where Beckett stood, tall, strong and commanding, waiting for her. Waiting to make her his wife.

"Daisy." He took her hand in his large and comforting one.

At his touch, her heart began beating again. Time seemed to move forward as she took her place beside him in the fragile, beautifully made dress with its inset lace, mother-of-pearl buttons and lacework skirt. When he looked at her, all his commitment, love and devotion lit up his midnight blue eyes, as bright as his heart. His love for her lived there—real, amazing and true.

"Dearly beloved," the minister began and as the ceremony started, it was easy to see their future. Peaceful evenings spent snug and warm in their lovely cottage with the fire crackling and Hailie finishing her homework. Nights tucked safe and cozy in Beckett's arms. Days lived with him and for him—every day—for the rest of her life.

This future as Beckett's wife was going to be wonderful, and as he slipped the ring on her finger, she could feel the magic of her dreams begin.

* * *

The ceremony ended, and Aumaleigh swiped tears from her eyes. There was nothing better than seeing true love win. Daisy and Beckett were going to be so, so happy. She could just see it. When she looked at them, standing hand-in-hand at the front of the church sharing their first kiss as man and wife, she knew they had the real thing. That their love would be strong forever.

"Excuse me," she whispered to Iris as she eased off the pew and onto her feet. "I need to leave early, but you stay here."

"Why don't I come with you?" Iris's eyes sparkled with happiness, too. "I want to help."

"For the final time, no. You stay here with your sisters. Daisy would want you here," Aumaleigh whispered.

"But she would want you here, too," Rose argued, her lashes spiky from happy crying.

"No arguing now." Aumaleigh winked, giving Rose's hand a squeeze on her way by. She tweaked Magnolia's nose and patted Verbena's hand and by the time she'd reached the far end of the row, all eyes were on Hailie who'd wrapped her arms around Daisy's neck, as the bride knelt before the child in a moment of sheer bliss.

"I have a ma now!" Hailie exclaimed. Absolutely touching.

It wasn't easy making her way to the back of the church, so she had plenty of time to look around. She spotted Seth Daniels, who was the only person in the church not gazing at the bride, groom and child. Very interesting. Call her curious. Aumaleigh craned her neck, trying to figure out what had the young man so absorbed—and suspecting she already knew.

Rose. Yes, Seth was certainly gazing raptly at her. The roof could cave in on top of him, and he'd never notice. Poor man.

"Aumaleigh?" Annie rushed up, meeting her in the vestibule. The dear girl looked lovely in her best blue dress, with her blond curls tumbling down from her simple up-knot. "Good, I was afraid I'd missed you. It's so crowded, that I couldn't get a good look to see where you were."

"Where's Bea?" Aumaleigh asked, fetching her winter coat. "Isn't she coming?"

"No, she's staying with Clarice. Clarice's family will be coming to the wedding supper," Annie explained, glancing over her shoulder into the sanctuary at the brawny, quiet young man who'd stood up to watch her go, towering over everyone in the row.

There was such a gentle tenderness to the man, it made Aumaleigh give a little sigh. Adam was the perfect match for dear, sweet Annie.

Louisa and Orla, both workers at the ranch, hurried into the vestibule too and donned their wraps. Talk turned to the preparations ahead—getting the food started and making sure the manor was ready for when the guests started to arrive. Oh, it was going to be a spectacular party, something Daisy and Beckett would remember all their lives.

Aumaleigh tossed her scarf around her neck and sailed down the steps, humming to herself. There was so much to think about, to get just right, and it was her pleasure to do it. She loved her nieces so much, and—

Her thoughts skidded to a halt as she reached the hitching post. Her foot missed the ground and for some reason the air whooshed out of her lungs as if she'd been struck hard in the chest with a two-by-four. Confused, puzzled, not sure what was happening, she grabbed the hitching post, steadying herself.

And then her conscious mind saw what her subconscious mind had already taken in—the driver of the passing horse-drawn sleigh. He held the reins in a loose, confident grip, his leather-gloved large hands so familiar, she would have recognized them anywhere, in any condition or circumstance. The man was finely dressed—that had changed—in a tailored black wool coat that encased his powerful arms and spanned his wide, muscular shoulders, still strong after all these decades.

"What is it?" Annie asked, sounding terribly concerned as she reached out, wanting to help, thinking something was wrong. "Are you ill, Aumaleigh?"

"N-no." The word stuttered from her, the only sound she could make as she watched the man in the sleigh turn toward her.

A black Stetson shaded his face, casting his eyes in shadow, but she didn't need to see them. She could draw up the exact shade of smoke from memory. His face was still strong and sculpted, his jaw like steel, and when he turned to her, as if sensing her gaze, it hardened invincibly. His gaze was piercing—as if unforgiving, as if seeing straight to the depths of the regrets and pain in her broken heart.

Then he was gone, carried away by the swiftly moving horses, leaving her shaken, leaving her gazing after him. She noticed there were others in the sleigh with him—she saw the back of Gabriel's Stetson, a woman's dainty hood at his side, and another Stetson in the backseat. The sleigh hooked around a corner and was gone.

Rattled, she tried to reach for Buttons' secured rein but missed. Her hand came up empty. Her mind spun, unable to make sense of what she'd seen. *Gabriel was in town. He was here.* Worse, she thought, squeezing her eyes shut, but the image of the people in that sleigh wouldn't leave, he'd come with his family. With his wife and a son.

Agony with a force unlike any she'd ever known pierced all the way to her soul, seemingly breaking bone and ripping through tendon, muscle and sinew. She leaned against the hitching post for support. The world became one big smear of white as something hot tracked down her face.

Tears, she realized numbly.

"She is ill." Orla took charge, gripping Aumaleigh by the elbow and steering her to the sleigh. "All that excitement, no doubt. I told her not to work so hard, but did she listen to me? No. Now sit down in the back and let me drive. I won't take no for an answer."

Dear Orla. Aumaleigh stumbled as she sat, hitting the seat with a rattling jolt. Her teeth clacked together, just missing her tongue, and she sat back, swiping at her silly tears.

What was wrong with her? Acting like that same young woman she'd been, who'd lost her heart to the man. That young woman who'd spent nearly a decade crying herself to sleep over him every night. She shook her head, fighting to stop the tears, trying to will the pain away.

Neither would budge.

"She's merely too tired," Louisa said in her quiet, timid way. The kitchen maid settled into the front seat alongside Orla.

"I'm not at all surprised." Orla took up Buttons' reins. "What did I tell you last night? Didn't I say you needed to rest? A body can't go and go and go without something going wrong."

"I'm all right," Aumaleigh argued, hating how weak she sounded, her voice thin and wounded. "Stop fussing, Orla, although I love you for it."

"Don't you tell me what to do," Orla said in her tough, gruff and entirely wonderful way as she gave the reins a shake.

"You lean right on back and rest." Annie moved in close, shaking out a folded blanket and leaning closer with it. "This will keep you warm. Snuggle in and just close your eyes."

How sweet. It had been a long time since anyone had taken care of her like this. Aumaleigh took the blanket from Annie and tucked it around both of them, to keep them both warm. She was still upset, but at least those foolish tears had stopped.

It was just the shock of seeing him after all this time, that was all. She was fine. She was strong. She wasn't about to let what was done and over ruin this special day. The past was gone—it was the now, the present that mattered. Her nieces mattered. Gabriel, for all he'd once meant to her, did not.

At least that's what she was telling herself.

Resolved, she closed her eyes as they drove through town, so she couldn't accidentally catch sight of him again.

* * *

In the church's sanctuary, Rose wrapped her arms around Daisy, hugging her hard, holding her long, hoping the pride, joy and dreams she had for her newly married sister came through in that embrace. There were no words that could possibly impart everything she felt and wanted for Daisy, but when she finally let go, the tears standing in Daisy's eyes told her that she had.

"You're Daisy Kincaid now," Rose said croakily. "That's going to take some getting used to. I'm still adjusting to Verbena's new last name."

"Me, too," Verbena sailed in to wrap Daisy in a warm, sisterly hug. "When I was at the mercantile yesterday buying groceries, I told them to put them on the McPhee account before I realized the mistake."

"Yeah, we don't want to buy your groceries," Magnolia teased, cheerful as always, her golden hair glinting in the lamplight as she took her turn giving Daisy a happy hug. "Think of poor Iris trying to balance that budget. It would be such a strain, maybe her head would explode."

"Very messy," Iris joked as she crowded in, quietly lovely in her new Christmas-red dress. She held Daisy for a long minute before letting go. "Look at you. The most beautiful bride ever."

"I feel like the luckiest bride ever." Daisy's gaze drifted across the aisle to where her strapping groom was being congratulated by several of his friends and tormented good-naturedly by a few of the ranch's cowboys (who were anti-marriage). "I don't know how I got this lucky, but I'm going to cherish this happiness and this love for the rest of my life."

"I know just how you feel," Verbena chimed in with a sigh as she watched her impressive husband make his way up the aisle toward her. She brightened, luminous with the kind of replete joy that Rose could never imagine. No one deserved it more. Verbena's hand drifted to her throat, rapt as she shared a secret smile with her beloved man. "Well, I've got to go. Zane is waiting for me. We'll see you at the manor?"

"Count on it." Daisy gave Verbena a final hug and they all watched their youngest sister go. It was like poetry come alive, the way she waltzed down the rows toward him, the sweep of her dress, the gleam of her hair, the way he held out one large hand to take hers.

"Now that two of you are successfully married, I'm next." Magnolia swirled away, her skirts rustling, a vision in her Christmas-red dress. "See you at home. I'm catching a ride with my Tyler."

"She says that so happily," Iris commented. "I hope it stays that way. Look at Tyler's mother. Mrs. Montgomery doesn't look any more approving of their engagement than when they announced it."

"That is a worry," Rose admitted, searching the departing crowd for the very proper, very distinguished Nora Montgomery. There she was, standing with her husband, talking with Doc Hartwell and scowling in Magnolia's direction. What were the chances the fine lady's opinion would change?

"Ma?" A little girl's tentative voice broke through Rose's thoughts. Beautiful little Hailie in her princess dress inched up, a vulnerable look on her face. "Can I walk you to our sleigh?"

"I would love that." Pure adoration lit Daisy's face and rang in her gentle words. Daisy held out her hand, taking Hailie's much smaller one in her own. "Your new aunts will have to excuse us. We have a sleigh to catch."

"See you at the manor!" Rose called out, watching a little wistful as Hailie escorted Daisy away. How wonderful it must be to have a beautiful little daughter. One day, she hoped she would be lucky enough to have babies of her own. One day soon, she hoped she would find the man—the one she could count on and trust and laugh with—who could change her life in such an extraordinary way.

"Good day, fair lady," a familiar tenor called out. Lawrence Latimer approached, his bowler hat clutched in one hand, dressed up in his Sunday best—a worn and patched but very carefully pressed suit. His thinning bald spot on top shone pink when a shaft of sun hit it. He gave what he probably thought was a dashing smile. "I've never seen you look more beautiful. You're an elegant, rare Rose."

Oh boy. Trapped, Rose looked for an escape, but there was no one to help her. Everyone was heading toward the door. Rats! If only she'd thought to dash away when she'd had the chance.

"Such an inspiring ceremony, wasn't it?" Lawrence started his monologue by sidling up to Rose and gazing out at the departing crowd as if with deep nostalgia. "Those time-honored words just fill you with hope, don't they? Throughout our history men and women have come together to repeat those vows, promising their lives and their hearts to each other."

Just kill me now, Rose thought. Please.

"Your sister and new brother-in-law are part of that honored tradition." Lawrence paused to emit a dramatic sigh. "Seeing them so blissful together makes a single gentleman like me turn his thoughts to romance, to finding that one special lady who is my match in every way."

"Er, I'm sure she's out there," Rose assured him. "I'm hopeful you'll find her soon. Very soon."

"I appreciate that sentiment more than you know, lovely Rose. And I think that wait is almost over." Lawrence's handlebar mustache wiggled as he spoke. "I heard from Deputy Wade that your romantic relationship with him has come to an end. Long have I been searching for just the right lady. It's not easy, you know, for a man like me. I'm discriminating, I like to think of myself as a true gentleman, looking to gallantly court that special bloom of a woman, one fragile and delicate, one lovely both on the outside and at heart, one who I can spend every day of the rest of my life to come—"

"Excuse me, Lawrence." Seth strode up, interrupting with apology in his voice and a twinkle of humor in his dark as obsidian eyes. "I need to spirit Miss Rose away from you. She's needed back at the manor. Preparations for the wedding party."

"Uh, right." Lawrence's narrow shoulders slumped with disappointment, then straightened again as if with new inspiration. "I could drive her. I would be most happy and honored to escort the beautiful Miss Rose to her abode. My donkey is parked very close by, it won't be a walk at all—"

"That's very kind of you, Lawrence." Rose interrupted, talking as kindly as she could over the top of him. "But I already have other arrangements."

"Oh." He ducked his head, trying to hide his disappointment, making her feel even more sorry for him. He made a tragic figure, standing alone in the emptying church as Seth grabbed her by the hand and dragged her off. Lawrence heaved out an unhappy sigh that seemed to echo through the sanctuary.

It was too bad Dottie from the Deer Springs Mercantile hadn't made it. Really too bad. Rose stumbled down the aisle and into the vestibule, where her coat hung on a peg, one of three left hanging on the wall. She reached for it, but Seth got there first.

"I might as well try being a gentleman," he told her, leaning in, smelling pleasantly of sweet grass hay, wood smoke and warm man. Very nice.

So nice she felt sort of sunny. Like she was shining from the inside out as she slipped her arms into the garment he held for her and settled the coat into place over her shoulders. She gave an involuntary shiver—perhaps from relief of having escaped an endless monologue with Lawrence.

"A gentleman? You?" she scoffed, as if she would never believe it in a hundred years. "Good luck with that."

"I know, but I've got to try." He flashed her a perfect smile—wide and white and wonderful—and it was so *familiar*, so beloved, as if she'd seen it every day of her life. Friendship with Seth was just that easy.

I really need to stay away from romance for a while, she thought, buttoning up. Friendship with Seth was the perfect alternative. "You know I'm catching a ride with Verbena and Zane, don't you?"

"I do." He stabbed one arm into his coat sleeve. "But I saw you with Lawrence, and I had to rescue you. Maybe, to save face and to keep me from being a fibber, you should let me drive you home. Besides, I think Wally misses you."

"Oh, Wally." She sailed through the door and into the brisk afternoon, squinting as the sun touched her face. "He's such a sweetheart. I have a confession to make."

"I'm all ears." Amused, Seth tromped down the steps alongside her.

"I'm sort of sweet on your horse." She landed lightly on the shoveled walkway, and the minute she came into sight, Wally lifted his head, tugging at the rein binding him to the hitching post and neighing an enthusiastic greeting. She waved merrily at him. "He's such a funny guy."

"Yep, that's Wally, a funny guy," Seth agreed, knowing just how the horse felt. Who wouldn't be halfway in love with gentle Rose? "How's it working out with Poppy?"

"Good." There was a slight hesitation in her tone as she caught sight of her sister and gave her a finger wave. Verbena, seated beside her husband in his expensive sleigh, waved back and leaned to whisper something to Zane. The matched set of fine horses jumped to life, pulling the sleigh down the road. Iris was in their backseat and noticed them together, too.

Seth waited while Rose rushed up to Wally and greeted him with a nose pat. The big buckskin held his head down for her so she could reach his ears too, his brown eyes full of bliss. That gelding knew how to work a horse-lover, that was for sure.

"That's what he did to me at an auction years ago." Seth offered his hand to help her into his sleigh. It took all his willpower to ignore the surge of longing that roared through him at the contact of her fingers against his palm.

"I can imagine." Rose landed on the seat in her graceful way, gazing up at him with her rapt, blue-green eyes. Eyes he would get completely lost in if he let himself.

Knowing Rose could never be the girl for him, he pulled away, circling back to the hitching post. His hand felt cold and empty without her touch. Poor Wally, the lovesick fool, strained ardently against his tie, struggling to keep his eyes on Rose. It was rough on a guy when his heart belonged to a woman who didn't realize it.

Because his heart *did* belong to her, Seth realized. He could fight it, he could ignore it and he could deny it, but that didn't change the unalterable fact. He was falling hard for Rose, and he didn't know how to stop it.

"I bet he strained against his rope just like that trying to get to you at the auction," Rose went on, unaware of his feelings, looking at him the way she always did—as a friend.

Thankfully, he thought with relief (although a part of him felt differently). Why did it have to be Rose? As much as he wanted her, as much as he longed to make her his, he knew better than to make the same mistake again. He'd learned the hard way that he couldn't hold a woman like that. He didn't want to get his heart shattered again.

"I mean, how could you say no to him?" Rose pulled her gloves out of her coat pocket, finally remembering to put them on. "You obviously couldn't. You can't fool me, Seth. You are so in love with that horse. You two are best friends, aren't you?"

"Guilty as charged." He gave Wally a gentle pat on the nose as he untied the team. Beside him William stood curious, wondering where they would go next. They were good horses, and he was lucky to have them. All his life, horses had been his best friends.

Unless you counted Rose. Trying to hold his heart in check, Seth settled into the sleigh, turning the conversation to the funny story of the day he'd met and bought Wally and William. He liked nothing more than making Rose laugh.

CHAPTER FIFTEEN

Aumaleigh pushed opened the manor's kitchen door and stepped into the spacious kitchen. The girls had done a lovely remodeling job—the walls were creamy white, the floors and cabinets a lustrous polished red oak, the accents of soft green and butter yellow cheered up the sunny space, but none of its brightness touched her. Aware of Annie and Orla coming up the stairs behind her, she wasted no time. She marched straight to the stove where Josslyn was already settled in and checking a pot, more upset than she wanted to admit.

"Why didn't you tell me?" she demanded, unbuttoning her coat. "Why didn't you tell me he was in town?"

"I thought it was best not to." Josslyn let go of the pot lid and turned around, worrying her bottom lip. Concern etched lines into her face and darkened her hazel eyes. "I mean, I warned you he would be coming, but I had hoped you would be so busy with the wedding and then with Christmas, you'd never cross paths with him. Besides, he must have only just arrived. I didn't know he was in town already, to be honest."

"Well, he definitely is." For some unknown reason, she started trembling. Annie, Louisa and Orla had stepped through the door, talking together and getting out of their winter things, so she lowered her voice. This was a wound she didn't want anyone else to see. It hurt enough as it was. "Trust me. He's here."

"What did you say to him?" Josslyn was back to biting her lip again.

"We didn't s-speak. He j-just drove by is all." And there was nothing else she intended to say on the subject. Aumaleigh grabbed the apron she'd left on the back of a chair and tied it on. Annie, Louisa and Orla had hurried over to Josslyn at the stove, eager to help with the cooking. Not even close to feeling better, Aumaleigh tied a bow, straightened the skirt of her apron and drew in a deep, calming breath. She needed to let this shock and pain go. They had guests to prepare for and a party to throw.

"I should have told you, in retrospect." Josslyn tapped over in her no-nonsense way, leaving the girls at the stove, busy with plenty of work. She pushed a lock of auburn hair out of her eyes. "I was trying to protect you, but it backfired. Don't be mad at me."

"I'm not. You are the only one who knows what this means to me." Aumaleigh reached out and drew Josslyn into a hug, her dearest friend. "Now, your brother is here to see *you*. So get out of this kitchen and go home, be with him and his family."

"Oh." Josslyn teared up, blinking hard to keep them back. "You saw his family?"

"They were in the sleigh with him when he went by." Aumaleigh had to turn away to stare out the big picture window at the snow-covered orchard and the mountains rising upward, so glorious and rugged you had to tip your head back to see their peaks. She wished she could be as frozen cold as that view so that she could feel nothing, nothing at all. "They've come a long way to see you, Joss. I want you to go."

"But I promised you I would be here to help today." Josslyn shook her head, scattering auburn curls. Boy, could the woman be stubborn. "I won't leave. You can't make me. Not until I get supper served successfully and every guest here is stuffed full."

"What if I drag you out the door?" Aumaleigh arched a brow, biting the corner of her mouth to keep from laughing.

"Impossible," Josslyn declared. "I'm tougher than you. Everyone knows it. You can't tell me what to do."

"Technically, I'm your boss, so I'm supposed to." Aumaleigh shrugged. "But I know a lost cause when I see it. I give up. Do what you want."

"Excellent." Josslyn glanced over her shoulder to check on the women. Annie had the oven door open and was peeking inside, Louisa was donning oven mitts, and Orla was manhandling baskets of sliced bread out of the pantry. "But first, I have to make sure. Are you all right?"

"Perfectly." Aumaleigh forced a smile. "It was a shock, I can't lie. But I don't want you to feel like you need to hide things from me. You must be ecstatic to see him again after all this time."

"I will be," Josslyn grinned, giving her apron a tug to straighten the skirt. "When I see him, that is. But I'm in no hurry. I've waited decades. Another few hours won't make a difference."

"It's hard to believe it's been that long." Aumaleigh closed off her memories, refused to look back as she headed to the sink to wash up. "Don't you dare stay to do the dishes, do you hear me? It would be my pleasure to do them, and I mean that."

"You're taking this better than I ever imagined." Josslyn bustled around the end of the counter, all business. "Annie, close the oven door—yes, it does need more time. Orla, put those baskets right here for Annie to warm the bread when it's time. Aumaleigh, you might want to keep out of town until the day after Christmas."

"You're warning me now?" Aumaleigh reached for the soap, trying to make light of it and trying not to feel the shadows taking over her heart. "Isn't it a little late?"

"Well, you just said not to hold back, so here it is. He's staying at Seth's house."

"All right. Good to know." Aumaleigh rinsed off and reached for the towel, very aware of Annie and Louisa's puzzled looks and Orla's curious one as they listened in on this part of the conversation. She didn't elaborate, because this wasn't their business. It was the past, and it was over. She had to find a way to keep it from hurting her.

After all, all those years ago she'd been the one to end things. She'd made her choice, she had no one to blame. When Gabriel had proposed to her, she'd said no and he'd left town. It was as simple as that. There was nothing more to be done now that she'd recovered from the shock, but to move forward. To try and let go of that regret and the pain of it.

But with any luck and if she followed Josslyn's advice, she'd never see him again.

* * *

""That is hysterical." Rose laughed, hand to her stomach. Boy, her sides were hurting. She fidgeted on Seth's sleigh seat, talking over the merry chime of jingle bells. "I can just picture Wally going crazy trying to get your attention. But seeing him pull up the hitching post and drag it after him through the auction? That's priceless."

"And he pulled poor William along with him." Seth shook his head, scattering his lightly curling black hair. His cheeks were pink from the burn of the icy wind, his obsidian eyes gleaming like black pearls. He held the reins easily in both large, gloved hands, guiding the horses with nothing more than an occasional flick of his wrist. William quirked an ear, listening in at the sound of his name. "William looked very aghast, like he wasn't at all sure they should be running loose in the auction. Men were starting to notice and pointing, laughing up a storm, and some had to jump out of the way of the wooden posts swinging wildly behind the pair. I looked up just in time to see Wally neighing shrilly, his gaze on me, charging around horses and people to get to me."

"He picked you out instead of the other way around." Rose noticed that Wally was listening in, too, arching his neck with a little bit of pride, as if proud of his strength and foresight. "It's unorthodox, but it seems to be working for the three of you."

"Yep. Me, Wally and William are buds. No doubt about it." Seth's affection for his horses came through in his words, and she couldn't help liking him more. He truly loved his animals.

She really liked him for that. Very, very much. In fact, she was feeling shivery again and as bright as summer.

"I had to buy the team after that, no one else would." Seth reined the horses around the corner, town far behind them. White blanketed everything all around them like winter's frosting, making everything new and sweet. "What good is a horse who is strong enough to pull up a hitching post? Any time you tied him up, you'd wonder if he'd be there when you got back."

"And the post too. I've been there, well, not with the post, but with Odie. It was stressful," she confessed. "I'm guessing Wally hasn't pulled up any more posts?"

"Wally doesn't know his own strength." Seth laughed at that, turning toward her, the intensity of his gaze deepening. His gaze held her, pulling her in with so much power, her heart skipped a beat. Then skipped another.

"Wally seems like a wonderful guy." When she spoke, her words sounded tinny and far away. Only Seth was at the center. His smile, his magnetic eyes, his warm humor.

"Oh, he pulls up a few posts now and then, but he doesn't mean it. Do you, big buddy?" Seth cut his eyes away to wait for his horse's response, releasing her from the powerful hold of his gaze.

As Wally gave a low nicker of agreement, Rose's pulse stopped all together. Maybe it was the letdown after the wedding and all the weeks of sewing and planning and baking and worrying. But when Seth leaned in so close, she'd run out of excuses. His arm pressed against her shoulder and she breathed in his warmth as he took another blanket from the floor at his feet and shook it out over her, taking care of her. Why hadn't she seen it before?

As he tucked in the blanket around her, a shudder quaked through her, from the crown of her head all the way to the tips of her toes. A shudder that felt silvery and sunny and thrilling. A shudder that knocked the air from her lungs and brightened the world.

As if it felt it too, the sun shone so brightly it washed out everything surrounding them. The trees faded away, the snow-mantled meadows disappeared and the mountains filling the horizon vanished. There was nothing—not anything—but Seth. His nearness, his handsomeness, his unguarded gaze found hers again. Her soul leaned toward his, like recognizing like. She shivered again at the heat of his touch against her chin as he gave the blanket one final tuck.

"There. Hope that makes you warmer. You're shivering pretty hard." He didn't inch back to his original place on the seat but remained right next to her, the warmth of his steely arm pressing against hers.

"Th-thank you." She didn't feel like herself at all. She slumped back against the seat, staring at Seth, at the strong angular lines of his profile and the slight swooping slope of his nose. There was something very endearing about him, the man, not the friend.

Wow, was all she could think. Just wow.

"I got lucky at Friday's auction," he went on, completely unaware that she was gaping at him, that anything between them had changed. "I got a couple really good horses."

"How many did you save from the slaughterhouse?" She was onto him by now. She saw who he was. All that he was.

"I picked up a nice gelding, and he is very affectionate." Seth arched his brow at her, leaning in, not fooled by her either. "In case Poppy doesn't turn out to be the horse of your dreams."

"She's a perfectly good horse. She's very well-behaved and easy to manage." Rose hesitated to say more, because she was hopeful. She wanted Poppy to love her. "Maybe she just needs time to get to know me better."

"Right. Well, you can go ahead and just say it." Seth's tone deepened with understanding, as if he already knew what she was struggling with, even when she hesitated to admit it to herself. "Poppy is a good horse, but she's not your dream horse."

"When I asked for a snuggly house, I didn't realize what I was asking of you." Rose shrugged, trying to make light of it. "I didn't realize how hard it would be."

"Are you kidding? I hunted for the right stallion for Maureen, back when she was alive, for two years before I found an animal that was what she wanted for the price she wanted. Trust me, this is nothing. I'm happy to help you, Rose."

"Maybe I don't want you to work that hard." Rose shrugged, trying to make light of it. She opened up to him without a thought, that's how much she trusted him. "Back when I was little and living in Chicago, the five of us would play make-believe in our backyard for hours and hours on end. It was a game that went on for years. I used to be a princess, you know."

"I'm not surprised." Seth arched a brow charmingly.

Little tingles spilled into her blood. She tried to pull her gaze from his, but her eyes wouldn't budge. She felt spellbound, tied to him as if by an invisible cord from her heart to his. She licked her lip, cleared her throat and went on. "We all used to be princesses of the realm. As my sisters love a good fairy-tale—"

"Who doesn't?" Seth asked with a wink.

"We were quite in demand by all the handsome princes in the land. And as nice as the princes were, I was always more interested in the imaginary horse my prince was riding."

"How did I guess?" That made him laugh. Wonderful little crinkles drew deep into the corners of his eyes, masculine and full of character, of life.

This was a man who laughed often, who cared deeply, who was no prince, just a good, flesh and blood hard-working man. Nothing could be more attractive. When had her heart started to choose him? She briefly closed her eyes, looking back, and realized there had been no specific moment. It had always chosen him, she just hadn't been paying attention.

"Let me guess." He reined his team off the country road and onto the tree-lined lane toward home. "Those imaginary horses loved you at first sight, too."

"How did you know?" She leaned a little closer against him, into the hot press of his iron-hard arm against hers. Was her heart even beating? She didn't know.

"It all makes sense now, looking back, why you wanted a snuggly horse." He winked at her, drawing the horses to a stop. His movements were fluid but confident, innately masculine as he climbed out of the sleigh, leaving the reins on the dash. "It's not the first attribute most folks ask for when they're horse shopping."

"What can I say? I know what really matters." She tried to make light of it, how much she had held onto that dream of the prince, so kindly and stalwart, riding the biggest horse in all the realms. That for all her prince's towering might and his greater strength, his horse was the clue to his true nature—gentle of heart. Was it foolish to think of that now? It had been so long ago, and she was no longer that little girl in an impoverished backyard pretending to be royalty. "I'm all grown up. Maybe I should be more realistic."

"Why do you say that?" He held the blankets for her, making it easy for her to scoot out from beneath them, across the seat warmed by him and then his hand was there, helping her from the sleigh. "If you want a horse to snuggle, I will find one for you. I won't give up until I do."

"That's what I'm afraid of," she admitted. He hovered over her, his grip firm and supporting, pointing out a patch of ice when she stood up, standing to protect her from the frigid wind. "It's like wasting your time when you've already found me a perfectly nice horse. For no fee, I might add."

"Well, don't forget the cookies you promised." His hand settled against the middle of her back (so wonderful), guiding her along. "Cookies are really important to me. I don't have anyone but Ma to bake for me, and she's too busy cooking and baking for the cowboys. I get nothing from her."

"Life is unfair," Rose agreed, a little breathless and definitely lightheaded. All because of him. Her skin buzzed with awareness, the fine hairs on her forearms stood on end and when she breathed, she drew *too* much air. Like a balloon, she was in danger of lifting right off the ground. Only his steady hold on her arm and the heat of his hand on her back kept her grounded. "I won't forget the cookies."

As she passed by Wally, the giant horse gave an affable whinny and blinked his long curly lashes at her. He had melted chocolate eyes and a dishpan face, so finely sculpted it could have been a masterpiece. His black forelock tumbled rakishly over his forehead in striking contrast to his golden-tan coat and the sugary-white blaze running down his nose. He nibbled her cheek as she waltzed by, stealing her heart.

"Oh!" She glanced over her shoulder, feeling fuzzy warm inside. "Thanks for the kiss, Wally."

Wally arched his horsy brows and gave her his best dashing smile.

Too cute.

"He's a charmer." Rose's hand flew to her cheek. "I bet he's like that with all the ladies."

"Not at all," Seth assured her. "It's only with you. He's very discriminating."

"Okay, that's sweet. Really sweet. But how did you teach him to do that?"

"I didn't. He came that way. Very needy. I'm embarrassed for him. That's no way for a big, tough horse to act."

"I'm a little in love with him," she confessed, blown away by the awareness that rushed through her, straight to her soul, when Seth took her elbow to help her up the porch steps. There he was, taking care of her again. It felt nice. More than nice. "I was kind of wondering if I could teach Poppy to be like that."

"You want her to pull up posts by mistake? Well, she's a little bit of a thing, so probably not." Mischievous midnight-blue flecks gleamed in his obsidian irises as he crossed the porch beside her, keeping a protective hand splayed on her back.

What was going on? She felt dizzy, she felt breathless, she felt as if her entire being—heart, body and soul—were alive in a way she'd never been before. As if she'd just taken her first breath, her heart its first beat. Never had she felt like this before. Not ever. She rolled her eyes. "You know I meant the horse kisses."

"With Wally it's more that I can't get him to stop." Seth swung open the door, holding it for her, standing to block the wind as she crossed the threshold and into the house. "He's a natural born kisser."

"He *does* give nice kisses." Warmth and light washed over her. They weren't alone, (she could hear the ring of voices in the nearby rooms), but it was Seth who dominated her senses, Seth who was her center. He closed the door behind him and helped unwind her scarf, standing so close, she couldn't breathe.

"I've tried everything," he confessed good-naturedly. "Scolding him. Staying out of reach of his lips. I even explained how it's embarrassing for me to be kissed by another guy, even if that guy is a horse. He doesn't listen."

Oh, this man could make her laugh. She could laugh with him for the rest of her life. What she felt was unexpected and so powerful it was scary. This was way more than friendship and far more than she'd ever thought she could feel. Spellbound by him, she pulled off her gloves, pocketing them, to unbutton her coat. "Something tells me you don't mind those horse kisses too much."

"In private is one thing," Seth joked on, his hands at her shoulders helping her out of her coat. "But he does it in public. In full view of the town. It's bad for business. Next thing you know, folks are going to stop patronizing my business. If I can't handle my own horse, what chance do I have handling theirs?"

"Something to consider. Come to think of it, maybe I should find a more competent liveryman and blacksmith." She stepped out of her coat, dangerously close to him. Goosebumps broke out over her arms. "Can you recommend someone?"

"Sure, maybe he can find you a kissy horse." With a wry twist to his mouth, Seth hung up her things on the coat tree. "I wish him luck."

"Actually, Poppy is just fine." It was the truth. High expectations scared her. She remembered her ma telling her once, *don't be like me, Rose. Don't let life break your heart the way I did. Be smart, keep your expectations realistic.* And that's what she'd done, that's the woman she'd grown up to be. Sure, she was optimistic for her sisters, but personally? She'd never believed she could find Mr. Wonderful. Or, at least, that Mr. Wonderful would be dazzled by little old her.

And she was standing in front of Mr. Wonderful, and he probably just saw a plain, regular girl, no beautiful princess. Just a girl he could be friends with.

I'm falling in love with him, she realized, her palms going damp. Her heart skipped three beats. *Really and truly in love with him.*

"Poppy's everything I could ask for." Disappointment rolled through her, and she pretended it was from lowering her expectations for the horse. "I'm sure she will warm up over time."

"And what about the snuggly thing?" He arched an eyebrow, not fooled.

"On second thought, maybe it will reflect poorly on the bakery business to have a kissy horse smooching me while I am delivering a customer's cake. It's far from professional." Breezy, that's how she meant to sound, but her voice croaked a little. Maybe because she was absolutely sure Seth didn't feel breathless and enamored. "I have to think of the good of the bakery."

"I know what you're doing." He reached out, his fingers like flames as he brushed her cheek, folding a lock of errant hair behind her ear. "Don't you worry. It's no trouble for me, and I like a challenge. But really, I just want you to have what you want."

"Ma always said growing up was learning to let go of childish things." Rose felt the brightness dim from the lamps, the heat drain from the fires. What she was feeling toward Seth was far from childish—it was affection, rising up like a dawning sun, casting the most beautiful pure gold on an awakening world. That's what she felt. And it was too much, far more than she'd ever expected to feel, so she took a step back, putting a little distance between them, enough to remind her of what else her Ma always told her. "Fairy-tale dreams are for children. I need to be sensible."

"Sensible?" Seth shook his head, his eyes as dark as night. "No, it's better to keep dreaming. Or how else will something extraordinary happen for you?"

"Extraordinary?" There she went, feeling lightheaded again, unable to breathe. This indescribable power coming to life in her heart definitely felt extraordinary. "It's over-rated. I'd rather have ordinary. Typical. Average."

"Sorry, that's not going to happen, not to you." Seth retreated too, tipping his Stetson to her in a silent farewell. His guards seemed down too, and the soft gleam of affection in his eyes surprised her. Then, in a blink, it was gone and he was opening the door. "You are far from ordinary, beautiful Miss Rose. Ordinary is never going to be your destiny."

And there was a hint of sadness in his voice as he opened the door and left, walking away as if the moment between them had never been. Her heart ached with a strange, mighty yearning.

"Rose, there you are!" Oscar limped down the hallway from the kitchen, carrying a box full of chopped wood. She hardly recognized him in a borrowed suit (Aumaleigh must have found one for him somewhere). With his light brown hair slicked back, he didn't look like a man who'd ever been homeless. He dipped his chin humbly. "I just want to thank you again. It feels great to be working."

"Good, because we'll be keeping you busy today." Rose tried to force her thoughts off Seth, but it was impossible. He stayed in the back of her mind. "It looks like they've got you on fire duty."

"Yep, it's my job to keep all the fires going, so everyone is warm and safe." Oscar hesitated at the library door, balancing his heavy wood box carefully. "And the candles on the Christmas trees too. It's good to feel useful again."

Pleased, Rose wrapped her arms around her middle, watching as Oscar disappeared through the doorway. Maybe this could be a turning point for him. His foot was almost healed. Maybe he could find full-time work soon and get on with his life.

"Rose! Oh, good, you're here." Iris stood at the archway into the kitchen, a wooden spoon in hand. "We have appetizer trays to fill. Why are you standing around staring into thin air?"

"I'm lazy," she teased, just to make her sister laugh. It worked, Iris shook her head, retreating into the kitchen.

Rose couldn't say why she stayed where she was, as if locked in place, or why she glanced over her shoulder to catch a glimpse of him, of Seth through the window. Affection, so new and shiny, strengthened when she saw him in the yard blanketing the horses that had begun to crowd the end of the driveway. Everyone was arriving, and he was lending a hand with the horses and vehicles. What a sight.

It took all her willpower to walk away.

CHAPTER SIXTEEN

"Woo-ee." Junior took one look at McPhee Manor and nearly fell off the crude make-do sled he and Giddy had built yesterday out of fallen timber. His jaw hung, and all he could do was stare. Sure, he knew the sisters were rich—they'd wound up with money that didn't belong to them—but even he hadn't expected *this*.

Three stories of windows. They were everywhere, from first floor to attic. Bay windows, bow windows, picture windows, stained-glass windows. And look at that porch. It was one of them fancy ones, with curlicue wood decorating the roofline, railing and support posts and from what he could tell, it wrapped around at least half the house. The mansion was enormous—there had to be more than a dozen large rooms, all from what he could judge by the front windows.

He grimaced. What did five women need with such a big house? Jealousy burned in his chest, sharp as a razor, as vicious as hate. He knew he wasn't the only one feeling like this.

"What in the blazes?" Giddy looked crestfallen. He hadn't expected this either. Up close, the mansion was even bigger and more impressive. "What did those worthless women do to get this? It was just handed to 'em. That's what. Now I hate 'em even more."

"Me, too." Red hazed Junior's eyes as the horses came to a stop. The turn-around area at the bulb of the driveway was a traffic nightmare.

Horses, vehicles and people were everywhere. Happy people all decked up in their finest, be it fancy frocks or plain calico, all excited and smiling and looking happy for those dang sisters. Happy that one of the heiresses had found some sucker to marry her.

Of course, if a woman was that wealthy, that might be a reason to stand before a minister. A woman with money might have some worth after all.

"There he is." Giddy gestured through an opening as the crowd parted, giving a good view of the groom. "Lucky. Now he's in control of some of that money and I'm guessin' a fifth of that house."

"Do you reckon this house and land is part of the ranch, too?" Junior reached down for his crutch and heaved himself off the uncomfortable board seat.

"Nah. I asked at the feed store when I was playin' checkers with some cowpokes there, and they said it was legally separated." Giddy shook his head. "Too bad. If it weren't, think of what that poor sap would be worth."

"Almost puts me in a marrying mind." Junior leaned on his crutch, searching through the crowd of women (they were everywhere, all yakking away, streaming toward the house), but he didn't see a single one of the sisters anywhere.

"That's the wrong leg," Giddy told him sharply, his mouth a hard, stern line, like Pa's used to do right before he reached out and smacked someone. "Be smart, Junior. Use that head of yours. This is important."

"Right." He switched sides and leaned heavily on the crutch. He doubted anyone had noticed. No one was looking this way, no, they were all too enamored with those McPhee girls. That's because they were filthy rich. He scowled sourly. That's what money could do for a person. Gain them respect they didn't do a dad-blamed thing to deserve. Bitterness flooded his mouth like bile, and he spit just to get rid of the taste.

"Let me take care of that horse for you." A black-haired man pounded over with a friendly air—the kind of fellow you just knew was one of them lucky men—he'd got every break in life. Everything always went his way.

Junior recognized him as the livery owner in town. He nodded in answer and put on his best fake smile. "Thanks. We appreciate it."

"It's pretty crowded here," the liveryman jabbered on as if they were old friends.

Phony idiot.

"And there's no shelter for the animals here," he went on to explain. "We're moving the horses next door to the ranch, unhitching them and getting them stalled and rubbed down. When you want to go, just speak to one of us near the door. We'll run down and drive them back for you."

"That's mighty nice." Giddy answered this time, climbing out of the sled. No one could put on a false front like Giddy. "Thanks. I've seen you around town. You own the livery, right?"

"That's right. My name's Seth Daniels. Drop by any time." He took charge of the reins, giving the useless old swayback gelding a gentle pat on the shoulder. "I haven't seen you boys before. Did you drive up from Deer Springs?"

"Something like that," Giddy lied easily, tipping his hat. The instant he turned around, his back to the liveryman, he gave Junior a wink. Men like that were easy to fool—they wanted to see good in everyone.

"Walk slower," Giddy advised as Junior limped along.

"I'm trying," he shot back under his breath. The crutch was uncomfortable, digging into his armpit as he hitched down the path. Folks had to slow down for him, bunching up in a crowd behind him, but he kept up the ruse, dragging his "crippled" right leg.

"What the—?" Giddy didn't finish his sentence because the instant he led the way across the threshold, he fell silent, gazing up and around, his jaw dropped so far it was a shock that spit didn't dribble out. His eyes had widened to saucers as he slowly turned around.

Then Junior saw why. He crutched carefully onto the polished hardwood, aghast at the stunning sight. A soaring, ornate ceiling domed over them, light shining from the windows above. An elegant staircase curved up to the second story, its polished wood gleaming like a dark pearl. He caught a glimpse into a sunroom halfway ceilinged by glass with walls of glass letting sunshine burnish the thick, colorful imported carpet.

That wasn't all. There was more. The parlor was behind him. When he spun around, forgetting to lean on his crutch, the air whooshed out of his lungs as he caught sight of the glass paneled French doors and the stunning stone hearth that dominated one wall of the room. Palladian windows framed the view of trees, the sloping hillside falling away downhill and the rolling view of the Rocking M Ranch.

The ranch. Acid pooled in his stomach as he marched around guests talking away and sipping what smelled like expensive wine and fancy champagne. His crutch caught in the dense softness of the area rug as he charged toward those windows. The drone of conversation, the press of people, the sparkle of the Christmas tree became nothing but background as his gaze glued to the sight of that expensive, expanse of ranch. A *profitable* ranch. He ground his teeth together, rage building.

"Remember your leg," Giddy whispered, sidling in to join him at one of the windows. He carried two crystal glasses and handed one over. "They sure got a good view here, don't they? Reckon it's a *million dollar* view."

"I reckon so." He unlocked his jaw enough to take a sip of the bubbly stuff. Not bad. A man could get used to this lifestyle, he thought, glancing around. A fancy life, a leisurely life, and money enough to have everything a man wanted when he wanted it. Thoughts like that could set a man to dreaming.

"Look at 'em." Giddy nudged him in the side with a strong elbow. He jutted his chin across the parlor to the open double doorway looking out into the hallway, where Rose carried a tray full of tasty little treats.

All dolled up in that Christmas-red gown, with the wispy blond curls around her face and that elegant little shape of hers, that could get a man dreaming too. Dreaming of her money.

"Rich like this, no wonder she's smilin' like that." Giddy huffed under his breath, taking a long pull from his glass. "I would be too. You ready to be friends with her?"

"You know I've been tryin'." How else would they be able to figure out the easiest way to part the sisters from their money? Junior caught a movement from the corner of his eye—Giddy taking something off the tree. Something golden and glittering.

"It's real gold." Giddy had a talent. He pocketed the ornament so smooth and slick no one would have noticed, even if they'd been looking right at him. "That ought to help make our Christmas merry."

Giddy winked.

Yep, coming here was gonna pay off. Junior drained his glass, the champagne tickling on the way down. Strange stuff, but he liked it. He was going to get used to a lot of fine things, he decided, starting with Rose McPhee.

JINGLE BELL HEARTS

* * *

"Oscar, you're doing such a wonderful job," Rose praised, meaning every word as she held the tray with one last appetizer on it in his direction. "The fires are crackling and the candles on the tree are perfect. I fear you've been running nonstop. At least take a moment to get a snack. I worry about you."

"Oh, pshaw, you don't need to fuss over me." Oscar blushed until his ears turned pink. "But I won't say no to whatever that is on your tray. I've never seen food like this. It all looks real good."

"It is. Aumaleigh is the one behind the appetizers. She grew up in a house very much like this, so she knows all about fancy things." Rose held the tray steady as Oscar plucked up the last mini meat pie, bit into it and rolled his eyes.

"Delicious," he said around a mouthful. "Best thing I've ever tasted."

"Then I'll send Magnolia over your way with a plate of your own. Where did she go off to?" Rose went up on tiptoe and strained to see over all the heads in the crowd (that was the problem with being short). "Or maybe you should just retreat to the kitchen, grab a plate and help yourself to the supply there. Have Aumaleigh get you some tea and sit down, so you can rest your leg."

"I don't need a break," Oscar insisted, staunchly. "In fact, let me take that tray back for you on my way."

And he snatched it from her hands before she could protest.

"You'll be busy anyway, I expect." He gave her a gentlemanly nod and limped off, tray in hand, heading down the hallway to the kitchen.

But Rose didn't notice anything else after that because of the tall, burly man winding his way toward her through the crowd, his black hair tousled by the wind, his angular jaw set. She felt the impact of his gaze like a blaze and, breathless, she felt glued to the spot. Her heart didn't beat again until Seth had reached her side and caught her hand in both of his.

"I saw you with that tray." He tugged her into the sunroom, where a familiar sound met her ears—the beginning strains of a waltz. Doc Hartwell and his buddies were gathered in the corner, coaxing notes from their violins. Seth guided her into the center of the room. "You've been working since the party started. It's time for you to relax a little."

"Dancing is not relaxing," she informed him, noticing a few other couples had the same idea and had paired up, hand in hand, dancing to the music. She frowned. "I have a lot of worries when it comes to dancing."

"Is that so?" Laugh lines bracketed Seth's smile as he pulled her close, his strength unmistakable. His hand settled on the small of her back, commandingly. "There's nothing to worry about with me."

"There's always something to worry about," she informed him as his shoe nudged hers, moving her feet along in time to the music. She had to try hard to keep from going majorly tingly at his nearness. "I have lots of worries. Sweaty palms for one."

"Your palm isn't sweaty," he assured her, those laugh lines digging deeper into his lean cheeks. "So that's one worry knocked down. What else?"

"I have this little bald spot in the middle of my head," she confessed. "Magnolia bumped a candle accidentally when she was a toddler and a blob of hot wax landed on my scalp. It's been hairless ever since."

"Ouch." Dimples cut into his lean cheeks. "I knew I'd get to some of your secrets. A bald spot, huh?"

"Don't make me regret telling you."

"You're secret is safe with me." His baritone dipped, sounding almost tender, not in the way of a friend at all.

But as a lover.

Wild hope seized her heart. Exhilaration snapped through her veins, and yet she felt comfortable and cozy at the same time—like friendship on fire. But when she studied his face, he looked the same—laughing, easy-going, friendly Seth. Disappointment arced through her, and she stared hard at the button at his shirt collar. So, he wasn't feeling this at all.

Not one bit.

"No fears," he told her with a wink. "I can't see your bald spot from here."

"I disguise it," she informed him. "It's really small, but if a hairpin slips, you'll see it."

"I'll be a gentleman and I won't look," he assured her. "Any other worries?"

Like she was going to tell him that! She arched an eyebrow at him. "This amuses you, doesn't it?"

"Absolutely. I'm having a grand time." His black eyes glittered gaily.

"How about you?"

"Sure, as long as I don't stumble over your foot and trip."

"No need to worry. I'll catch you," he promised, sure of himself. "I have excellent reflexes."

"Good to know. My reputation can't survive another falling incident. Especially since I'm not wearing long johns today."

"You're making me laugh." Pleasant crinkles cut into the corners of his eyes. "It's a little hard to waltz and laugh at the same time."

"I'm noticing." How could she feel two different things at once? Laughing so hard with no real reason why—not a single one—and stubborn disappointment that wouldn't let go. "Why are we laughing? I didn't say anything that funny."

"I know, but I can't stop."

"Neither can I." She laughed harder, because he was laughing harder, and she knew he was picturing it too, the ruckus it would cause if she landed sprawled on her back with her skirt above her knees. "Why didn't I think to wear long johns today?"

And that did it. He roared. She roared. Finally he gave up and stopped waltzing. He leaned his head back, laughing hard, a wonderful, deep low ripple of sound, probably the best thing she'd ever heard in her life. A sound she could get used to. A sound she wouldn't mind hearing for the rest of her days.

"My eyes are watering," he confessed, blinking hard.

"My side is aching." She glanced around, laughing harder. "We're starting to attract attention."

"Won't be the first time." He swiped at his eyes. "This happens when I'm with you. People start staring. I wonder why?"

"Because I'm nuttier than I seem at first glance?" Her stomach muscles felt ready to burst. "It's my deep dark secret."

"Trust me, it's no secret." His hand snared her wrist, and moved up her arm in one searing caress that ended at the back of her neck.

The weight of his hand settled on her nape, and he guided her straight to the glass door that led out onto the deck. It happened so fast, as if in a dream. He opened the door and they tumbled out into the cold together. She hardly noticed the slap of the icy wind against her face because she was still laughing and he was laughing with her.

And then he wasn't.

"Rose." When he said her name, his eyes went dark, turning to a sheer, unfathomable black she lost herself in. She drew in a quick breath, startled because she wanted this too.

More than anything.

"You make me hope," he said. He leaned in, his free hand coming up to cradle her chin and jaw. A heady combination, that blend of his scorching hot touch and the frigid cold air—both seemed to meld on her skin. Heart hammering, she resisted the urge to reach up and touch his silky, thick black hair or to rub her fingertips across the line of his jaw. His lips, carved granite and soft tenderness, hovered over her mouth coming closer—

The door whipped open with a rasp of hinges. The crescendo of voices and music spilled out in a noisy rush.

Startled, she broke away and Seth did too, his mouth aching with the promise of that interrupted, almost kiss. He was standing there like a fool, heart racing like he'd run ten thousand miles, as Elise Hutchinson, friend to the McPhee sisters, stepped onto the porch, studying them with a puzzled frown.

Yes, they were standing very close together. Mindful of Rose's reputation and the swiftness of the town gossip mill, he took a big step back.

"Just getting some fresh air," he explained, disappointment hammering through him. Any instant now his common sense would return and Rose was going to let him down gently. Nicely, but it wouldn't be possible to soften the blow.

He loved her. He wanted her. He wanted to take care of her for the rest of his life.

"Yes," Rose said quietly, drawing herself up like the lady she was. "Just some fresh air."

"Well, if I'm not interrupting anything, my cousin was asking about you." Elise shoved a dark lock of hair behind her ear before wrapping her arms around herself, shivering a little. "I saw you two head out here, and I thought I'd come fetch you. Supper will be served soon and there might not be another chance to introduce you. We'll probably be leaving early because of the weather."

"The weather?" Seth asked, feeling dumb the instant he said it. Tiny flecks of white were raining down, fast and furious. He hadn't even noticed. "Right. It's snowing."

"Since we have a bit of a drive." Elise shrugged apologetically. "Are you sure I'm not interrupting anything?"

"No," Rose said uncertainly, and he felt the sweep of her gaze across his face, searching for an answer he couldn't give her. Something in her green-blue gaze softened, showing her caring heart.

For one moment, he let himself dream. To picture life the way he wished it could be—courting her diligently, proposing to her with all of his heart, standing at the altar in front of family and friends and vowing to cherish her for all their days to come.

But some things were impossible, some dreams too far out of reach. He'd never thought he'd feel this way again, but love had snuck up on him, coming softly, coming quietly, but like a river ran deep. He took one look at Rose—beyond gorgeous in her fancy dress, standing on the porch of her outrageously expensive mansion and he stared down at his hands. Working man's hands. And then he remembered Liz.

"Nothing." He planted his feet, sad he'd gone crazy for a moment there, given in to his feelings. "You aren't interrupting anything. Nothing was ever going to happen here."

He heard Rose's little gasp, and he hoped she'd heard the intent behind his tone. He'd gentled those words the best he could, it was the kind thing to do, but this was the right thing.

"Sure, Elise," she said, her voice thick with surprised hurt. "I should head in."

He did his best not to look at her as she walked away, jamming his fists into his pockets and holding his ground when every bit of his being screamed at him to go back to her, draw her into his arms and kiss her until she knew how he felt.

But they lived in two different worlds. And so, defeated, he stayed where he was, alone in the icy cold listening to the light knell of her shoes on the porch boards, then the rasp of the door closing and then silence—and then nothing at all.

* * *

"Are you all right, Rose?" Elise asked, leading the way around the dancers taking up the entire middle of the sunroom. Her beautiful silk dress rustled as she walked, so poised and elegant she outshone nearly everyone else in the room. "I can't help feeling I interrupted something. You and Seth were laughing so hard, I saw you two head outside, and honestly, I was talking with my cousin at the time and he was fascinated by you. He said he had to meet a lady who could laugh that beautifully."

"Which cousin are you talking about?" Rose shook her head, but it still felt vague and fuzzy, as if it were stuffed with cotton, the noise in the room tinny and far away. Her lips buzzed with anticipation for a kiss that was never going to happen. Seth really had been about to kiss her, but he'd stopped. No, she thought, skidding to a halt. He'd changed his mind and then he'd dismissed what had almost happened as nothing. *Nothing.*

Her chest wrenched tight, full of pain. She'd wanted his kiss so badly. More than she'd ever wanted anything before.

Sadness hit her as she glanced over her shoulder, searching past the swirling couples and the crowds of people conversing along the sidelines for any sign of Seth. Had he followed her inside, or was he still out there? She fought the urge to race to him and demand to know the truth. Why had he tried to kiss her if he hadn't felt anything for her? Confused and torn, her chest was one open wound.

Then Seth came into sight, striding through the doorway and into the sunroom. He didn't look at her. He purposefully turned his head away.

Clearly dismissing her. That hurt even worse.

"This is my cousin. He came all the way from Deer Springs." Elise's voice held a hint of excitement. "Ian has just taken over his family's ranch, which is almost as big as the Rocking M."

"Really?" Rose tried to focus, but her head felt fuzzy, in a daze. She looked up to find a striking man with thick blond hair, probably in his thirties, wearing an expensive navy blue suit.

"I've been most eager to introduce you two." Elise beamed, gazing up at her cousin as if she thought he was the best cousin in all the world. "I've told him all about you, and he's quite eager to get to know you, now that you're suddenly without a beau."

So that's what this was about. Rose gaped, trying to find the right words. She wasn't ready for this. Not at all.

"It's a great pleasure to meet you, Miss McPhee." Ian bowed courteously, granting her a kind smile. As amazing as he undoubtedly was, he couldn't compare to Seth.

No one could.

And thinking of him only confused her more. Why had he dismissed what had almost happened so easily? Did he truly care that little?

"I couldn't help noticing you are a good waltzer." Ian held out one wide palmed hand. "Is there room for me on your dance card?"

She could hardly decline. It wouldn't be polite, and it would surely disappoint Elise. Vowing to give him her full attention, she placed her hand in Ian's capable one.

"Yes," she told him politely. "A spot on my card just opened up."

"Excellent." He led her onto the dance floor, but when he took her in his arms, it felt all wrong. Just as flat and platonic as it had once felt with Wade.

The problem was that now she knew the difference. She feared the one man she wanted did not want her.

CHAPTER SEVENTEEN

It tore Seth apart to see her in another man's arms. He took a swig of punch, draining the cup. It didn't help. Nothing would. He set the dainty crystal cup back on the table, watching her whirl around the floor, so stunning and sweet it made the backs of his eyes sting. Everything, *everything,* inside of him ached for her. Only for her.

It was a lucky thing he actually hadn't kissed her.

"More punch?" Verbena asked from her place behind the lace-covered table, a dipper in hand. The big crystal punch bowl glittered in the lamplight, full of fresh, tasty lemonade style punch, but he'd had all the sweet and sour he could take. He shook his head, unable to say anything more. Seeing Rose smile up at Ian Hutchinson cut like a knife.

"Seth." Verbena broke into his thoughts. "Are you all right?"

"Fine. Just wondering if I should go and check on the horses." It sounded like a good reason to escape the sight of Ian holding Rose, and to try and forget the feelings that still haunted him. He cleared his throat. "It's bone-chilling out there."

"Is that why you and Rose went outside?" Verbena asked sweetly with an expectant arch to one slender eyebrow. "To check on the temperature?"

Her question made him wonder what she had seen. While they'd been next to the windows and not in front of them, from this angle it was possible Rose's sister had caught sight of that moment—that almost disastrous moment.

Then again, he thought as he battled down embarrassment, maybe Verbena couldn't have seen. It was hard to tell.

"Something like that," he said with a shrug, his eyes cutting sideways to Rose, so prim and pretty, like a china doll come to life. Yes, checking on the horses was sounding better and better. He pushed away from the table and circled the room, taking care not to get too close to certain people dancing.

"Seth! Where are you going?" Aumaleigh appeared in the hallway, carrying two big cloth-covered baskets of delicious smelling bread. "Supper is about to be served. Don't you dare leave before the meal. I've been cooking for days. I'll never forgive you."

"No, you'll forgive me. What you mean is that I'll never hear the end of it from my ma." He stopped short of the coat tree. Blissful escape had been so close. "Any chance you'll let me just take a plate with me?"

"Forget it. Stay or pay the consequences." Aumaleigh gave him a breezy wink before disappearing into the library and out of sight.

"You can sit with me," a soft, feminine voice snared his attention. Miss Shalvis, the new schoolteacher, stood in the parlor's doorway. Her brown hair was caught up in a loose bun, tendrils falling down to accentuate her porcelain cheekbones and kind smile. She was just the sort of person who ought to be teaching kids. "I'm here by my lonesome, too. I'm not seeing anyone, and the older married ladies in this town keep trying to set me up with their grown sons."

"So sitting with me would be doing you a favor?"

"Desperately so." She gave a little shrug, making her high, lace-edged collar brush one of those tendrils. "Unless you are going to pick up where they left off and try to match me up, too?"

"Not a chance," he assured her. "You'll be safe with me."

"Excellent. I promise to be good company." Understanding shone in Penelope's eyes.

While he appreciated her kindness, it hurt his pride. And having to stay and watch Ian move in on Rose wasn't going to be easy. From the first instant he'd set eyes on Rose and realized there was something special about her, something that pulled at his heart, he'd known how this was going to end.

It had been a lucky break that he'd been interrupted before he could kiss Rose. Kissing her, regardless of how much he wanted to, would have been a terrible mistake.

* * *

The party was a success in every single way—but one. As Rose stood in the library late that night, all she could think about was the one thing that hadn't gone right. Seth. He hadn't sat beside her during supper. Worse, he'd avoided her afterwards as if he was embarrassed he'd tried to kiss her (or horrified). He'd left early to take care of the horses, and she hadn't seen him since. He hadn't even said goodbye.

"Rose?" Iris huffed in frustration. "This is going to take all night at this rate. Look at you standing there. You're a hundred miles away."

"Sorry." She blinked to find her other sisters staring at her—Magnolia and Iris, that is. Daisy had gone home with Beckett and Hailie to their cozy cottage down the hill. Verbena had left arm-in-arm with her rugged husband. It was just the three of them. "I guess I've got a lot on my mind."

"Don't tell me it's losing that mercantile customer." Iris's forehead creased up in furrows. "I'm not sure we should be spending time delivering all the way to Deer Springs anyway. It's not exactly cost-effective."

"She's not thinking about the business." Magnolia waggled her brows. "At first I was shocked, shocked I tell you, at learning about her break-up with Wade from Fred the post office guy, but then I saw her dancing with Elise's cousin. Clearly she's over the deputy and has a very gorgeous rancher on her mind."

"Wrong on both accounts." Rose heaved up her end of the sofa.

"You look tired," Iris observed, hurrying to lift the other side of the sofa. Together they hefted it across the library floor and back into place. "Maybe we should leave the rest of the clean-up for the morning. Goodness, is that clock right? It's nearly midnight?"

"Tell me about it. Time flies when you're being tortured with housework." Magnolia grabbed an end table, carried it across the room and set it beside the sofa. "That's it. I'm going to bed. I need my beauty sleep."

"No kidding," Rose piped up, unable to resist teasing her little sister. "You need it bad. Bad, I tell you."

"Funny." Magnolia retrieved the lamp she'd set on the floor and rearranged it on the end table. "Is Elise's cousin as nice as he seems?"

"I guess." Rose backed away from the sofa, wanting to escape while the getting was good.

"What does that mean?" Iris wanted to know. "You danced with him at least half a dozen times."

"Not to mention sitting with him at supper," Magnolia pointed out, waggling her brows again. "You two looked pretty cozy."

"He was telling me about his horses." Rose hesitated at the doorway. Her sisters were only trying to be hopeful for her, but it was misery because the man she'd needed to talk to, the man she'd missed all evening long, wanted to avoid her. She shrugged. "That's it. That's all. Stop trying to match me up. Good night, you two."

She stepped into the hall and almost rammed into someone.

"Sorry, Rose," Oscar apologized, nearly dropping the little shovel and poker set he carried.

"You're still here?" She rubbed her forehead, frustrated at herself for not thinking of checking on him sooner. "It's really late, Oscar."

"I don't mind. I just need to go into the library and put out the fire for you ladies, then I'll be done." Courteously, he bobbed through the doorway, limping as he went. "Miss Magnolia, Miss Iris. If you want to go on upstairs, I'll finish up down here and lock the door behind me when I leave."

"That would be great," Magnolia said enthused, her voice echoing in the large room, so empty now after being crammed full of partiers that it felt strange.

"You've done such a good job," Iris praised. "All through the party, every time I looked up, the candles were perfect and the fires crackling merrily. It's been good to have someone so dependable looking after things."

"Glad I could ease your burden some, Miss." Oscar hunkered down in front of the hearth.

As Rose looked through the doorway into the room, she saw the straight line of his shoulders, not to mention the determination and dignity there as he broke apart the embers in the hearth, the iron poker clinking against the grate. How much pain was he in after being on his injured foot for so long today? And it was a long walk back to his tree hut, not to mention the snow was really coming down out there. She bit her bottom lip, debating, feeling another idea coming on.

"Oscar." Iris's soft voice resonated above the *clinks* as Oscar covered the last of the glowing embers. She moved in, pulling cash from her skirt pocket. "Here's what we agreed on, plus a little bonus. You worked far harder than I expected. We're very grateful."

Good for Iris, Rose thought with approval. It was hard for her to loosen the reticule strings, as if she hadn't quite accepted they had so much money. Maybe that would come in time, especially with the plans Rose had for the bakery. But those plans didn't hold the excitement or the appeal they once had. In fact, the shadows felt endlessly bleak and the night bitterly cold. Seth was the reason. She'd really wanted his kiss tonight. She wanted more than his friendship.

"Thank you so much, Miss Iris." Oscar stood, shoulders slumped, staring at the fold of dollar bills in his hands. Rose wondered how long it had been since he'd been able to earn a wage of any kind. He swallowed hard, as if it meant everything to him. "It's been a great pleasure working for you ladies. I'll be on my way now, unless there's something else you need?"

"No, we're all done for the night," Iris assured him gently, as if she had noticed how hard he was swallowing too. "Wait a minute. You filled up the wood boxes for us, too?"

"So you wouldn't have to worry about bringing in wood come morning," Oscar said, bobbing his head once in a farewell nod as he pocketed his earnings and turned away. "Likely you all will be pretty tired tomorrow. It was the least I could do."

Rose glanced over her shoulder, peering into the shadowed parlor. Yep, the wood box was piled high in there, too. Not that she was surprised. "For what it's worth, I don't think you should be walking home."

"Don't even think about driving me, Rose." Oscar's chin jutted up, firm. "It's not good sense for a lady to be out there this late at night on her own. I'm happy to walk."

"Not tonight." Rose gestured to the parlor behind her. "We've got more than enough room and a sofa of your choice. You should sleep here."

"Uh, Rose?" Iris rubbed her hands together, upset now. "That would destroy our reputations. It just can't be done. Not that I want you to walk in this cold and at night, Oscar."

"Here's an idea." Magnolia sashayed into the hallway. "Why doesn't he spend the night at the bunkhouse? It's not a long walk, just down the hill, and no one will mind. The cowboys can find room for him."

"Excellent idea." Rose rolled her eyes. Why hadn't she thought of it? At least it was one night Oscar would be warm and safe in a comfortable bed.

"That's too generous, but my foot is paining me enough that I'll accept your offer." Oscar took his coat from the tree. "As long as the cowboys don't mind."

"You tell them we sent you," Iris spoke up, sympathy on her face as her gaze traveled down to his foot. "How did you get injured?"

"I worked at a logging camp west of Deer Springs." He pulled on his coat, quickly buttoning up. "A big log rolled off the skid, killed the man next to me and crushed my foot and ankle. I was lucky they didn't have to amputate it, but it's taken a long time to heal up."

"And the company didn't keep paying your wages after you were hurt, of course," Magnolia spoke up, hands fisting, angry on his behalf. "Typical company."

"They fired me." Oscar shrugged. "I came away with both my life and my foot, so I'm grateful for that. Maybe it won't be much longer before I can get back to work. You have a good night ladies, and be sure and lock up after me."

"Good night, Oscar." Rose closed the door behind him and turned the bolt. Sadness clung to her—she wanted to pretend it was for Oscar's sake, but that wasn't entirely the truth. Seth was on her mind—and in her heart. She couldn't get him out.

"Well, that was a great party." Iris turned down the lamp and the library descended into darkness. With a sigh, she emerged through the doorway, exhaustion bruising the skin beneath her eyes. "Do you think Daisy liked it? She seemed happy."

"She seemed blissfully happy," Rose corrected, not mentioning how empty it felt now with both Verbena and Daisy gone. It was just the three of them rattling around this enormous house.

"Ooh, my bed is calling me." Magnolia dragged her feet wearily down the hallway. "Come on. I'm totally exhausted and it's not over yet. Christmas is coming, and we've got a lot of preparing to do."

"Don't forget we've got baking to do in the morning!" Iris trailed after them, turning out the few lamps left on as she went. "And when we aren't baking, we're sewing. We need to step it up if we're going to get all our gifts done on time."

"Not now, Iris," Magnolia rolled her eyes. "I don't want all that on my mind. I need all the sleep I can get."

"Me, too." Rose admitted, feeling oddly alone. It didn't make sense. She wasn't alone, since she was with Iris and Magnolia, but the loneliness stuck like glue to her soul anyway as she accompanied her sisters through the house and up the stairs.

* * *

In the glacial pre-dawn cold, Seth clutched the jug of coffee, tucking it in the crook of one arm as he let himself out of his mother's house. While her sofa had been fairly comfortable, that wasn't the reason his eyes felt scratchy and his body haggard as if he hadn't slept a wink. He closed the door quietly, so it wouldn't make noise enough to wake his ma in the next room and waded through the snow to the street.

Alone, he trudged his way down a block and up an alley. His house loomed on the large corner lot with property behind it, surrounded by evergreens, boughs weighed down with snow. His two-story home was dark except for one window. Someone was up at this hour. That surprised him. As he plunged through the deep snow in the side yard, he caught sight of Uncle Gabriel through the kitchen window making coffee. His uncle spotted him and waved, so Seth wasn't surprised when the lean-to door popped open.

"What are you doing out and about at this hour, boy?" Gabriel shrugged into his coat one hand at a time, since he was also carrying a coffee cup. "Come in and get some breakfast with me. The kids are still asleep."

"I can't." Seth wouldn't have minded the distraction, but he had an early rental to gear up for—the Fletcher family needed a team and a sleigh to drive to Bear Hollow for Christmas. He didn't want to make them wait in this cold. "I just came by for something in my stable out back."

"You've got an entire livery. You need a stable, too?" Uncle Gabriel grinned. "Let me guess. You use it for storage."

"That's right. Are you all settled in here?" he asked. "Do you need anything? We weren't expecting you until today, or I would have had the pantry fully stocked for you."

"We made good time, so I didn't expect to be here early either."

Gabriel took a sip from his steaming cup. "We're doing fine, don't you worry. The kids have found everything they need. I appreciate the use of the house, it's mighty comfortable. I'm just glad you and Josslyn got to go to that party. I didn't want to mess up your plans."

"It meant a lot to Ma." Seth felt his ribs tighten, remembering last night. The images of Rose sitting with Ian Hutchinson at supper and being held in his arms while they danced tormented him. She was everything he wanted—everything he could not have. "Although Ma's not working today."

"Good." Gabriel took another sip of coffee, looking thoughtful. "That ranch she works for should give her time off. No one is a harder worker than Josslyn. Someone said a woman owns that ranch?"

So, Seth thought, Gabriel didn't know about Aumaleigh. Sorry for his uncle, he turned away, staring at the porch posts that would need a new coat of paint come spring. "Yes. Ma is pretty happy working there, the happiest she's ever been. Watch out, she was sleeping when I left, but knowing Ma she'll be up before long and marching over here ready to whip up breakfast for you all."

"Thanks for the warning. It's good to know my sister is still as bossy as ever. Some things don't change, I guess." Gabriel gave a soft laugh, retreating back into the lean-to. "It's cold out here. I'm starting to freeze."

"Can't have you frozen solid for Christmas. Guess we could always use you to keep the food cold?" Seth joked. He'd like to stay and talk more, but work called. "I'll try to drop by for lunch."

"Let me guess, Joss is planning to be here then, too?"

"She has plans. I don't know what they are entirely, but beware. It's good to see you, Uncle. I was sorry to hear about Aunt Victoria."

"It was a hard couple of years." Gabriel's face tightened, standing in the shadows behind the doorway, grief carving its way onto his features. "But we got through it, and things are better now. I saw the livery on my way through town. You've built yourself quite a business. I'm proud of you."

"That means a lot." Seth tipped his hat, fighting emotions as he tromped to the back of his property. He cared about his uncle. He couldn't imagine what it must be like to lose your wife. Gabriel had been lucky. He had a good and loving marriage. But then again, he had married the right woman. And that seemed to be the key.

As he wrestled the stable door open and reached inside for the coiled up string of sleigh bells, Rose flashed into his head again. Rose, laughing hysterically as he'd held her in his arms, pink-cheeked and full of life, as sweet as Christmas candy. Rose, so relieved to see him in the church when she was cornered by Lawrence Latimer's desperate attempts to court her. Rose, her mouth softening as if wanting his kiss—

You weren't going to think about that, remember? Seth looped the string of bells over his shoulder, slammed the stable door shut and trekked down the snow-bound alley. The night shadows were gray now, making it easier to see as he hiked several blocks over to the back entrance to his livery.

A friendly whinny greeted him the instant he stepped through the door. Wally, snug and safe in his stall, popped his head over his gate and stretched as far as he could into the aisle, eager for first contact. Silly horse, he thought, affectionately.

"How's it going for you this morning, buddy?" Seth stopped to love him up, rub his nose and stroke his forehead. He received a few horsy kisses to his jaw for his efforts. "It's a day of leisure for you. Nothing to do, no place to go. How does that sound to you?"

Wally nibbled Seth's hat in answer. It was hard to tell if he was excited by the prospect of a lazy day or just unable to resist the hat.

"Can't say the same for you two fellas." Seth opened the neighboring stall. The gentle gelding inside obediently stepped out with his head down, so Seth could easily grab hold of his halter. "You're a good guy too, aren't you, Peanut?"

Peanut seemed to think so as he gave a big nod of his head, happy to be led down the aisle to the front of the barn. The horse stood patiently while Seth set aside the string of sleigh bells and measured out some grain (every other horse neighed in protest).

"You all will get your turn," he called out, but no one seemed happy about that. No surprise there. The complaints continued, whinnies echoing in the rafters. Only one horse stood quietly, ears up, watchful and hopeful. The sweet older gelding he'd picked up at the auction for Rose, just in case. After their talk, Seth was pretty sure she needed to take Charlie out for a spin. Maybe he would be a better match.

But the thought of seeing her again felt like a bullet to his chest. The worst sort of agony dug deep, down to his core, so powerful he had to stop, prop one hand against the wall and take a moment to steady himself. No doubt about it, it was going to be tough. The only thing harder than seeing her again was knowing he would have to walk away, that she could never be his.

Well, that was his own fault. He'd made the mistake of falling in love with the wrong woman. Because Rose was definitely the wrong woman. He knew, because Liz's parting words came back to him now. *If I can do better than you, then I should. It's my life and I deserve to be as happy as I can. If I choose you, then it will always be a matter of me knowing I could have had more.*

Those words had killed him at the time, but as the years had passed, he'd come to see the wisdom of them. Resolved, he grabbed the brush and began cleaning Peanut's coat. Bits of hay dust rose up along with the pleasant scent of warm horse.

"I'll get you all gussied up for the Fletchers," he explained, because Peanut was probably wondering. "Mr. Fletcher drove you last summer, remember? When they went to visit their family? Well, you'll be taking them there again."

Peanut gave a little nicker, like he was good with that. The gelding lapped up his grain, consuming every kernel and crumb in the trough.

"After we're done with the Fletchers, I'll take you out to McPhee Manor, Charlie." Seth bent, carefully brushing Peanut's underbelly, doing his best not to flinch at the thought of facing her. "I know you're going to like Rose. Everyone does."

Charlie pricked his ears curiously, as if happy to hear this new piece of information while Wally, farther down the aisle, gave an ardent neigh the instant he heard Rose's name.

Who could blame him? Seth thought. It was how he felt, too.

CHAPTER EIGHTEEN

"Daisy, Daisy, Daisy. Shouldn't you be busy at your own home?" Iris frowned her disapproval as she gave one more stir to the mixing bowl she held in the crook of her arm.

The McPhee kitchen was a madhouse and a crazy mess, with a lot of baking going on in preparation for the holiday. Rose glanced up from finishing the last frosting rose on the top of little Sadie Gray's birthday cake.

"Wilhelmina has everything covered," Daisy said with reassurance, shucking off her snowy coat and hanging it up near the door. "I love Wilhelmina. She was so worried we would let her go after the wedding. Not a chance. No way, no how. She needs the job and Hailie would be lost without her nanny. They've been together for so long, Wilhelmina is family. So she stays, and that means I can hop up here to help out when you're wildly busy."

"Oh, don't hop," Magnolia teased, oven mitt in hand as she knelt in front of the open oven door. The gingerbread cookies looked perfect and she reached in to slide them out. "It would be much better to walk. Or sprint. Or run. Or skip. But hopping uphill is just too much work."

Everybody groaned at Magnolia and her wacky sense of humor. Undaunted, Magnolia shut the oven door and grabbed a spatula. "What? It's true. Anyway, we only have a busy morning. After this, our orders are finished."

"Because tomorrow is Christmas Eve," Rose stepped back to study her masterpiece critically. All the little green leaves looked perfectly pointed, vining their way around the two layer cake. A variety of colorful frosting flowers dotted the white frosting like a fanciful flower garden gone whimsical. She hoped Sadie would be happy as she reached for a bakery box. "I can't believe it's here already. What if we aren't done with the presents?"

"I have most of the baskets done," Iris piped up, lifting her mixing bowl over the prepared cake pans set side by side on the counter. She expertly poured the batter, shepherding it with her wooden spoon. "It's just the perishable stuff left to do."

"And the sewing," Rose added, winding a length of string around the box to secure it and tying it up in a bow.

"We'll get it finished in time," Daisy said blithely, tying on her apron. "I'm here to help."

"And doesn't the new bride look blissful this morning?" Rose asked her sisters.

"Yes. Glowing," Magnolia agreed.

"Absolutely radiant." Iris scraped her mixing bowl to get every drop of batter. "Marriage must agree with you."

"I'll admit, it's not bad so far." Blushing prettily, Daisy sauntered up to the counter. "The first eighteen hours or so have been magnificent. The best eighteen hours of my life."

"Good to know," Magnolia said mischievously, rearranging the gingerbread men on the cooling rack to make enough room for the last one. "After all, I'll be having a wedding soon. And a wedding night."

"Please, you're making me blush." Daisy washed her hands at the sink, and gave a little huff. Apparently back to the no-nonsense Daisy they knew so well. "How many cakes do we have left for today?"

"Just two," Iris said on her way to the stove with a round cake pan balanced carefully in both hands. Magnolia rushed to open the oven door for her. "After this, that is."

"Then I'll whip them up." Daisy reached for the hand towel. "Magnolia can bake the bread for tomorrow's mercantile delivery and then we're done with the baking. That leaves decorating and delivering, and that won't take long."

"I can run out and deliver a few things while we're waiting for the cookies and cakes to cool." Rose maneuvered Sadie's boxed cake into one of her crates. "We still have today's delivery at the mercantile to do and I want to drop off Gemma's present, in case she doesn't work tomorrow."

"Right, then. Go on." Iris nodded her approval, rushing over to pluck the fresh bread off their racks. The delicious, doughy scent filled the air. Yummy. "I'll pack these up, you go get your coat. We're on a tight schedule here."

"Don't worry, we'll get it all done," Rose assured her much more confidently than she felt. She forced a smile to her lips, so no one would guess the truth. As long as she didn't think about Seth, her chest didn't hurt. She'd slept terribly last night, tossing and turning in her comfortable bed. At a loss, she crossed the kitchen, hurrying to grab her coat.

"I miss Oscar." Magnolia's voice followed her down the hall. "The wood box is empty again. He was so good at keeping it full. I'm too busy to go fill it."

"We could hire him." Rose skidded to a dead stop, spun around and fought to keep the excitement from her voice. This was exactly what she was going to suggest once she'd figured out a way to bring it up so Iris would say yes! "It would be great. We wouldn't have to haul in wood, and he could use the job."

"It would be wasteful." Iris carefully piled the last loaf into a basket and settled it into one of the crates. "We can carry in our own wood. It doesn't cost us a thing."

"But we need to think bigger than that." Rose retraced her steps toward the kitchen. "Especially if we want to expand the bakery."

"*You* want to expand." Iris hefted one of the crates off the counter, hiding a smile. "I'm happy with the way things are."

Rose bit her lip, not wanting to point out that things were changing. Come spring, it would be just the two of them running their business. It felt a little lonely to think about that, only Iris and her in this big kitchen stirring up batter and whipping up frosting. It just wouldn't feel right. "Wouldn't it be better to do some good with our money? Think of all the people we could help by providing jobs. Not just Oscar, but there are other people struggling right here in our town. It's just something to think about."

"When you say it like that, I feel like a Mr. Scrooge by saying no." Iris sidled past her, lugging the crate. "But I do miss all the excitement of the bakery we used to work at. The families coming in to order goodies at the counter. It was rewarding to hear all the children exclaiming over the decorated baked goods."

"Remember those cookies you used to make with animal faces?" Rose saw that soft spot in Iris—the one for children.

As a former schoolteacher, Iris adored kids. It hadn't been her choice to leave her former profession—tragedy had made that decision for her. But Iris couldn't hide a longing look as she set the crate by the front door. "Yes, I do remember those cookies. The cow shaped cookies were my favorite. And the kids would get so delighted over them."

"You made a lot of children and families happy with those cookies." It was merely the truth. Rose shrugged into her winter coat, aching for her sister. Iris had lost so many dreams all in an instant. Didn't she deserve at least having one wish come true? "Remember when we were working at the bakery in Chicago, and we would talk about owning a bakery one day while we worked in the kitchen?"

"I remember." Iris's sigh was wistful as she gazed up at the ceiling, momentarily caught in those memories, of a time when they'd dreamed. "We always made plans about how our bakery would be. A striped awning out front. A display in the window. Free cookies with every purchase for the children in the family."

Then she seemed to shake herself out of her reverie. "That was a different time. We were just playing, that was all."

"You don't have to be afraid of having this dream, Iris." Rose felt her eyes burn as she buttoned her last button. She reached out, squeezing her sister's hand. "I know it's scary because it makes you vulnerable. If you want something and risk your heart on it, then you can lose it, too."

Seth popped into her mind, but she pushed him out. This wasn't about her heart. It was about Iris's.

"Just think about it," Rose encouraged, hearing the *clip-clop* of steeled hooves outside. Cal must be pulling up with Poppy. "In the meantime, don't work too hard. I'll be back in a jiffy."

"Drive carefully," Iris advised. "And I put a shopping list in with the bread. Tell Gemma we'll pick up the order with tomorrow's delivery."

"Will do!" Rose heaved up the crate, waited for her sister to open the door and sailed out into the brutally cold morning—only to skid to a stop and nearly drop the crate (Sadie's cake!). Panicked, she caught it just in time, but her heart kicked up into a panicked, adrenaline-fueled fury. Hard to tell if it was because she'd almost ruined the cake or if it was because of the grim-faced man holding the reins of a new horse.

"I know you said Poppy was just fine." Seth had no smile for her, no friendly greeting. His black Stetson, pulled at a low angle, hid his gaze but she could feel the impact of it—as impenetrable as steel. He gave the gelding next to him a pat. "Why don't you give Charlie a try for today? He is a good boy, I promise. He won't run away with your sleigh."

"I l-like that in a horse," she stuttered, trying to get her bearings, but it was impossible. She felt knocked off center with the way he stared at her like that—like he was seeing right through her, as if she didn't exist to him. He could have been talking to a closed door instead of to her. She forced her feet to carry her down the steps and into the falling snow, knees feeling like jelly, her feet completely numb. Her heart hammered crazily. "You didn't have to go to the trouble, Seth."

"It's my job. I put on some jingle bells, too." A muscle jumped along his angled jaw. "I want every customer to be a happy customer."

"Is that what I am, just a customer?" Rose wasn't exactly sure where the boldness came from, but it filled her up until she charged down the walkway with the power of it. "I thought we were a good deal more than that."

"Well, I suppose you could say we've been friends forever." His tone was light, an attempt to be friendly, as if he were trying to go back to the easy, natural conversations they'd had before everything went wrong last night. Before the almost kiss.

"You know that's not what I mean." She saw him reach out to take the crate from her, and she jerked it away. As if she would let him. "Friends don't avoid eye-contact all evening. Friends don't refuse to say another word to you. Friends don't leave a party without saying goodbye."

"I get it. We're friends." His baritone boomed, his large hands fisted as he stood there, all black from head to toe, bleak against the crisp white snow.

Like a shadow, she thought as she eased the crate onto the floor between the first and second seats. There was something about the way he'd said the word *friends* that made her let the silence stretch for a few longs beats.

She straightened up, facing him, determined not to let him know how much he'd hurt her. By not wanting to kiss her. By not wanting anything more between them. So, he wasn't falling in love with her. That was loss enough. But she knew she'd lost his friendship, too.

She'd missed him last night. She'd wanted to sit next to him at supper and spend the evening laughing with him. Right now she missed the easy-going accord between them. She missed the man who made her laugh, who took care of her, who would search the whole county if that's what it took to find her a kissy horse.

"Maybe you're acting this way because you want to stay friends." The words popped out, more honest than she'd ever been, moving toward him when common sense told her to get in the sleigh and drive away. Preserve her dignity, keep her affections to herself and escape before he figured them out. But she couldn't do that, not to Seth. "Maybe you don't see me in that special way. So why did you try to kiss me last night?"

"Because I was an idiot. I wasn't thinking." His answer sounded honest too, so sincere she couldn't begin to doubt it. He planted his fists on his hips, booted feet braced apart, a man who meant what he said, a man who didn't give his heart easily.

She knew that. So why had she thought he could fall for her so effortlessly? She hung her head, staring at her footprints in the snow for a second, just to try to get hold of her feelings. A lot of disappointment. A ton of disillusionment. Another painful crack in her heart.

"Well, that was blunt but honest and very good to know." She let out a small sigh and climbed blindly into the sleigh. Maybe her vision was a little blurry—or maybe it was the icy wind burning her eyes. She found the reins by feel and lifted them off the polished wood dash. "Thanks for Charlie."

"No problem." His words came out clipped, almost sharp, as if he were angry and frustrated. His boots made scrunching sounds in the snow as he paced closer.

She didn't want him close. What if he saw how upset she was? Really saw, you know, like the tears in her eyes and the heartbreak she wasn't sure she could hide. Staring hard at the dash in front of her, she tugged on the right rein. "I'll have him back to you by the end of the work day."

"It doesn't have to be today." Nearer now, Seth's deep voice didn't sound as steely. "Go ahead and—"

"No, I'll have a decision for you today," she interrupted, firm and clear. The sooner she got this over with, the better. He was the kind of man she'd never thought she would find. But he hadn't fallen madly in love with her, he hadn't fallen at her feet. She'd let herself get caught up in a fairy-tale—of falling in love with her friend, her best friend—and that was her own fault. She should have listened to her mother's advice.

Why wasn't the horse going? Feeling foolish and horribly embarrassed and really, really wanting to leave, she tugged harder on the right rein. But Charlie didn't move a single step forward. He just turned his head to the right and gave a puzzled nicker.

"You forgot to give him the signal to go." Quiet, Seth's words, resonating with understanding.

Perhaps not fooled at all.

Instead of giving the gelding a light slap on the flank, to get him going, Seth reached over the traces and grabbed both reins, holding the gelding in place. "I hurt you, didn't I?"

"Not really." No, she realized. This was all her doing. She'd been the one to fall for him, when he'd done nothing but be a good friend to her. It killed her to lift her chin, but she blinked hard to clear the emotion from her eyes before she met his gaze.

Maybe, if she held her chest perfectly still so that not even her heart could beat, nothing would show on her face and he'd never know what she truly felt for him. She tightened her grip on the reins. "The heart feels what it feels or in your case doesn't. That's not your fault, Seth."

"I can't let you drive off like this." He didn't let Charlie take a single step. "Rose, I—"

"Let go of the reins," she interrupted, her jaw tight. "I mean it, Seth."

"No, I won't do it." This was too important. He could not let this moment pass. He could see the pain he'd caused her. That was the last thing he'd intended. He ran his hand down the reins until they met hers. Through the layers of his leather glove and her hand-knit ones, he felt that kick of awareness. It arced into him like an electric charge, firing through him, lightning to his soul. "I thought it might be best to just back off, but I was wrong. I didn't realize. I've been trying so hard to convince myself that I can't feel what I feel, I've convinced you, too. That isn't fair, because what you think about me *not feeling* isn't true."

"That's a pretty complicated way to say something." She looked past him, staring hard at the pricked ears of the horse. Judging by the tightness of her jaw, she might be ready to rip the reins out of his hands and smack him with them—or at the very least, drive off.

His heart squeezed, so full of love for her he couldn't see straight. He let go of the leather straps and braced one hand on the dash and the other on the seatback, so close to her he could smell the lilac fragrance of her hair and see the green swirls of color in the blue of her irises. Pain lived there. That tore down the pathetic defenses he'd tried to put up. In the end, nothing could protect him against Rose. What he felt for her was too powerful.

"I really care for you." He didn't bother to keep the tenderness from his voice, he let his own hurt show. It was too powerful. "But I know how this ends. You're going to break my heart, Rose."

"Me?" Confused, she blinked up at him, so sweet and kind-hearted that it was clear she really didn't see it. She really didn't know. Her lower lip trembled. "You're the one doing the breaking here."

He squeezed his eyes shut, trying to survive the impact of her words. So, that's how much she cared. He hadn't realized it. It was everything he wanted. Everything. He winced, wanting to forget his hard lessons learned, haul her into his arms and kiss her until she was breathless and clinging to him, until nothing mattered—not the future or the past—just the two of them and their love.

But down deep, he knew better. He felt torn apart, cleaved in two as he eased onto the seat beside her. There was no other way to do this, he had to be direct. "I love you, Rose."

"You do?" Her slim eyebrows arched up in surprise. Hope made the green swirls in her eyes shimmer like emeralds.

Seeing that, it made everything worse. He bowed his head, staring hard at his hands, hating reality. It was much better living in the dream of Rose—of laughing with her, dancing with her, wanting to kiss her in the snow.

"I've been here before," he told her. "When I was courting Liz. Like you, she was financially much better off than me."

"You think I'm like the lady who broke your heart and left you for a richer man?" Rose's sweet face crinkled up with distress and hurt.

"No, not at all," he told her swiftly, seeing he was hurting her again without meaning to. He unfisted one hand and laid it over the top of her left one, ignoring the wrench of his heart at the contact. Touching her felt so *right*. That could not be denied. "But we are now in different worlds, you and me. You belong in that fancy mansion over there, and I'm just a blacksmith. I can't offer you the kind of life a wealthier man can. It's a plain fact."

"Love isn't about money or big houses." Tears stood in her eyes, gathering but refusing to fall. "But that's not the real reason you're saying all this, is it? You seem very sure I am going to break your heart."

"I am," he admitted, simply shrugging one shoulder. He knuckled back his hat, accidentally knocking a little snow off the brim. "Liz hurt me very badly. I did not see her answer coming. I felt sure she would accept my proposal."

"I'm really sorry for that." Rose's lower lip trembled even as she struggled to keep it still. "I wish she hadn't hurt you. I can see how deeply you must have cared for her."

"I was angry for a long time," he admitted. "Not to mention humiliated and disillusioned."

"Sure. You were planning a life with her." Rose tilted her head to one side, empathetic, her soft alto full of caring. "You wanted to love her for the rest of your life. Otherwise you wouldn't have proposed to her. Anyone would be devastated. I can see you still are."

"Not in the way you think," he admitted with a grimace. "One day I saw her down the street when I was heading to check out a horse in Deer Springs. She looked good, beautiful in a fine gown with lots of ruffles and lace. She was walking down the boardwalk with her sister, laughing away. She looked happy. Truly happy."

He stopped, stared down at his hands again and gave a heavy sigh. "That's when I knew she was right. She made the wise decision. Marriage is hard. Love is harder. I've watched my ma struggle through two marriages and a heap of unhappiness. I saw how my father fell apart when he got hurt and couldn't work. I saw how my stepfather took out his anger at life's hardships with the business end of a belt."

Rose winced, remembering the story Seth had told about his stepfather's abuse. Of course he'd seen a lot of unhappiness. So had she. Her parents had once loved each other so, so much, only to have that precious love fade away. But Seth, he straightened his shoulders, not a broken-hearted man at all. Whatever was hurting him was not his former fiancée's betrayal.

"Liz did us both a favor," he confessed, his voice dipping low with sincerity. He meant this. "The two of us would have been doomed from the start. I would always have been trying to make up for what I couldn't give her. There would have come a day when she wished that the life I'd given her could be more—that I could be more."

"Oh, Seth." A single tear fell, tracking down her cheek. She curled her fingers through his, soaking in the warmth of his hand and the summery feeling in her heart at the connection. She savored it, because she knew this was the last time she would ever feel it. He wasn't going to change his mind. A thousand arguments crowded onto her tongue, but the sorrow and grief lining his handsome face stopped her. This was hard for him. Very hard. And he believed every word he said.

"Here's the truth." He turned toward her, leaning in to press his forehead to hers for a moment—just a moment—before leaning back, letting the snow tumble down between them. His eyes darkened to pure, hopeless black as he unlaced his fingers from hers and took his hand away. "I love you. In fact, I love you so much I want to give you the best life there is, the best happiness, the best of everything. But I can't give you that, I can't give you the best."

"Oh, Seth." She tugged at a frayed piece of yarn on her glove, watching it unravel a few stitches. That's how her heart felt, coming apart, thread by thread. He loved her. The words she'd wanted to hear, that were so precious to her. Love was the reason he was letting her go? "You have this all wrong. Money isn't that important."

"Are you kidding me?" He shook his head, stubborn, not willing to consider her side of things. "This isn't about money. This is about love. I want you to have the happiest life, and if you find someone who can give you that, then that's what I want for you. You have all the options in the world, Rose. You're gorgeous and sweet and kind. And there are a lot of men around here who can give you your every dream."

"But what do you know about my dreams?" Those tears shimmered, growing, ready to spill over at any moment, seeming to magnify the green-blue of her eyes and her pure honesty. "It seems to me you're deciding what's best for me."

"One day I want to see you walking down the boardwalk looking radiant and joyful, on top of the world, a woman who has everything.

Even if I have to let you go to get that." He reached out to brush a few snowflakes from her hair, tender. So tender. "Ian Hutchinson is a good guy. I know his family. I've shoed all their horses, even a few of his. You can tell a lot about a man by the way he treats his animals. He's a good catch, Rose." Seth's voice cracked, low and revealing, as he turned away.

"Maybe I don't want to catch Ian Hutchinson." A hint of anger worked into her voice. "And I don't like much of what you think of me. I'm not materialistic. I'm not that shallow."

"I know that. You are amazing." He climbed off the seat, landing solidly in the snow. Feet planted, back straight, shoulders set. Determined, he forced himself to face her, wincing at the hurt and anger playing across her delicate, oval face. "Let Ian court you. Marry him. I want you to have the best of every great happiness there is."

Because I love you so much. That's what he didn't add. She deserved a fancy house and every luxury, servants to do the work, cooks to prepare her meals and a man who could give her all she'd ever wanted. That was his dream for her. He loved her that much. He figured he wasn't her greatest dream, but she was his.

"I'm mad as Hades at you, Seth Daniels." She grabbed up the reins again, chin jutting out mutinously, tears spilling down her cheeks. "If that's what you think of me, if you think what I want is a rich man and a fancy house, then you don't know me at all, and I'm glad we're no longer friends. In fact, I don't ever want to see you again."

"I'm sorry, Rose." He truly was. Seeing her like this, crying and hurting, killed him. His instincts shouted at him to run to her, to haul her into his arms and kiss her pain away, but he'd made his decision. He'd made the right decision for her. He was protecting both of their hearts.

As Charlie trotted away with Rose in her new sleigh, jingle bells chiming, it felt as if his heart had fallen to the ground at his feet, raw and bleeding. Nothing in his life had ever hurt more than watching her go because she was the one. The only one he would love forever. He would never love anyone as deeply or as mightily as he loved Rose McPhee.

CHAPTER NINETEEN

Men! What was wrong with them? All of them? Rose dried her eyes with the last dry corner of her handkerchief and gave a little sniff. She was so mad at Seth, she could beat him with a bread loaf. Smack him up-side the head with a cake. Whack him with the wicker basket over and over until it knocked some sense into him, but that wouldn't help, that wasn't what she really wanted. More hot tears seeped into her eyes thinking about him standing beside the sleigh, with love and regret lining his rugged face.

She'd never been angry like this before, wanting to hit a man with baked goods. What was wrong with her? Clueless, she collapsed back against the cushioned sleigh seatback, stopped at the far end of the driveway, safely out of sight of the house (and Seth). Worse, she couldn't seem to calm down.

Furious, she pocketed her handkerchief. Furious. She snatched up the reins and signaled Charlie to go.

The gelding obediently pulled her onto the county road, his head up, completely unaware of her tragedy. He clomped along, his steel horseshoes ringing on the hard-packed snow, taking her far away from Seth. For that she was grateful. The stupid, stubborn, wonderful man. He loved her? She arched a brow scathingly. Well, clearly he did not. He'd practically given her away to Ian Hutchinson—as if he had that right.

Now she'd lost him. She hung her head, feeling her chest collapse. There would be no more sleigh rides spent talking and laughing, no more funny incidents shared over misbehaving horses. He'd opened a door in her heart she hadn't known was there. He'd been her friend, then her best friend. How was she going to get over that?

She didn't know. As the countryside whizzed by in a blur of white, she felt as if she'd left every piece of her heart and soul on the snow at his feet. She'd wanted to give him everything, and he'd rejected her. Because he loved her.

More tears stung behind her eyes, but she didn't let them fall as Charlie pranced into town and came to a stop at the mercantile. Hollow and painfully empty, she climbed out of the sleigh. How come her entire body hurt, when only her heart was broken? She felt like she was one hundred and eighty years old as she scooped up the big basket of bread from the backseat floor and hobbled the short distance to the hitching post.

"Good morning, Rose!" a voice called out. Fred, the post office guy, tromped down the boardwalk, looking chipper and eager to start his workday. "That was quite a wedding celebration last night. Me and the wife ate so much of that good food and cake, we were ready to pop. Then we danced until way past our bedtimes. I'm payin' for it this morning. You McPhee girls really know how to throw a party."

"Glad you had such a good time." She forced a smile as Fred hurried on by. At least thinking of the party helped get her mind off her shattered heart. She reached for Charlie's rein and he bared his teeth at her.

Big, long, yellow teeth. He gave a terrifying high squeal. His brown gaze turned fierce, focused intently on her arm as if he wanted to take a big bite out of it.

She leaped back, safe behind the rail as he glared at her furiously. Apparently he didn't like her very much.

"What is wrong with that horse?" Lawrence Latimer rushed up to the rescue, his bowler hat balanced perfectly on the top of his round head. "Step back, fair lady. Let me help you with your troublesome steed."

"Thank you, Lawrence." She hated to admit it, but she was a little glad to see him. He might be a strange little man and he could talk without a break for longer than anyone she'd ever met, but he did have a heroic side.

"Odd, he calmed right down." Lawrence gave the knotted rein a tug with a flourish. "He's as gentle as a kitten with me. He didn't hurt you, did he?"

"Not at all." She blinked, staring in wonder at the gentle horse standing pleasantly at the hitching post, tied up and docile. You never would have guessed he'd tried to bite her. Maybe something startled him. Maybe he wasn't used to a woman's skirts swirling and rustling, and that had riled him up. She'd have to be more careful when she approached him next time.

"What happened to the little mare you were driving?" Lawrence asked, bowing to her like a duke at the queen's court, making a sweeping gesture with his hat. "She seemed much more agreeable for you."

"I was test-driving her. I still am, I think." She wasn't exactly sure if Seth had taken her back or not, but she didn't mention that as she headed down the boardwalk with Lawrence. It was best not to encourage conversation with Lawrence.

"In my humble experience," he began, launching into another one of his monologues. "It's best to stick with a horse that is easy to manage. If you find one that suits, it's wise to keep that horse. Looks are overrated. Sure, that's a fine gelding, but what good is a horse that attempts to bite you every time you approach him? I believe manageability is the key. That's why I drive a donkey. She might not be as eye-catching or as reputable as a pedigreed Arabian, but her temperament is what matters here—"

"I appreciate your thoughts, Lawrence, and your assistance." She stopped at the mercantile door, waiting as he opened it for her. Loneliness seemed to emanate from him. Maybe that was why he tried so hard in social situations—too hard, in fact. She stared down at the basket still tucked into the crook of her arm and gave him a loaf. "Merry Christmas to you. Do you have anyone to spend the holiday with?"

"Uh—" He blushed beet red and took the loaf from her. Judging by the way he hung his head, he didn't. "Thank you kindly for the bread. This smells wonderful. Reminds me of the baking my mother used to do. She could make a loaf of bread that could be a meal in itself."

"I hope you enjoy it," she said, meaning every word. She hesitated just inside the doorway. "Lawrence, if you do find yourself wanting some company on Christmas Eve, stop by the Rocking M. I mean, you're a neighbor, so it won't be much of a drive. We're all putting on a big supper for the cowboys who couldn't go home for Christmas. You don't need to bring a thing, and you'll be very welcome."

"Why, thank you, Rose." Lawrence's Adam's apple bobbed up and down. "I will. That means a lot."

"Be there by five o'clock," she advised. It was easy to remember that last year at this time, she was much like Lawrence, wearing secondhand clothes, carefully washed and pressed and patched. Trying to make ends meet and failing miserably, no matter how hard she and her sisters tried. Spending Christmas alone together with no presents—they had combined their extra pennies to buy yarn to knit an extra afghan for each of their beds.

"Don't come a moment too late. The cowboys are like a wild horde of barbarians before mealtime," she told Lawrence over her shoulder as she waltzed deeper into the store. "They snatch up all the food in a matter of minutes. We'll look forward to seeing you there."

"Thanks, Rose." Lawrence's throat worked and he had to look away. Finally, he closed the door and continued on his way down the boardwalk.

"Whew, I missed a bullet with that!" Gemma popped around the corner of a tall shelf, weaving around several groups of shoppers. "For a minute there, I thought he was coming in. I don't have the time today for his long-winded, uh, presence. Great! You brought the bread. We're completely sold out and folks are complaining."

"Good thing I came by early then," Rose told her, handing over the fragrant basket. "Although I owe you one. I gave it to Lawrence. I can drop it by on my afternoon delivery."

"That sounds fine, but one thing." Gemma handed the basket over the counter to her mother, who looked stressed and disapproving, perhaps due to the line of shoppers standing at the counter waiting to be helped. It was a busy morning. Gemma led Rose to the door, dropping her voice so it wouldn't carry. "I'm afraid I have some bad news. I begged my father to tell you myself, hoping maybe I could soften the blow."

"What is it? What's wrong?" Rose skidded to a halt, barely missing a wild pair of identical twin boys dashing to the candy display (school was out for the week). She hated seeing such distress on her friend's dear face. "What can I do to help?"

"Oh, it's Pa. He's as cheap as they come, a regular Scrooge when it comes right down to it. He's a miser and that's what this is about." Gemma flushed with anger. "I'm not speaking to him, if that makes any difference."

"I don't understand." Concerned, Rose reached out and caught Gemma's hand. "I hate seeing you so upset, though. Just take a deep breath. I'm sorry you and your father are arguing."

"Over you and your sisters." Gemma wrinkled her forehead apologetically. She gave a stray black lock a shove out of her copper-brown eyes. "Another bakery came in and gave Pa a lower bid for baked bread, and he took it. I told him not to, I told him you were my friends, and we should be loyal to you, but he accepted the deal anyway. I'm afraid this is the last morning we'll be needing your bread. I'm sorry, Rose. Maybe I should have fought harder for you."

"Gemma, that's okay." As distressed as Rose was, she was more so over poor Gemma who looked on the verge of tears. "You did more than anyone for us, and I'm so grateful for that. It's only bread. Don't be upset. The only downside here is not getting to talk with you every morning."

"You're not mad at me?" Gemma gave a watery sigh, the worry carved into her face fading away.

"Not in the slightest. It's only business, but you're our friend. That's far more important." She squeezed Gemma's hand as reassuringly as she could. "I don't want you to be upset about this anymore. You're still coming to the Christmas Eve party at the ranch, right?"

"Right, but I saw you talking to Lawrence." Gemma cast a dubious glance at the front window and the boardwalk beyond. (There was no sign of Lawrence). "Something tells me you invited him, too."

"That's because I have an idea," Rose confessed. She was certainly full of them. "Do you know what Lawrence needs?"

"A different hat? A clue?" Gemma answered with a wry sparkle in her eyes.

"A girlfriend." Rose dug into her coat pocket and pulled out a pencil and a bakery order form. She turned it over and handed it to Gemma. "You know your friend, Dottie at the Deer Springs Mercantile? Would you write her a note and ask her to come to the party tomorrow? I'm going to swing by and give this to her on my delivery run. If she needs a ride, we can send someone for her."

"That would be great. She's really nice. It would be fun to see her there." Gemma took the pencil and the slip of paper, setting it flat on the top of the pickle barrel before scribbling down a few sentences. "You aren't going to introduce her to Lawrence, are you?"

"That's exactly what I'm gonna do." Rose took the note and pencil when Gemma offered it and shoved it back into her pocket. "I have a feeling. Maybe they'll be a good match."

"You're devious, Rose. I like it."

"I know!" Rose took a backward step toward the door, checking to make sure there were no more children dashing around nearby to barge into. "By the way, what was the name of the bakery that beat us out?"

"It's called Dobson's Bakery." Gemma reached out and opened the door. The bell overhead chimed as frigid air rushed in. "I know nothing about them. I've never even heard of them before, but I did overhear them say they are located in Deer Springs and they're expanding."

"Expanding, huh?" That didn't sound good. There was a limited amount of bakery business in a county this small and she wasn't going to lose out to low-bidding under cutters. "Well, thanks. See you tomorrow, oh! I almost forgot my shopping list."

"Oh, right. For your Christmas gifts. It's a nice thing you and your sisters are doing."

"Oh, it'll be more fun than anything, especially since it's a secret only you and Penelope know, besides us, that is." Rose dug the shopping list out of her pocket. "We'll need this by tomorrow morning."

"I'll have it wrapped and ready." Gemma plucked the list out of Rose's hands. "Have a good day."

"You too! Talk to you soon." She bounced onto the boardwalk, where snow hazed the air and gave a crisp, Christmassy feeling. She just wished she could soak it in, but her heart was too heavy to do it justice. Not to mention losing out on another account.

With her mind on this mysterious Dobson's Bakery, she paraded up to the hitching post and reached for the knotted reins. Charlie opened his eyes, took one look at her and lunged, huge teeth bared. A shrill, terrifying *"Eeeeee"* rang in the air as he hit the hitching post rail with his chest.

Rose rocked back, dropping her empty basket, adrenaline surging into her veins. Her heart stuttered thickly, afraid, as Charlie snapped his teeth at her, trying hard to get over the rail and bite her.

"Calm down, Charlie. Easy now. Why don't you like me?" Rose eased back a few more feet until the gelding judged her to be a safe distance away and let his lips fall back over to cover his teeth. Within seconds, he'd relaxed, looking like the most mild-mannered gelding in all of creation.

"Having a problem, there?" Seth's baritone rumbled through the air, full of care and wonderfulness.

Oh, no! Why did it have to be Seth? She squeezed her eyes shut, not wanting to see him, wishing he wasn't the one to come to her rescue. Where was Lawrence when you needed him? And what kind of world was this when she was hoping for *Lawrence?*

The steeled *clink* of horse shoes came to a stop and a horse's friendly neigh sang in the air like a song. Up and down it went, full of horsy gusto.

"Hi, Wally." Focusing on the friendly draft horse was much easier than facing the man. She made a wide birth around Charlie, tossed her basket into the back of the sleigh and stepped into the street to give Wally a nose pat.

Ecstatic, Wally gave one final, excited whinny before nibbling her chin with his velvety lips. His long whiskers tickled, but it was sheer sweetness. His unbridled affection was like sprinkles on frosting—it made everything better. It eased the shock and discomfort of seeing Seth again.

"If I hadn't seen it with my own eyes, I wouldn't have believed it." Seth's boots hit the snow with a scrunching thud and pounded over to the now docile horse. Charlie even offered his nose for petting. Seth frowned. "I don't think he likes you, Rose."

"I know, and why not? I'm nice to animals." She tried to swivel her eyes away from Seth and focus them on Wally, but they didn't want to obey. They kept trying to cut sideways, as if drawn to the tall, burly blacksmith. She loved him. He was in love with her too. And he made her angry.

"I see the problem," Seth said, his voice drown out by Charlie's vicious *"Eeeeeee"* and a woman's startled gasp as she darted away from Charlie lunging at her as she passed on the boardwalk. "I don't think he likes women. Any woman. Tell you what. I'll trade Wally for him, just for today. What do you think?"

Oh, she was tempted to tell him what she thought. Too bad she wasn't armed with a bread loaf. She missed him. She missed that sparkle in his eye whenever he saw her. She missed the way his easygoing grin tugged up the corners of his mouth when he talked with her. She missed that singular, one-of-a-kind connection to him. If only she could tell him. If only telling him would make any difference.

Look at him, head down, all business, treating her like a customer. He'd closed his heart to her. He'd rejected her, he'd insulted her by saying she was just like Liz, a woman who clearly didn't mind using and hurting people. How could he accuse her of such a thing?

"You don't have to bother." She just wanted her best friend back—and she wanted that kiss he'd never delivered on. She lifted her chin, too proud to let him know it. "I have one delivery to make, and I can walk from here. It's no big deal. I can wait until Magnolia swings by on her delivery route. She can pick me up."

"But what about your sleigh?" Seth asked over the jingle as he unbuckled Charlie's harness. "You don't want to leave it in town."

"*My* sleigh? Isn't it one of yours or something?" She arched a brow, really seeing the vehicle for the first time. Okay, it was gorgeous, all sleek polished chestnut with shining brass trim. Royal blue cushions contrasted with the rich wood and a string of twinkling silver bells raced up and down the harness, giving the occasional jingle as the wind caught one of the bells. She'd been too upset to notice.

"You said you wanted your own sleigh," Seth explained as he led Charlie out of the traces and tied him up. "I have my eye on a smaller one if you'd rather, but I thought the two-seater might suit you better with all those deliveries you make. Last time I saw your sleigh, it was so full there was no room for your feet."

"I managed to squeeze them in." She gave Wally another pat. He responded by nosing in beneath her hat brim and lipping her bangs gently, moving across her forehead to leave a row of kisses behind. She just melted. "You're a good horse, Wally."

Wally nodded, gazing down at her with sweet chocolate eyes, as if he was so glad she thought so too.

"If this two-seater is too big for you, let me know." Seth tromped over to free Wally from his bindings. "We can get you a smaller one. Are you all ready for Christmas?"

"Really? We're going to make small talk?" Rose spun away because she couldn't look at him for a single second longer. In fact, a second was too long. She started marching. "I'll walk."

"Remember the last time you walked down the street?" Seth called after her. It was hard to tell if it was humor or concern in his tone. "You fell down and showed off your long johns to half the town."

"That's okay, because I'm wearing my pretty flowered ones today," she shot back, carefully extricating Sadie's cake from the crate. "Really, I'm fine."

"When a woman says that, it means she's not fine." Seth led Wally out of his traces, one gentle hand on the gelding's bridle. "I might not know much, but I'm smart enough to know that."

"Smart wouldn't be the word I would call you." She struck off down the street, letting her words ring out, carrying on the wind. While she didn't look up, she could sense the curious gazes of several shoppers watching from the boardwalk. She kept going.

Okay, she was angry. She had every right. He'd made her fall in love with him and then he'd broken her heart—and he'd done it so nicely she couldn't even call him out on it. So she kept walking, blinking against the snowflakes hurling into her face and sticking on her eyelashes, trying to drown out the distressed whinnying of Wally who seemed to be trying to call her back.

For some reason, the story Seth had told her about Wally and the horse auction popped into her mind and she had the hysterical mental image of the gigantic gelding tearing off down the street after her, perhaps dragging Seth and the sleigh heedlessly along behind him. A snort of laughter bubbled out of her and then she wasn't laughing anymore, she was on the verge of crying and that wasn't going to happen. Not right here in the middle of town with everyone watching. Gossip like that would move like greased lightning. She was already notorious enough. She refused to add to it.

Chin up, fighting to look dignified, she cut across the street and headed down the residential lane. Trees lined the streets, silent and stoic, bare limbs lifted up to the sky as if to catch the falling snow. A few dogs barked from front porches and yards. Children's laughter belled in the air as she passed kids in their yards building snowmen or snow forts or rolling up snowballs to pelt each other with.

"Miss Rose!" A girl in trousers bounded into the street with a snowball tucked in each mittened hand. Her blond hair was tied into two stiff braids, her bangs peeking out like fringe from beneath her boy's wide-brimmed hat. "Is that my cake?"

"It sure is. A flower cake, just like you wanted." She couldn't help but adore the girl who was as cute as a button. "How does it feel to be nine years old?"

"Just the same." She gave a one-shouldered shrug, eyes bright with excitement. "Except for the presents and the cake. Is it chocolate? You didn't forget?"

"I looked over Iris's shoulder to make sure she did it right. Of course it's chocolate." Rose hiked up onto the shoveled walkway. A small legion of kids, both girls and boys, parted, snowballs clutched in hand as they gazed hopefully at the bakery box, knowing what was inside. "She put in extra chocolate, so it's going to be extra special. The best cake she's made so far."

"Yum." Sadie beamed with anticipation, skipping along beside her, fearless of falling in the snow (sure, because she was wearing trousers. What a good idea).

The front door swung open and Milo the sheriff grinned out at her, looking less polished and put together than he usually did when he was out on the street, working to protect the citizens of Bluebell from criminals. He looked harried. Running a child's birthday party must be seriously challenging his skills.

"Rose, so glad to see you." He took the box from her, relief lining his handsome face. He really was a nice looking man. Rose couldn't help but remember a little incident between him and Iris a few months back. A rather heated discussion, and she was curious as Milo glanced around, checking the yard and the street. "Did your sister come with you or are you by yourself?"

Now, wasn't that just a tad interesting? Rose couldn't help smiling. "Just me. Iris is home finishing up the last of our baking. How are you doing?"

"Managing." He set the cake down on a small table beside the door and reached into his back pocket. "Here's your payment. Tell Iris thanks for me, for that extra chocolate in the cake."

"You must have super good hearing to have overheard that," Rose commented, but then, when a man cared about a woman—really cared about her—he did little things like that. Went the extra distance to take an interest in her, to do things for her, never to hurt her. Clearly that was not Seth.

"I do have good hearing, which comes in handy when I have so many kids to keep track of. I was just interested in what you had to say about the cake." He turned his attention to the group of snowball battling munchkins who had gone back to their hurling snowballs and howling with laughter.

Well, the handsome sheriff might be denying his interest in Iris, but his ears had gone pink, so that had to be a sign, right?

Totally pleased, Rose pocketed the money. "Thanks, Milo. Have a good rest of your day."

"Oh, I'm sure I will survive it." He flashed a grin.

What a nice thing it was that a man like that was interested in Iris. Rose bid farewell, dodged four snowballs and spotted Wally standing at the curb all by himself, hitched to her new sleigh. When the horse shook his head, the jingle bells gave a shivery jingle. He neighed to her in sheer excitement and held out his nose for some love.

Now that was the way to show affection, Rose thought as she rubbed his super-soft nose. The big gelding's chin landed on her shoulder and nudged her forward against his neck, where he held her there in a horsy version of a hug. Full of sweetness, Rose wrapped her arms around his neck as far as they would go. This was a perfect horse, and a little loving comfort was exactly what she needed because she realized something, standing there in the street.

Seth had lent her his horse, his best friend. Seth might be treating her like a customer, but Wally was his personal horse. A horse he never rented out. Here Seth was, taking such good care of her, making sure she had a good horse to drive, even when he'd broken her heart.

He wasn't over Liz, she realized. That's why he'd done it. Tears blurred her vision, because it was hard to be angry about that.

CHAPTER TWENTY

Aumaleigh McPhee wished she hadn't left those final few items on her Christmas gift list for the last minute, but there was nothing to be done about it now, she thought as Buttons pulled her around the corner and town came into sight.

She sat up straighter on the sleigh seat, full of purpose. She could absolutely do this. It would be quick in and out of the post office and the mercantile. Her chances of catching sight of a certain former beau would be slight anyway. Probably miniscule. Likely Gabriel, his wife and son were tucked away in Seth's house enjoying family time. So, no need to worry, right?

"Good afternoon, Miss McPhee." Oscar called out to her as the post office came into sight. He was limping along the side of the road carrying a metal pail.

She smiled instantly in greeting. He was bundled up well against the cold in his layers of ragged clothing. She'd seen him around plenty of times, always in the distance, always wondering about him, but she'd never tried to search him out. That Rose had done so and offered him a job felt almost shameful now.

For so long, in those difficult years of taking care of her difficult mother, she'd had no time or energy to look beyond the demands of her own life. And then, once Mother was gone, she didn't have the means, struggling to pay what she could of Mother's debts. But now she had time and means. And after the way Oscar had worked so hard for the girls, he'd caught her attention. Not to mention splitting and carrying wood into the kitchen house in exchange for his breakfast. That had told her all she needed to know about Oscar.

"Hello, there." She drew Buttons to a stop. "That's a big fish you have. That must be your supper."

"My Christmas supper, ma'am." He gave a sheepish nod and stared down at the snow between his patched boots.

"Fresh salmon is one of the tastiest things there is." She had no idea where he lived or what his circumstances were, but she knew he was alone. "Do you have Christmas Eve plans? We would love to have you join us at the kitchen house for supper. You don't have to bring a thing, we're just getting everyone together to celebrate. There's nothing better than good food and good company. Will you come?"

"Rose has already invited me, ma'am." Oscar released hold of his bucket with one hand to tip his battered hat. "I told her I wouldn't miss it. She told me it would hurt her feelings if I didn't come."

"That sounds like Rose to me." Aumaleigh lifted her reins to give them a light snap. "Come by around four-thirty or so. Looking forward to seeing you."

"Thank you, ma'am." Courteous and gentlemanly, Oscar gave a chin jut of farewell.

The truth about people was this: No matter their outward appearance, a person's inner character will always shine through. You just had to wait for it.

Buttons seemed happy to get going, for the wind was picking up, blowing colder than it had been all winter. Brrr. Aumaleigh shivered and reached down for the extra driving robe at her feet. She shook it out, layering it over the other two, snuggling in for warmth. Fortunately that gave her something to think about as she sped into town instead of looking for Gabriel under every Stetson she saw.

"What a good girl," Aumaleigh praised when Buttons came to a free spot at the hitching post as close to the post office as they could get (it was crowded, everyone was out and about). She grabbed her reticule, letting it dangle by her wrist, and hopped out of the sleigh. "I know it's terribly cold, but you haven't complained one bit."

Buttons nickered low in her throat, as if she didn't mind. What a dear mare. Aumaleigh snatched the horse blanket from the floor, unfolding it quickly. She'd been lucky to get such a mare. Seth had found Buttons for her at one of the many horse auctions he attended in the county. She'd been a sad and neglected little thing back then and, surprisingly, was exactly in her price range.

"That Seth," she told Buttons as she went up on tiptoe to drape the warm wool blanket over the mare's back. (The blanket was a pretty light blue shade which complimented Buttons' gray coat and snowy white mane and tail wonderfully). "I've always suspected he took a loss when he sold you to me."

Buttons blew out her breath in a raspberry, batting her sweet eyes as if she suspected it too. Lovingly, Aumaleigh stroked the mare's forehead before looping one rein around the post, not bothering to knot it. Buttons would never leave without her.

"I'll be as fast as I can, pretty girl." Aumaleigh promised, turning her attention to the boardwalk that was as crowded as she'd ever seen. Women and children scurried from shop to shop. Men stood in front of display windows looking puzzled as to what to buy. But she headed away from the shops, intending to do the quickest errand first.

That's when a familiar curve of a muscled shoulder, covered with fine black wool, caught her attention. The familiar man stood on the street with his back to her, chatting with Doc Hartwell. The two men's voices carried on the wind, blowing in the opposite direction, so she couldn't hear more than the low rumble of his baritone. But it was still deeply memorable, even after all these years. Tears burned behind her eyes as she snuck a quick glance at Gabriel. He stood as tall as ever, so strong and true.

Overcome, she dashed down the boardwalk and yanked open the post office door, landing inside the shop with a breathless thump of her shoes on the floor. Hardly decorous or dignified, but at least he hadn't spotted her.

"Aumaleigh!" Fred greeted her from behind his counter, giving his cap a tug upward to see her better. He was grinning wide, full of cheer. His red suspenders, bright against his white shirt and black trousers must be a nod to the Christmas season. He spun around, pulling mail out of one of the cubbyhole boxes lining the wall behind him. "Your ears had to be burning. Doc Hartwell was just in here not a few minutes ago, and we got to talking about the food you served at your niece's wedding party. Might I say it was the tastiest vittles I've ever put in my mouth? Too bad we didn't meet when I was a young bachelor. I would have scooped you up so fast, it would have made your head spin."

"Josslyn did a lot of the cooking too." Aumaleigh arched a brow at him, used to his cheeky ways. "Maybe it's her you should be praising."

"Not the way I hear it, and I'm usually right about these things. I talk to a lot of folks." With a friendly wink, Fred laid the handful of envelopes on the scarred wooden counter. "We're all still talking about that party. Christmas is bound to be a let-down now. It's a sad thing you did to us, Aumaleigh."

"Magnolia's wedding will be in the spring." She gathered up the envelopes, tucking them into a neat stack so they would be easier to hold. "We'll be throwing another party then."

"Not sure I can wait that long," Fred teased. "But I guess that's my burden to bear. Say, you have a fantastic Christmas. So glad you have those nieces of yours to celebrate with."

And there it is, Aumaleigh thought, her chest twisting at the sight of sympathy dark in Fred's well-meaning eyes. Her throat tightened up. She'd spent a lot of Christmases entirely alone, it was true, back when her mother had been alive. She managed a smile as she opened the door. "Merry Christmas to you and your family, Fred."

The burn of the bitter wind scorched her face as she took a tentative step onto the boardwalk. Her gaze zeroed in instantly on the spot where Gabriel had been, but no one was there. He'd gone. Relief washed through her as she started down the boardwalk on shaky knees.

You're being silly, she told herself. Trying to avoid Gabriel like this, well, it was almost childish. Not at all an adult thing for a woman in her fifties. But that didn't stop her from studying every man in a black coat and Stetson on the street and boardwalk as she went.

"Did you find what you needed?" His—Gabriel's—buttery deep voice somehow rose above every single sound on the street, drowning out the ring of the bell above the mercantile, the *clink, clink* of horse shoes on the icy snow and the drone of conversations as neighbors stopped to talk and friends called out to one another.

Aumaleigh skidded to a stop, panic rattling through her. She could lecture herself all she wanted, one truth remained. She did *not* want to see this man. Not at all. But against her will, as if that part of her who'd loved him so purely had taken over, her gaze cut to him.

He stood right outside the mercantile, his back to her once again, holding the door for someone she couldn't see. The impressive span of his shoulders still looked the same, as did the shaggy dark hair at the back of his collar. His Stetson sat at the same dashing angle and he stood with that familiar, powerful feet-braced-apart stance.

Gabriel. Her heart seemed to whisper his name. The scars and old wounds from decades ago ached like an arthritic bone in winter. But the brightness of that long ago time came back too, and she remembered the hot blaze of the sun on her back as he drove her home from their first date. The grass-scented breeze caressing like a kiss against her cheek. The warmth of his hand as he helped her down from his buckboard at the side of the road, safely away from her mother's watchful gaze. Oh, she'd never forget the light of love soft in his gray eyes as he promised to pick her up next Sunday. Or how that wonderfully joyous feeling rushed into her.

She found herself smiling ear to ear. Why, it was just a memory from long ago, but she would never forget what it had felt like to be wanted by Gabriel. Not ever.

"I found just the right thread." A young woman's voice broke into Aumaleigh's thoughts. A dark-haired girl (maybe eighteen or twenty) swirled onto the boardwalk, spinning to speak with Gabriel. "Disaster adverted. I can have my Christmas dress finished in time for Christmas Eve supper. I'll show Aunt Josslyn. She said it can't be done."

"That's because she doesn't know you well enough." Humor laced his voice as he released hold of the door and headed the other way down the boardwalk, a hand landing on the girl's elbow. His *daughter's* elbow. He chuckled. "She'll learn soon enough. You are every bit as stubborn as she is."

"I like that I'm like Aunt Josslyn." The girls' bell-like voice lilted briefly above the surrounding noise until the hammering sound of a team of horses pounded by, stealing her words completely.

Aumaleigh stared after them, watching father and daughter cross the street and continue down the next block of the boardwalk, stopping to turn into another store. Even when they were out of her sight, she couldn't move. She'd been staring at everything she'd never gotten—at everything she would never have.

"Aumaleigh, I'm so sorry to hear this." Penelope clipped to a stop on the walk beside her and held up a piece of paper. In her other hand was an envelope, freshly opened. "The girls have worked so hard to start up their baking business, and now this...competition."

"Competition?" Aumaleigh repeated, her mind spinning, struggling to focus. She shook her head, confused.

"I received this in the mail. I think everyone did." Penelope bent her head to read off the parchment. "Greetings, neighbor. Dobson's Bakery has exciting news. We are now expanding our delivery area to include all of Bluebell and surrounding vicinity. Come give us a try with an introductory fifty percent off your first order. We've enclosed our menu. Don't forget, delivery is free. We bake the tastiest cakes around. Sincerely, Fannie Dobson."

"Well, this is unexpected." Aumaleigh shook her head, not wanting to believe it. Her nieces had so much fun with their little baking business. She shuffled through her mail. "I see I have one of these announcements, too. Oh, this is bad news for the girls. I'm so glad you told me about this, Penelope. With the state of mind I'm in, I might have forgotten to open my mail for days. Maybe more."

"It is a busy time around Christmas," Penelope sympathized, adorable as always. She was such a good friend to the girls. She folded up the letter and stuffed it back into its envelope. "Well, I'm not giving this company a try. I'm one customer they can't convert, so there. I've got errands to run, so I'd better get going before the shops start to close, but I'll see you on Christmas Eve. I've been invited to supper."

"I'll look forward to seeing you then. Have a good evening, Penelope." Aumaleigh waved the girl off, her thoughts returning to Gabriel. She cast her gaze down the stretch of boardwalk just in time to see a shop door swing open and his daughter emerge.

She looks like a sweetheart, just a doll. Aumaleigh bit her lip, feeling the pain, loss and grief inside her transform into something as bright as a Christmas star. The young woman clutched a few packages, excited with her purchases, her rich dark hair drawn up into a loose knot. Carefully curled tendrils tumbled down to fall around her face and shoulders. Tall and slender, lovely and graceful, Gabriel had to be proud of her. She wore an expensively tailored red wool coat, which draped over an equally fine blue dress. The fancy flounced hem swished and swirled over her new, perfectly polished black shoes.

Gabriel emerged, closing the door, laughing at something his daughter said. For an instant, Aumaleigh caught the chiseled glory of his profile—straight nose, sculpted lips, carved, strong chin. Then he turned away, ambling down the boardwalk with his back to her, alongside his daughter.

Aumaleigh remembered the letter he'd written her all those years ago, which she'd found not long ago hidden in her mother's things. *I married, I have two fine sons and a daughter,* that letter had said. *I've found everything that matters. I hope you've found the same. A good man to love you, children to fill your life, the happiness you have always deserved, that I've always wanted for you.*

It's what I've always wanted for you, too, my dear Gabriel, Aumaleigh thought, blinking a tear from her eye. It was hard to say if it was a sad tear or a happy one—maybe a little of both. She opened the mercantile door and ducked inside.

* * *

"Okay, handsome guy." Rose gave Wally's knotted rein an extra tug (remembering Odie who'd known how to untie himself) and eyed the sturdiness of the hitching post (remembering the story Seth told of Wally's strength). "You'll stay right here until I get back, won't you?"

Wally nodded his head up and down emphatically, as if he understood and promised to be good. His rich, chocolate eyes fastened on hers, beaming adoration.

"Yeah," she told him, leaning in to kiss his nose. "That's how I feel for you, too."

Wally gave a deep, emotional sigh in response.

Yep, he was definitely a love. She sailed down the boardwalk, dodging shoppers and doing a double take (was that Aumaleigh's horse and sleigh near the mercantile?) and wondered if her aunt was finishing up last minute gift buying. Probably. Rose opened the door of the shop next to the post office. Through the post office window, she spotted Fred bounding around his counter to come and see what she was up to.

"Right on time." Dark-haired Tyler, Magnolia's fiancé, flashed a welcoming smile as he paced across the room, his footsteps knelling in the empty shop. He was a friendly, good-natured man who had given up daily work in his carpentry business in order to fulfill his family duty and work for his father's real estate company.

It was different seeing him in a suit instead of his regular muslin work shirt and denims (which is what he wore when he'd been renovating

McPhee Manor), but his wide grin was the same. He looked as if he was making the job adjustment well. "I kept my word and didn't say a thing to Magnolia when I saw her at lunchtime, but it was tough. I'm sure if she knew what you were up to, she'd approve."

"Thanks for that. I may use you for further information gathering," Rose teased, closing the wood-framed glass door firmly behind her. She did not want a single bit of their conversation to carry over to nosy Fred next door. "Like I said, it's going to take some doing to get Iris to agree to this, but it's the next logical step. I like the space."

"It's a nice corner shop," he pointed out, gesturing to the row of windows lining both the side walls and the front. "The pot-bellied stove in the corner will heat the front of this space nicely, especially if you have the counter right here, say, out of the draft of the door by the side windows. You'll get a lot of sunshine, which should brighten things up in winter for you."

"How much would it cost to put in a kitchen?" She eyed the long rectangular space that stretched all the way to the back wall. She took a step, her voice echoing in the emptiness. "Would we have to hire it done?"

"No, I can make it part of the lease agreement. Father won't be too happy with it, but you're going to be family, Rose. We'll do right by you." Tyler lumbered over to the front window, studying the boardwalk outside. "This is a good location, visible for everyone who drives into town. You could have a lot of walk-in business being next to the post office and all."

"Just what I'm hoping for, too." Rose tried to picture it—the glass bakery display crossing the front half of the store full of beautiful and tasty treats, enticing shoppers in off the boardwalk. Pretty, ruffled white curtains at the window, framing the cheerful sunshine. Cute tables and chairs for customers who wanted to sit and rest a spell while they nibbled on cookies—Hmm. Rose tilted her head, considering. Maybe they could also serve coffee, tea and lemonade.

"You know, I can picture it." She spun around trying to see it with creamy wallpaper covering the board walls and Iris at the counter handing out sample cookies to children. The ring of a little bell above the door, the doughy smell of fresh bread ready to come out of the oven.

"I can picture it too." Tyler leaned one shoulder against the wall, relaxing as he looked around. "I can do a modern kitchen for you, put in the best range and the best ovens. Give you lots of counter space. Put up a wall here, say, behind the counter. You'll blow your competition out of the water."

"Ooh, Dobson's Bakery, you mean?" Rose scrunched up her mouth, trying not to have ill will toward the people who had snatched business away from them. "Wait, how do you know about those people?"

"Because they just sent me a flyer. I think everyone in town got one." He pushed away from the wall, his granite features gentling. "Didn't you know? They are delivering here now and giving everyone who orders a half-off discount."

"What?" Rose's vision hazed over for a few seconds—just a few—before the surprise vanished and indignation took over. "Why, they have all of Deer Springs to deliver to. Why they feel the need to horn in on our business, I don't know, but I'm not going to allow it. We need this business."

"Because you're not rich or anything," Tyler teased dryly.

"Because Iris needs this, and I need to help her. Plus, I love frosting things." Rose airily lifted her chin, feeling purpose take over like a tornado racing across the plains. "I've made a decision, and Iris will just have to learn to live with it. We're taking the space. Haul out that lease and I'll sign it."

"Well, this is about to get interesting." Tyler's amused grin said it all as he opened the door for her. "Come on, let's walk over to my office, and we'll get everything signed and official. Just so I know and don't make a blunder I'll come to regret, are you going to tell your sisters about this before or after Christmas?"

"Are you kidding? This is the kind of thing that has to wait until after the holidays." Rose marched through the door, shivering as the icy wind blew right through her. "Iris is going to have an apoplexy. That's no way to spend Christmas."

"Then my lips are sealed." Tyler closed and locked the door.

While she waited for him, she felt a shiver skate down her spine, but when she turned around, no one was there.

* * *

Junior stayed hidden behind the far wall of the post office, peering around the corner when he was sure Rose was far enough away not to spot him. He hadn't brought his crutch to town with him, because they were just stopping for a few supplies before heading off to visit Pa. The last thing he wanted was for Rose to realize he didn't need that dad-blame crutch at all and that he'd been playing her all along.

Look at her, he thought sourly, easing onto the boardwalk. Walking like she owns the place, like she thinks herself so fine. With her fancy duds and a stunning horse for every day of the week—not to mention a whole passel-load of sleighs. No woman ought to have the right to own that many vehicles.

"It makes you want to grab your gun and start shooting her up, don't it?" Giddy settled the package of the groceries into the back of their sled. "It'd be a good way to get some satisfaction."

"I can't say you're wrong." Junior hiked over to the hitching post and untied their gelding, the ugly, swayback thing. It wasn't fair that they had to endure the humiliation of driving a run-down animal like this.

But not for long. That thought sustained him as he climbed onto the seat and took up the reins. Not for long.

CHAPTER TWENTY-ONE

Crouched in a comfortable stall in one of the three barns on the Rocking M, Seth lowered Jane's hoof to the ground. The mare gingerly put some weight on it—not much, but the deep crack hadn't worsened on the slow walk from town.

"You did a good job caring for her." Gil Blackburn planted his forearms on the top of the stall's half-door. He was second in command on the ranch and married to the McPhee sisters' distant cousin, Maebry. "We're much obliged. No one else could have saved her from foundering the way you did."

"She was a good patient and that helped." Seth shrugged off the compliment and stood, taking the time to stroke the mare's neck. "She's a good old girl. She'll be ready to run the sisters around before you know it."

"Heard you are staying home this year instead of spending Christmas Eve with us." Gil swung open the gate. "Must be nice to have your uncle's family visiting, but it won't feel the same without you and Josslyn."

"It won't feel the same not being here." That was simply the truth. Seth marched into the aisle, ignoring the heavy weight dead-center on his sternum. "But it's nice to have family visiting."

"Sounds good to me." Gil secured the latch and ambled down the aisle, slow and easy, a happy and contented man. The right woman and a happy marriage could do that to a guy. "Say, I don't know if you will be doing much smithing as long as your uncle stays in town, but—"

Gil's voice faded away into silence, into nothing at all. Nothing could compete with the sight on the other side of the open double doors. Seth stopped stock-still in the center of the barn aisle, riveted by Rose as she hopped out of her sleigh with a swish of Christmas-green skirt ruffle beneath gray coat.

The sunshine worshipped her, glinting gold in her hair, kissing the ivory curve of her cheek, laying a sparkling path on the snow at her feet. It was as if she walked on diamonds and sunbeams as she circled around, gloved hands up, voice like a melody as she caught Wally's chin in her delicate, gentle fingers.

"Who was a good boy today, the very best boy?" She planted a big smacking smooch on the top of Wally's nose while Wally stood like a perfect gentleman, neck arched, eyes so full of love anyone could see it from a hundred miles away.

"You. *You* are the very best boy, Wally." Rose continued to praise, going up on tip-toe to rub her fingers up the length of his face all the way to his forelock. "You're the most perfect boy ever."

Wally gave a casual nicker, as if this was not news to him.

"Thank you for being such a great friend today." Rose, little Rose, gazed into the horse's eyes with rapt adoration. Oh, she was sweet—like Christmas candy and Christmas snow and starlight on a Christmas Eve night.

Wally, giant Wally, gave a sigh of agreement, lifted his muzzle to her pink cheek and gave her a nibbling kiss. As she laughed, he raised his mouth to her hat and lipped the blue pompom on the top before stepping into her, using the underside of his chin to draw her against his neck in a hug. Rose's arms went around him, holding on tight.

"Uh, Seth?" Gil cleared his throat, amused, glancing tellingly at Rose. "Something seems to have caught your interest."

"No," he denied, although they both knew it was a lie. It didn't stop the longing ebbing into his chest, one wave at a time, lapping at the edges of his heart. "Sorry. What were you saying?"

"After Christmas is over, we're going to need to engage your services." Gil gestured toward several stalls where horses stood watching the men in the aisle curiously. "We've got shoeing to do.

You'll stop by?"

"Sure." It took all his willpower, every strap of inner strength, but he didn't look down the aisle again. Safely out of her sight in the shadowed depths of the barn, he kept his attention focused squarely on Gil as Rose's dulcet alto carried on the wind, thanking the stable boy Cal for coming to get Wally and the sleigh for her.

"Thank you, Wally!" she called out. "Thanks for spending the day with me."

Wally whinnied high and long, distressed as she walked away from him, trudging through the snow and out of sight.

Yeah, Seth thought with a heavy heart. I know exactly how you feel.

"Go ahead and come by when it's good for you," Gil was saying, stopping to give one of the horses a rub on the nose, but it was hard to hear him over Wally's sorrowful neighing. The horse lowered his head and gave a shuddering sigh, forlorn.

That's when Seth knew what he had to do. If he couldn't have Rose to love and keep, then Wally would.

* * *

At a loss, that's what she was. Rose trudged across the back lawn along the shoveled path and stomped her boots off on the steps as she went. The whole day had felt off, like waking up to find out the sun had gone out. She missed Seth. There was a big, aching emptiness in her life. Would it always be this way? She shrugged, not sure what to do about it, but something in front of the back door caught her attention, diverting her thoughts. It was a little collection of wooden figurines lined up at the back door.

Ornaments, not figurines, she realized, kneeling down for a better look. Beautifully carved in soft cedar and honeyed oak, each piece had its own character. There was a round-bellied Santa with a friendly wink and a smile. Three wise men in their robes, gifts in hand. A manger with farm animals—a lamb, a calf and a foal. Five angels with flowing gowns and fragile dragonfly wings—one with Iris's oval face, one with Daisy's heart-shaped one. There was Magnolia laughing, Verbena curtseying and Rose touching the nose of a carved horse. Wooden snowflakes and carved Christmas stars.

A scrap of paper peeked out from beneath the horse and she tugged at it, fingers shaking.

To five special ladies. Thank you for your kindness. Oscar.

Oh, Oscar. Rose scooped up each ornament, wondering how much time this had taken him. Sitting in his tree hut, he must have spent endless hours on these, working by candlelight. This had to be the most thoughtful present they had ever received.

The door swung open and Iris frowned out at her. "Rose? What are you doing? It's late...and what is that? It looks like—"

"A Christmas gift from Oscar." Rose rushed into the house (the warm air felt delicious), and headed straight for the round oak table in the bay eating nook.

Lamplight pooled cozily over the pretty red Christmas tablecloth and provided an excellent background for the ornaments. She set each one down as Magnolia scurried over, a fork in hand from having just used it to check the doneness of the boiling potatoes.

"Ooh!" Magnolia crowded in. "He's talented. They're really good."

"And think how great they will look on our parlor tree." Rose ran her fingertip over the horse, marveling at the detail etched into the wood. The mane and tail looked in motion, the horse as if it could turn and leap right off the table. "This was really nice of him."

"It was." Iris picked up her angel ornament. "I was a little afraid of him at first, you know, because I didn't know him, but this is sweet. I feel as if we should have done more for him. He was so grateful for the job."

"Well, I've been saving this up for the best time to tell you." Rose shucked off her coat and tossed it onto a hook by the door. "He was so grateful because he's homeless. He's living in a shelter he made out of tree branches. I found him sitting by the river bank one day just out of town, with his head in his hands. A bear had found his trap and had taken every last fish and tore up the trap. Oscar looked so defeated, I gave him the half sandwich from my lunch pail I hadn't eaten."

"And let me guess." Iris arched one eyebrow. "You've been feeding him ever since?"

Rose couldn't deny it.

"Poor Oscar." Magnolia's forehead wrinkled up with sympathy. "I can't stand the idea of him in a tree branch house. We should do something."

"We could hire him permanently." Rose lifted her angel from the table by its plain white string and headed through the kitchen. "He could split the wood for us and fill the wood boxes."

"He could shovel the snow for us," Magnolia piped up. "That way I wouldn't have to do it."

"He could fetch the horses for us, especially when Cal is too busy to bring the horses by," Iris added, quite easily. "What? Don't look so surprised. I've been thinking about things all day, about how lucky we are. I mean, I've known this all along, but with Christmas upon us, it's been especially heavy on my mind. I remember working so hard when I first hired on at the Chicago bakery, because having that job meant everything. I needed it so badly."

"And Oscar reminded you of how that felt," Rose guessed, nodding. She crossed the parlor, so beautiful with its soaring, coved ceilings and impressive stone hearth. Fire danced merrily in the grate, warming the room. The three sisters glanced around at the luxurious, comfortable furniture, the grand piano, the expensive knick knacks. Of all the things they had, nothing mattered more than each other. Family was a great gift, one they were deeply thankful for.

"Oscar is coming to the supper at the ranch, right?" Magnolia asked, reaching up to hang her wooden ornament next to a glittering crystal star. "We'll talk to Aumaleigh then and see if she will let him stay on at the bunkhouse. I think she will."

"She's more of a softy than you two are," Iris said drolly, but no one was fooled. Iris was a softy too.

As they hung the ornaments one by one, their conversation turned to other things. Rose had decided to keep Poppy for good. It was official, she was a new horse owner. Lucile Breckenridge nearly cried when she saw the cake for her Christmas dinner (Rose had put in a little extra time on the decorating—she hadn't been able to resist). Magnolia reported on the state of the gift baskets they were assembling for their Christmas Eve surprise. Iris admitted she was behind in sewing her Christmas gifts, too.

It looked like a pleasant, crazy-busy evening ahead, Rose thought, hanging the little lamb from the manger scene carefully, thinking of the exciting last minute sewing and hemming and fussing to get their gifts just right before wrapping them.

What fun it was going to be. This was her life—just about perfect—only one thing was missing. Seth.

* * *

JINGLE BELL HEARTS

All night long that image of Wally hugging Rose stuck with Seth, creeping into his dreams. Worse, that shining image of her, luminous with happiness, light with laughter tormented him all night, through the morning and into the afternoon when he was supposed to be enjoying this rare time with his uncle and cousins.

He really missed Rose. She'd come along, filled up his life and now it felt desolate and meaningless without her. He tightened his grip on the pitchfork, tossing fresh straw into the stall. When he'd told her it wouldn't work between them, he'd figured it would be easier than this to let go.

He'd figured wrong.

"Thanks for letting me help you out." Uncle Gabriel leaned on his pitchfork, looking pleased. "I'm not much of a vacationing man. Since I sold my ranch, I've been at loose ends. Don't know what to do with myself."

"Hey, if mucking stalls makes you happy, I can hire you on for good." Joking, Seth lifted the last fluffy tangle of straw from the wheelbarrow and tossed it into the clean stall. "Sometimes it feels like that's all I do. Come in the morning, muck out the stalls. Turn around at day's end and do the same thing. Day after day."

"You're not fooling me." Gabriel lumbered over, tossed his pitchfork in the wheelbarrow and grabbed the wooden grips. "It's work that suits you. You're happy here. You've built a fine business."

"I like my life." That was simply the truth. He settled his pitchfork into the wheelbarrow. "I spend my day with horses. There's nothing better than that."

"Oh, I can think of one thing." Gabriel flashed a wry grin over his shoulder as he headed toward the back door. "A pretty lady, perhaps? My son mentioned seeing you with a pretty young woman in town yesterday. You switched horses with her? Now, my son has the gift of exaggeration, but from the way he told it, there was something between you and the lady. Am I wrong to think you've set your cap for her?"

"As wrong as you could be." Dark emotions moved in. Loss, sorrow, grief. It wasn't supposed to be like this. He'd thought he was smart ending things now. Another thing he'd been wrong about. He untied the horse cross tied in the aisle. "Rose isn't the one for me."

At the sound of her name, the horse bared his teeth.

"Easy, Charlie." Seth patted the gelding's neck and led him into the fresh stall. He still couldn't believe the horse had tried to bite her. "You are trouble, boy."

Charlie gave him an innocent look and went straight to his trough where he lipped up grain with great gusto.

"Rose?" Gabriel parked the wheelbarrow against the back wall where it belonged. "Haven't you fallen for a Rose before? It was a long time ago, but I see a pattern here."

"It's the same Rose." The words were out before he could call them back, whirring through the air like weapons. Seth grimaced, angry at himself for not thinking. The last thing he wanted was to cause his uncle any upset.

"You mean, Rose McPhee?" Gabriel's forehead wrinkled, drawing his brows together. Stunned, he missed a step, rocking to a stop in the middle of the aisle. "What a coincidence that she's here in Montana Territory. Well, she must have come to see her aunt. Is she here alone?"

"She lives with her sisters." He wasn't sure if he should say more. How many times had Ma warned him not to bring up the past? Even though Gabriel had found happiness, it would always be troubling for him to remember that time in his life spent with Aumaleigh. Seth worried his bottom lip, deciding to say nothing more. He double-checked the latch on Charlie's stall door instead.

"It must have been strange seeing those girls after all this time," Gabriel mused. "They were just little back when your mother was working for Maureen. I'd see them playing in the grass picking wildflowers when I'd come calling on their aunt."

"The sisters rolled into town last summer, and I couldn't believe my eyes. They've grown up into lovely ladies."

"So, tell me more about Rose. You're not just sweet on her, are you?" Gabriel took a careful step, holding himself very still and bowing his head, staring at the straw-strewn floor. "You love her, don't you?"

"And trying hard to fall out of love with her." He suspected that if anyone would understand, it would be Gabriel, but he didn't want to do that to his uncle by bringing up the past. "I'm going to be smart about this. Rose and I just won't work."

"I see." Gabriel drew himself up to his full height, his gray eyes darkened with understanding. "Is there any particular reason why you two can't be happy?"

"Not that I want to share." He was never going to get over her. She was his heart and soul. The knell of steeled horseshoes on icy snow echoed out front. Must be a customer. Grateful for the interruption—any interruption—Seth launched down the aisle.

Wade dismounted from his roan gelding, landing with a thud. The deputy looked tired and depressed. His blond hair looked a little uncombed, peeking out from beneath his Stetson. The badge on his coat was unpolished.

"Hey, Seth," he greeted, handing over the reins. "That's it for the day. I'll need him early tomorrow, the sheriff has me working my regular shift on Christmas. Will you be here?"

"I'm closed tomorrow, but I'll mosey on over and saddle your horse for you, no problem." Seth took the reins, giving the gelding a nose-rub of greeting. The roan answered back with a friendly nicker. "It's too bad Milo is making you work."

"Guess that's what I get for having no family." Wade straightened his shoulders, trying not to look so glum. "I was gonna propose, you know, at Christmas dinner. Guess having to work the holiday will keep me busy enough I might forget what I lost, what I almost had."

And that's exactly how I feel too. Seth hated to admit he had anything in common with Wade, but it was the truth. Rose, who didn't see how beautiful and special she was, had no idea the broken hearts she left in her wake.

"I saw her dancing at Daisy's wedding party with that rich fella, Ian Hutchinson." Wade took a hesitant step back. Instead of leaving, he clearly had something on his mind. "Did you see it, too?"

"I think everybody did." Seth didn't think he would ever forget that revealing moment when Ian Hutchinson had first taken Rose into his arms. She looked as if she belonged there, the lovely wealthy miss and the stately handsome man, and Seth tried to remind himself of that—even if his heart remembered how right it had felt when she'd been in *his* arms. "Ian seemed pretty smitten with her."

"Yeah, I saw that, too." Wade's chin sank down almost to his chest. "I was hoping to get her back. Do you reckon I have a chance against Ian?"

"I don't think anyone does." He said the words as kindly as he could.

"Yeah, I was afraid of that." Wade shrugged, saying nothing more, and ambled off, trudging through the snow with a dejected, heavy-footed gait.

Seth watched him go, knowing just how he felt. Rose was the kind of lady a man waited his whole life for.

"I think I see the problem." Gabriel came over to unbuckle the roan's cinch. "You aren't the only man competing for her heart."

"I'm not the richest man competing for her heart." It was the truth, no sense sugarcoating it. He hefted the saddle from the roan's back, lugging it over to the tack room. Gabriel said nothing else, letting silence fall between them—another reason why he liked his uncle so much.

A friendly neigh rang out, echoing over the sound of jingle bells. Rose's sleigh, drawn by Marlowe, zipped to a stop near the open door. Wally, tied behind the sleigh, lifted his head in an eager greeting, his brown eyes full of sparkles. His ears up, his mouth open in a horse-like smile, Wally wagged his head up and down enthusiastically and, as if he couldn't help himself, leaned forward to nibble the back of someone's neck in the backseat—Rose.

At the sight of her, every bit of his heart and soul came to life, longing for her.

"You're not driving today?" He cleared his throat, trying to sound casual, reminding himself of all the reasons why they didn't belong together. Ignoring the rapid strum of his pulse in his veins, he headed over to the sisters. It was hard to miss his uncle's sudden interest as he peeked curiously around the doorway at the three McPhee sisters in the sleigh.

Rose didn't answer him.

"It's my turn to drive," Iris arched a brow at Magnolia as if to silence her. "*Someone* always tries to get the reins before the rest of us."

"Yeah, I wonder who?" Rose piped up to her sisters from the backseat, leaning forward to try and escape Wally's nibbling.

"It's me," Magnolia admitted good-naturedly. "How else am I supposed to become a better driver if I don't practice?"

"Maybe there's no hope for you," Iris teased back sweetly, and the sisters shared grins, but Seth hardly heard whatever they were saying, because Rose was there—Rose, who refused to look at him from her perch in the back.

"What are you ladies doing out and about?" he asked, trying to sound like nothing was wrong—not one thing. "Last minute deliveries?"

"You could say that." Magnolia looked full of mischief.

"This late on Christmas Eve day?" He looked everywhere except at Rose—down the street, at the tips of his shoes, at the sky above. "Don't you have a big supper on the ranch tonight?"

"They do, I don't." Magnolia gestured at her sisters. "Tyler is taking me to supper at his parent's house. This is going to be interesting."

"Tyler's mother just has to get to know you," Iris assured her in her kind, big-sister way. Beneath the fur lining her hat, her strawberry-blond locks shone in the waning sunlight. "To know you is to love you."

"It's true," Magnolia joked cheerily. "I don't know what I'm worried about."

Seth laughed. He couldn't help it. Tyler's mother was a woman he didn't like much, but he hoped it would go well for Magnolia's sake. She was funny and nice—plus, she was Rose's sister and how could he not like that?

"So these are the McPhee girls." Gabriel moseyed over, hands in his coat pockets, peering down at the women seated before him. "I knew your parents when you were very young. But then your family moved away."

"You mean you knew our folks when they lived in Ohio?" Magnolia asked, leaning forward, riveted. "Back on our grandparent's farm?"

"That's right." He tipped his Stetson in a cordial greeting. "It's good to see you all grown up. You all are as lovely as your mother. How are your parents?"

"They passed away," Rose croaked out an answer, her voice rough and raw, as always, when she spoke of Ma and Pa.

"I'm sorry to hear that." True sympathy boomed in the low notes of his voice, and he swept off his hat. "They were good people."

"Yes, they were." Rose shifted in her seat, fighting a dreadful feeling that she knew who this man was. Standing alongside Seth, it was easy to see the similarities—the slightly curly dark hair, the carved chin, the granite lines of cheekbones and nose. "Did you used to work for our grandparents?"

"No," Seth cut in, his gaze finding hers with a hint of apology. "This is my Uncle Gabriel."

"Gabriel?" Magnolia and Iris whispered in unison.

Poor Aumaleigh, Rose thought, not bothering to try to rescue the pompom of her hat from Wally as he decided to nibble on it. Did Aumaleigh know her long lost love was in town? And how would she feel if she did?

"It's a pleasure to meet you." Rose's words came out croaky again. She didn't know why she turned to Seth, but in those obsidian depths she saw his concern too. "Maybe we should be getting on with our errands. Seth, I've come to return Wally. I'm going to keep Poppy after all."

"Sorry, but that's not possible." He circled around to the back of the sleigh where Wally released his hold on Rose's hat to grab hold of Seth's scarf. "I already returned Poppy to the Hutchinsons."

"Why did you do that? I hadn't made up my mind. She was the best horse of the bunch." Anger—irrational and overwhelming whipped through her with blizzard force, and she didn't care if her sisters and Aumaleigh's Gabriel were watching, she was mad. Mad, mad, mad. "Now go and get that horse back—"

"I'm sorry, Rose, but—" he interrupted patiently, wonderfully, in that gentle way of his.

"No buts," she interrupted his interruption. "Do not talk to me. Do not argue with me. You do not get to go around making decisions for me. Not now, not ever, mister. So go get that horse back or I'm going to—" She sputtered, the red haze of fury fading, and she realized everyone was staring at her—Iris aghast, Magnolia interested and Gabriel amused—and that wasn't all.

"Merry Christmas, Rose," Fred the post office guy called out, tipping his hat as he walked home for the day. "You too, Iris and Magnolia. Don't mind me, I'm a married man. I've heard a lover's spat before."

"A lover's spat? You could not be more wrong," Rose informed him, no longer caring who heard what. After all, this wasn't the first time she'd embarrassed herself on this street. "We are not together. I wouldn't be caught dead with this man."

"Oh, is that right?" Fred called over his shoulder, always ready for more gossip.

"It's no wonder he's single after all this time." Rose was on a roll. The fury was back because he'd hurt her, because his heart wasn't ready for love and hers was. "You've hurt me enough, Seth. I know you're not over Liz, but I can't keep doing this. I need this horse business done and over, because I can't see you again. Not like this."

"Rose, I didn't mean to hurt you so much." He lowered his voice, ringing deep with apology, and he leaned in, splaying his hands on the side of the sleigh. "That's on me. That's my fault."

"You bet it is. Now take your horse—" She had to stop because Wally was swiping his tongue across the side of her face, very concerned over why she was so upset. "Oh, Wally. Now you're breaking my heart, too."

"We can't have that." Seth knelt down so he could meet Rose's gaze, hoping maybe she could see through her hurt and rightful rage at him to recognize the truth—how very much he loved her. "I returned Poppy to her owners, because I found the perfect horse for you after all."

"You did?" Her words came out angry, but her green-blue eyes were shadowed with vulnerability.

"Wally is the perfect horse for you. I'm giving him to you, Rose." This was killing him. When he wanted to lean in and capture her lips with his, to hold her until her pain left forever, but he took her hand in his instead. As a friend might do, he told himself.

"No. He's your horse." She shook her head, scattering golden curls, her face scrunching up with tears even as she fought to blink them away. "No way, Seth. I'm not going to let you do that."

"Too bad, it's a done deal." He withdrew his hand, stood up and backed away. Everything he loved was right there on the backseat of that sleigh—he loved her so completely that he wasn't sure where his heart ended and hers began. "Wally is yours. It's not my decision. Look, it's his."

Wally batted his long lashes, tilting his head adorably as he leaned in beneath her hat to nibble her cheek. Tears stood in her eyes.

"I want the best for you," he told her. "And Wally is the best."

Wally nickered, high and proud, because that was his opinion too.

"Merry Christmas, McPhee sisters," he said, tipping his hat in farewell. Everything within him cried out not to let her go, but he stood his ground. It wasn't easy.

"It was nice meeting you, sir," Iris said politely, and Magnolia seconded it. Rose may have said something too, Seth couldn't say for sure as the sleigh dashed off, taking more than his heart with it.

As the sun slanted long and low, casting golden shafts across the street and through the barn, Seth saw his future vanishing—the one he'd never allowed himself to see until now. Rose in the same wedding dress her sisters had worn walking down the aisle toward him, beaming with happy anticipation. Rose, wearing his ring and greeting him at the door, with supper on the table and a baby girl in her arms. Rose, silver-haired and ever-lovely, surrounded by their grandchildren on Christmas day.

This is what she took with her when she drove away.

CHAPTER TWENTY-TWO

"Someone is pretty mad at you." Gabriel Daniels pondered that interesting fact as he turned down the flame on one of the livery's lanterns, lifted the glass chimney and blew out the light. "And when a woman is angry like that, you've got to know you've done something wrong."

"Not me. I always do the right thing." Seth strolled into the barn with a hang-dog look on his face. His shoulders seemed deflated, like the life had gone right out of him. "That's me. That's what I do. Rose will get over it."

"Let me tell you something about women. They don't get over it." That was one thing he knew for sure. As a man who'd negotiated a long and happy marriage, he'd learned a few things along the way. He replaced the chimney carefully, heading to the next support post with a lantern hanging on a hook. A few horses eyed him with interest from their stalls, likely hoping for more grain. "If you get a woman mad at you, she'll stay mad until her dying day. Maybe even beyond that. Who knows the true magnitude of a woman's anger? It's one of life's great mysteries."

"So you say." Seth rolled his eyes, as if he was thinking he knew a lot about women. Sure, all men did until they married one of them—then they figured out just how truly clueless they were. Seth shrugged, like it was no big deal. "Rose will get over this. My guess is a few dates with Ian Hutchinson and I'll be out of her mind for good."

"Is that what she said?" With one eyebrow arched, Gabriel blew out another lantern.

"No, but that's what will happen. I practically told her as much." Seth shut the tack room door a tad too hard and latched it with force. "I just saved us both a lot of heartache."

"It doesn't look that way to me." It was hard not to be both amused for the boy and concerned for him. He blew out the last lantern, and the dark shadows took over. "You look like you might die of heartache. That girl looked pretty heartbroken to me too."

"Yeah." Seth bowed his head, wrestling one of the front double doors closed. "I feel pretty bad about that."

"Then what are you going to do about it?" Gabriel caught the other half of the door, wrestling it closed. "And don't try to tell me you aren't in love with that girl. I've seen that look before. I used to look like that, back in the day, when I was torn up by a woman."

"Fine, I am in love with her, but I'm not going to do anything about it." Seth hiked off down the street and around the corner, plunging his hands into his pockets, utterly miserable. "She inherited a good chunk of her grandmother's money, which means Rose is seriously wealthy. She could land any husband she wanted. There's no way she'd be happy being a livery owner's wife when she could have much more."

"Did you ask her that?" Gabriel asked patiently, because he knew what it was like wrestling with this dilemma. Funny how history repeated itself. Sweet memories from that long ago time dawned in his heart—Aumaleigh McPhee waiting for him to come to pick her up for their first date, sitting on that wooden fence. She'd been as pretty as a summer rose with the wind ruffling her molasses-dark hair and hope making her heart-shaped face even more beautiful.

Yes, he thought with a pang to his heart. That had been a sweet time. He'd messed that up royally. There was no reason why his nephew had to do the same.

"I guess I didn't ask Rose exactly," Seth admitted, squaring up his shoulders like a man ready to take a hit for the woman he loved. "But it's obvious. I'm not a rich man, and I know how it ends. Either she winds up with Ian Hutchinson or someone like him, or one day she realizes she settled when she could have had a much more exciting life. I don't want that for her."

"It's a beginner mistake." Gabriel tightened his scarf around his neck, gazing down the shadowed residential street. They'd come to an intersection and so they could see a lot of houses down the block as twilight set in. The sun set early this far north, and it felt later than it was to him. The kids had been called in the hour before supper, the air smelled like snow and wood smoke, and mothers were no doubt at their stoves cooking up a tasty meal for their families.

That's what he wanted for his nephew—a good life, a happy marriage, a family. That's what made a man's life complete. All it took was one look at the boy to know he desperately wanted forever with Rose McPhee. In truth, he might not even know the entire depth and reach of that dream. Sometimes a great love came softly, grabbing a hold of you so gently you had no idea how rare and vital it was until it was forever gone.

Those old places in his heart ached.

"You might as well learn this right now, Seth, it'll save you a lot of trouble in the end." Gabriel spotted a familiar buckskin (the horse Seth had given Rose) tied to the back of a sleigh pulled to a stop up the road a ways. A few faint jingle bells chimed as two sisters climbed out, skirts rustling and swishing, hushing one another to keep quiet. He turned to his nephew, determined to help him out. "Never assume you know what a woman wants. You've got to ask her. And there's an even more important rule when it comes to women. Never think you know what she's thinking. Women aren't like us. There's no way to guess what is going on in that head of theirs."

"What *is* she doing?" Seth didn't seem to be listening. Maybe the poor guy couldn't. Look at him, so lovesick he couldn't see anything else but her. "She's delivering something, but it isn't a cake."

"It's a Christmas basket." Gabriel could see the details that Seth missed, for the boy was too riveted by Rose McPhee and her sweetness to notice anything else on this earth. Gabriel smirked, remembering when he'd felt the same. He'd been lucky. He'd fallen in deep love twice in his life, a rare thing. "The girls are leaving food and gifts for that family."

That poor family, he didn't add, watching strawberry-blond Iris keep watch on the windows, while the other two sisters crept up the walk, careful not to make any noise. The basket looked heavy, full of food—a ham, bread, potatoes, beans, bacon and cookies—and what looked like clothes. Children's clothes. If he went up on tiptoe, he could see through the front window into a small parlor where two little girls played with corncob dolls, their dresses patched in many places.

"They are giving gifts to the Collins family." Seth's voice cracked with surprise and emotion. "Mr. Collins was killed in an accident on their farm this past summer, and they lost their land. His wife and daughters moved to town and they are just scraping by. I bought their horses from them for three times what they were worth. I felt so sorry for them."

The men stood, watching in silence as Rose settled the big basket in just the right spot on the step and darted away. Magnolia stayed, fist ready to knock the instant her sister was back in the sleigh. She gave two rapid raps and ran at top speed down the walk, tumbled into the sleigh, and Iris sent the horse dashing into the darkness. When the door opened, a little girl looked out, her red corkscrew curls bobbing.

"Mama!" She went down on her knees and dug through the basket, pulling out a lavender knit cap that would fit her perfectly. "Looky! Santa *did* come. He really, really did."

"Ma!" The second little girl, maybe a year older than the first, dashed into sight, her eyes wide, squealing with delight. "It's a ham! And pretty dresses. Oh, that one's just my size!"

Seth bowed his head, putting it all together now. *We're doing Christmas up right this year,* Rose had told him. He'd assumed with lots of presents and frills, a big feast and jolly festivity, but he'd been wrong.

This gift basket, given to the poorest family in town, wasn't some token charity donation from wealthy folks so they could feel better about themselves. No, this was a gift the sisters had made with their own hands. Bread they had baked and food they had shopped for. This was the selfless gift of women who had known poverty, women who carried the true meaning of Christmas in their hearts.

"Seems to me your Rose is a lady who hasn't let all that money she inherited turn her head one bit." Uncle Gabriel sounded sure of it. "A lady like that knows what is real in this life. Do you?"

* * *

"Did you see the tears in Mr. Redmond's eyes?" Iris swiped at her lashes and gave a little sniff as she set down the reins on the sleigh's dash and took a moment to compose herself. "This last stop was my favorite. Four small children and no mother. They have had a very hard year from what Penelope told us."

"We can't forget Penelope's thank you gift," Rose spoke up, drying her eyes on the backs of her gloves. It was a sight she wouldn't soon forget, the widower standing in the wavering candlelight, staring down in shock at the gifts left on his stoop. Food and warm clothes. The hand he'd put to his face, the gratitude that he obviously felt for the sake of his children, that was the best gift Rose could get this Christmas. Finally Grandmother's money, selfishly horded and ill-gained in her lifetime, was now doing good. And if Rose had her way, it would continue to. "We wouldn't have been able to know which families needed help or the sizes of clothes to make for the kids if Penelope hadn't told us."

"Swing by her place first before you drop me off at Tyler's mother's house." Magnolia gave a big sniffle, trying to compose herself. "I want to see the look on her face when she sees what we made her. I—"

Magnolia fell uncharacteristically silent, her eyes widening in the light of the single lantern mounted onto the dashboard.

A shadow emerged from the dark—a tall man, his Stetson shading his face, his gait strong and familiar. Rose's heart leaped, forgetting to beat. She knew him before he stepped into the reach of the light. Seth. Her Seth. At least that's what her heart called him. She'd tried to stop it, she'd ignored it, she'd raged at it and yet still it endured.

That's when she knew it always would.

"Rose? Can I speak to you for a moment?" He strode closer, tall and strapping, brawny of chest and shoulder. His black, slightly curly hair tumbling down around his sculpted, granite face. Remorse shone in his dark eyes. "It's really important."

"Uh, Penelope's house is just down the street." Magnolia's voice came as if from a mile away, faint and tinny. "We'll drop off her thank you gift and meet you there."

Rose vaguely nodded, hardly aware of the sleigh driving away or the clomp of horse hooves or even the fact that she'd climbed out of the seat. All she knew was that she stood in the middle of the dark-swept street, the wind blowing her skirt ruffle, listening to her pulse drum like a Comanche in her ears. All her anger, all her hurt, all her pride ebbed, fading away until there was only her love for Seth, strong as forged steel.

"I came to say I'm sorry." He eased in, towering over her, so close she could see his chest rise and fall with each breath. "I was wrong about taking Poppy back without asking you. I was wrong about ending our relationship without consulting you. And I'm sorry if you think I was comparing your character to Liz's in any way."

"That's exactly how it felt." She fisted her hands, determined to hold her ground. Of course she'd already forgiven him. Her heart had decided that, too.

"It's not what I meant. In no way have I ever thought you were materialistic or that you value someone based on their total yearly income." His mouth curved up in a faint smile, hard to see in the shadows, but it was there, reminding her of all the times they'd smiled together and laughed together and how their friendship quietly became something incredible. "That's not what I think at all."

"Well, that's good to know." It was the warmth in his tone that got to her, that melted her completely. All her defenses came down. There was nothing but her affection for him—achingly vulnerable and true. "I'm sorry I got so mad at you. You just rile me up like no other man ever has."

"I have that effect on ladies." He reached out, his hand catching hold of hers.

Even through his leather glove and her wool one, snaps of lightning charged through her. The chemistry between them was still there, still undeniable. He grimaced, as if he felt it too. Regret carved lines into his handsome face and weighed down his words. "Now that I've admitted what I did wrong and apologized for it, it's your turn."

"Mine? What did I do?" She couldn't think with his touch blazing through her system, hot as desire, sweet as innocence.

"You accused me of not being over Liz." He tightened his grip on her. His fingers warm and thick, twined between hers, his palm wide and warm pressing against hers.

The heat, the connection bolted through her with enough force to curl her toes and touch her soul. Her eyes burned harder and a sob wedged halfway up her throat.

"You're wrong about that." The angular line of his jaw snapped tight, as if he meant that. "I got over her long ago. I told you that she did us both a favor, one I'm very grateful for in the end. We wouldn't have been happy. Once I realized that, it was easy to let go. You, however, are not. Far, far from it."

"Why did you say those things? Why did you end this between us then?" She blinked at the tears gathering in her eyes. "You said it was to protect both our hearts, but look at us."

"We're both a mess, no doubt about it."

They gave a little laugh together, and it felt right, like old times, connecting again—one heart, one soul. It also felt sad, because it was over. It felt too broken to be fixed.

"My ma used to say to be smart and keep my expectations realistic when it came to love," she confessed quietly. "To look for someone good and safe, not to be carried away by powerful emotions and the hope for fairy-tale love, but this happened so unexpectedly. You were looking for safe, too, remember?"

"Oh, Rose." His baritone dipped, lulling and soothing her like the stuff of dreams. His free hand caressed up her arm, from wrist to elbow, stopping to hold her there, achingly tender. "You are the most incredible beauty, the sweetest and loveliest woman I've ever known. You would be a lot to lose, Rose. You can't blame me for being afraid of that. This is such a great, great love. No man on this earth will ever love you more."

"That's the greatest treasure to me." Their gazes locked and the connection was like stars colliding—so powerful it hurt the eye, so bright it would burn forever. "That's my greatest dream. You are, Seth. To be loved by you."

He leaned in, closing the distance between them. This time he did not hesitate, this time there was only sweet anticipation and breathlessness until his mouth captured hers in a kiss so perfect, it made time stand still. She clung to him, her fingers curling into the wool of his coat and she held on, joyful beyond compare. They'd been friends, then best friends and best friends in love, but nothing could be more perfect than this—true love's kiss.

EPILOGUE

Christmas Day, McPhee Manor

Everyone gasped in surprise and delight as Adam took Annie's left hand in his and knelt before her on the parlor floor. Rose put down her cup of tea on the end table, leaning forward on the cushion, bursting with such happy excitement. Beside her, Seth took her hand, lacing their fingers together. On the other sofa, Magnolia held her breath, Iris smiled joyfully and Daisy clasped her hands together. All eyes in the room turned toward the couple seated next to the Christmas tree.

"My dearest Annie," Adam said in his quiet, steady way. "I have waited a long time for this day. I love you so much. Will you be my wife?"

"Oh!" Tears spilled over Annie's flushed cheeks, and a sob of joy escaped. "Yes. You know I will. Yes!"

You could see the love they shared, deep and real. Adam slipped his ring on Annie's left hand. Bea clapped, bouncing on her seat by the fire. Aumaleigh swiped her tears. Verbena smiled into Zane's eyes, happy with one another and for the newly engaged couple. Beckett slipped his arm around Daisy, holding her close.

Then congratulations rang out, conversations echoing through the parlor, filling McPhee Manor with more joy and happiness. Annie squealed in surprise, Adam must have told her about the house, but Rose's attention drifted to the man beside her. Her Seth, her dream come true.

"Now it's present time!" Hailie called out merrily, the sweet little girl in her Christmas princess dress. She'd accessorized with a matching tiara and sword. She dashed to the tree, landed on her knees and began to hand out gifts. "Bea, you gotta help me. There's a lot of stuff here. How much of it do you think is for us?"

"Lots," Iris assured them, moving in to help. She knelt in her graceful way and plucked the first wrapped gift off the pile. "This is from Aumaleigh to all of us."

"Open it now," Aumaleigh advised, rising from her seat, calm elegance amid the excitement as Hailie ran around as fast as she could go, stacking presents in piles around the room. "I don't think I can stand waiting a moment longer. I can't wait for you to see it."

"You open it, Daisy," Rose said, giving Seth's hand a squeeze before leaving his side. "After all, you are our fearless leader."

"Yes, you led us here to Bluebell," Verbena spoke up, crowding in next to Rose. "You brought us here to happiness and to love."

"I'm dying here. Just open it already!" Magnolia rolled her eyes, laughing, so Daisy untied the ribbon. The rectangle of cloth fell away to reveal a wooden frame holding a charcoal sketch.

Iris gasped. Daisy gave a cry of surprise. Magnolia's hand flew to her mouth. Verbena blinked back tears.

"Oh, Aumaleigh," Rose gasped, reaching out to touch the gilded frame as if by touching it, she could draw it farther into her heart. Her eyes soaked up the picture of a family—her family—sketched when they lived in Ohio. "It's wonderful. Just wonderful."

"It's amazing," Magnolia whispered croakily.

"It's us," Iris said, wiping her eyes.

"I remember when we sat for this." Daisy sniffed, fighting tears. "We were just little. Verbena, you weren't born yet."

"Yes, Verbena, you were just a twinkle in your mother's eye." Aumaleigh gave a watery smile.

"No, she was left on our doorstep," Magnolia teased through a sob. "She's not one of us at all."

"Right." Iris rolled her eyes, not bothering to wipe away any of her tears. They streamed down her face unchecked "Look at Ma and Pa."

"It's so good to see their faces again." Rose sniffled.

"It does my heart good," Daisy agreed.

"Mine, too," Magnolia added.

"Mine, three." Verbena dripped several more tears.

"They're beautiful people," Annie added, going up on tiptoe to peer over Rose's shoulder.

"It did my heart good to see those beloved faces again." Aumaleigh pulled a handkerchief from her skirt pocket. "To remember when they were happy."

"Happy," Rose repeated, clinging to that word, hungry to savor every detail of the sketch. As adorable as her sisters were when they were little, it was their parents who riveted her. Those carefully drawn faces—Pa's round and smiling, youthful and carefree, before hardship had come into his life.

Lovely Ma with her sparkling eyes and gentle smile, full of joy and contentment.

Joy, loss and longing rushed through her, driving the tears that tracked down her cheeks. All the grief came rushing back too—but so did the love so strong, it overpowered all the sorrow. If she closed her eyes, she could still hear the light trill of Ma's laughter and the deep, good-natured rumble of her father's voice. They'd had such an unhappy marriage in the end, but it hadn't started that way. No, Rose could remember the easy accord between her parents, the laughter and gentle teasing, the soft looks and kisses.

Love was so precious. It was everything there was in this world. The only treasure, life's greatest gift. And for all the wealth they had inherited, what made this family rich was the love they shared and the love they'd found. Her gaze cut across the room to where Seth stood, watching her and waiting for her, true love bright in his eyes.

Here was one big truth about life: It isn't what you get, it's what you give. And she looked forward to a long and blissful future giving Seth all the love in her heart. Their destiny was going to be extraordinary.

* * *

Montana Territorial Prison

"It's about time you boys showed up." George Klemp clunked to the bench in the visitor's room, his ankle chains jangling against the stone floor.

JINGLE BELL HEARTS

"We're sorry, Pa." Junior hung his head. It just went to figure he couldn't even do this right. "We got slowed down by the weather in the pass."

"Yeah, it was a bear," Giddy added, raking his fingers through his hair. They'd tried to gussy up, but the clothes they'd stolen off a clothesline weren't much better than the ones they'd had. "We got through though."

"What'd you bring me?" Pa bit out, dropping onto the bench. "I gotta tell you, this place ain't no picnic. They work us so hard in the quarry, it takes the life outta ya."

"I'm sorry, Pa. Really." Junior handed over one of the boxed meals they'd picked up in town. "Merry Christmas. It's turkey and all the fixin's, thanks to those McPhee sisters."

"Those horrid, thieving McPhees." Pa spat bitterly, tore open the box and cried out at the food inside. He dug in with one hand and shoved a glob of garlic mashed potatoes into his mouth. "Hmm, that's good. We don't get real food here, just slop. You boys done all right."

"We love you, Pa," Giddy spoke up, taking a spot on the bench on the other side of Pa and opening his boxed meal. "It's real nice us getting together. We haven't been in a long time."

"You make sure the McPhees, they keep payin', you hear?" Pa laughed, grabbed a turkey leg and bit into the drumstick like a starving animal. "They did this to me. Those women took what was mine, what belonged to me and by God above I'll make sure they pay for it."

"We won't let you down," Giddy promised.

"Yeah," Junior agreed. "You can count on us. They won't see it coming until it's too late."

"This was just the news my old heart needed," Pa said, giving them a nod of approval.

That nod, that approval, felt mighty good. Junior just wanted his pa to love him. This was finally the chance to make up for all the times he'd let Pa down, all the times Pa had been disappointed with him. Hopeful, he lifted the lid on his box, breathed in the mouth-watering scents of a finely prepared meal and dug in.

The McPhee Clan continues in Penelope's story, *Sweet Forever*, coming soon.

ABOUT THE AUTHOR

Jillian Hart makes her home in Washington State, where she has lived most of her life. When Jillian is not writing away on her next book, she can be found reading, going to lunch with friends and spending quiet evenings at home with her family.

Made in the USA
Lexington, KY
28 April 2014